Praise for *W.*

"Jean Hegland is a compassionate novelist whose characters are at once archetypal and personal. In *Windfalls,* she has created an elegy to motherhood in all its painful, beautiful complexity."

—Joelle Fraser, author of *The Territory of Men*

"Harrowing and vividly real, Windfalls offers a lyrical portrayal of two women's lives, one of privilege, one of poverty. Hegland writes with precision about the many facets of motherhood—the necessary courage and the inevitable compromise. Her book is a terrific act of sympathy and understanding."

—Lisa Michaels, author of *Grand Ambition*

"As in *Into the Forest,* Jean Hegland continues to ask the questions most of us avoid, and offers answers that surprise and sustain us all."

—Kathleen Alcalá, author of *Treasures in Heaven*

"Here is a lovely novel by a writer who understands the consequences of the greatest blessing we can bestow upon one another, that of our physical touch; and who knows that all we really have in common in this world are the ways we can be broken."

—Don J. Snyder, author of *Of Time and Memory*

WINDFALLS

JEAN HEGLAND

WASHINGTON SQUARE PRESS
New York London Toronto Sydney

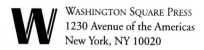 WASHINGTON SQUARE PRESS
1230 Avenue of the Americas
New York, NY 10020

ISBN: 978-0-7434-7008-7
          0-7434-7008-7 (Pbk)

First Washington Square Press trade paperback edition June 2005

10 9 8 7 6 5 4 3 2 1

For information regarding special discounts for bulk purchases,
please contact Simon & Schuster Special Sales at 1-800-456-6798
or business@simonandschuster.com

Manufactured in the United States of America

For Heather Fisher and Russell Shapiro
and the family that they make

for Hannah, Tessa, and Garth
whom I love more than words

and—again—for Douglas

Nothing could have prepared me for the realization that I was a mother, one of those givens, when I knew I was still in a state of uncreation myself.

—ADRIENNE RICH

Of all the means of expression, photography is the only one that fixes forever the precise and transitory instant. We photographers deal in things which are continually vanishing, and when they have vanished, there is no contrivance which can make them come back again.

—HENRI CARTIER-BRESSON

Praise the mutilated world
and the gray feather a thrush lost,
and the gentle light that strays and vanishes
and returns.

—ADAM ZAGAJEWSKI
(translated from the Polish by Clare Cavanagh)

WINDFALLS

AFTER ALL

A tree stands on a windswept hillside. Alone between the darkening heavens and the stony earth, it raises bloom-filled branches toward the sky. A low sun kindles the storm clouds that brood above it, warms the wood of its broken trunk, ignites the blossoms that cram its gnarled limbs.

The tree has been split almost in two—perhaps by lightning, perhaps by wind, or by the weight of its own fruit in some too-fecund autumn long ago. Half of it now sprawls unflowering along the ground. But the living half of the tree still reaches skyward, its limbs so cloaked in bloom that the blossoms seem to hover in the storm-charged air. White flowers cluster on even the smallest twig, and in the photograph each bloom shines like a candle flame.

It is that cloud of flower-light that first draws the eye. Soaring and trapped beneath the glowering sky, that unlikely multitude of blossoms holds the viewer cupped inside a single moment. Gazing at it, a viewer may be transformed, turned from an onlooker into a witness—and, perhaps, from a witness into a partner.

It is a lovely photograph, even a stunning one. Large but not huge, it has been printed full-frame on double-weight matte paper, and its velvet blacks, its pewter grays, its whites as rich as satin all attest to the craft—and maybe the heart—of its maker. But the purest white on the photograph is not the *living white of storm light through apple petals, not the roiling brightness of slant-lit clouds. Instead it is the dead white gash that runs the length of the print—from ominous sky to bloom-laden branches and down through the rocky earth.*

Someone has folded the photograph in half. Someone has folded it as if it were a letter or a newspaper clipping, and that fold has cracked the print's emulsion and left a long unhealing scar in its wake. It is shocking to see that photograph defiled. But the longer one studies it, the more one wonders.

Spread flat, the print buckles and curls, its corners bent, its edges worn. It appears to have been folded and unfolded so many times that the white crease now seems almost like a hinge. Simply by looking, it is impossible to say whether the photograph has been rescued or ruined, impossible to know if the person who last held it in her hands considered it a treasure or would have called it trash. But gazing at that marred and glowing image, a viewer—or a partner—might have to ask whether it hasn't served some purpose, after all.

BECAUSE

THE SHADOWS OF EARLY EVENING HAD LONG SINCE BEGUN TO seep into the room. For over an hour Anna had watched them thicken in the corners and beneath the chairs that lined the walls. She had studied how shadow deepened on the faces of the other students, how it gathered beneath their hands and in the folds of their clothing, and for a while she had even tried to fix her thoughts on wondering whether it was one single shadow or many that filled the health center's waiting room as the brief midwinter day wore on.

She had been waiting so long that everyone who had been there when she'd taken her seat had long since been called out, and other people had taken their seats, and most of them had left, too. For the last fifteen minutes, a skinny man with a scrawny beard and a stained Irish sweater had sprawled in the chair next to her. He reeked of fresh and stale tobacco, and the smell filled her throat so tightly, she wondered if she would gag. She was thirsty by now, too, and she needed to pee again, but she hated to leave the room in case her name was called while she was gone.

Instead she tried to focus her attention on her surroundings. It was an old game, a trick she'd first learned as a child. Long before she'd ever held a camera, she had discovered that just by looking, she could transform an ordinary object into something strange and rare. The same sensation other kids achieved by spinning in circles or rolling down hills, she got by giving her whole regard to the brass spigot on the side of her house or the sparrow bounding across the polished earth beneath the playground swings, concentrating until all that remained in her awareness was the worn sheen at the lip of the spigot or the glint in the sparrow's eye. There'd been a fierce thrill to it, even then, as though she were an explorer laying claim to something no one else had ever seen, like Robert Peary at the North Pole the year her grandmother was born or Neil Armstrong on the moon the year that Anna turned ten.

At first glance the room in which she sat was ugly, but its ugliness was inadvertent, so unplanned and undisguised that there was something nearly touching about it, too. The enameled walls were grimy with age, and the chairs that ringed the room were battered and scarred. A coffee table sat in one corner, its surface covered with a sprawl of magazines and earnest pamphlets that all the waiting students ignored. Afraid of meeting anyone's eyes, Anna avoided studying their faces. Instead she looked at the twisted leather laces in the boots of the man next to her, noticed the dirty pennies in the loafers of the girl who sat across the room, examined the way the shadows beneath the coffee table grew denser as the minutes passed.

Shifting in her seat, she snuck a glance at the wristwatch of the man beside her, and then raised her eyes to study the casement windows on the wall above the girl's head. The building was one of the oldest on campus, and the windowpanes were wavery with age, their texture like the smooth ripples in the sandy bottom of a pond. Despite the grayness of the day, there was something gentle about the light they let into the room, something so tender and wistful that for a moment that light bypassed all Anna's anxieties, soothing and moving her so that she all but forgot how long she'd been waiting, and what she had been waiting for.

The door at the far end of the waiting room opened. A nurse stood on the threshold and glanced at the manila folder she held.

"Anna Walters?" she asked the room.

At the sound of her name, Anna cringed. She wanted to hide, but she forced herself to stand, as though being responsible and agreeable could, even now, affect the news she was about to hear.

"You're Anna?" the woman asked. Her eyes flicked over Anna's patched denim skirt, her muslin blouse and black army boots, although her face said nothing. Anna nodded, then bent awkwardly to pick up her backpack and her portfolio.

"This way," the nurse said. She turned and led the way down a narrow makeshift hall. Anna saw how the nurse's shoulder blades jutted against the polyester fabric of her uniform, how her flat rear remained motionless even as she walked. It was unnerving to think that that dry stranger knew the truth Anna could not yet know for certain about herself. She felt her need to pee intensify, felt her shoulders tighten, tasted a bile of black coffee and fear at the back of her throat. Please, she begged the universe. Please, she begged the treacherous reaches inside her body. Please let my nausea be nervousness, let my exhaustion be stress. Please let me off this one time, and I'll never risk anything again.

The nurse opened a door at the end of the hall and motioned Anna inside. The little room smelled of rubbing alcohol and iodine and the nurse's perfume, and inside of each of those smells was the new smell that everything had held recently, a weird smell with an unidentifiable edge. Anna saw an examining table, a sink, two chairs. Tacked on the ceiling above the table was a poster of a tabby cat dangling from a bar by its claws. "Hang In There!" it said in pillowy letters along the bottom of the poster.

The nurse motioned toward one of the chairs. Anna shrugged off her backpack and sat obediently, leaning her portfolio against her knee like a faithful pet.

"You're here for test results," the nurse said, sitting in the other chair. Test results, Anna's mind echoed. Put that way, it seemed nearly trivial, as though they were only discussing another class. She had never failed a class, never failed a test. She had always liked tests for the tidy challenge they offered, for the proof that she was doing well. *Why was I so worried?* she thought—*it's only a test.*

Catching sight of the nurse's immobile face, Anna was suddenly embarrassed to be wasting anyone else's time with her own unfounded fears. She thought of the newly developed prints she'd had to abandon in the wash water in order to make it to her appointment on time. She hoped that no inept undergraduate had torn their soft emulsions or stained them with contaminated tongs. While she waited for the nurse to affirm what she was suddenly certain she'd known all along, she cast her eyes around the room. A single drop of water hung from the lip of the faucet, its pendent surface bright as a star. On a photograph that speck of light would be pure white, the brightest spot. She stared at that drop, already anticipating the wash of sheepish relief she suddenly felt certain would follow the nurse's news.

The nurse opened her file, glanced at the top page. The world stopped, poised between two possibilities, teetering. Anna watched as the drop grew heavier, slowly elongating like a tiny ripening fruit, while all her terror came coursing back. She wanted to stand up, wanted to leave the room before the news could reach her. She wished with all her heart the nurse weren't so thin and stern.

The nurse was speaking. "—was positive." Her voice was neutral, flat. "Of course you'll need to schedule a physical exam to make sure."

The words churned in Anna's mind. For an unhinged moment *positive* seemed like a good thing. But then its new meaning slammed her like a fist.

"No." She gasped and clutched involuntarily at her portfolio.

"I'm afraid so," the nurse answered matter-of-factly. She wore black mascara that smudged her eyelids and her cheekbones, a pale shade of lipstick. Her skin was large-pored, devoid of light.

"It can't be," Anna said, though even as she spoke, she could feel the truth of it like a stone in her gut, the reason she'd felt so odd and shaky, so half-there, the reason the world had smelled all wrong, the reason no food had tasted right.

"Why can't it be?" the nurse asked, studying her with an unexpected curiosity.

"I'm not a mother," Anna explained, the logic of it clear until the words left her mouth. The nurse's face flattened, and Anna gave a nervous laugh. "I mean, I . . ." she said, but her voice faded into baffled silence. I'm too young, she argued silently. I'm busy doing important things. I'm a graduate student, a photographer. I'm no one's wife. Besides, no one would want me for a mother. Her eyes swept the room, landed on the faucet. The gleaming drop was gone.

"It takes a while, sometimes, to absorb," the nurse said. She pulled a packet of papers from the folder and handed them to Anna. "Here's some literature explaining your options. You'll want to read it as soon as you can."

Anna stared at the papers. Words jumped out at her—*complications, relinquishment, curettage*—a barrage of words whose meanings she couldn't begin to fit inside her head.

"You're not the first person this has happened to," the nurse said, and Anna thought she could detect a wisp of sympathy in her tone.

"It was a mistake," Anna said, suddenly desperate for comfort or forgiveness or understanding. "An accident. I wasn't, I mean, I didn't—I never—"

"As I said," the nurse answered, "you're not the first." She shut Anna's file and rose to leave, adding as she reached the door, "You'll want to make an appointment to see the doctor on your way out."

It was like facing the end of the world with a body full of novocaine. Somehow she managed to gather her things, managed to find the restroom and pee long and hard, huddled on the toilet with her face buried in her hands. Somehow she made her way back into the waiting room to make an appointment to see the doctor, even trying to schedule it around her seminars, although she had to struggle to remember what they were and when they met. She took the little card the receptionist gave her, and as she turned to leave, she caught sight of all the other waiting students. She imagined their simple problems—strep, pneumonia, herpes—and she wished that she could weep.

Out in the linoleum-floored hall, the empty elevator was waiting. She rushed into it and pushed the button for the ground floor. The elevator lurched beneath her like a ride at the fair. She gripped her portfolio and thought of the prints it held and of the exposed rolls of film in her backpack, their long strips curled like promises inside the darkness of their canisters. She'd been doing such good work, she thought, had been making such exciting photographs.

There was a bump and another shudder, and the door opened, revealing a sudden wall of people that seemed to face her like a jury. She pushed blindly through them as they moved in to fill the elevator. At the back of the crowd was a young woman carrying a baby. Anna looked at it, and the baby looked back, its gaze cool and level. The woman entered the elevator, the doors closed, and suddenly Anna was alone in the empty foyer.

The baby made her think of her sister Sally's sons—her nephews— the only children she'd spent any time around since she'd ceased being a kid herself. Jesse was four already, but Dylan was still a baby, the size of the infant she'd just seen. "I don't know how we ever lived without him," Sally had crooned into the phone the day after Dylan was born. Sally's voice was thick with a pleasure that sounded almost sexual, and talking to her, Anna had expected that Dylan would be remarkable, would somehow shine with his own irrefutable light. But she'd arrived home for Christmas to discover that Dylan was just a baby like any other— cute enough, she guessed, in a kind of vacant way, with his round head and soft fists and rosebud lips—but only a baby all the same, a fat, blank bundle who did little more than sleep and fuss and mess his clothes.

"Isn't he wonderful?" Sally had demanded that first night. She was ensconced like a queen on the couch in their parents' living room,

Dylan asleep in her arms like a bland cocoon. "He and Jesse are the best things that ever happened to me."

Anna had taken a sip of her eggnog. She'd held the slick cream and warm brandy in a puddle on her tongue, rubbed the peppery flecks of nutmeg between her teeth, and then swallowed, welcoming the silken fire at the back of her throat. She'd wished she could say what she knew she never would—how terribly meager it made Sally's whole life seem, to think that one grubby boy and one damp baby could be its best thing. Sally had been a painter before Jesse was born. She had studied in Italy, had won awards. She had sold paintings and been part of successful shows, but the woman she'd been then seemed to have vanished into the abyss of motherhood, leaving behind her a complacent cowish creature who worried when Jesse wouldn't eat his peas and laughed when Dylan's leaking diaper left yellow stains on her lap.

It's just biology, Anna had thought, staring at her parents' Christmas tree until the lights grew into one great blur and none of the needles remained distinct. Motherhood was just a trick, just a hormone-driven strategy to keep *Homo sapiens* alive until they could themselves reproduce. Mothers were tools, nothing more than nature's dupes. Looking at her sister's limp hair, at the lax skin beneath her eyes and the beatific expression on her face, Anna wondered how much art was lost to the world each time another baby was born. With a ferocity that nearly frightened her, she'd thought, I could never be like that.

Now she crossed the foyer on leaden legs and left the building. The world outside looked strange, somehow both flat and sharp, as though it had been smashed into two dimensions. The late winter light was greasy, the sky low and gray. Students pushed past her from every angle, their chins buried in their coats, their feet heavy in their boots. They were hurrying to their final classes of the week, or else racing home, drawn like a tide to the promise of Friday night. They were all born, Anna thought dumbly. They all happened to someone. Each one of them had interrupted someone else's life.

She stopped, stared at the brick wall of the building she was walking alongside, the mortar frozen like stone icing between the cold brick. Reaching out her forefinger, she fitted it in the groove, ran it along the mortar furrow until the pad of her finger hurt. Then she headed off across the cold campus, her body aching with the ugliness of everything she saw—the mounds of old snow crusted with dust and gravel, the sodden yellow lawns studded with a winter's worth of dog shit, the passing students huddled against the gritty wind. Who would want to be born? she wondered.

When she reached the decrepit Victorian mansion on the edge of campus where she rented an attic room, she paused for a moment on the broken sidewalk to look up at it. An American flag hung upside down in a second-story window, and a string of faded Tibetan prayer flags festooned the railing of the widow's walk, fluttering in the cold breeze like last year's leaves. From where she stood she could feel the throb of the sound system in the living room—Mick Jagger singing about some girls—and she knew that a party was already percolating inside.

A car filled with frat boys careened past, shedding its own music as it went, its wheels sending an impersonal spatter of gravel across the sidewalk. She took a last breath of icy air and headed up the weathered steps and past the department-store mannequin that stood like a sentinel on the porch. Someone had dressed the mannequin in a new outfit—a bikini, a muskrat coat, and a Ronald Reagan mask.

When she opened the door, she was assailed by a blast of sound. Music pounded inside her rib cage like an extra heart, and the smoke that billowed out at her was so dense, she had to fight to keep from gagging. Peering through the gloom, she could see that the front room was packed with students and strangers, and even several hip professors. Everyone was yelling and laughing and passing things—joints, cigarettes, jugs of wine—in eccentric circles. Strings of bulbous Christmas lights hung from the ceiling, and a black light illuminated the room with its menthol glow. In front of a blaring speaker, a woman in a glowing white dress danced by herself, flipping her waist-length hair like a feathered whip.

Ducking her head and clutching her books, Anna dove into the room. She thought she heard someone call her name, but she kept moving, pushing and twisting through the crowd as though she were running an obstacle course. She had almost reached the hall when she felt someone touch her shoulder and heard a voice in her ear. "We've been looking all over for you."

She turned and saw the dancer in the white dress—Estelle—her face flushed with excitement. Beneath the taut fabric of her dress her breasts were lithe, precise, her rib cage a series of descending ripples. "Go get your camera," she cried, opening her mouth in a wide laugh that the music swallowed.

"Not now," Anna answered. "I—"

"Arden and Rick made a mold of Samantha's body and cast it in Jell-O. They're in the kitchen right now, handing out spoons. Hurry," Estelle urged.

"I'm not—I really . . ." Anna hesitated, passing her hand across her forehead.

She was grateful for the volume of the room, which hid the wobble in her voice, but even so Estelle suddenly looked concerned. "Are you okay?" she yelled. "You don't look that great. Have you been at another party already? Maybe you need to lie down for a while."

Anna nodded and pushed on through the crowd and then up the cold back stairs to her room. Inside, she dropped her backpack on the floor, set her portfolio against the wall, and slumped against the door. The stillness was so complete it felt congealed, though below her the sounds of the party continued. She was too weary to take off her coat, too weary even to cross the room to turn on the space heater. She flung herself down on her mattress, wrapping herself in her grandmother's quilt and burying her face in her cold pillow. For a long time she lay there, listening to the throb of the party, inhaling the faint scent of herself embedded in the pillowcase, feeling the air press against her shoulders like a cold washcloth, and watching as the last light seeped slowly from the room. She remembered the light that had flickered through the high windows in the waiting room, how moved she had been by it, how comforted by its watery calm. But that was before, she thought. And this is after.

She felt a cavernous loneliness. She wanted to find someone who would promise her that things would be okay. She wanted to weep in someone's arms, wanted to be comforted by someone, and forgiven. But she'd only been in Indiana since September, not long enough to have made any real friends yet. All of her old friends were dispersed around the world like dandelion seed. For a moment she considered trying to find a secluded telephone and calling one of them. But even if she could manage to sort out what time it was in New York or Paris or on the North Slope, and even if she could arrange to pay for the call, she couldn't imagine what she would say. She saw herself clutching the receiver and trying not to sob while the expensive seconds ticked by.

For a moment she thought of her family—her parents, her grandmother, her sister—but they were both too near and too distant to trouble with this. A new record came on, Stevie Nicks singing about changes. Anna thought of the sculptor. She remembered his mane of auburn hair, the curves and planes of his shoulders and chest, his proud hooked nose and tawny-green eyes. For an instant she let herself imagine that he would be glad and tender when she told him, that he would wrap her in his finely muscled arms and lift her into another life. She saw them together, on a farm somewhere in springtime, he working in his foundry, she in her darkroom, the two of them meeting in the evening for a meal of brown bread and red wine and steaming soup. She imagined him cupping her growing belly with his sinewy hand, imagined her smiling up at him, imagined their shining eyes meeting.

The record quit, and a fresh burst of laughter rocked the house.

"Bullshit," she scoffed into the pillow, though the word smelled sour after she'd spoken it, and sounded way too small. That was what had caused all this to begin with, that kind of gooey stupidity. She forced herself to remember the last time she'd seen him, how he'd called her *babe* and draped his arm around her as though she were a thing he owned.

She wondered where he was tonight, what he was doing while she lay alone in the darkness of her cold room, the bundle of cells they'd set in motion snowballing inside her. It's his fault, she thought. He did this to me. But before her anger grew large enough to matter, it was toppled by a futile truth. He hadn't done anything she hadn't thought she wanted. He couldn't be blamed for the fact that she'd decided to let him into her bed. He couldn't be blamed for the fact that her diaphragm had failed.

It was after midnight when she finally unwrapped herself from the quilt. She groped through the darkness until the lamp chain tickled her fingers. She pulled it, and a red-tinged light spilled from the beaded shade into the room. She forced herself off her bed and across the dry pine floor to the space heater in the corner. She plugged it in and waited as it clattered to life. Holding out her palms, she stood unthinking, staring at the red, glowing rods, soaking up the elementary comfort of heat and light until the color stung her eyes and her palms began to itch and tingle. Then she went back to the mattress, took the sheaf of papers the nurse had given her from her backpack.

Literature, she thought, as she spread the pages across the bed, hearing the nurse's word and remembering the English classes she'd taken as an undergraduate. You're not the first one, the nurse had said, though of all the novels that Anna had ever read, she could not think of one about a woman in a rented attic room at midnight, half nauseous and alone, studying the mimeographed pages spread before her like the tarot cards that would reveal her future.

Below her the party continued to surge while she read and reread every word the nurse had given her, looking for the choices she'd been promised, seeking the hidden meanings she'd learned to search for in her English classes, trying to identify the decision that would return her life to the way it had been. She read until she'd memorized the words, read until her vision was thick and her head throbbed with unshed tears. But as hard as she tried, in the end she could find no choices, no safe havens, no way out.

CERISE UNLOCKED THE FRONT DOOR AND PUSHED AGAINST IT WITH her armload of schoolbooks. A sigh escaped her as she stepped inside, and it was as though the house also gave a sigh, exhaling the breath it had held all day in her absence. Inside it was still and utterly quiet, exactly as she and her mother had left it that morning, and yet as always, it seemed to hold a little edge of strangeness, as though she were returning to an alternative world, like in some old *Twilight Zone* rerun. There was her mother Rita's pastel sofa, her cream-colored carpet, her glass-and-chrome coffee table still strewn with the little debris of Cerise's breakfast. There were the new drapes Rita was buying on time, and the original oil painting she'd picked up last week at the furniture store closeout. It was all as Cerise remembered it, and yet everything seemed slightly different, too. Or maybe, Cerise thought resignedly, it was she who was different, she who did not quite belong, not even in her own home, not even alone.

Standing in the living room, she inhaled deeply, partly out of relief at having made it through another day at school, and partly so that she could fill her nose with the smell of the place that was her home. Just for a moment she was able to examine the scent she could never detect once she'd been there for a while—that particular mix of perfumes and disinfectants, and below that, the slight sourness she always associated with her mother, a smell of unwashed nylons or unacknowledged disappointment.

It was a smell that interested and unnerved Cerise, a whiff of foreignness at the core of who she was. It reminded her of how she felt each spring when she opened the envelope that contained her school photographs and drew out the sheets of little, identical Cerises. She knew that the girls on the glossy paper were supposed to be a more accurate reflection of herself than the glimpses she caught in windows and mirrors, but even so, she couldn't help feeling that they were only a distant cousin of the person she really was.

Despite the silence of the house, it was a comfort to be home again. Passing through the living room and down the mute hallway, Cerise could feel her face slacken as the expressions she had struggled all day to cover it with slid off. Her shoulders sagged, her spine collapsed, even her pelvis relaxed. But a moment later, climbing the stairs to her room, she felt the same little ache she experienced each afternoon as the quiet closed in around her once again.

Only it was worse today.

She allowed herself one quick thought of Sam, as though the memory of what he had just done wouldn't be so bad if she took it like a scalding drink, one careful sip at a time. But despite her caution, she was unable to control the hot spill of it, the way shame and yearning burst over her in a blistering flood. She remembered his fingers lingering in her palm, how, even though he'd never looked at her, he'd made it seem as if they shared a secret, as if he knew how often she thought about him—riding on the bus and sitting in bonehead algebra and lying in her bed at night.

Upstairs in her bedroom she dumped her books on a chair and kicked off her brand-new loafers, half hoping she might scratch the leather as she toed them from her feet. For her birthday she had asked her mother for secondhand boots from the army surplus store because she loved how used and rugged they looked, because they were what the girls wore whom she most admired at school. But Rita had said she wouldn't hear of paying good money for her daughter to wear some strange man's worn-out boots, and her fifteenth-birthday present to Cerise had been penny loafers instead.

It was an old contention between her mother and herself, Cerise's love of hand-me-downs. Outcasts, castoffs, any object that had once been used and valued and was now ignored, had always touched Cerise in a way that nothing new ever could. It used to infuriate Rita when Cerise would pull a cracked piggy bank or a scalped rag doll from a stranger's garbage can and bring it home—germy and stinking—wash it with dish soap, mend it with ragged stitches, and then play with it instead of with the dolls that Rita bought for her.

Rita's dolls came with outfits and tiny high-heeled shoes that clamped onto their permanently S-shaped feet. With their shiny hair, their pert expressions, and their hard, unnippled breasts, those dolls seemed to have no need of Cerise, and Cerise, unable to imagine how to animate them, had had no need for them. Instead, when she was five and six and seven and eight, she used to sit for hours alone in the room her mother had decorated for her, playing with the creatures she'd rescued from the trash. Downstairs in the living room, her father yelled and her mother cried while Cerise huddled behind her closed door and made up stories of hardship and redemption for her dolls, saving them again and again from witches and robbers, slapping their chipped cheeks or spanking their plush rumps when they were bad, and then kissing them, rocking them, forgiving them. So she had comforted herself with the rich slosh of her own emotion while her parents raged and wept below her.

Rita's dolls still lined the shelf above Cerise's bed, and for a moment she paused, considering them. With their dust-grimed skins and fading dresses, they now looked almost like the sort of toys Cerise would once have loved. Fleetingly she imagined washing their clothes and wiping their faces clean. But then, remembering Sam, she reminded herself that she was too big for dolls.

Back before she got too old, Cerise would sometimes come home from school to find her room smelling of lemon and pine and ammonia, a grim-faced Rita poking the roaring vacuum beneath the canopy bed, and all her trash-dolls gone, deported like illegal aliens back to where they'd come.

"You should have seen your room," Rita would announce, as though Cerise had been staying somewhere else. "I don't know how you can stand to live in a pit like that."

But by the time Cerise entered third grade, all that had changed. Her father gave her a TV to remember him by and moved south, leaving Rita and Cerise on their own in Rossi, the city that had sprung up almost since Cerise's birth between San Francisco and the Central Valley. After her husband left, Rita's hair turned shiny, her breasts hardened, and her feet seemed to grow S-shaped in the high-heeled shoes she always wore. She got a job and arrived home each day at suppertime with a headache and a bag of takeout steamed sodden in foil wrappings. After that, the treasures Cerise salvaged from the garbage remained undisturbed, and sometimes it seemed the only thing that changed from one year to the next was the weight of the books she carried home from school.

Standing beside her bed, Cerise slipped out of her bell-bottoms and tossed them toward the laundry basket. At least she'd worn her nicest blouse, she reminded herself as she shrugged it off and pulled a T-shirt from her drawer. At least she'd maybe looked a little okay.

She'd spent the whole bus ride home trying to decide whether or not she should stop at the market for a Coke. It was Friday, and she'd wanted that little reward for making it to the end of another week. She'd wanted to begin her solitary weekend with a treat, and she'd also thought that if Sam were working that afternoon, she would be able to catch a glimpse of him, though she was so afraid he might notice her that by the time the bus reached her stop, she'd decided to skip the Coke. But as she stepped down onto the diesel-scented street, she found herself heading toward the market, after all.

She'd seen him the minute she'd opened the worn screen door. He was leaning against the counter beside the cash register, reading a magazine. Standing in the doorway, she'd felt a hot buzz of confusion, and only her fear that he would look up and see her sneaking away convinced her to enter the store. Like a timid thief she'd eased her Coke from the cooler and then stood for a long time, pretending to study the cans of Spam and Spaghetti-Os before she worked up the nerve to carry the bottle to the counter.

Sam hadn't said a word as he rang up the sale, not "Hi," or, "That everything?" or even "Want to use the opener?" Keeping her eyes on the upside-down picture in the magazine between them—a girl in a bikini straddling a shiny motorcycle—she'd handed him her dollar bill, mutely held out her hand to receive the change. When, along with the trickle of dimes and pennies, she felt the press of his forefinger inside her palm, she'd looked up, startled.

But although his finger was caressing slow circles around the coins cupped in her hand, his face was as blank as if he were watching TV. She'd snatched her hand away, and her change shattered across the counter and down onto the sticky floor. Hurriedly, she knelt to pick up her pennies, and when she'd ventured a glance at Sam, he was studying his magazine, though she thought she saw a private smile flicker across his face.

Now, as she crossed the strewn floor of her bedroom and turned on her television, she felt a fresh flush of shame. The laugh track from an *I Love Lucy* rerun frayed a small hole in the silence of the house, and she stood before the TV, watching as Lucy wrung her hands and Ethel tried to comfort her. Still staring at the screen, Cerise reached beneath her bed and drew out the box of cake mix she'd snuck from the kitchen cupboard and hidden there. She fed herself spoonful after spoonful, sitting on the floor of her room, almost choking on the chalky flour, and rubbing the sharp grains of sugar against her palate with her tongue until the sweetness disappeared, her mouth was scoured sore, and she could taste the secret salt of her blood. But even after she'd eaten half the box, she could still see Sam's half smile, still feel his finger in her palm, still feel the roar of confusion it caused inside her.

She left her bedroom to roam the house, drifting like a wraith from room to room. Downstairs, she stared so long at Rita's new painting that the floppy-eared puppies almost seemed to move. She felt such a helpless cramp of love for those creatures that for a moment she was tempted to draw them. Back in junior high, when she found a picture she liked on a calendar or a greeting card, she used to tear a sheet of paper out of her binder and draw a copy of it for herself. The lines on the paper always made the baskets of flowers or the kittens or colts look as though they were behind bars, but even Rita used to remark how much like the real pictures Cerise's copies were.

"Where you got that knack from," Rita would say, "I don't know. Not me, and for sure not your dad. He couldn't even draw a paycheck," she'd add with bitter humor, and Cerise would feel a guilty compunction, as though she'd dragged her ability for drawing home like another doll from someone else's trash.

Now she imagined Sam finding her copy of Rita's painting, imagined him looking up from her drawing to eye her with a new admiration. But then his face as she had last seen it bullied its way inside her daydream, and she winced and turned away, left the puppies to frolic on their own.

In Rita's room, she shoved aside the stockings draped like perished ghosts across the rumpled bed and sprawled there herself, flipping through the *Cosmo* that lay beside her mother's pillow and gazing at the skinny, suntanned models until a keen self-loathing filled her soul. Unlike the models' breasts, and unlike the breasts of Rita's dolls, when Cerise's breasts arrived, they came with silver stretch marks and with nipples that tightened or softened as inexplicably as the moon that was sometimes round as a pizza, sometimes skinny as a torn-off toenail, and other times entirely absent in the sky above Rossi. Cerise's feet had grown, too, stretching out flat and long in front of her, and though the hair on her head had remained dense and blond, new hair grew in the sticky V's of her armpits and her crotch.

It seemed as though she had never even had a body before her breasts began to grow. Back in grade school, her body had been unremarkable, reliable as a machine. But in junior high that machine betrayed her, growing so tall and thick and smelly it seemed as if Cerise had turned into some kind of animal instead of the sleek creature the pictures in Rita's magazines promised she would be if she became a woman. Suddenly she was the largest kid in the whole school, and the tiny boys and compact girls who the year before had ignored her now gawked and whistled and whispered when she passed.

Cerise Center, the boys called after her as she hurried down the halls, her schoolbooks clutched against her chest as if she could press her breasts back inside her. But she was too clumsy and self-conscious to play basketball, and later, when the sting had worn from *Center,* the boys changed it to *Centerfold,* and snapped her bra and inquired about her cup size.

"Hey, Centerfold," they yelled when she ignored them. "Whatsa matter? You on the rag?"

"My name's Cerise," she said once, after Rita told her she had to stand up to them, that no one could do for Cerise what she was too spineless to do for herself. But she said it so halfheartedly, her voice rising at the end, that she turned her own name into a question, and her protest only added to their joke.

"Cerise?" they jeered, "My name's Cerise?" and when she finally submitted to tears, they asked her, "Is Cerise? sad? Is Cerise? on the rag?"

She slapped the magazine shut in self-disgust and headed toward the kitchen. Standing in the draft of the open refrigerator, she swallowed a full-throated swig of milk, gnawed on a cold drumstick from the Kentucky Fried box, helped herself to a fingerful of Cool Whip. She glanced at the clock above the stove, saw that it was almost time for *Star Trek,* and closed the refrigerator.

But a note on the kitchen table snagged her attention, CERISE—
FOLD LAUNDRY & IRON. She stared at her name until her vision blurred,
nearly washing those words from the page. She had always hated her
name. It was awkward and unusual, and it seemed to have more to do
with Rita's pretensions and aspirations than with Cerise herself. Once
she had looked it up in a book of names for babies and found herself dismissed in three words—"French for cherry." Cherries were okay, she
guessed, but French was foreign, foreign was strange, and she was
already strange enough without a name that substitute teachers, to the
pooled delight of the rest of the class, always mispronounced—Shir-ice?
See-rise?

Sighing, she crumpled the note, tossed it in the trash, and set off
through the house, assembling the iron and ironing board, the basket of
laundry and the spray starch. Back in the kitchen, she plugged in the iron
and waited listlessly for it to heat. When the air above the sole plate wrinkled with heat, she licked her forefinger and flicked it across the surface of
the iron, felt the sizzle of evaporating spit. It was satisfying, the tidy quick-
ness of it, but it was oddly exciting, too, that small proximity to danger.

"Cerise!" she exclaimed suddenly. Ruthlessly and without warning
she cocked her wrist and thrust it against the hot edge of the iron. The
hurt was quick and wicked. She made a little sound like someone else's
moan. Tears flung themselves from her eyes, but she used her other hand
to keep her wrist pressed against the iron. This is me, she thought, burning, and for a moment she felt a kind of triumph that overshadowed all
her pain. When she could stand it no longer, she yanked her wrist away,
first lifting it to her nose to sniff, and then holding it out so she could
study the tidy white stripe of ash running like a broken bracelet along
the inside of her wrist, across the tender skin where a razor might be
pressed. That was strange, she thought, pleased by her courage, by her
ability to punish herself for her awkward size and awful name. She imagined Sam seeing her wound and being impressed—and maybe even a little intimidated—by what she was capable of doing.

Looking at the burn on the pale inside of her wrist, she couldn't keep from remembering Sam's finger in her palm. But somehow all the shame and confusion of that moment had vanished like a lick of spit against a hot iron. She felt clear and focused, as near happy as she'd been in a long while. This time, as she reached toward the iron, she had a swell of feeling that could only be known as hope.

BY THE TIME THE BUS FINALLY REACHED ANNA'S STOP, HER MIND WAS scraped so raw from a week of working through the same sad set of facts and coming to the same inevitable conclusion that she'd almost ceased to think at all. Mechanically she lurched down the aisle, stepped blindly onto the street, and stood for a moment amid the diesel fumes and dust, blinking in the gritty light and trying to get her bearings. A large cluster of people was milling on the sidewalk in front of the building where she was headed. At first she thought there'd been an accident. But the crowd seemed too purposeful to be waiting for an ambulance. A second later it crossed her mind to wonder if she had made a mistake about the address or the time of her appointment, but even as she scrambled to recheck her memory, she knew she could not possibly have got those details wrong.

She'd brought a book to read in case she had to wait, and now she clutched it to her chest and began to walk faster. As she drew nearer, the group resolved into individuals, though to Anna's eyes they all looked much the same—the women in thick hose and knee-length skirts, the men in crew cuts and polyester jackets. There were also several children, scrub-faced kids in tidy hand-me-downs. With a jolt of alarm Anna realized that the whole group was watching her.

Her thoughts clattered together, and her steps began to slow. For a split second she thought she should try to speak to them. But before she could think of what to say, she saw the suspicion on their faces, and her apprehension sharpened into fear. One of the men was holding a placard toward the passing traffic. When he turned his sign in Anna's direction, she read its scarlet word and started as though she'd been slapped. A protest blurted up inside her, inadvertent as vomit. Part of her wanted to turn and run, and another part wanted to stop and rage at them. But instead she focused all her attention on walking.

When she realized that she would somehow have to pass through those people to reach the building where her appointment was, a new confusion fluttered through her chest. But as she was hesitating, the crowd parted grudgingly in front of her, creating a rough corridor down which she might pass. Her shoulders cringed in anticipation of the blows it seemed would surely come if she tried to reach the doors at the far end, but she forced herself to start walking, passing so close to the bodies of the protesters that she could smell the spice of aftershave and the acrid musk of nerves, so close she could hear the censure in their breathing. She kept her eyes down, watching the fringe of weeds that was already beginning to grow in the cracks in the sidewalk, watching the toes of her boots as her feet propelled her on.

"I'll raise your baby," a man said to her when she came abreast of him.

His voice was low, insinuating. Glancing in his direction, she saw his shiny face and the way his belly distorted the plaid of his shirt beneath his jacket, and she looked away, repelled at the thought of giving anything of hers to him. The doors loomed ahead, double doors with metal handles like twin halves of a moon. She stretched out an arm as though she were an exhausted swimmer floundering to reach a dock. But suddenly a child darted between her and the doors, a girl of ten or twelve.

"Miss?" the girl asked. "Would you read this?" She kept her face twisted away from Anna so that she seemed to be speaking back over her own shoulder as she thrust a pamphlet blindly in Anna's direction. Anna reached out to take it from her only because the girl seemed so uncomfortable—more miserable, even, than Anna herself. Then, in an attempt to reassure the girl and to prove to the watching crowd that she was no monster, Anna tried to smile.

But the muscles in her face trembled so violently it seemed she had forgotten how a smile was made. A sound came from the back of her throat, involuntary as a glob of coughed-up phlegm, and the child shot a startled look at Anna's face. Their glances met and held. The girl's eyes were blue and somehow strangely familiar. For a crazy second Anna had the sensation she was looking into a mirror, although Anna's eyes were brown and she was twice the girl's age.

From somewhere in the crowd a man's voice rang out, "Remember Jesus." The girl's eyes filled with fear, and Anna glanced down at the pamphlet in her hands as a way of protecting them both. But the photograph on the cover of the pamphlet was so appalling that even before Anna could react to its lack of contrast, bad focus, and cluttered composition, she was staring aghast at the image itself.

It was a photograph of a newborn baby, an infant even younger than Dylan had been at Christmastime. Only instead of lying in its mother's arms, this baby was sprawled lifeless on top of a trash-filled can of garbage. It was as sickening and fascinating as pornography, and for a second, as she stared at it, Anna forgot about the crowd. A moment later she felt the horror of it slap her, and she flung the pamphlet to the ground.

"That's your baby," she heard the male voice boom as she reached the clinic door. "Don't throw your baby away."

She was shaking when she entered the waiting room. Her legs felt porous, too frail to bear her weight. She sank into the scoop seat of the plastic chairs that ringed the room, and for a hysterical second she wondered if she had wet her pants. The thought came to her that she should leave. She could catch the bus back to the university and deal with everything tomorrow, but her fear of the crowd outside kept her rooted where she was.

There were other people in the waiting room, six or eight women

and several men. Anna snuck a quick check of their faces to assure herself that they had not witnessed the encounter outside, that they were
not watching her now. Most of the other women sat as Anna had
instinctively sat, with an empty chair between her and the person next
to her. They all appeared both shaken and resigned, as though they had
just heard bad news and were now waiting for a bus. Of the two men in
the room, one was little more than a boy, a scrawny-haired teenager who
held the hand of the girl sitting next to him with a furtive defiance. The
other man was middle-aged and sat stolidly reading the newspaper,
ignoring the woman who waited beside him.

At the front of the room was a counter. A sign below it read, "Please
Confirm Your Appointment Before Taking a Seat." Anna crossed the
room to stand before the receptionist.

"I'm Anna Walters," she made herself say, although her voice rasped
like sand against her throat.

"Walters?" the receptionist echoed, without looking up.

Anna cleared her throat. "Yes."

The woman reached for a stack of files, and Anna saw that her fingernails were so long that she had to handle them with a splay-fingered
dexterity. It made her movements seem squeamish, as though everything
she picked up was something she would rather not have to touch.

Anna said, "My appointment's at eleven."

The receptionist nodded and began to shuffle files. When she found
the one she wanted, she opened it, studied it, and asked, "You have the
money?"

Anna had known she had to bring money, but even so the question
seemed so crude and the receptionist's voice so loud that her throat
clogged again. She coughed and answered, "Yes."

"Cash? Or cashier's check?"

"Cash," Anna croaked, opening her backpack to get the money
she'd withdrawn from the bank, almost half of what she had to live on
for the rest of the semester. Even though she could have used his help

with the money, Anna had not told the sculptor. Getting him involved seemed as silly as seeking out the person who had been sneezing the day before she caught the flu and insisting that he pay for her aspirin. Besides, she'd been reluctant to reveal such an intimate failure to a stranger. But now, standing alone in front of the receptionist with her rent money in her hand, she wished for a fleet moment that she'd told the sculptor, after all.

"Here's your receipt," the receptionist said, handing a slip of paper across the counter to Anna. "You have the consent form?"

Anna nodded. Pulling a folded piece of paper from the pages of *On Photography*, she laid it open on the counter. Words snagged her eyes— *perforation, hemorrhage, infection, death.* A woman had died in Texas only last October.

"You can sign it now," the receptionist said, handing Anna a pen.

But this is different, Anna told herself as she wrote her name. She was paying cash for this, in a clinic. This was legal and safe. It wasn't even an operation. A surgical procedure, it had said in the literature the nurse had given her, eleven times safer than birth.

"Okay," the receptionist said, tucking the form with Anna's signature into her file. "Sit down, and the nurse will call you as soon as they're ready." The woman looked up, and the warmth in her black eyes was so startling that Anna turned away in confusion.

She returned to her chair, opened her book, and stared at the page until the words doubled and smeared. There was a bathroom off the waiting room, and after a while one of the women got up and went inside. Through the closed door Anna heard the heave and splat of vomiting. There was the sound of water running, the roar of an institutional toilet flushing, and a moment later the woman reentered the room, her face empty of color.

Another door opened, and a nurse stood in the threshold, calling a list of names. At the sound of her own name Anna felt a jolt of fear. Each of the women in the room stood and glanced uncertainly at the others. They made an awkward cluster around the nurse, who shepherded them through the door.

"They're going to do us all at once?" someone asked nervously as they shuffled down a narrow hall.

"You have the procedure one at a time," the nurse answered over her shoulder. "But you get prepped and you recuperate together."

She led them into a room filled with cots, like the sleeping cabin at a summer camp.

"Find a cot and get your gown on. The opening goes in back," the nurse said.

"Will it hurt?" the girl who had been sitting beside the boy asked timidly.

"That's what the medication is for," the nurse answered crisply. "And you'll be given gas during the procedure itself."

As Anna turned her back to the roomful of strangers to get undressed, several of the other women began talking. Their voices were flat and loud, and they followed everything they said with a laughter that made Anna think of fiberglass insulation, pink and fluffy and sharp.

She was tucking her socks into her boots when a voice from a nearby cot said, "I wanted to keep it, but my boyfriend's not ready." At first Anna thought the woman was talking about a plant or a pet, and when she realized what the woman meant, she was startled to discover that she had never thought of it that way herself, had never thought of keeping anything or not. For her it had been a question of being or not being.

A mother.

She was not a mother, so how could she have a baby? It would be an accident if she were to have a baby, a failure, a great mistake. If she were to have a baby, she would lose all she was and all she wanted to become, would lose all she hoped to do and to create. And where would that leave the baby, with a mother who was not the person she was meant to be?

She folded her clothes with icy hands, tucked her underwear beneath her skirt and blouse, and then she sat on the edge of her cot with her eyes closed, willing herself to be still, to wait patiently, to be ready for whatever came next. Names were being called. Anna could hear women leaving their cots, could hear them returning. It occurred to her to meditate, but when she tried to say her mantra inside her head, it was like running through sand.

"Anna Walters," the nurse announced. Anna's eyes burst open. She stood, clearing her throat, clutching her gown behind her like a child. As she followed the nurse out of the room, she saw that a few of the women who had already returned were lying with their faces turned to the walls, while others were sitting up, eating Oreos and drinking purple juice from tiny paper cups. The feeling in the room was subdued, the chatter and sharp laughter all leached away.

Barefooted, still holding her gown closed with one hand, Anna followed the nurse down the hall into a room dominated by a stainless steel operating table. A squat machine sat in a corner. A tray stood next to the table, covered with a set of tools like curved screwdrivers and another gadget that looked like a plastic crochet hook.

"Hop up," the nurse said, her voice matter-of-fact, "and fit your feet in the stirrups." Anna climbed on the table and lay back. When she placed a heel in each of the steel cups, she could detect the faint residual warmth of the feet of the stranger who had lain there before her. For a moment she felt oddly comforted.

Then the nurse began to strap down her arms.

"Is this necess—" Anna said, attempting to sit back up.

"It just reminds you not to move," the nurse answered, pressing her back onto the table.

Another nurse arrived, her face already covered with a surgical mask. A man came in, the doctor. His face was masked, too, and he wore a blue shirt. He gave a curt nod in Anna's direction, although he did not meet her eyes.

"Open your legs," the nurse commanded.

No one had said it would hurt so much. No one had said the nurse would thrust a black mask over Anna's face, a heavy rubbery mask that stank and threatened to suffocate her. No one had said that the man in the blue shirt would bark, "Be still," while he twisted his succession of instruments up inside her. No one had told her that he would try to split her open, to core her like an apple, the pain red and mean and inescapable. A machine came on, roaring like a carpet cleaner, but Anna was too occupied with pain to think what that noise might mean. No one had said she would writhe, that a thick sweat would soak her all at once, that she would cease to care how her gown hung open, or worry about the noises she made. No one had told her that, as she fought the pain and the hissing mask, she would hate the people who were helping her as much as she hated the sculptor and herself.

When the machine was finally silent, Anna lay panting and defeated on the table, the sweat on her neck and belly and thighs suddenly cold while the doctor removed his last instruments. Watching the expressionless eyes above the nurse's mask as she began to unstrap Anna's arms, Anna remembered the girl outside the clinic, remembered the broken baby in the photograph and the man's sign with its red word—MURDER.

Still lying on the table, Anna blurted, "Can I see it?"

"It's over now," the nurse answered. "Time to go back to recovery."

"I want to see," Anna persisted, startled by the urgency of her own request. "I need to see—what came out."

There were furrows in the nurse's brow as she cast a glance at the doctor. He shrugged and answered, "Sometimes they do." He addressed Anna directly for the first time since he'd ordered her to be still. "Are you sure?"

Unable to trust her voice, she nodded. Beating down great raw wings of panic, she elbowed herself up to sit, wobbly and wet, on the edge of the operating table. The nurse removed a glass jar from the machine and held it out toward Anna. As she leaned forward to look, she felt terrified and also vaguely embarrassed to be studying a product of her body in public. But what she saw when she peered into the jar was so astonishing, it made her forget about herself.

Suspended in the clear fluid was a billowing cloud of tissue. Like a strange flower or a rare sea creature, it was all tender pinks, iridescent whites, delicate webs of crimson. Anna bent closer, and for a moment she thought she glimpsed an elfin hand—a hand so tiny a doll that size might sleep forever stretched out inside a walnut, like Tom Thumb.

"Oh," she gasped. She gazed, soaked in emotions she couldn't begin to name, until the nurse made a small, impatient movement that set the contents of the jar swaying. Then, tearing her gaze away, Anna whispered, "Thank you," as, trembling, she climbed down from the table.

THE STRIPES ON CERISE'S WRISTS TURNED TO SCABS THAT CRACKED AND caught on whatever she happened to brush against, and tore and bled. Sitting in the back of U.S. history or sophomore English or bonehead algebra, she sucked the ooze, thinking, This is me, and before the burns healed, she took the iron out again.

In the beginning she had almost hoped that someone would discover those burns, like a row of mouths seared shut inside each wrist—maybe one of the teachers at her school, or Sam, or even Rita. She'd imagined that person would ask her what had happened, and hoped that in explaining it to them, she would come to understand it, too. She'd hoped that someone else would be able to give her the sympathy she craved, that someone else would finally recognize what she couldn't seem to realize for herself. Sometimes she even envisioned Sam running his fingertips across the rutted surface of her wrists, only in her daydream his fingers were cool and gentle, as tender as a girl's.

At first she believed that things would change once someone noticed her wrists. But later she began to be embarrassed by their ugly skin and ragged scabs. The wrists of the other girls at school were fresh as clean sheets, and it wasn't long before Cerise realized that there was something wrong with her, something sick and shameful about what she did. She began to worry that her wrists would betray her, and she started wearing long-sleeved shirts that hung below her palms. Now she dreaded being caught, dreaded being made to confess or to explain, dreaded having another of her weaknesses exposed to the whole school's ridicule. But every afternoon when she got home, she had to battle with that craving to burn herself.

The first time Sam asked her to wait for him until he got off work, one of the reasons she agreed was so she wouldn't have to be alone at home with the iron perched like a squat, hot idol on the kitchen counter, taunting her. Sitting on the bench in front of the market, she stared at the inexplicable equations in her algebra book, dug her finger-nails surreptitiously among her blisters and scabs, and felt as terrified as if she were about to take a pop quiz. But she was thrilled, too, for it seemed like her real life was finally beginning, now that Sam had noticed her, now that someone had singled her out.

There were things she wanted for herself. However—unlike Rita—she could not fit her desires directly into words, couldn't say she wanted a Cadillac DeVille and a new shag carpet and a trip to Hawaii. Instead, she yearned for the life she felt must surely be waiting just beyond the life she currently inhabited, and although she was helpless to say exactly what that life consisted of, she felt hopeful that Sam might be its start.

Sam was taller than she, nineteen, and out of school. He took her to the apartment he shared with a group of other guys, showed her how to inhale the skunky smoke of a joint until her lungs convulsed for lack of oxygen and then how to exhale in a triumphant dizzy blast. He was impressed by the size of the tokes she took and, after they'd smoked the joint down to a damp nub, by the fact that she claimed she didn't feel much different than before. Later, he was pleased by how quickly she agreed to lie down beside him on the mattress in his room, though on subsequent afternoons he complained about how little interest she seemed to take in what he did to her there.

The times with Sam that Cerise liked best were the times after sex, when all the pushing and grunting was over and she could press her ear against his bare chest and listen to the naked booming of his heart. She liked to feel little in his arms, longed to be able to sleep with him all night, curled up safe like a baby, instead of having to get up and dress and rush home before Rita got off work. She sometimes startled Sam with her desire to burrow against him or the ferocity with which she inhaled his smell. But on those rare occasions when he was so moved by lust or dope or pride that he said he loved her, she never answered him, and when he came inside her body, he was always alone.

School was almost over before Cerise began to worry that she might be pregnant. She couldn't remember having had a period since sometime in January or maybe even December. Still, it wasn't until the end of March that she started to wonder about it, and another week had passed before any real anxiety began to seep into her bones. It was impossible to imagine saying anything to Sam that would require her to use words like *period* or *pregnant,* so instead she made a deal with the universe or fate or God that if she let her wrists heal and did not burn them anymore, her period would come.

She kept her part of the bargain, though she had to suffer through waves of panic and desire so mean they made her dizzy. But despite both her torment and her victory, the crotch of her panties remained pure white. Night after night she lay beneath the canopy of her bed, kneading her stomach or pounding it with her fist. Sometimes she even tried cramming her hand inside herself in an attempt to dislodge whatever it was that kept the blood from flowing. But she had no idea what she was groping for up there, and no matter how hard she hit or prodded, she could not get the blood to come.

Each night she promised herself she would do something about it in the morning, but in the morning the worst edge of her fear had been blunted by sleep. Besides, in the morning it seemed impossible to believe that what Sam did to her could make her pregnant, especially since she'd experienced none of the wild desire she'd seen on TV, had felt none of the overwhelming need the teacher in her health class had warned that girls should guard themselves against.

It was the end of the first week in April before she finally dialed the only number she could find in the whole phone book that seemed to promise help. She called from the phone booth outside the market while Sam swept out the stockroom. Sticking her finger in the cold chute of the coin return, she stared out through the scratched glass and listened to the ringing of a stranger's phone. "Problem Pregnancy?" it had said in the Yellow Pages. "We Can Help."

Three hours later she was sitting in the LifeRight office, almost buried in the cushions of a broken sofa, while Jon and Sylvia sat in folding chairs in front of her, smiles of pained tenderness on their faces as they told her that the plastic cup of hot yellow pee she'd shyly handed to Sylvia had proven that she was pregnant.

Jon was broad as a fullback, with wide hands and ears that angled out from his head like semaphores. Sylvia was small, demure, in a skirt that covered her kneecaps when she sat and a blouse that remained unwrinkled despite the spring heat. Her eyes shone, and she held Jon's hand and leaned toward Cerise.

"Sometimes when we think we're looking for someone to love us," Sylvia said, "we're really looking for God's love instead. God never loves our sin. But He always loves us. And Cerise, He's blessed you with the most wonderful chance of all to prove your love for Him—He's entrusted you with the life of a baby."

On the floor beside Cerise's feet a mint tea bag oozed a faint green into a mug of tepid water. They had already passed a plate of store-bought cookies, and Cerise, in her shyness and sugar-hunger, had taken four, while Sylvia abstained and Jon chose two, swallowing them both in a single gulp, like vitamins.

Now Sylvia was saying, "God can try us in some really hard ways, if He thinks we're strong enough. And you are strong, Cerise." She smiled and reached out to give Cerise's knee a little shake of encouragement.

"God asks us to honor our parents, but He wants us to do that because they gave us life. You'll do the right thing. We know you will. We'll pray for you."

Cerise was embarrassed to be talking about that thing they called her sin, and by the pile of cookies on the paper napkin on her knee. But she liked the way Jon and Sylvia held hands. She liked the way their eyes sought each other out, as though they were each mirrors in which they could admire their shared reflection. She could not imagine Jon doing to Sylvia what Sam had done to her.

Jon said, "Just because the government made the mistake of legalizing infanticide doesn't mean it's right—or even safe. We want you to know all the facts. Not just what they'll tell you at the abortion mill."

They said her baby's heart was already beating, that her baby was already breathing inside her. They said her baby was sucking its tiny thumb, that it would cry and struggle when the baby-killer tore it from her body. They said, "God doesn't make trash."

They told her that abortions hurt, that the pain could be unbearable. Abortions were risky, they said. If Cerise had an abortion, she might die, or might never be able to have another baby. They said that women who had abortions had a higher risk of drug addiction and suicide, and for a second Cerise thought that meant she was safe, because she was only a girl. They showed her pictures—color photographs of tiny limbs and perfect hands projecting from jumbles of bloody tissue that made Cerise think of road-killed animals. They showed her grainy black-and-white photos of dead babies heaped in garbage cans like discarded dolls. They said her baby trusted her. Her baby would love her forever, they promised, their eyes tender and shining, whatever she chose to do—give it to a childless couple or even raise it herself.

They said, "We'll be there for you, all the way."

She looked at them holding hands, leaning toward her in the eagerness of their conviction. It was nice to think that her baby loved her, and she wanted Sylvia and Jon to like her, too. She imagined walking down the street between them, she in the middle, small and safe, holding a hand of each. She thought of the baby they claimed was inside her, like a tiny perfect doll she'd rescued from the trash. And she imagined later, when that baby had grown into a little girl who would, as Sylvia had promised, love Cerise more than all the world.

When Jon described the lawyers and procedures it would take for her to give her baby to strangers, Cerise knew she was too shy, too easily flustered and quickly confused, to ever to go through with an adoption. That night, when Rita came home and handed Cerise the bag that was their dinner, Cerise unpacked the hamburgers and fries, poked a straw into each waxed cup of Coke. After she'd laid the food out on the table, she lowered her chin to her chest and told her mother that she was going to have a baby.

The fries wilted and the ice melted while Rita yelled and wept. She called Cerise a slut and asked her what the hell she intended to do about the mess she was in.

"Keep it," Cerise answered.

"Oh, no, you aren't."

"Yes," Cerise said, and though she was speaking to the floor, she felt a tight triumph as she spoke, like when she'd pressed her wrist against the iron.

Rita said she would pay for Cerise's abortion. She would pay for Cerise's abortion and give her a hundred dollars besides for new school clothes, but she would be damned if she'd help Cerise raise a baby.

"I've got more important things to do," Rita yelled, while Cerise scraped crescents of wax from her Coke cup with her fingernail and rolled them onto her napkin, where they lay beside her burger like a litter of tiny moons. Finally Rita's voice went hard and low, and she said, "If you want to ruin your life, go ahead. I don't guess there's much I can do to stop you. But don't come crying to me to help you later on. I'm already doing all I can. Every day I work my butt off so you can go to school and have a good time, and this is the thanks I get. It's time you learned about the consequences of your actions."

She stormed into her bedroom, slamming the door behind her like a fist, and Cerise waited until she heard the laughter coming from Rita's television before she ate her limp hamburger and drank her watery Coke.

AFTERWARD THERE WAS BLOOD—MORE BLOOD THAN ANNA HAD expected would come from the loss of that feathery, floating thing. On her way home from the clinic, as she leaned her head against the rattling window of the bus and waited wearily for her stop, she could feel the warm blood seeping out of her, and she was afraid she would not make it back to her room before the blood overflowed the pad that chafed between her legs.

She was tired and cramping, and she longed in all her bones for the hot bath the sheet of instructions the clinic had given her said she shouldn't have. But her nausea had vanished, and despite her exhaustion, she felt as relieved as if she had just survived a traffic accident and were now standing in one piece on the solid shoulder of the road.

She made it home without meeting anyone she knew. Collapsing on her bed, she toed off her boots, shrugged her way out of her coat, and then crawled beneath the covers with her clothes on, toppling into a sleep so deep it was as though some huge hand were holding her beneath the surface of consciousness. She woke fourteen hours later and rose and showered and dressed and left her room. It wasn't yet dawn, and for once the kitchen was empty of people, though the counter was cluttered with last night's empty bottles and full ashtrays. An overflowing compost bucket sat like a toad amid the waxen husks of burned-out candles. She heated water on the great black range and dripped a mug of coffee for herself. Standing by the window, she ate a bowl of granola and yogurt, savoring both her hunger and the rightness of the flavors, exalting in the restoration of her senses. She rinsed her dishes in the stained sink, left them to dry in the musty dish rack, and let herself out of the house into the cold dawn, hurrying down the broken sidewalk toward campus.

She was at the end of the block when she heard someone calling behind her, "Hey, Anna! Wait up."

She turned and saw Estelle hurrying toward her. Her hair was scraped back in a ballerina's bun, and beneath the hem of her trench coat Anna could see her striped leg warmers and black Adidas. "It's too damn early," Estelle groaned as she drew nearer. Her breath left her mouth in a dense gray cloud. She shuddered and flipped the end of her scarf a second time around her neck. "Where are you off to?"

"The darkroom," Anna answered, stepping over an ice-filled gutter. She had not been back inside the darkroom since her visit to the clinic. She thought of the finished prints that needed matting, of the negatives waiting for her like unread fortunes, and her pace quickened. Turning to Estelle, who was nearly jogging along beside her, she asked, "How about you?"

"Rehearsal," Estelle answered. She gave Anna a shrewd glance, and asked, "What have you been up to, anyway?"

"Me?"

"We were talking about it last night. No one's seen you for weeks."

Anna's mind stuttered to a stop. They were walking past a row of fraternity houses. On the sidewalk ahead of them an orange tomcat had planted its head and forefeet inside an open paper bag and was tearing ravenously at whatever the bag contained. I had an abortion, Anna thought. But even inside her head the words sounded both too harsh and too meager to describe what had happened. Behind the frat houses and the telephone lines and the skeletal maples, the sky was stained a pink as delicate as the color inside a shell. In her mind she saw the jar the nurse had held for her, its contents wafting and drifting like a sea anemone.

"You're like the ghost in the attic or something," Estelle offered, looking over at Anna. Startled by their approach, the cat bolted across the street, leaving the bag yawning in the middle of the sidewalk. It would be possible, Anna realized, to tell Estelle. She could explain the predicament she'd been in and what she had done about it, and she saw how by saying those words she could reduce the whole thing to a single memory, could turn it into something flat and manageable, a thing she could complain about and forget, like drinking too much on a Friday night, or having too many finals in a row. Something in the back of her throat yearned for the simplicity of that. She longed for Estelle's quick sympathy, longed for the whole thing to be over.

But she remembered the iridescent tissue floating in its lonely jar, and she felt a strange ache, like an emptiness turned inside out. She did not believe the protesters were right, did not believe that the tissue the doctor had taken from her was a thing capable of dying, and yet, as she gazed toward the coming sun, she knew it was undeniable that it had lost the chance to live. A sudden loyalty welled up inside her, a strange desire to protect that ethereal bit of matter, to preserve the way it shimmered inside her head.

"I've been busy," she said, the dense mist of her words mingling with the strengthening light.

"Doing what?" Estelle persisted.

"Nothing, really," Anna shrugged. "School stuff. Not much." They entered the student commons. For once the wide brick courtyard was empty of people, and the sound of their footsteps echoed eerily between the surrounding buildings.

"Why—" Estelle began, but Anna interrupted her. "Have a good rehearsal," she said, and darted away across the courtyard.

As she passed through the doors of the fine arts building, Anna inhaled the clay dust and varnish-scented air deep into her lungs. I'm home, she thought exultantly, passing the main office and heading down the echoing concrete stairs. It's over now. I'm back. I made it through.

Inside her cubicle she went straight to the drawer that held her most recent photographs. She'd thought she would start the morning by matting a print or two, and then, if she felt up to it, she might work in the darkroom for a while. But when she set her new prints on the table, the photograph on the top of the pile was so empty and uninspired that she wondered how it could have gotten mixed in with her best work.

It was an image of a lace tablecloth she'd found in a secondhand store. Two months ago she'd hung the lace across the window of her attic room and then spent a weekend shooting it in every possible light. At the time, she'd loved how its broken folds draped between the aged window jambs, how the torn mass of it lay in a weary, graceful heap on the sill, and later, when she'd made that print, she'd been pleased by the tension she thought she'd caught between the exact froth of the handmade lace and the causal damage of time. *Every Thread a Web,* she'd planned to call it when she hung it in her graduate show. But this morning it seemed strained and mundane—an old tablecloth hanging awkwardly from a splintered window frame. Looking at it now, she saw only the vast distance between what she had hoped for and what she had achieved.

I was really off there for a while, she thought as she remembered back over the last six weeks, how scared and sad she'd been, how sick she'd felt. Hurriedly she began to flip through the rest of the pile, seeking to comfort herself with better examples of her work. But she couldn't find a single print she liked. Every photograph was trite and amateurish and immature, its composition stiff, its tones muddy, its subject sentimental or clichéd. It made her feel hot and flushed to realize she had ever meant to show those prints to the world. It made her heart falter to think of all she had given for them. Standing in the empty hallway, she wondered, How could I have been so wrong?

SYLVIA AND JON WENT WITH CERISE TO THE WELFARE OFFICE. THEY helped her gather the documents the caseworkers required, helped her fill out the forms to claim she was an independent minor, the forms to apply for food stamps and Medi-Cal and welfare. They took her to the clinic, where a gray-haired doctor twisted a speculum inside her and prodded her stomach and pressed the cold lozenge of his stethoscope against her breasts. They helped her find an apartment on the other side of Rossi, helped her move her clothes and her TV and the mattress from her bed while Rita was at work.

Cerise's apartment consisted of four rooms lined up like train cars, a tiny living room in front, a stale bedroom in the rear, a dark slice of kitchen and a damp bathroom sandwiched in between. Sylvia helped her clean it, and Cerise cut pictures from magazines to decorate the walls—photos of flowers and baby animals and bright butterflies, and one strange picture with no color at all but the smooth curve of a silver river leading toward a wall of rugged mountains. There was something fierce and fearless about that picture that tugged at her, though when Sylvia asked her why she'd chosen it, Cerise shrugged shyly and answered, "I don't know."

At first, when she told Sam she was pregnant, he acted like a boy who'd been accused of hitting a baseball through a neighbor's window, but later, when he realized that no one was going to make him pay for what he'd broken, he swaggered with a newfound sense of accomplishment and referred to Cerise's swelling belly as "the kid."

Jon and Sylvia said that Sam should marry her—for the baby's sake, as well as for the sake of Cerise's eternal soul. But it was hard for Cerise to think of a child's welfare or even her own soul when there seemed to be no child, when it sometimes seemed more likely that she would give birth to a beach ball than a baby. She couldn't imagine Sam as a father any more than she could imagine herself as a mother, or as Sam's wife.

Sometimes she tried to pray about it, like Sylvia and Jon had said she should. But the answers that popped into her mind when she tried to address her thoughts to God and seek His guidance never seemed to be the ones that Sylvia and Jon would approve, which made Cerise think that she was doing something wrong, that her prayers were missing God entirely, like when she misdialed a phone number and a stranger answered by mistake.

She had received special permission from the principal to return to her high school when it began in the fall. Although the teachers showed their disapproval of her condition by pretending she did not exist, for once the other kids clustered around her in the halls, awed and envious and a little scared because she had her own apartment, because she had so obviously had sex. They all vied to touch her stomach and offer their suggestions for baby names. But later, when she quit attending classes because she had grown too tired to try to study and too large to fit in any of the desks, none of the schoolkids ever came to visit her.

For days she sat in her apartment with the television on and waited dully for whatever was going to happen next. She liked the thought of a baby like a living doll she could dress and kiss and hold, but she had never changed a baby's diaper or fixed a baby's bottle. She couldn't remember ever having held a baby, though now she tried to pay close attention to the babies on TV. The TV babies advertised tires and laundry soaps and paper towels. They brought sitcom families back together, and wailed from the depths of their cribs at funny times, and all those babies seemed more real than the baby that was supposedly inside her, giving her heartburn and hemorrhoids and bruising her ribs with its kicks.

The kids at school had debated names, which ones were cute and which were cool, and Rita, who had relented enough to take an interest in what name her grandchild was given, had a list of her own picked out. But Nicole or Scott, Tanya or Zachary or Jason—it was hard for Cerise to imagine any of those people inside her. Occasionally she draped a newborn-size sleeper across her bulging uterus, and it seemed both too small to fit something human, and too large to clothe anything that could ever be gotten out of her.

At night, lying alone on her single mattress, she would sometimes lift her T-shirt, crane her neck so that she could stare down at her stomach, and try to imagine what it was that she contained. Sylvia had told her that already she and her baby shared a sacred bond, but when Cerise tried to beam her thoughts through her bloated belly to the baby, she felt like Captain Kirk, attempting to contact an alien spaceship that might not even exist.

When she became so big she couldn't stand to have Sam on top of her, grinding away between her legs and squashing her belly until she felt she might burst like a water balloon, he suggested that there were other ways they could do it. But she was too uncomfortable and too embarrassed by her bulk to submit to trying anything new. And it wasn't long after that that Sam let slip he was seeing another girl. He made sure Cerise knew how the other girl begged Sam to do all the things to her that Cerise refused. She knew how Sam's confession was supposed to make her feel, and when she realized she didn't care how much that other girl wanted to have her twat sucked, didn't care that the other girl loved to slurp Sam's thing as though it were a double-dip cone on a sweltering day, a part of her felt as though she had failed at something yet again.

When Cerise was nine months pregnant, Jon and Sylvia moved away.

"It's God's will," Sylvia said, smiling sorrowfully from her seat on Cerise's sofa. "We'll miss all our dear friends here, but the Lord has challenged Jon with a new work in Chicago."

Jon grinned at Cerise and patted Sylvia's hand. "You let us know the minute that baby comes."

Cerise turned to Sylvia, "But you said you'd help me, when—you know—it's being born."

"Of course I'll help you," Sylvia answered staunchly. "We'll both help you, with our prayers." And when Cerise looked stricken, she added, "Even if we stayed here, I couldn't actually be with you in the delivery room. Cerise, you have to believe that God will never give you more pain than you can bear. Besides, if things get to be a little much, you can always ask the doctor to give you an epidural."

Epidurals were a wonderful new procedure, Sylvia told her, that let a woman pray or even watch TV while her baby was being born. But when, after hours of an agony Cerise had never imagined existed, she timidly asked for hers, the nurse glanced at her chart and said, "Sorry, sweetheart. You're Medi-Cal. The state won't pay for epidurals for Medi-Cals. Epidurals are for ladies with insurance."

The shot the nurse injected like a consolation prize into the heparin lock on Cerise's wrist didn't make the pain go away. Instead it made Cerise forget she had ever felt any other way. She lost herself in the doze between contractions and then woke time after time to a bewildering savagery of hurt whose source she could not remember. Hours after the pain had squeezed her into the furthest corner of herself, a new nurse came to her bed and said, "Let's give you another check."

She twisted a gloved hand inside Cerise and gazed up at the ceiling as though she were listening to far-off music. Then she said, "Looks like you're finally ready. We'll go ahead and move you to delivery."

They made Cerise skooch from her bed to a gurney, rolled her down the hall to a room filled with bright lights and machines, and then had her crawl from the gurney onto a bed so high and narrow she wondered if she would fall off it and break on the floor like Humpty Dumpty.

"Are you going to cut me open?" she asked when she saw all the gleaming equipment. But the nurse answered, "No such luck. You gotta do this one the hard way, all by yourself."

Then the room was filled with people all staring at a monitor like a TV screen on which a blue light traced out mountains. At first they told her she could push when she felt like it, but when it became clear she didn't feel like pushing, they began insisting that she push while they all gazed at the screen where the mountains grew and fell, and yelled "Now—push! Push!"

She wanted to please them, but she was too tired and too confused about what it meant to push—push what with what? Besides, she knew if she pushed anything very hard, she would push herself apart, and even though she wanted to die, she didn't want to have to endure more pain to do it. They brought something to help pull the baby out of her, and when she saw what looked like a giant copy of Rita's salad tongs and realized that they were meant to fit inside her, she was certain that she would be disemboweled and that whatever was stuck inside her would be torn apart, but by that time she had almost ceased to care.

When they finally laid the baby in her arms, Cerise's first thought was that she'd done something wrong. Inside its flannel swaddling its face was so squashed and raw and broken-looking that it reminded her more of the photographs in Sylvia's brochures than any of the round-eyed babies she'd studied on TV. Gingerly she touched the bruises on its temples, gently traced the impossible softness of its mottled cheek, and when it did not scream an objection, she laid her open palm against its chest, felt it breathe beneath her hand. It whimpered a little, its eyes wide and unfocused. She bent to sniff it, inhaled the smell of the inside of her which the baby had brought with it into the world, and a sudden greedy passion swelled up in her.

The nurse looked at her sharply. "Don't you even care what sex it is?"

"Sure," Cerise said shyly, staring at the baby's puffy face. "I guess."

"It's a girl," the nurse answered almost angrily.

"A girl," Cerise echoed, gazing.

A moment later the nurse whisked the baby away, and Cerise raised her eyes to look around the room. She saw the doctor in his green scrubs bending between her legs as he stitched her back together down there, saw the other nurses wadding up bedding and fussing over the machines, and she realized with a start that all those people had once been babies, too. Someone had had to keep the doctor alive, had had to feed and clean and clothe him, and that person had also been borne and cared for by someone else. The nurses had once been little girls. She imagined the hands that now uncoupled cords and tugged sheets into place making mud pies and dressing dolls.

"How are you going to feed?" the doctor asked, peering into her crotch as he drew the needle up and gave a little tug.

She cast a bewildered look at the nicest nurse, who suggested, "Bottle or breast?"

Rita had said that nursing would make her fat, and before Sam left, he'd once observed that only cows made milk. Besides, she felt too shy to say the word *breast* out loud in that roomful of near-strangers. Instead she whispered, "Bottle?" and everyone nodded as if she'd just got the right answer on a test.

Later, while her baby slept in the nursery, Cerise ate the gray mashed potatoes and wooden roast beef from her supper tray and placed a long-distance call to the LifeRight office in Chicago. But the stranger who answered said that Sylvia and Jon were out at a rescue. She ate her watery apple crisp and called the fort in Texas where Sam was in his third week of basic training. When the corporal asked whom he should say was calling, Cerise answered, "Just tell him it's a six-pound baby girl," and hung up before the corporal could ask anything more.

Late that first night, long after Rita had come and cooed and complained and gone and the ward was dim and quiet, a nurse brought the baby from the nursery so that Cerise could practice giving it a bottle. As Cerise tried to work the rubber nipple into the infant's mouth, the nurse stood above her bed, watching so critically that it seemed the baby was really the hospital's and not Cerise's at all.

But finally the nurse was called away, and Cerise was alone with her daughter for the first time. Long after the bottle had been emptied and the baby had produced a belch so large it seemed yet another proof of its prodigious gifts, Cerise cradled the little creature in her arms, bending over her, peering into her face, studying her for signs, for meanings, soaking her being deep into her bones. She was astonished that her baby already knew how to suck and swallow and breathe, astonished that such a perfect creature would consent to rest uncomplaining in her arms.

A feeling squeezed her so tightly that she began to cry, though when she tried to identify the sadness in it, the only evidence of sorrow she could find was that she hadn't known before how wonderful it would be to have a baby. The word *blessed* came into her head, and although it was Sylvia's word and Sylvia was gone, the word remained, shining like a candle in that stern room.

When Cerise looked down at the newborn sleeping in her lap and saw that her tears had dripped from her face to land on the baby's cheeks, she quickly wiped the teardrops away, afraid they were unlucky or unsanitary, afraid the nurse would return, catch her crying on her baby, and question Cerise's right to keep the infant who had birthed in her such an unexpected joy.

As she daubed her tears from her daughter's cheeks, another word came to her—a name this time. It was a name like a poem, the most beautiful name she'd ever heard, the word she knew she wanted to say every day of all her life, the name she wanted to whisper in the night and yell across the playground after school. She knew Rita would be indignant and her former classmates would be disappointed, but before the nurse came to reclaim the baby and return her to the nursery for the night, Cerise had named her daughter.

Melody.

She named her baby Melody because it sounded small and calm and feminine, and because it was a word that everybody knew. She named her baby Melody because, as she remembered the elementary school music teacher explaining on one of her rare visits to Cerise's classroom, a melody was at the center of every song.

When the hospital said they could leave, Cerise took Melody home to her apartment, despite the fact that Rita wanted them to move back in with her.

"You don't know the first thing about having a baby," Rita said as she drove out of the hospital parking lot with Cerise beside her on the front seat, holding Melody.

"I know the first thing, I guess," Cerise answered softly. She bent to sniff the bundle in her arms and nuzzle her face in the fuzz that hovered above Melody's small warm head.

"What will you do when she gets a fever? What will you do if she won't stop crying?"

"I'll figure it out."

"If that's the way you want it," Rita said, smashing her foot against the accelerator as the light they'd been waiting for turned green, "you're on your own. It's one thing if you're living with me, but you better not go calling me in the middle of the night when I have to work the next day."

"We'll be okay," Cerise said doggedly. "I have a thermometer."

But after Rita left the apartment, and Cerise was all alone with that strange, limp creature, she felt as raw and scared and awkward as she had the first time she'd been alone with Sam. When Melody began to whimper and suck her fists, Cerise panicked and reached for the phone. It would be easy as going to sleep to surrender her baby to Rita. Rita would put Melody in Cerise's old room, Cerise could stay in the guest room in the basement, and next fall she would go back to school as though nothing had happened. Even though Rita would complain about the extra work and trouble, Cerise knew that Rita would secretly be glad to have Melody, especially since Cerise was already certain that Melody would be prettier and tidier and more popular than she had ever been.

But before Cerise could dial the number, Melody's whimpers blossomed into cries. They weren't very loud, but they reached inside Cerise like fingers, clutching at her empty womb. She imagined Melody in the room where she'd spent her own lonely childhood, and an objection rose inside her. When the voice inside the phone directed her to please hang up and try again, she returned the receiver to its cradle and fixed a bottle for her baby.

After the formula was warm, Cerise tested its temperature carefully, pressing the rubber nipple against the faint scars on the inside of her wrist until a few white drops bled out. Then she sat on the sofa and tried to tease the nipple between Melody's tiny gums. For a while Melody fought the bottle, twisting her head from side to side or butting blindly against the nipple with her cheek. But just as Cerise was ready to give up, she suddenly clamped down on it, engulfing the nipple with such a look of surprise on her little, screwed-up face that Cerise laughed out loud.

Later, when the bottle was empty, Cerise held the bundle of her daughter against her shoulder. She patted Melody's back with the palm of her hand until the burp came, and then she pressed her against her aching breasts and held her while the light drained slowly from the room. In the darkness beyond the locked door of her apartment, sirens wailed, car horns honked, and people yelled out greetings or obscenities. But inside the walls of her small rooms, Cerise held Melody while she slept. Suffused with a savage happiness, Cerise sat for hours, sat until her arms tingled from lack of circulation and her back ached and her bladder stung, secure in her bone-deep certainty that nothing would ever prevent her from keeping her baby safe.

GRADUALLY THE LAST GRAVEL-STUDDED HEAPS OF SNOW DISAPPEARED from the streets, leaving behind little piles of grit like shrines to something no one wanted to remember. Gradually Anna's bleeding diminished to a few dirty clots and then finally stopped altogether while the spring sun strengthened, the air grew nearly creamy with new warmth, and the semester trudged toward an end. But still all of her work looked vain and pointless. Still all her efforts to find something new to shoot and print and tone and mount and sign and frame dissolved into an overwhelming sense of fruitlessness.

On Friday of finals week, Anna gathered all her prints and negatives and burned them, hunkering over the pale little bonfire she'd built from the slats of a broken bed frame in the weedy yard behind the house. The air above the flames wrinkled like vision through tears, but she liked the bite of heat and smoke, liked the authority with which the fire claimed her work. As each print buckled and curled, it seemed more alive than it had ever been before. Squatting beside her little blaze, she thought it proved her commitment to art, that she could destroy anything that wasn't perfect. When all her prints were blackened crusts and ashes, and her final negative had been reduced to a dark little knot like a melted heart, she felt a kind of triumph, felt so purged and proud that she wished there were someone to admire her conviction.

But a moment later the fire began to ebb and smolder, and she stared at the lace of ash that was all that was left of her work and thought, What now? She had a sudden fear that someone had been watching her. Lifting her eyes from the fire, she scanned the windows of the house for faces, and then peered sheepishly around the yard. But she saw only empty windows, only the battered lawn and the skeletal remains of a bicycle leaning against the back steps, a cluster of stunted daffodils spearing up through its twisted spokes. She saw how the world went on about its business regardless of her little hurts and wants, and a sudden anguish speared her to the core.

She left the next day to spend the summer living in Spokane with her parents and working in her father's insurance office. She had no better plan for the next three months, and she needed the money she could save that way, but driving west across the shining prairies and over the gleaming Rockies, it made her want to weep, to be twenty-two years old—young and grown and living her one and only life—and reduced to spending her summer with her parents.

"How did your semester go?" her father asked the first night as she sat in her mother's clean kitchen eating things she hadn't had since her last visit home—herbed chicken, deviled eggs, and lemon pie—while her parents watched her like attentive hosts.

"Fine," she answered so brightly she was sure they would hear the lie. Then, trying to strain the rue from her voice, she added, "It's a good program."

"When will you get your degree?" her father asked.

She hesitated half a second too long, so that in the end she had to say, "I'm not sure."

"Not sure?" her mother asked.

"There's a lot of factors," Anna began, but an edge of worry was already building in the room. She saw it in the nearly imperceptible tightening of the lines that framed her father's smile, and in the careful casualness with which her mother wiped the spotless counter. The moment wavered like air above a fire. For a second she considered saying—what? I had an abortion. I burned all my work. But when she tried to imagine her parents' response, she realized that no matter how they took it, no matter what they said or did, she could not bear to have to add their sorrow or worry or anger to her own.

"There are a lot of variables," she repeated, reaching across the counter for the pie. "But my show's scheduled for December." Picking up the knife, she said, "If my committee likes it, I'll graduate next spring."

The moment became solid once more. Her mother nodded quickly, as if she'd known it all along, and although the shape of her father's expression did not change, he relaxed back into his smile. "Next spring," he said heartily. "That's just fine."

"How're the boys?" Anna asked, ignoring the little punch of loneliness in her gut. Placing the point of the knife at the center of the pie, she pressed the blade down through the foamy meringue. "Sally said Dylan is already crawling."

She spent the next two months answering phones and filing claim forms and coming home to watch David Brinkley on the evening news and eat her mother's quiches and pork chops and spinach salads. On weekends she roamed Spokane with her camera, wandering the riverfront and Division Avenue and the Arboretum, seeking something to replace the photographs she'd burned. She hung around the lobby of the Davenport Hotel, loitered past the pawnshops down on Mission, drifted through the Japanese Gardens. But she couldn't bring herself to expose a single frame. By mid-August, fall semester was looming like an iceberg in a dark ocean, and she wondered—sometimes vaguely and sometimes desperately—what she should do about it. It made her frantic to think of returning to school empty-handed, but when she imagined remaining in Spokane, she felt a despair so heavy it was hard to breathe.

"You need to visit your grandmother before you leave," her mother said one night at supper. "She keeps asking when you're going to come."

"I know," Anna answered contritely. "I meant to go down earlier. It's just that I've been—" busy, she thought, though she anticipated the look her parents might exchange and didn't say it. Instead, to camouflage the way her sentence failed, she said, "I'll go this weekend." Turning to her father, she asked, "Hey, boss—can I have Friday off?"

That Friday she worked until noon and then left the office, stopping at a drive-in for a cup of coffee on her way out of town. Just west of the city, she turned off the freeway and headed south on the state highway, following a route she'd traveled all her life. But after the flat Midwest and the forested Rockies, the land she drove through seemed almost foreign. The sky was cloudless, and a late-summer light covered everything with its rich gloss. The fields spread out in all directions like earthen waves, unfenced, treeless, a vast maze of swells and curves.

Occasionally a breeze rippled through the nearly ripened grain. Once a red-tailed hawk dropped from a telephone pole and swept in a low arc across the road while Anna watched dispassionately. She reminded herself that time was getting shorter, that she had to get to work, but she still could not bring herself to stop the car and take her camera from the trunk.

Steering with one hand, she raised the plastic cup to her mouth. The coffee tasted bitter, chemical, its harshness like a penance. She thought of where she was headed, of the staid farmhouse alone in the open fields, of her grandmother sweeping the clean front steps or waiting on the front porch with her knitting. She wished she could be ten again, thrilled at the thought of a weekend alone at Grandma's. She felt guilty for not having gone to visit her grandmother sooner, though at the same time she chafed at the thought of giving up a weekend to visit her now. In recent years it was as though she'd somehow outgrown her grandmother. These days her grandmother seemed too simple and too sweet to understand the person Anna had become, seemed too frail and old and timid to be exposed to Anna's world.

Eighty miles beyond Spokane Anna entered the little city of Salish. She drove past the pioneer museum, past the entrance to Spaulding University, where Sally's husband Mike taught English, past the public pool where her grandfather used to drop Sally and Anna on summer afternoons while he went to the John Deere dealership or to the Grange. Two miles outside of town she turned off the state highway and headed south on a county road. After the whine of asphalt, the crunch of gravel beneath her tires sounded sturdy and secure, a small comfort that did not quite belong to her.

She passed the Levitt elevator, which loomed like a lone wooden skyscraper above the empty railroad tracks, passed the Hopkins's place and then the Joneses', passed the grove of bull pines where she had once seen a fox. As she drove, memories moved through her, intense as the sour candies her grandpa used to bring from the Grange. She remembered perching with Sally on top of a load of grain while the farm truck raced down the road to the elevator, remembered how the hot wind had whipped their hair, how the dusty load had shimmered in the sun, how they'd chewed handfuls of wheat into a glutinous gum and gazed like sunburned princesses out across the golden land. She remembered picking roses with her grandmother and going hunting with her grandfather in his pickup. "Don't look for deer," he'd told her as he drove. "Look for where you can't see field. Sometimes you have to try to find what's missing before you can see what's really there."

The car began to labor up a hill, and she shifted into second. When she reached the crest, she eased back on the accelerator and paused to look down into the valley that held her grandparents' house. Amid the golden fields, it sat in a tidy island of green yard, dwarfed by the spruce tree her grandfather planted the year the stock market crashed. Grandpa's dead, she remembered, and the stab of pain that followed seemed nearly welcome for the way that—for a moment—it thrust all the other emptiness aside.

She descended into the valley, turned up the drive, parked in the wide shade of the spruce. The front door opened, and her grandmother stepped out onto the porch, one hand shading her eyes in a worried salute. She was wearing a housedress and an apron, opaque hose and solid black shoes. Anna saw how small she had become, how lined and strained and faded, and an odd flicker of anger seared her. For a moment she felt impatient with her grandmother because she had allowed herself to get so old.

"You're here," said her grandmother, coming down off the porch and holding out both her hands toward Anna. Her fingers were stained a deep maroon, and when Anna took her hands in her own, she was startled to feel how smooth they were, as if the lines and ridges of her fingertips and palms had been rubbed away.

"I didn't expect you before suppertime," her grandmother said apologetically. "I'm working on the beets."

"The beets?" Anna asked, dropping the smooth, stained hands and reaching out to give her grandmother a careful hug. She felt her narrow shoulders and staunch spine beneath the fabrics of her apron, dress, and slip, smelled lavender and Ivory soap and the earthy scent of beets.

Her grandmother reached up to pat Anna's shoulder as though she were a small girl or a good dog. "Irene Hodge brought by a bushel. I doubt I can eat that many, but I hate to let them go to waste. I'll send some home with you," she added brightly.

All that work for beets, Anna thought wearily. She said, "I don't think I've ever canned beets."

"No?" her grandmother asked, pulling back from the hug and peering into Anna's face with a mixture of pleasure and consternation. "My."

"But you can show me how," Anna offered awkwardly.

"Surely," her grandmother answered. "Though first," she added warmly, "I want to hear everything about how you've been."

It was the world's most innocent question, but it caught Anna off guard. Hastily she tried to scrape together a response from the stock of answers she had used all summer. I've been fine, she thought, looking out across the empty acres of wheat. I've been just great. Everything's going really well. But before she could say those words, other words escaped instead. "Don't ask me that."

Her grandmother shot a quick look in Anna's direction, and Anna flinched and caught herself, appalled at the rawness in her voice, terrified at the thought of what might spill out next. "Please," she added, casting a quick imploring glance in her grandmother's direction.

The old woman's face held an expression Anna had never noticed on it before—keen, unflinching, kind, and nearly shrewd. She studied Anna for a long moment, and then she nodded briskly as though she were making—or keeping—some kind of promise. Motioning toward the car, she asked, "Would you like to bring your things in now?" and the moment healed over itself so seamlessly that, except for the trembling of Anna's hands as she lifted her suitcase from the trunk, it might never have happened.

That evening, after the mountain of beets had been boiled and peeled and sliced and salted and packed into jars, after the hot lids had been screwed down and the filled jars had been submerged in the great kettle of boiling water and then heaved up, dripping and steaming, and set on the counter to cool, after Anna and her grandmother had eaten pot roast and mashed potatoes and boiled green beans and sipped an inch or two of the sour chablis her grandmother kept in the refrigerator to serve to company, after the dishes had been washed and dried and replaced in the china cabinet and the floor had been swept and mopped and the leftovers wrapped and put away, they went outside to sit together on the porch and try to catch a wisp of evening breeze.

The sun had just set, and a last ruddy light filled the world, burnishing the fields and illuminating the roses that grew beside the porch railing, deepening the crimson Mr. Lincolns so that they looked nearly black and causing each of the Bridal Whites and the Summer Snows to glow like the core of a flame. But studying them from her seat on the top step, Anna felt only a dim nostalgia for how that light might once have stirred her.

From the kitchen came the faint ping that announced another lid had sealed.

"Nineteen," her grandmother said, her voice almost smug. She sat in a white wicker armchair, a skein of pastel yellow yarn in her lap, her knitting needles flashing in the rosy light. "We accomplished a lot today."

"Yes," Anna murmured, gazing out across the quiet fields. The sound of knitting ceased, and Anna looked up. Her grandmother was counting stitches. Despite her dexterity with the needles, her fingers were bent, the knuckles thickened with arthritis. Anna remembered how smooth those hands had felt when she'd held them that afternoon, so smooth she wondered if her grandmother's fingertips would even leave a print. It seemed as though her grandmother had shed her very identity in the anonymous, endless labor of housekeeping, and now, looking at her grandmother's hands, she shuddered to think how small and sheltered her grandmother's life had been. She thought, It's no wonder we've got so little to say to each other.

"What are you knitting?" she asked, in penance for her thoughts.

"A sweater for Dylan," her grandmother said, holding up her needles so that Anna could admire the sweater the size of a tea cozy that was skewered between them.

"It's sweet," Anna answered. "Sally will love it."

Another silence draped them, broken only by the little tapping of needles. From the kitchen came the ping of a lid sealing.

"Twenty," her grandmother counted.

Anna murmured a small assent. She wondered if it was too early to excuse herself and go to bed.

"I have a conceit about canning," her grandmother said.

"A conceit?" Anna asked politely. "You mean you're proud of it?"

"Well." Her grandmother gave a quiet laugh. "I expect conceit's an old-fashioned word. I mean a little idea—a fancy, you might say. It came to me years ago, when the boys were all still babies. I used to spend all of August in the kitchen back then. When I wasn't cooking for the harvest crews, I was canning everything I could get my hands on. Seems like we needed every bean and berry to make it through the winter."

The pale yarn danced and jerked briskly between her needle tips. "It came to me one day back then that what I was really doing was preserving light—the sun's light, you know, caught in those vegetables and fruits—I was putting up light in those glass jars, saving sunlight down cellar until we needed it, in the dark of winter." She cast a shy look at Anna. "I expect you'll think that foolish," she said.

"No," Anna said, looking across the yard at the quiet fields and trying to keep the ache out of her voice. "I think it's a nice idea—preserving light."

Above them in the deepening sky the first stars were appearing. Anna felt the ache widening inside her, felt the gaping yearning returning.

"I was always so practical," her grandmother said lightly. "It frightened me, when I first started thinking like that. Later I got used to it, I suppose."

"Hmmm," Anna answered, and then roused herself to ask, "What made you think that way? At first?"

There was a pause so long Anna thought her grandmother hadn't heard. Then she said, "I lost a daughter."

Lost? Anna thought, trying to make the words fit inside her head. A daughter? A sizzle of warning ran along her spine. She felt a moment's disbelief, a refusal as if her grandmother were joking or even lying, or as if she'd somehow gotten the facts of her own life wrong. Anna darted a startled glance at her, but she appeared as serene as ever, looking quietly out toward the darkening garden. She said, "I doubt your father ever told you."

"No," Anna answered cautiously. "Dad never said a thing."

Her grandmother nodded. "It was before he was born—or Charles or Henry, of course." She was silent for a moment, and then she gave a gentle laugh. "I haven't spoken of her for years—decades, maybe, by now."

Anna thought, I cannot bear to hear this. "What happened?" she forced herself to ask.

"She died," her grandmother answered, "being born." She spoke so mildly she might have been talking about a recipe or the weather. "I carried her to term, but I lost her before she ever took a breath."

Anna made a small involuntary moan, a little sound of pain and sympathy.

"It was a difficult birth," her grandmother continued, the yarn still jigging between her needles. "A dry birth, was what they called it back then. It took so long to get her out, I'd nearly given up on living myself by the time she came. I used sometimes to wonder if that was what had killed her, me forgetting about her in all my pain."

"Oh, no," Anna answered ardently, reaching her hand toward her grandmother, although she sat too far away to touch her. "That couldn't—"

"I know that now," her grandmother said. "But then I wanted so much for there to be a reason. I needed some way to understand it, something to blame. Even if the blame was mine, it seemed easier to bear. It's hardest, you know, just to let things be."

Warm as the light from a candle flame, a glow was widening low in the sky behind the crest of the farthest hill. The moon, Anna thought, and beyond all expectation she felt an answering bloom of hope.

"Afterwards," her grandmother went on, "everyone had an explanation for why I shouldn't take it too hard. They said the Lord needed her in heaven, or that her heart was so weak she would only have suffered had she lived, or that it was a blessing I hadn't had her longer and come to know her more and love her better before she left me. But I just wanted to hit them when they talked like that, all of them—the doctor and the preacher and even my own mother. I wanted to spit at them, and kick and scream. There was a wildness," she said awkwardly, "I'd never known before. Sometimes that winter I wanted to tear off my apron and all my clothes and run into the fields and lie down in the snow and die. I had a longing to let the winter wheat sprout up through my ribs. I wanted to join her—my only daughter—in the dirt."

All the crimson roses had vanished into the evening, although the white roses still remained, hovering like glowing ghost-flowers in the darkness.

"What was she like?" Anna asked, and then cringed, afraid she'd asked something wrong.

"She was the loveliest thing," her grandmother answered promptly, her voice ringing as though she were reading from the Bible or telling a story she knew by heart. "Though I got only a glimpse of her, in the nurse's arms. They said it would be too upsetting if I held her. But I never forgot how she looked. She was the prettiest of all my babies, the very prettiest one."

The edge of moon rose above the horizon, spreading a wide nimbus of yellow light in the dark blue sky. "How did you stand it," Anna asked softly, "losing her?"

So harshly it almost sounded like a rebuke, her grandmother answered, "I didn't have a choice."

"I—know," Anna said. "I'm sorry." She pressed her open hand against her stomach.

"No one has a choice," her grandmother added gently. "You always think, 'I couldn't bear that,' but when it happens, you see you have no option but to bear it."

The moon broke free of the horizon, rose full and huge and golden into the clear night sky. Her grandmother spoke again. "You fold it back into your life, as best you can. I suppose a corner of my heart died when she did, and it never came back. But the rest of my heart compensated somehow, like the way they say a blind person's other senses get more alert.

"It's funny," she went on. "The boys all outgrew me, moved on into their own lives. But she stayed with me, all these years. Of course I imagined a life for her, how old she'd be, what she'd be doing, the kind of woman she'd have become, but she never left me, never moved on."

Gentle as a whisper Anna asked, "What was her name?"

"They buried her before I had a chance to name her. They said that was for the best, not to wait. But later I named her anyway, in my thoughts. I would have called her Lucy, had she lived. It's queer," she added softly. "But I only just now realized—I don't believe I've ever told anyone that before."

"Lucy," Anna repeated, looking at the moon. She wished she had the courage to cross the porch and fold her grandmother in her arms. She wished her grandmother would come across the porch to hold her.

"It's from the Latin," the old woman explained, "for light."

The breeze they had been waiting for suddenly arrived, rustling through the wheat like a sleeper shifting, wafting the scent of roses over them, licking Anna's bare arms so that she shivered and pulled her knees tighter to her chest. In the darkness the roses still bloomed, offering up to the night the shapes and colors that could no longer be seen by human eyes.

"I suppose," Anna mused, though she spoke so quietly she wasn't sure her grandmother would hear, "you just go on, in spite of everything."

There was a silence so long that the moon had risen higher in the sky before her grandmother finally spoke again. "Not in spite of," she answered above the soft clicking of her needles. "Because."

By now the moon was small and high and white. Around them, the fields seemed to be floating in the moonlight like pale roses. Looking across their curves and shadows, Anna suddenly felt as though she were seeing them for the first time. It was as though her vision had been doubled, as though her sight had expanded to include what was lost. She felt a deep ecstatic ache, felt the slow burn of tears rising in her eyes, felt the emptiness inside her thrumming like a gift. "Because," she whispered, gazing out on the glowing fields through the living film of her own tears, "because."

INTO THE FLUX

S ATURDAY MORNING WAS ALWAYS THE WEEK'S SWEETEST TIME, when the last five days of hurry and hard work and being apart from Melody had already begun to recede into the past, and the whole weekend still stretched out ahead, like a beach untouched by footprints, like a cake without a single bite gone. Saturday mornings Cerise did not have to punch in at the nursing home two hours before Melody's school began. On Saturday mornings they could get up together, Cerise waking long before Melody and then lying in bed, warm and grateful and dozing, waiting for Melody to crawl up from her mattress at the foot of Cerise's and worm her way into her mother's arms. On Saturday mornings Cerise did not have to worry about Melody getting up and dressing and fixing her own bowl of cereal and getting herself to school while Cerise was fifteen miles away, mopping her way down Woodland Manor's endless halls.

Saturday mornings they could have breakfast together, the two of them kneeling next to each other at the coffee table in the cramped front room, eating toaster waffles smeared with Jiffy and pooled with Aunt Jemima while cartoons flickered across the TV screen. It was their favorite breakfast, their Saturday breakfast, the breakfast Cerise splurged on once a week. It was the breakfast they fixed together for each other, working elbow to elbow in the cramped dark kitchen—Cerise keeping watch over the treacherous toaster while Melody spread peanut butter soft as shortening across the surface of each steaming waffle.

It was the breakfast they could savor, Cerise eating her waffle slowly, while Melody raised her plate to her face to lap up the last sticky goo. As they ate, Melody talked about the kids in her class and what her teacher had said, about what she had to do for homework and the kind of clothes she thought were cool, and Cerise, remembering her own unhappy days in school, listened in proud astonishment to her daughter's chatter.

There was a rhythm to Saturdays, a progression of pleasures that repetition only seemed to hone. After they had finished eating, Cerise cleared their dishes off the coffee table while Melody ran to the bathroom to get the hairbrush and the box that held their collection of sprays and gels and bows. On weekdays Melody had to brush her own hair. But Saturdays Cerise could fix it for her. On Saturdays she could take her time, glorying in the golden heft and gloss of her daughter's hair, brushing until it shone and crackled, and then, when it lay across Melody's shoulders and down her back like a tamed waterfall, trying out the styles she'd imagined all week as she dusted and mopped.

Once the first mean snarls were out, Melody would grow dreamy beneath the strokings of Cerise's brush. Sometimes she would sit for over an hour, gazing at the TV, her lips slightly parted, her eyes halflidded, her head bobbing to the rhythm of her mother's work.

"When you're older," Cerise would promise, pausing in her work to study the girls on TV, "we'll find the money to get you in one of those modeling schools." Her fingers flew, firm and deft and certain, twisting and smoothing strands of hair. "You'll like that, won't you?" she said, nodding at the screen. "When you're on TV, too." It was a rainy Saturday in mid-November, but the grimness of the weather only made their apartment feel cozier. With her hands busy in Melody's hair and the TV murmuring to itself and Saturday morning not even half over, it seemed impossible that everything would not turn out the way Cerise knew it should. Melody would become a model, and maybe they could afford to rent a bigger apartment or even buy a house, but nothing else would change. They would still have their Saturday mornings, would still have their waffles and the rest of their weekend pleasures.

They kept a box of crayons and a stack of coloring books beneath the sofa, and every Saturday, once Cerise was satisfied with Melody's hair, they got the crayons out. Coloring was another of their rituals, a weekend passion begun so long ago that by now it seemed they'd always done it. Together they had developed their own tastes and techniques for coloring, their own rules for how a finished picture should look. They knew all about shading and outlining, knew when to make their strokes parallel or when they should fill a space with tiny circles. They had an abhorrence for letting their crayons cross over a printed line or for pressing so hard that the colors left crumbs of wax on their work. They had learned how to keep their crayons pointed as they used them, turning them in their fingers so that their ends stayed sharp, and how to peel the wrappers off in tidy strips.

It was Melody who insisted they keep the box organized "by the rainbow," and they had long ago memorized the names of all the colors, reading them off the sides of the sticks like taxonomic facts—Indian red, carnation pink, Pacific blue, flesh. Magenta and gold were their favorites, and those they had to ration while they forced themselves to use the ugly colors, too—olive and brick and seal gray.

Once or twice Cerise had tried to amuse Melody by drawing her own copies of the pictures in their coloring books. But rather than being pleased by her mother's talent, it had only frustrated Melody that she couldn't make her own drawings look as good. So Cerise had abandoned drawing and returned to coloring, to the simple pleasure of choosing colors, to the little challenge of keeping within the lines, to an activity at which she and Melody could work as equals.

Now, taking her place beside her daughter as the rain came down outside, Cerise flipped through the book Melody had laid out for her and chose the page she wanted to work on first. Pulling the plum crayon from its spot between wisteria and violet, she started in on Snow White's skirt. Beside her, Melody chose aquamarine and began on Peter Pan. For a long time the patter of the rain, the rhythmic whispers of their crayons, their own soft puffs of breath, and the TV's chortle were the room's only sounds. It was hypnotic, the way each stroke left its color on the rough paper, fascinating the way the colors sang or jangled against each other. Cerise knew it was just a kid's thing, coloring, and yet it was so soothing on Saturday mornings to kneel beside Melody and rub their crayons in matching rhythms on their separate pages. It was so satisfying to inhale the woody scent of newsprint and the butter and Vaseline smell of the Crayolas. And sometimes it felt oddly urgent, too, to fill those empty shapes with color.

Cerise traded plum for butter and began to work on the collar of Snow White's dress. Gradually she forgot the ache in her back and the sick feeling of the worries she carried in her gut all week long. She forgot about the electric bill and the broken oven, forgot about her sore molar and her promise to call Rita, forgot about the new gym shorts Melody said she had to have for school, and once again two of them—she and Melody alone together—filled all the world.

When the knock came on the door, her first impulse was to ignore it, to sit in silence until whoever was on the other side gave up and went away. But glancing down at Melody, she realized that would be too much like lying to pretend they weren't at home, so she rose and answered the door.

"Grandma!" Melody cried when she saw Rita standing outside. "We're coloring."

"That's nice, darling," Rita said. Beneath her raincoat she was wearing black leggings and spike heels, and when she came inside, she filled the room with the smell of her perfume. Turning to Cerise, she said, "I got you a date."

"A date?" Cerise echoed in surprise.

"Tonight. Fred has a cousin whose wife just left him. He has a little boy about Melody's age. Fred and I'll take care of the kids, and you two can go out and have some fun."

"A boy?" said Melody, looking up from her picture and wrinkling her nose.

"I don't know," Cerise said warily. "Maybe not tonight."

"What," Rita said as her glance raked the room, taking in the coloring books, the crayons, the grainy TV screen, the shabby sofa, "you have other plans?"

"Well, Melody—"

"Melody can stay with us. She can make a new little friend."

"A boy?" Melody repeated indignantly.

Turning to Cerise, Rita said, "You need to spend more time with people your own age. You need to find some outside interests. And so does Melody. She needs friends."

"I have friends," Melody spoke up. "Lots of friends, at school. Girls," she added staunchly.

"She needs more going on at home," Rita said, speaking to Cerise. "She's nearly ten, for godsake. That's way too old to spend her weekends coloring. She needs a father."

Cerise felt a jab of confusion and concern. As much as she dreaded going on a date, she wanted what was best for Melody. "I didn't have a father," she said.

"Not because I didn't try," Rita answered curtly. "And besides, look what happened to you. You'd be in a lot better place right now if Fred had come along sooner."

"I don't mind it," Cerise said softly. "Where I am."

Rita looked around the room disdainfully. "You've lived in this dump ever since you moved out on me. That sofa must be ninety years old, at least, and it was junk when it was brand-new. You need a man to help you get ahead. How long have you been working at that place, anyway?"

"Woodland Manor? Four years, last month. Ever since Melody started kindygarden."

"See? You're never going to get anywhere, working there. All those old people." Rita gave a delicate shudder.

"They're okay," Cerise answered. "I like them. They can't help it that they're old."

"Fred's nephew's a great guy. He has his own business. You're probably a little tall for him, but he's already been in AA for eighteen months."

"I'm sure he's nice. I just—"

"It's not good for you to build your whole life around a kid. What will you do when Melody grows up and moves away?"

Melody looked up from her coloring indignantly. "I'll never move away," she said. "I love it here. I'd never leave my mommy in a million years."

For a moment Cerise gazed at her daughter, her heart swollen with so much gladness that it was hard to pay attention to what her mother was saying next.

"When you get older," Rita said, her voice somewhere between sugar and acid as she looked down at Melody, "things will change. You'll want a husband and a nice house of your own."

"I'll never want a husband if he's a boy," Melody exclaimed.

Turning to Cerise, Rita said, "Don't say I never tried to help you. Don't you ever say that. You got where you are all by yourself."

"I know," Cerise said mildly, bowing her head.

"Coloring!" Rita scoffed, taking a last disdainful look around the room before she swept back into the rain.

But even after Cerise closed the door behind her mother and Rita's footsteps echoed away down the steps, Rita's scent remained, her perfume lingering like a reproach that kept Cerise from returning to the morning. Rita was probably right, she thought as she watched Melody bending over her page, her lovely face intent, her French braid following the perfect curve of her head. Melody needed more in her life than a mother who was always tired and a weekend filled with coloring and toaster waffles. Melody needed more than the promise of modeling lessons someday.

But even if she managed to satisfy Rita and find herself a husband, she didn't like the thought of having to share Melody with someone else. She didn't want to have to divide her weekends between her daughter and some stranger Melody was supposed to call Dad. She didn't want to risk changing the way her life was now by trying to make it better. Besides, hadn't Melody herself just said she'd never leave her in a million years? And even if Melody did change her mind someday, even if she grew up and moved away, wasn't that all the more reason for Cerise to spend every minute that she could with Melody, right now?

A WEEK AGO THEY'D TAKEN A TOUR OF THE LABOR AND DELIVERY WING at the Salish hospital, Anna and Eliot and the other members of their childbirth class shuffling along behind their instructor like curious tourists, all of them shy and awkward and a little awed by the hurrying nurses, the gleaming halls and looming machines. Their childbirth instructor was a crisp, warm woman with a boyish haircut and a waist that seemed to grow smaller with each class meeting. At the end of the hall beyond the nurses' station, she'd stopped in front of a closed door and waited while her class clustered around her, the women with their lank hair and placid faces, the men looking small and cowed beside their swollen wives.

"This is our birthing room," she'd said, motioning to the door behind her. "I'd like for you to be able to see inside, but it's being used right now. If you want, you're welcome to stop by later and have a peek." As she continued talking, Anna's attention had been drawn from the instructor's description of the birthing bed to the sound that was coming from behind the closed door. At first it was so low, she wondered if she were really hearing anything at all, but slowly it grew in volume and urgency, increasing until it seemed to fill the hall. It was disturbing and embarrassing, the sound of something mating or someone dying. On and on it went, raw, unceasing, increasingly impossible to ignore as it forced its way through the scrubbed air. A wave of nervous giggles swept the class, and Anna felt hot and dizzy and exposed. Finally, with one last grinding exhalation, the moan had ended, although the echo of it seemed to linger around them like a foul smell.

Now she was inside that room herself, though it looked more like a medieval torture chamber than the pleasant place the childbirth instructor had described. Its walls were hung with chains and spikes and iron hooks, its floor was blotched with sinister stains, and instead of the oak birthing bed the instructor had mentioned, a rough wooden table dominated the room. Anna didn't feel any of the symptoms she and Eliot had learned about in their childbirth class, but she knew that she was supposed to be in labor, knew that she was expected to give birth as soon as she could because there were other pregnant women waiting outside the door. Obediently she climbed onto the table and lay back on the rough-hewn boards.

Hurry, came a voice, either from somewhere inside herself or from somewhere beyond the stone walls of the room. But although she strained her legs and tightened her stomach, she realized she had no idea how to get her body to produce a baby. She raised her head and looked around for Eliot. But the room was empty, and when she opened her mouth to call his name, no sound came out. An answer came to her anyway, from that same disembodied voice that was both her own and that of some distant authority. Forget about Eliot, it said. No one else can do this for you.

I can't do it alone, she pleaded. I don't know how.

You asked for this, the voice answered dispassionately. You said you wanted it.

She realized that in order for the baby to be born, she would have to give up some part of her own body—an eye, maybe, or an arm or a leg, or even her head. But though she wanted to do anything that would allow her to leave that room, she couldn't decide what piece of herself she could bear to lose. I need my whole self, she pleaded. I can't be a mother if I'm not all there.

In desperation she clambered off the table and grabbed one of the heavy iron hooks from the wall. Scrambling back up, she lay down again and, ignoring her bulging belly, plunged the hook directly into her heart. The baby can come out here, she thought with satisfaction, stabbing the hook into her chest, hacking herself open, jabbing deeper. She felt no pain, but when she craned her neck to look down at what she had done, she was suddenly appalled by the mess she'd made. A red hole gaped where her heart had been, the meat of it torn and raw and oozing, and she realized with a thickening horror that she would never again be the same.

She woke with a gasp and a shudder. She was lying on her side like a beached whale, breathing as heavily as though she'd been running up a hill. For a long moment she could still feel the hole in her chest, and she was sick with fright. But slowly that sensation began to yield to the feel of sheets, the press of blankets, the stir of cool night air against her face. A dream, she thought, relief pouring through her like brandy. She opened her eyes, saw the room that had been her bedroom for the last three years and her grandparents' bedroom for the sixty years before that and felt a surge of gratitude for those uncurtained windows and moonlit walls, for the gift of her intact chest, and the baby still safe inside her, for the warm bulk of her husband next to her on the bed.

Eliot, she thought, and heard his patient breathing answering her. She turned to face him, heaving herself over like a seal on a dock. Wriggling as close to him as her belly would allow, she tucked his butt into what was left of her lap, bent her knees to fit inside the crook of his, and draped her arm across his chest.

"Umph," he groaned.

"I had a dream," she said, speaking into the back of his neck.

Deep in his throat he made a sympathetic noise.

"I shouldn't wake you," she said remorsefully.

Reaching back, he gave her hip a drowsy pat. " 's good practice," he mumbled, his voice sticky with sleep.

"Good practice?"

"When the baby comes," he answered vaguely.

"I couldn't get it out," she said.

"Uh?"

"The baby. In my dream, I didn't know how to get it born." She stopped, and then blurted the thing she'd been afraid to say before. "What if I can't?"

"Can't what?"

"Can't have the baby." She shuddered, remembering the table like a chopping block or a sacrificial altar, remembering the bloody hook.

"You have the baby already," Eliot answered, his voice beginning to come into focus.

"What?"

Reaching behind him again, he placed his hand on her stomach, rubbed it as though he were polishing a great brass bowl. "The baby's right here."

"I mean, get it born," she insisted.

"You'll do fine."

"In my dream I didn't." She winced at the whine of fear her voice held.

"You're serious, aren't you?" He turned to face her, his face a pale shadow in the moonlit room.

"I guess so, yes."

For a moment he was so silent, it seemed to Anna she could hear the hush of the dark fields beyond the house. Then he said, "Remember how well we got that baby into you?"

"How well we got the baby in?"

"Last summer? Remember?"

"Yes, but that's diff—"

"Remember?" he said, his voice firm and warm. "On the butte?"

In the long dusk of a late June day they'd hiked up the western flank of the butte that rose behind the house like an island above the ocean of hills. They'd arranged their quilt so that the whole world seemed to spread out beneath them, green and clean and hazy with evening, and then, as the sunset flared behind the distant mountains, they'd shared a meal of bread and wine and cheese and the garden's first tomatoes.

Undressed, their bodies seemed more naked than they ever did inside, both of them pale and vulnerable, ephemeral as flowers. When he entered her, she'd felt the delicious shock of it in every cell. Eliot inside me, she'd marveled, rising up to welcome him. Above them in the darkening sky she could almost see the shimmer of the coming stars, could almost feel the little ache of their near-presence. Deeper and deeper inside herself Eliot took her, down into the dark cave of her own being, down to the molten want at her core, down until she'd forgotten the distant fields the deepening shadows the gathering stars forgotten the poke of the weeds beneath the quilt forgotten the sharp stones against her spine the air licking her thighs her toes digging into the earth until in the whole sweet evening it was only the two of them only the one of them and she'd given herself up to that one opened so wide it seemed the whole world came shuddering in I want it all, she'd thought or said or yelled, Everything.

"Remember?" Eliot asked gently, dangling his fingers along the place where her waist was hidden, tracing the underside of her swelling belly, fitting his palm to hold the curve that held their child.

She nodded against his chest. She remembered the pure sound of their coming ringing in the twilit air and how, a second later, a robin had cried out as though it were answering them, its voice piercing the evening like the star that was suddenly in the sky above them—the star that had been above them all along.

"You knew what you were doing then," he said, running his palm up her thigh. "You knew how to make a baby," he whispered, bending to lick her nipple. "Of course you'll know how to do what comes next."

She let him nuzzle her breast, let his fingers trail between her legs, inhaled his smell. She ran her tongue along his clavicle, tasted the salt of him, his warm skin. She felt his penis stir against her thigh, and she reached down to cup it in her hand, felt the push and press of it inside her palm. He kissed her, his mouth soft and sleepy-tasting. Inside her the baby kicked and stretched. She felt its head against her cervix, banging that disk of muscle that kept it separate from the outside world. Someone else inside me, she marveled, smiling into Eliot's kiss. His mouth widened, his smile answering hers. They pulled apart to grin at each other, the baby frolicking between them like a puppy.

This time when he entered her, the baby grew still, not sleepy but attentive, as though it were soaking their tenderness into its forming bones, squirreling their urgency away inside its brand-new brain, as though it were letting their happiness shape its heart.

Afterward, as they lay askew in each other's arms, ebbing slowly back from that astonishing beyond, the baby suddenly roused itself and stretched, one foot jamming Anna's ribs, its head butting against her cervix so firmly that it nudged Eliot's softening cock, and, in their laughter, he slipped away.

"See," he said, nuzzling her shoulder, "You'll know exactly what to do."

"I hope," she answered gratefully.

"I'll be the one who's clueless," he said. "I'll keep asking everyone where I left my cigars."

"Go back to sleep," she groaned.

"Okay," he answered instantly, settling into his pillow. Reaching over to give her belly a last companionable pat, he added, "You, too."

But long after Eliot's breath had grown slow and even, Anna lay awake, thinking over the web of choice and chance that had made her life. She lay awake beside her husband in the farmhouse her great-grandfather had built while her great-grandparents and her grandparents lay in the pioneer cemetery west of Salish, and her baby twisted inside her like a salmon. Memories passed through her with a logic that merged on dream. She remembered the first night she and Eliot had spent together in that room, how bereft she'd been to be there without her grandmother, and yet how satisfied she'd felt, too, to be buying the house that had sheltered her family for so long.

Low in her abdomen, Anna felt the poke of tiny foot or hand. Pressing her own hand against the spot, she thought of her grandmother's hands as they had been when Anna saw her last, in the nursing home in Spokane where they'd had to move her in the end. Someone— probably an aide or a volunteer—had painted her grandmother's nails with pink polish, and in her dementia those dabs of color had puzzled and pleased her. "Will you look at that!" she'd exclaimed over and over again, studying her twisted, pink-tipped fingers as though she couldn't imagine what they were or where on earth they'd come from.

The baby gave another leap, and Anna's memory shifted to Eliot's hands offering her a glass of wine on the night they met. She saw his ragged hair and his eyes as blue almost as glacial ice, but kind and warm. That was six years ago, at a party Spaulding University had hosted for new faculty. The gathering had been stilted and the wine was sour, but twelve months later they were married, and three years after that they'd moved out to the ranch, and even when the rest of the land had to be sold to settle the estate, it had not really troubled her, because she had Eliot and her work and the family home, because she knew she could never not own that land—not as long as she could see it every day.

"Perennial wheat," Eliot had answered that first night when Anna asked him what his research interests were, and she'd been enough of her grandfather's girl to laugh at the paradox of it, enough of her grand-mother's child to let herself be stirred by its promise. "I work with wheat, too," she'd answered almost coyly, taking a sip of the bad wine and thinking of her photographs. "But I teach in the art department."

"It might take a lifetime," Eliot had explained later that evening as he walked her back to the apartment she was renting at the edge of campus, "to develop a sustainable strain of perennial wheat. But it would be a life well spent. Right now, every bushel of wheat we harvest costs the earth two bushels of eroded soil. We have to find a way to farm sustainably, or our whole civilization will collapse." He'd been so ardent, saying that, his voice so clear and sure in the autumn darkness, and something inside her had opened in answer.

She was still so immersed in her memories that when the first pang came, she hardly noticed it, a tightening that seemed to crawl across her stomach like the squeeze of a blood-pressure cuff, though it eased before it caused her much pain. But later, when she was finally hovering above sleep's abyss, it came again—this time a groundswell strong enough to send her bobbing back to consciousness like a cork. It's probably nothing, she thought, pressing her hands against her belly as the last of it ebbed away.

It was too soon to wake Eliot, but she knew she couldn't sleep. As quietly as she could, she heaved herself out of bed, slipped her arms into the sleeves of her robe, and pulled it taut across her great belly. She tucked her feet into the slippers that lay scattered on the floor and shuffled across the hall to the room her grandmother had always called the guest room. Standing in the doorway, she could just make out her grandmother's rocking chair and the antique dresser Sally had refinished for them, its drawers newly stocked with diapers, tiny T-shirts, and thumb-size socks.

Another contraction caught her, a stronger one. Leaning against the door frame, she tried to let it pour over her, though she felt a little startled by its force. After it receded, she crossed the room to the rocking chair, tugged it in front of the window, and sat down. The moon had set, and the world the window looked out on was utterly dark. She stared at the blackness in front of her, waiting for morning to come or for another contraction to begin while snippets of thoughts continued to flow and eddy inside her.

In the early-morning darkness, the room she sat in seemed nearly eerie, waiting less for a guest than for a stranger, a person no one on earth had ever met. "Having a baby is exactly like falling in love," the art department secretary had said at the baby shower last week, and Anna had smiled and nodded and swallowed another forkful of Sally's lemon cake. But now those words came back to her cloaked in warning. Gazing through the black glass at the featureless cold, she thought of all the wrong ways there were to fall in love. She thought of all the mistakes she'd made before she met Eliot, of all the insight and oversight it took to keep even her good marriage alive, and it struck her yet again how much was at stake, how precarious one small baby made everything. With a shudder she realized that labor might be the easy part.

You asked for this, the voice in her dream had said. You said you wanted it.

I thought I did, she answered that dream-voice now. But maybe I didn't know.

Perhaps a tentative light had begun to seep into the eastern sky. Gazing out the window, she studied the darkness intently, trying to catch the instant when the land first emerged from the night. But, as always, that one moment slipped past her guard. It was impossible to say precisely when the yard and fields appeared, but suddenly there they were—vague shadows in the slowly brightening morning—and before she'd had a chance to appreciate it, the moment she'd been waiting for was gone. It was like standing in the darkroom, watching for the one second when the first shadows stained the blankness of a sheet of paper drifting in the developer tray.

She felt a little twist of sorrow, thinking of her darkroom. She hadn't developed a sheet of film or made a print since before she conceived. At first, she'd tried to appease her need to work by exposing film, even though she knew she would have to wait until the baby was weaned before she could develop or print it. But after a while she'd given up. It had been half a year now since she'd even exposed any film, and though she still yearned for the way her work scrubbed and sharpened her, the way it left her open and awake and made her whole life feel valuable and right, she had also begun to wonder if, once the baby was finally weaned, she would have the time to teach and be a mother and make photographs, too. Sometimes that question made her feel vaguely desperate, as if she, too, were trapped inside her womb, though at other times it was almost appealing to think that her life could be complete without the work of making art.

Outside, the light was returning more and more texture to the world. Earlier in the week there'd been a Chinook wind, and now the land the dawn revealed was bare of snow. Down in the yard her grandmother's dormant roses huddled like heaps of sticks beneath their blankets of cold straw. Across the raw hills Anna could make out the merest mist of green—the billion tiny blades of winter wheat waiting to be woken by the longer light of spring. Her grandmother had once longed to let that wheat grow through her bones, and now, looking out on the strengthening morning, Anna remembered how learning of her grandmother's loss had given her a way to face her own.

It would be ten by now, if it had been—that wisp, that ache, that pearl, that seed of light. Even now it sometimes hovered just beyond her inner sight, like a star before the fall of evening brings it into view. It was still an emptiness too precious to be dissolved by words. She'd never spoken of it to anyone, not even Eliot. She'd never told anyone, and she had not forgotten. For ten years it had been her talisman, her charm, her reminder of all she owed the world.

Not in spite of, her grandmother had said; Because. And the next day Anna had taken her camera from the trunk of the little Subaru she used to drive. She'd exposed three rolls of film before sundown, hungrily shooting everything she saw—the rough heaps of beets, the filled canning jars gleaming like secrets in the dim cellar, the grain-covered hills rippling with the pattern of the wind, the tousled roses, her grandmother's long-veined hands. Because, she'd thought like a mantra or a blessing or a plea each time she pressed the shutter release. Because.

The squeeze of her uterus began again, slow, insinuating, growing until she felt a bite of hurt. Two years ago at harvest time she'd made an exposure with her field camera looking out that very window. *Because,* she called it, and now a print of it hung in the Whitney in New York. She liked to think of the strangers who paused in front of it. She liked to think that perhaps some few of them understood.

Her belly continued to tighten. The pain was sturdier this time, wicked, unexpected. A whiff of her dream returned. She felt a spike of panic, remembered the hook, the table, her mangled heart. The pain drove deeper, widening inside her, climbing up her spine, filling her pelvis, seeping down her legs. It pushed from her a moan, low and guttural, a near-growl that fit perfectly inside her throat. She heard in her own voice the sound that had appalled her in the hall of Salish Hospital, but she understood it now and answered it, let that same moan pour out of her.

I am having a baby, she thought in astonishment as the contraction began to ease. Despite her pain, elation blossomed in her chest. She remembered Eliot's sleepy answer, You have the baby already. Looking out the window at the morning, she felt shivery, thin with excitement, entirely alive. I asked for this, she thought as the next contraction came.

MRS. SONNEGRAD HAD DIED IN THE NIGHT, SO 304 WAS EMPTY. THE mortician had already come for the body; the aide had stripped the sheets and left the window open so the summer heat could bake the smell of death from the room. Now it was Cerise's job to pack up Mrs. Sonnegrad's things and prepare the room for the next resident. It was a chore she'd had to do dozens of times in the nearly seven years she had worked at Woodland Manor. Even so, she entered 304 cautiously, though once she was inside it was hard to see the threat lurking in that quiet room or in the dresses and knickknacks Mrs. Sonnegrad had left behind her.

Cerise got to work, spraying the plastic mattress cover, wiping it down, and then horsing the mattress off the bed so she could clean the frame. It had been less than a month since the last time she'd disinfected 304, so it was an easy job, not like other times, when the residents who died had been there for years, and along with the dust on the mattress springs, she'd had her own sadness to deal with. Cerise had only a fleeting image of Mrs. Sonnegrad, a shrunken woman lying silently between the raised railings of her bed as her gray-haired son leaned over to hold her hand.

She tore a plastic trash bag off the roll on her cart and began placing Mrs. Sonnegrad's things inside. It seemed so strange to think that Mrs. Sonnegrad was gone when her nylon underpants and her pink hearing aid remained. Cerise tried to imagine where Mrs. Sonnegrad was now, and she felt as though she were standing on a high tower, looking down into endless space. She shuddered and went back to work, sorting and folding Mrs. Sonnegrad's clothes, tucking her terry slippers together heel to toe, setting everything neatly at the bottom of the billowing trash bag. On top of the pile of folded clothes she laid the things from the bureau—a pocket calendar, a color portrait of two red-haired toddlers, a black-and-white photograph of a mild-faced woman in a beaded evening dress.

The final item on the bureau was a figurine, a little fawn made of dime-store china, and Cerise paused to study it before she added it to the bag. It looked so cute, with its wide eyes, splayed legs, and dappled sides, but when she turned it over in her hand, she saw that it had once been badly broken. Its legs were marred with yellowing lines of epoxy, and one had been set a little crookedly. Her heart gave a sudden clench of pity, to think that someone had valued that little thing enough to fix it, to think that of all the knickknacks a woman like Mrs. Sonnegrad must have owned, that little dime-store fawn had stayed with her to the end. It seemed important, somehow precious, and she hated to think of shutting it away inside the dark plastic.

In all the years she had worked among the feeble and the senile, handling their watches and wallets and wedding rings, she had always taken a stubborn pride in the fact that she had never stolen or broken anything. But now she imagined she might save that fawn. Suddenly she felt an impulse to tuck it in her pocket and take it home—not for herself, but as a gift for Melody.

Thinking of Melody, she felt as though she were standing back on that high tower, looking down. Melody was nearly twelve now, and almost as tall as Cerise herself. In the last few months it seemed as though a whole new person had taken up residence inside her gawky body. The pudgy nubs of breasts were swelling on her chest, and lately she'd begun to turn her back to Cerise when she undressed. Even her smell was changing, growing sharper and earthier and more complex, no longer the clean animal scent she'd carried in her hair and on her skin the year before.

Over the summer Melody had taken to sleeping on the sofa in the front room instead of on her mattress at the foot of Cerise's bed. On the weekends, rather than coloring with Cerise or letting Cerise fix her hair, she wanted to go ice skating or to the movies, wanted to hang out at the mall with her friends, and when Cerise said No, she had to stay at home and do her homework, or Sorry, they had no money for skates or Cokes or movies, Melody rolled her eyes in disdain.

The women's magazines Cerise picked up in the Woodland Manor staff room claimed that preteens could be sulky and private, and warned that parents needed to use good communication skills and set limits now, before their kids became real teenagers. That made it seem like Melody was a time bomb that must somehow be disassembled before she exploded, but although Cerise wanted desperately to do whatever she could to make things right, she had no idea where to begin. Recently it seemed that being nice to Melody was like pouring water into sand, while insisting that Melody clean the kitchen or do her homework or not talk back only made things worse.

It seemed like only yesterday that Melody had vowed she'd never leave Cerise, and now it felt like she was already gone. Now when Cerise looked back along that chain of days that led from Melody's birth to the present, it seemed they were linked not by the firsts the staff room magazines were always talking about, but by hundreds of unnoticed lasts. She could remember when Melody got her first tooth, could remember when she took her first step. She could remember Melody's first word and her first day of school. But somehow those milestones were not nearly as significant as all that Cerise could not remember—the last time they'd colored together, the last time Melody had let Cerise fix her hair, the last Saturday breakfast they'd eaten side by side.

Cerise gazed at the trinket on her callused palm and imagined teaching Melody the tricks she'd learned in her own childhood, imagined showing Melody how to clean the little fawn with a damp washcloth so the epoxy wouldn't give, and helping her to dress it with scraps of fabric. She imagined Melody talking to the fawn, and inventing little stories about it, imagined Melody snuggling up beside her and telling those stories to her, too. No one would ever know, she told herself, if she rescued the fawn for Melody. And even if they did, why would they care? She envisioned the gray-haired son opening the sack that held his mother's final possessions and tossing the broken fawn into the trash.

But suddenly she saw how worn and grubby and faded it was. With a knowledge so swift and certain it sucked her breath away, she realized that Melody wouldn't want something that old and ruined. Melody liked mall things—slick, brand-new, and bright. At best she would be indifferent, distantly polite. "Thanks, Mom," she might say, and stuff the figurine into the back of her underwear drawer. But at worst she would ask coldly, "Where did you get that thing?" and then Cerise would have to choose between the disgrace of lying to her daughter and the humiliation of telling her the truth.

Her shoulders slumped. She wrapped the fawn in a wad of facial tissues, set it on top of the little pile in the depths of the bag. Shutting the bag with a twistee, she placed it, tidy and hapless as a hobo's bundle, on the disinfected mattress and headed down the hall to 306.

* * *

SALLY KNELT ON THE CANVAS DROP CLOTH THAT COVERED THE FLOOR OF her family room and pried the lid off a gallon of paint with a screwdriver. "I learned a new word last night," she said.

Beneath the humor in her sister's voice there was an unexpected sharpness that reminded Anna of sandpaper or vinegar. "A new word?" she asked, gingerly shifting her position to avoid waking the baby sleeping against her chest. Lucy. She bent her neck, buried her face in the down that crowned Lucy's head, and inhaled. The scent of her infant hit her brain like a pheromone, like a necessary drug. Lucy, she thought gratefully, and her eyelids fluttered closed for a second of near-ecstasy before she opened them to fasten a questioning glance on Sally.

"Being married to an English professor's a real vocabulary builder," Sally answered dryly. Lifting the can in both hands, she tipped it so that a column of mustard-colored paint poured down into the tray that sat on the floor beside her. Then, giving the can an expert twist, she cut the flow of paint without spilling a single drop.

"What was last night's word?" Anna asked. It was a brilliant afternoon in mid-September, and Sally had propped the door to the backyard open for ventilation. The air that entered the room carried with it the musky tang of falling leaves. From her place on the draped couch, Anna looked hungrily out through the door to the light-drenched maples that rimmed Sally's yard. Even as she soaked their loveliness deep into her bones, she was calculating camera angles and shutter speeds, imagining how she might shoot them. It had been fifteen months since she'd been able to make a print, but in the six months since she'd had Lucy, she had used her field camera to expose another thick stack of film sheets. It was as if Lucy's arrival had given her yet another set of eyes, and though she still had to wait until Lucy was weaned before she could develop and print that pile of negatives, thinking of it made her warm with promise, as though she were hoarding secret riches or gestating something new.

"Teenful," Sally answered, hammering the lid back on her paint can and giving Anna a glance that held as much grimace as smile. "Last night's new word was teenful."

"Teenful?" Anna echoed doubtfully. "As in, full of teen?"

"Teenful, as in 'causing trouble or sorrow, vexatious, wrathful, malicious, injurious, spiteful,'" Sally recited angrily. She pushed a thick strand of steel-colored hair from her temple with the heel of her hand. Sally was already forty—seven years older than Anna. Over the last few years it had seemed to Anna that Sally's face was somehow growing younger beneath her prematurely graying hair, but looking at her now, Anna noticed a tight new strain around her mouth, a kind of hardened resignation in her eyes.

"Is everything okay?" Anna asked. It had been a while since she'd stopped by for a visit, and she wondered belatedly what had been going on with her sister while she'd been so absorbed in Lucy.

"Everything's fine," Sally answered, her voice brittle. "It's just that Jesse borrowed the car last night."

"Wow—I guess I didn't realize he had his license yet."

"He doesn't," Sally said grimly. "But he does have a girlfriend, and he thought it would be a really nice idea to sneak out at midnight and take her for a little ride."

"Oh, my God." Anna gasped and clutched involuntarily at Lucy. "What happened?"

"We got the call at two this morning. My Chrysler was in a ditch out on Hodge Road, and Jesse was being held at the police station until he could be released into our custody."

"Is he okay?" Anna asked. Panic begin to rise inside her, and she was bewildered that Sally seemed so calm. "How about his girlfriend?"

"Everyone is fine," Sally answered. Her voice was bright and sharp, more angry than relieved.

"He must have been terrified." Anna said. She felt Lucy's slack, warm weight against her chest like a gift. Like a given, Anna thought, soaking up the feeling of her daughter, grateful for the way Lucy's flesh served as a comfort and an anchor, even now.

"Jesse wasn't terrified." Sally laughed harshly and turned to face Anna. "He was teenful. On the way home he had the gall to yell at me because he claimed we'd treated him like a child in front of his girl-friend." Her voice went shrill with fury. "Of course we treated him like a child. He is a child. Do grown-ups run around stealing each other's cars? I told him we'd treat him like an adult the minute he started to act like one, and not a goddamn second sooner."

To escape the blast of her older sister's rage, Anna bent her face and pressed her lips to Lucy's head. Beneath her down-fine hair, Lucy's scalp was damp with sleep. When Anna pulled her mouth away, Lucy's hair clung to her lips, as weightless as light. She asked, "What are you going to do now?"

Sally shrugged. "What can I do? The police are still deciding whether or not to press charges. It's out of our hands."

"Yes, but, I mean—"

"He's grounded, of course, and he's lost his allowance until Christmas."

"Aren't you going to talk with him?"

"We told him he'd better not ever pull a stunt like that again."

"But don't you want to find out why he did it?"

Sally looked at her sister strangely. "He did it to impress his girl-friend."

"Maybe in the short term, but—"

"But what?"

"He's fifteen," Anna answered, groping. "Don't you think he's trying to figure things out?"

"Figure things out?" Sally scoffed. "Like where the clutch is?"

"Like how to live, what matters, and what it all means? You know—the same stuff we were trying to figure out back then."

"Not Jesse," Sally said acidly. "He's convinced he's already got every-thing figured out. Besides, trying to talk to Jesse is like trying to talk to a sack of turnips." She made her voice drop an octave, " 'I dunno. Yeah. Fuck, no'—that's the extent of a conversation with Jess. Living with an English professor hasn't done a thing for *his* vocabulary." Glancing over at Anna, Sally added darkly, "Just wait. Your time will come. Before you know it, little Lucy there will be joyriding around the countryside with a beer in one hand, a joint in her mouth, and a boy groping her thigh."

Not Lucy, was Anna's instant thought, Never Lucy. She knew that utterly and instinctively, but she could find no way to say it that didn't sound either smug or naïve, no way to say it that wouldn't make her sister scoff. "Maybe," she said reluctantly. "We'll see."

"You'll see, all right," Sally said, tearing open a package of sea sponges with her teeth.

Sally's face was stark. Her eyes above the package looked so bereft, it startled Anna. This wasn't the first time she'd seen Sally struggle with Jesse, though always before, her anger had seemed like the logical conclusion of her love. But today it was as though some elemental thing had changed, as though some essential part of her connection to her son had ossified or soured, like a marriage gone bad. She's given up, Anna thought with a shiver.

Sally dipped a sponge into the mustard-colored paint and then pressed it nearly dry against the side of the tray. "This had better be right," she announced grimly. "Yarrow on barley. But it always looks different when there's a whole room of it." Methodically she began to daub the sponge against the wall. It left a mottled pattern on the cream-colored surface, like a dappling of light or a crayon scrubbed across concrete.

"How's that?" she asked, stepping back to study the effect.

"It's nice," answered Anna, more heartily than she felt. She wanted to beg Sally to do something, but she had no idea what to suggest. She wondered if she should maybe try to talk to Jesse herself, but then she was afraid that Jesse would resent it as much as Sally and Mike probably would if she tried to interfere. Besides, Jesse was no longer the creamy-faced boy who used to love to visit Eliot and her at the ranch. In the past few years he'd grown sullen and reluctant, resentful of all adults. It might not be as easy as she imagined to reach him now.

"This'll take a while," Sally was saying as she dipped her sponge back into the paint. "But it should be worth it. This room has never been cozy enough," she muttered as she turned back to the wall.

In Anna's lap, Lucy made a little moan. Arching her back, she stretched one soft fist above her head and squeezed her face into a waking grimace. Her eyes opened, and she looked around solemnly, giving equal attention to everything in her line of vision—the door frame, the ladder, the glowing maple leaves. She's like me, Anna thought with an odd shudder of pride and fear.

She lifted her shirt and opened her bra, and Lucy began nursing, her dark eyes staring gravely out the sunlit doorway, one small hand resting light as a breath against Anna's stomach, her fingers scrambling gently over Anna's skin. Flesh of my flesh, Anna thought, reaching down to stroke her daughter's arm.

She looked up to see Sally studying them, the sponge poised in her hand. There was something clinical in her look, but something wistful, too, as though she were hearing a far-off music that triggered an even more distant memory. "I once got kicked out of the Chicago Art Institute for nursing Jess," she said.

"Really?" Anna asked. "I don't remember that."

"It was the summer Mike was finishing his dissertation. Jesse and I used to spend every Tuesday at the Institute, because on Tuesdays it was free. It was air-conditioned, too." She replenished the paint on her sponge and began to dapple a new patch of wall. "Anyway, I was sitting in front of one of Gauguin's bare-breasted Madonnas, and suddenly a guard came up and told me I needed to go to the bathroom."

"Go to the bathroom?" Anna puzzled.

"At first I didn't get it, either. But when I finally realized what he meant, I asked so loud that everyone in the gallery could hear, 'Do I look like I need to take a crap that bad?' "

"You're kidding." Anna's laughter made Lucy give a startled jump and pull away from her breast. For a moment she looked around perplexedly, and then, catching sight of her mother, her face bloomed in a milky smile.

"I was pretty brash," Sally said, pride and rue mingling in her voice. "Back then."

Anna smiled down at Lucy. "Not unlike Jesse . . . ," she suggested gently.

"Unlike Jesse," Sally answered with surprising fervor, "I never stole my parents' car. I never drove without a license. That little bastard could have killed himself. He could have died. And his girlfriend, too. He could have killed that girl, and I would have been stuck trying to explain to her parents what my goddamn son had done." Sally had stopped sponging. Her voice was high and loud, and her eyes glittered. A streak of mustard paint decorated her cheek like a fading bruise. "I just—" she began helplessly, and then she stopped and gathered herself. "It's hard," she muttered. Turning to Anna, she said, "I suppose I should have warned you."

"Warned me?" Anna asked perplexedly.

"About having kids."

"Oh, no—" Anna began, clutching Lucy as though she might even now be taken back.

Sally studied her sister dispassionately for a moment and then, with a bitterness that broke Anna's heart, she added, "Maybe you can do better than me."

"But, Sally," Anna began fervently. "It's not too—"

"Or maybe I should just shut up. I'm sorry," Sally said. "I'm not being fair. You don't need me to tell you all this right now. You need to just enjoy things while you can."

I'll enjoy them forever, Anna answered inside her head. But looking at her sister standing in the warm autumn light, her handsome face stiff with anger and grief, she was suddenly gripped by a fear so fierce that for a moment she couldn't remember how to breathe.

* * *

WHEN CERISE ENTERED THE WOODLAND MANOR DINING ROOM, THE morning sunlight was slanting through the tall east windows. Great rectangles of brightness lay on the linoleum, and the whole room seemed as peaceful as a chapel. The kitchen staff had already cleared the dishes, though the tables and chairs were littered with clots of oatmeal, shards of toast, soggy paper napkins. "We eat family style," Cerise must have heard the director announce a thousand times as he paraded potential residents' relatives through the dining room.

She parked her cart inside the double doors and got to work, spraying cleaner in swift arches, wiping the tabletops and the seats of the chairs and then piling the chairs on the tables. Her sneakers squeaked on the linoleum. She paused to push a wisp of hair back from her face with her forearm. She planned to take her break as soon as she finished the dining room. If she hurried, she might have the staff room to herself, and she could call home and see if Melody had managed to get to school. When all the chairs were off the floor, she took the broom from the cart and began to sweep. As she bent to chase a pile of toast crumbs and egg scraps into her dustpan, she wondered how many times she had cleaned that floor since she'd started work at Woodland Manor.

She knew she could figure it out—five days a week times fifty weeks a year times nine years, minus the days Melody had been too sick to stay at home alone, and the few days Cerise had had to take off for herself, to see a doctor at the health clinic that time when her back was so bad, to go to the dental school when her molar got abscessed. She could figure it out, she thought, as she tipped the gatherings from her dustpan into the trash bag on her cart, but it would only make her tired.

The door from the kitchen swung open. An aide came out to get the coffee urn, and a thick steam of meat and starch and bleach wafted toward Cerise, triggering the queasiness it seemed these days she always carried with her, as if her worry about Melody were another pregnancy pushing its constant nausea against the back of her throat. Her stomach lurched as though she might be sick when she thought of Melody as she had been that morning, sprawled across the sofa in a stupor so deep that none of Cerise's questions or pleas or warnings could cause her to do more than flop a limp arm and mutter, "Go away."

When the dining room was mopped, she pushed her cart down the hall to the staff room and peeked inside. It was empty, and she entered with a sigh. Usually she was able to resist the invitation of the soft-drink vending machine that purred next to the time clock by reminding herself of the generic diet sodas she kept in her refrigerator at home and rationed out to herself—a can a day—after work. But today, after only a moment's struggle, she dug through her pockets, found three quarters, and fed them to the machine. She made her selection, and a can of Diet Coke thunked down onto the shelf.

Standing in front of the grubby microwave, she pried the pull tab open, took the first sip, felt the icy carbonation bite her mouth, let its sweetness widen like a little gift inside her. She sat beneath the wall phone on one of the vinyl-covered chairs that edged the room, and when her can was half-finished, she lifted the receiver and called home. The phone rang, steady and lonely as the beating of a heart, until Cerise hung up.

Two dozen limp magazines—mostly parenting and fashion, a few on news or travel—were strewn across the coffee table in the center of the room. Gazing from their covers were an assortment of women as lush as tree-ripened peaches. These days Melody scoffed at her mother's dream of modeling. "Get real," she'd said last week when Cerise had suggested they enter her picture in a contest for modeling classes she'd seen advertised at the Rite Save pharmacy. "Do you remotely think I'd have a chance? Besides, it sucks, all that crap."

Melody claimed that modeling was bullshit. She said what she really wanted to do was be an artist, but Cerise could see no future in that, even if she believed that what Melody did could be considered art.

Melody seemed to have inherited Cerise's old knack for drawing. In the past few years she'd discovered she could copy pictures and even sketch the things she saw so that they looked as real as the originals. But instead of using her talent to draw pretty things—things that might soothe people or cheer them up—Melody made drawings of lizard skulls and road-killed rabbits, sketches of used lipstick tubes and crushed soda cans.

Last fall for the school art show she'd collected a bag of trash from the side of the freeway, spray-painted it gold, piled it on a pedestal, and called it *Harvest*. When Cerise protested that it was just a heap of junk, Melody had rolled her eyes and tossed her hair and groaned as though it was hopeless to even try to get Cerise to understand.

Melody fixed her own hair now, or rather didn't fix it, but instead found a new way to wreck it every week. The day after Cerise mentioned the modeling contest, Melody came home with her beautiful hair dyed midnight black, and since then she'd braided feathers and beads into a few random strands and let the rest hang like a dead mane down her back. When Cerise protested that she thought Melody had looked prettier before, Melody said that pretty sucked, that her new friends thought she looked way bad. Melody was proud of how much older than she her new friends were—girls of seventeen or eighteen, their faces smooth and hard as ceramic masks, and slouching boys already out of high school.

Melody had gone out with those friends last night. When Cerise observed it was a school night, Melody said they were only going to the library, to study for a quiz. "I thought you wanted me to get good grades," she'd snapped. But the library closed at nine o'clock, and Cerise had stayed up until two waiting for Melody to come home. For the last hour she sat with her hand on the receiver of the phone, both willing and dreading its ring. She had considered calling someone herself—the police maybe, or another parent—but she was scared of what might happen if she got Melody involved with the law, and she cringed at the thought of waking a stranger to admit that her daughter had not yet come home. Finally, because she had to be at work at six, she went to bed, and though she had not intended to, she slept so heavily she did not hear when Melody came in.

From beyond the staff room door Cerise heard the sound of voices. She looked up from the sprawl of magazines and blinked to regain her focus.

"Exterior only," a male voice said. "Obviously that's all that matters to the Man with the Money, what it looks like from the street."

The two men who pushed their way into the room were wearing work boots and canvas coveralls streaked like clown suits with a dozen different colors of paint. They brought with them a breeze of turpentine and sunshine.

"Oops," said the taller one when he saw Cerise.

"What?" she asked, jumping up as though she'd been caught at something.

He grinned at her confusion and asked, "Are you his daughter?" His brown hair was stiff with a dusting of white paint that made him look prematurely aged, although for a moment Cerise saw the boy he must have been, quick and brash in torn jeans, his hair cowlicked into confusion, his smile melting stones.

"What?" she said again, standing awkwardly in front of him, hating how she could never find the right words in time. But the man laughed as though she'd said something clever. "That's right—not who, but what. The Man with the Money. Herr Doctor Director. Mr. Harding—that's what."

"He's my boss."

"I knew you were too pretty to be his daughter," he answered, while the other guy dug into his pocket for soda change.

He studied her for another moment, then said, "Hey—he's my boss, too." He turned to his buddy. "Doesn't that mean she and me're related?"

Spreading his arms wide as though he were going to fling them around her, he said, "Sweetheart, remember me? Your favorite long-lost uncle Jake! Come here and give Uncle Jakie a great big hug."

But Cerise ducked his embrace. Tossing her empty can into the box by the machine, she said, "I got to get to work," and left, letting the staff room door swing shut on the sound of the men's laughter.

The apartment was empty when Cerise got home from work, although Melody's presence blared in the mess she'd left behind—clothing draped over the sofa, dishes strewn across the floor, schoolbooks stacked unopened on the coffee table. A note on top of the books said she was at the library, studying. It was signed, "Love Melody," like a command.

Cerise kicked her shoes off beside the door and crossed the room to turn on the TV. An image bloomed obediently on the screen, a pulsing montage of soft drinks and gaping mouths. She stood watching it, dazed by its flood of pep and urgency, until finally her own thirst drove her to the kitchen.

When she opened the refrigerator and saw that her six-pack of diet colas was gone, her immediate thought was to go buy more. But then she remembered she'd given the last of the grocery money to Melody so she could buy the leather boots she'd put on layaway last October.

"What were you thinking?" Cerise had asked when Melody told her she would lose the deposit if she didn't pay the balance that week, "to put something that expensive on layaway?"

"I had to," Melody said, her voice heavy with contrived patience, as though she were explaining something to a stupid child. "I didn't have the money at the time."

"You don't have the money now, either."

"It's only twenty more," Melody pleaded. "Otherwise I'll lose the eighty-five I've already paid."

"Eighty-five," Cerise echoed, thinking of rent, of the electric bill, of all she still owed the dental school. But when she gave Melody the money, Melody had flung her arms around her, hugging her so warmly and treating her with such friendliness for the rest of the evening that it was almost like old times once again.

Cerise ran a glass of tap water and fixed a bologna sandwich for herself. She carried her meal out to the coffee table, sat down on the sofa, and rummaged beneath the blankets for the remote. These days, with the TV as her sole companion at meals, it sometimes crossed her mind to get out the crayons and color while she ate. But when she imagined Melody's contempt if she were to come home and find her mother coloring, she always chose the television instead.

She took a bite of sandwich and began to surf, pausing to watch a news segment about a missing teenager. The newscasters said the girl had last been seen the evening before, climbing onto a motorcycle with a man she'd met at the party she'd snuck out after her curfew to attend. The newscasters' smooth faces held practiced little furrows of concern as they said the police were asking the public to help in their widening search.

Some talk about the stock market came on next, but Cerise was too overcome to bother to change the channel. It made her panicky to think what Melody might be doing at that very minute, where she might be instead of at the library. There were hundreds of ways that Melody could be killed, thousands of ways for her life to be ruined, and what scared Cerise most was that Melody didn't seem to care. These days it seemed that Melody's life meant more to Cerise than it did to Melody herself.

She should quit work, Cerise thought as she stared at the TV screen where a woman and a man ran toward each other across a flower-spangled meadow. Melody needed someone to keep an eye on her. She needed someone to insist she did her homework, to see she got to school every day, got home on time at night. She needed someone to be there for her, to listen like the articles and news shows said parents were supposed to listen to their teens. Things hadn't been easy for Melody, Cerise knew that— growing up with no money and no father, in a crummy apartment with a mother who was always working extra hours, who was always tired.

She felt a stab of remorse, remembering the times Melody had been sick and had to stay home by herself because if Cerise missed another day at work, she wouldn't be able to pay the rent. Occasionally there had been a friend to check in on her, or, before Rita and Fred moved to Florida, Rita would sometimes stop by on her lunch hour to see that Melody was okay. But mostly Melody had had to endure her fevers, colds, and flus alone, watching daytime TV and eating her solitary lunches from cracker boxes and soup cans.

She should quit her job, Cerise thought as the couple on the TV screen met in the middle of the meadow. Now, before it was too late, she should devote everything to Melody. They could make popcorn together, could watch the late-night shows. Cerise would try to help Melody with her homework. She would get to know Melody's new friends. They could eat their meals together again, family style.

But then her thoughts began a circle as familiar and as endless as the paths she mopped through Woodland Manor's halls—for hadn't she already devoted everything to Melody? Hadn't she lived these last fourteen years for Melody alone? Hadn't every hour of overtime been for Melody—to feed her, to pay for shelter, to buy her clothes? Hadn't she already done everything she could for Melody?

Besides, quitting work meant going back on welfare. Cerise watched as a squad of cartoon roaches fled from a giant can of bug spray. She felt the slump of defeat the thought of the welfare office always caused in her, its grubby rooms crowded with strangers as intent on their own needs as people in the betting hall at a racetrack. She remembered the rules, the stacks of forms, remembered the stream of weary caseworkers who all ignored the fact that her meager list of monthly expenses always came to more than her benefits ever did. Some of them were kind and some were mean, but all of them made sure to warn her that if she failed to report any extra income she could be sent to jail, and not one of them ever asked how she was able to cover the difference. She remembered how necessary it had been to accept Rita's grudging help, and thought how unlikely it would be to get more help from Rita now.

And what would it teach Melody anyway, Cerise asked herself as the roaches writhed and died, if she were to go back on welfare? Especially now, when every argument about Melody's blighted future swung back to Cerise's failed past, quitting her job and going back on welfare—even for Melody's sake—would only prove Melody's point.

It was the gunning of an untuned car that tore her from her sleep. Her half-eaten sandwich had fallen to the floor, and the apartment was dark, lit only by the TV and the streetlight outside the window. Her body ached from sleeping on the sofa and her brain felt glued shut, but she rose and moved unerringly across the room. She opened the door to find Melody standing in front of her, her head lolling to one side so that her black hair hung over her shoulder like a ragged shawl.

"You okay?" Cerise croaked through her sleep-drenched throat. Something about Melody looked so wrong that for a moment Cerise reinhabited the night Melody's fever had risen to 105 and she had woken to find the body of her toddler daughter jerking on the sweaty sheets, her eyes rolled up into her skull as though she were looking inside her own brain.

" 'm fine," Melody slurred, swaying vaguely in some private breeze.

"What's happened?" Cerise asked, the sound of the fear in her own voice pricking her into a painful wakefulness.

The light from the bulb above the door lost itself in the blackness of Melody's hair. She stumbled against the door frame and mumbled, "Nothin'."

A few moths battered their soft bodies against the lightbulb above their heads while the realization of what it was that each of them was facing seeped through Melody's daze and Cerise's exhaustion. Finally Melody flicked her hair back from her face in an awkward parody of the gesture she performed effortlessly a hundred times a day, and said in a thick voice, "Oh. You're up."

Cerise stood in the doorway, counting her words before she spoke them, checking under each for land mines.

"Where were you?" she asked.

"At the library. You mind turning off the tube? I wanna go to bed."

Melody pushed past her to tumble down on the sofa, and Cerise smelled the gluey-sweet scent of alcohol in her wake. She groped for the light switch on the wall beside the door, and a harsh brightness scoured the room. Melody squinted and gave a lopsided scowl. When she bent over and began to wrestle with her new boots, Cerise saw long gashes scratched into the leather of their shafts.

"What happened?" she asked, teetering between fear and anger. "Your boots are ruined."

Melody yanked a boot loose and almost lost her balance. But when she lifted her head to face her mother, her voice was tight with impatience. "You mind?" she said. "I'm tired. I wanna go to bed."

On Melody's neck and chest beneath her misbuttoned blouse, Cerise saw bruises, red bruises like crushed roses where someone had sucked her daughter's blood to the surface of her skin. She said, "It looks like you've already been to bed."

The TV screen was suddenly filled with a woman's face. Her brow was crowned by the tiniest frown, her mouth curved in the tenderest smile. Between her lips, her teeth were smooth as well-kept fingernails. Then she vanished, and in her stead a car sped along a road that hugged an ocean cliff. Light glinted off the car's bumper and rear window, off the surface of the road and the distant waves. For a moment mother and daughter were lost in that image, traveling together up that sleek road.

"What?" said Melody, as she tried to twist out of her jacket. "Wha'd you say?"

"I said, It looks like you've already been to bed."

That time the words reached Melody. She craned her neck to check her chest and clutched belatedly at the collar of her shirt as though she might still hide the love bites from her mother. But then she shrugged. Facing Cerise defiantly, she asked, "So?"

"Have you been sleeping with someone?" Cerise asked.

"What do you think?" Melody asked from beneath the screen of dead-black hair as she bent to battle with her other ruined boot.

"Who?"

"Back off, okay? It's my body. Jus' because nobody wants to sleep with you."

"Melody. You've got to listen. I—"

"I—I—I. Fuck you." The boot gave, and Melody jerked backward. She raised her face to glare at her mother. "What the fuck do you know? At least I know about birth control. When you were my age, you were pregnant." She spat the word out like a curse.

"I was older—"

"By what—twelve months?"

"—and I was pregnant with you, goddammit. I was pregnant with you."

"So? What's that supposed to mean? You're saying that makes it okay? Or you wish I hadn't been born?"

It was so hard to match feelings to words, like trying to pick lottery numbers, to somehow choose the winning combination that would open the world wide. "I loved you," Cerise said. "I mean, I love you. You saved my life. I've told you that. You were the best thing that ever happened to me. But it's not like it's been easy. And you—your life doesn't need saving."

Melody tossed her hair back with a deftness that defied her drunkenness. Her eyes hard as ice, she met Cerise's gaze and asked, "How do you know?"

THE SUMMER LUCY WAS FOUR, HER BREATH SMELLED LIKE CEDAR AND her skin was as smooth as the petals of her great-grandmother's roses. Her hair glowed like polished teak, and the fuzz on her tanned shoulders and arms and her knobby knees glimmered as though she'd been dusted with light. The summer she was four, she woke at dawn, ate Cheerios and just-picked peas for breakfast while the light grew in the kitchen until it blazed across the Formica and linoleum, stinging Anna's eyes like a kind of joy. The summer Lucy was four, she sang songs about spiders and whales and stars, belted out the alphabet, counted to twenty a thousand times. The summer she was four, she forgot to wear underwear, hated to wash her hair, made dolls out of the hollyhocks that grew behind the shed and pets of the frogs she found in the birdbath beneath her great-grandfather's spruce. The summer she was four, her shoulder blades angled from her back like sprouting wings, and her flanks and slender spine flooded Anna with a sensation of such helpless sensual love that it bordered, almost, on lust.

Sitting on the porch with her parents after supper, Lucy heard the insects humming and said, "The stars are purring." She watched the wind moving across the darkening fields and said, "The wheat is dancing." She twirled on the lawn like a dervish fairy, her dress ballooning from her suddenly skinny legs, her arms out-flung to grasp the spinning world, and when she tripped and sprawled akimbo on the lawn, she lay unmoving on the dense green grass and said, in a voice round with awe, "The world is breathing me."

She had been a lovely toddler, pert and fat and wide-eyed, but the summer she was four, that time was still so recent that what Anna most remembered of it was a blur of sleepless nights and unfocused days. She was not yet far enough removed from that time to wish it back again, to yearn for buttery baby-flesh or wordless love. Instead she marveled at how capable Lucy was, how interesting and entertaining, now that she could dress herself and feed herself, now that she could say where it hurt or explain why she was happy.

The summer Lucy was four seemed perfect even as they lived it, the bright days and broad evenings, the silken nights. In their test plots, Eliot's wheat crosses were thriving, and his plans for the future were firm and certain. Each morning he left the house at dawn, and every afternoon when he came home, his purpose had been leavened once again by his pleasure in his work, by the promise that he saw in it. On Independence Day, when Sally's husband Mike asked him how his research was going, Eliot lifted his beer to the sky and said, "It's getting closer all the time. It took one hundred years to turn wild emmer into domesticated wheat. If we can develop a perennial strain in half that time, it'll be nearly as miraculous."

That summer Eliot came home early so that Anna could work on the photographs for her Berlin show while he and Lucy tended the garden and fixed supper. Every afternoon the two of them looked so content—spraying rainbows of water across the yard or pawing through the pea vines for ripe pods—that it was hard for Anna to leave them for her darkroom in the cellar, with its musty air and stiff electric light. But once she managed to pull herself away, their very happiness allowed her to forget them. Alone in the amber-shadowed darkness, she became all mind and hands and huge-pupiled eyes. Swearing like a mechanic, muttering like a witch, she counted out seconds by the moon-round timer while the hours slid by unnoticed.

She was making prints the size of her kitchen window that summer, projecting the eight-by-ten-inch negatives from her field camera onto sheets of photographic paper so large she had to thumbtack them to the darkroom wall when she exposed them, and had to develop them in plastic garbage cans. In her prints every cloud and stalk of wheat and clod of dirt looked as God might see it, everything equal and exact and luminous. It was the way the world appeared to her that summer, each thing blessed and precious, each thing utterly itself and intrinsically connected to everything else. Alone in her sour-smelling darkroom, she could feel the gathering thrill of what she was doing, that knowledge that she was on the verge of something fine.

And when she was finished for the day, she hung her huge prints to dry on the clothesline her grandfather had strung decades earlier beside the shelves where the last of her grandmother's preserves still held some long-past summer's light inside their dusty jars. Then, climbing the stairs her great-grandfather built before the First World War, she emerged, blinking and squinting, to the lucid light of a summer evening and supper on the table.

"Thanks for us," Lucy said, throwing back her head to proclaim the grace she'd made, and Anna was suffused with such gratitude and easy joy that it seemed impossible that the future could ever be anything but a continuation of those shining days. The summer Lucy was four, Anna's life felt seamless, the whole of it enriched by all its parts. Spooning green beans onto Lucy's plate, passing the sliced tomatoes, helping Lucy with her drumstick, Anna thought that whatever it had cost to reach that time, and whatever hard times might be yet to come, they were all worth it for the riches of that summer.

Sometime in the deep middle of the summer Lucy announced that she wanted to sleep outside in the backyard, alone.

"Are you sure?" Anna asked, but Lucy nodded her head so vigorously that Anna had to take her seriously. "What if you wake up in the night?" she wondered, and Lucy answered, "I'll count all the stars till I go back asleep."

Anna kissed her sour-smelling hair and said, "Can Daddy and I sleep outside with you?"

"Uh-uh," Lucy answered, shaking her head so firmly that her eyes closed and her hair fanned out from her ears. "It's only a agventure if I do it all alone."

"What about the dark?" Anna asked, hesitant to suggest a fear that might not already exist, and yet reluctant to leave Lucy to discover it herself in the middle of the night.

Lucy said, "The dark will keep me safe."

"It will?" asked Anna in surprise.

"The dark keeps the light safe till day," Lucy said matter-of-factly. "It will me, too. I want to sleep in my red sleep pig bag."

That night, when Lucy was settled on the lawn, it gave Anna a pang to see how little of the red sleeping bag her body filled, to see how small her head looked against the white pillow, and how dark and cold the grass seemed all around her. But when Anna slipped out to check on her at midnight, her face in the moonlight appeared almost ecstatic, although she was so deeply asleep that even when Anna kissed her, she did not stir. She seemed so remote, in that cool light, so utterly inside her own life, her closed eyes as bland as eggs, her breath a tiny whisper in the night. She was a person apart from Anna, and kneeling beside her, Anna was bathed in the strangeness of it all—how Lucy had begun inside her, how she had opened Anna to get out. Gazing down at her smooth-faced daughter, Anna felt again the great stretch and push of Lucy emerging. In the vast silence of the brilliant night, in her own backyard, she was struck almost to vertigo by the unfathomable fact of life.

"How was your night?" Anna asked in the morning, when Lucy stumbled into breakfast with grass prints on her cheek.

"My night was nice," Lucy said solemnly.

"Were you warm enough?" Anna asked. She was shelling peas still chilled from the garden into Lucy's blue bowl, where each pea landed with a little musical ping.

"Yes," Lucy answered.

"Did you get lonely?" Anna asked, torn between wanting Lucy never to feel lonely, and wishing she might be missed.

"I had Noranella," Lucy answered, reaching for a pea. "I couldn't never get lonely with Noranella."

"Who's Noranella?"

"Noranella is my friend."

"Your friend from preschool?" Anna asked, puzzled.

"No," Lucy answered, placing the pea on the center of her tongue like a Eucharist wafer.

"From where, then?" Anna asked, racking her brains to remember a child named Noranella.

"She lives here," Lucy said, chewing.

"Here, on our road?"

"Here, in our house. She lives in our house because I unvited her and she has long blonden hair and she eats dirt and noodles and *her* mommy never makes her wash her hair."

The summer Lucy was four, there was a permeable membrane between reality and story, between what she wanted and what was. Later that same week, as she ate ice cream on Sally's newly tiled patio, she proclaimed, "I'm pertending this ice cream is ice cream," and after she'd buried her face inside her bowl and licked it clean, she announced, "Noranella needs some ice cream, too."

"Lucy," Anna said with mock sternness.

"Oh, it's just ice cream," said Sally, rising from her wicker chair beside the new fountain and reaching for Lucy's bowl. "We might as well indulge her while we can."

After Sally brought out another dish and Lucy had eaten it for Noranella, Sally said, "Run on now, sweetie, and show me how you can do a somersault or something." And once Lucy left the patio, Sally lowered her voice and told Anna that Jesse had been arrested the night before for painting graffiti inside the fountain at the Seattle Center.

"Oh, no," Anna gasped.

"Oh, yes," Sally answered. Her voice seemed tinged with a grim satisfaction, as if she'd been right about something, after all.

"Where is he now?" Anna asked.

"In Seattle," Sally answered crisply. "In jail."

"Oh, my God," Anna said. "Do you want Dylan to stay with us while you go get him?"

"He's eighteen," Sally said with an angry shrug. "He's old enough to face the consequences of his actions. He knows that Mike's in London, doing research for his book, and that I'm in the middle of a big decorating job. I'll be damned if he makes me sacrifice my life for his one more time."

"But—" Anna stammered. Out on the lawn Lucy had spread her arms and was beginning to twirl.

"But what?" Sally said sharply. In the sunset's lurid light the lines in her face were harsh and deep.

"Maybe he needs you," Anna offered feebly.

"Of course he needs me," Sally said acidly. "But he won't admit that for a million years. And where does that leave me?"

He's your son, Anna wanted to plead. She gazed at Lucy, staggering in joyful, ragged circles on the lawn, and answered cautiously, "Maybe if you helped him now, things would be better, later."

"What am I supposed to do?" Sally asked, her voice tight with suppressed fury. "Tell my client her house won't be ready in time for her daughter's wedding? Leave Dylan with you guys while I race to Seattle, make Jesse's bail, and drive him home—reminding him all the way about the dangers of paint fumes and freeways and gangs and criminal records? Install him in his old bedroom, feed him, buy him new clothes, and then, when I ask him to take out the garbage or to tell me where he's going with my car, listen to him tell me that he's eighteen and doesn't have to take that shit from me anymore? No, thank you. I'll cut my losses right now."

Lucy's laughter floated across the yard to them, its sound twining with the lilt of water in the fountain. The last time Anna had seen Jesse was at the party Sally had thrown in honor of her new patio. Anna and Eliot had arrived early, and while Eliot and Mike barbequed mountains of jumbo shrimp and Sally organized the trays of hors d'oeuvres, Anna had worked out on the patio, arranging sunflowers in tin buckets for Sally to set around the fountain. She'd been surprised when Jesse had come up to her, looking as angry and awkward as ever in his enormous pants and his green-tinged hair.

"Wanna see one of my pieces?" he'd asked almost sullenly.

"Sure," she'd said, looking up from the sunflowers in surprise. In the last few years Jesse hadn't spoken more than a dozen words to her. "Pieces of what?" she asked, trying to keep her voice easy, though it suddenly occurred to her he might be talking about a gun.

"I'm a writer," he'd answered shyly, digging into his deep back pocket and pulling out a rumpled photograph.

"A writer?" she echoed bemusedly.

"An aerosol artist," he'd explained gruffly. "You know—graff stuff. And I thought, well, maybe, since you're an artist, too . . ." His sentence trailed off, and he'd jammed the photograph at Anna, who took it in surprise. It was a snapshot of a huge sound wall covered with a colorful tangle of letters that made a word she could not read, all arrows and angles and pillowy curves.

"You did this?" she'd asked, glancing from the snapshot to his baggy pants and slumped shoulders, looking at his still-pudgy face beneath the green hair.

"Don't tell my folks," he'd said quickly, and before anyone joined them, he'd told her about what it was like to paint in the dark, about how he chose his colors and modified the nozzles of his cans. He talked about a technique he called can control, and described how he might work on a design for months, sketching it over and over again before he finally decided it was ready to execute on a wall. He told her about the hot thrill of being an illegal artist, and how it felt to look at his work afterward, to see his art so anonymous and so public. Gazing at the vases of sunflowers, he'd said, "It's like flowers, I guess, or fireworks, or something. I don't know. Even when you're doing it, you know it can't last. But still, you gotta make it as perfect as you can."

He'd been as earnest and passionate as any undergraduate who'd ever sought her out in the halls of the art department, and Anna had recognized a similar hunger in his eyes—that great want to make a thing that mirrored the ache and awe inside him. She'd thought, Why didn't I see this before?

"Have you ever thought about art school?" she'd asked, but just at that minute Sally had appeared on the patio with her exquisitely decorated trays, and Jesse's face had gone hard and blank and he'd crammed the snapshot back into his pocket and turned away. For the rest of the evening she'd been on the lookout for him, but he must have slipped out of the house, for despite her vigilance she hadn't seen him again.

Since then, lingering in the back of her mind had been a kind of half-resolution that she would get in touch with him, maybe invite him out for lunch, or take him to an art show up on campus, or even to some galleries in Spokane. But all summer she'd been so busy, had been so happy, had been reluctant to risk trouble inside the family. And now Jesse was in jail in Seattle.

Sitting beside Sally's fountain, she wondered how her sister would respond if she were to offer to drive to Seattle herself, wondered how complicated it would be if she were to invite Jesse to live with them at the ranch for a while. But then she wondered if he were taking drugs, if he had joined some kind of gang, wondered what sort of threat he might be to Lucy.

Out on the lawn Lucy was staggering beneath the weight of her dizziness. Her arms outstretched as though the air could catch her, she toppled gleefully to the dusky grass. She lay there giggling for a second. But a moment later she began to scream, her scream soaring in the air like a siren as she leapt to her feet and stumbled desperately across the yard. Panic thickening in her veins, Anna leapt out of her chair. "What's wrong?" she cried. "What happened, Lucy? What?"

"A bee, a bee, a bee," Lucy shrieked, plunging her head into her mother's abdomen. "A bee," she cried, burrowing against her mother and staring in horror at the white welt rising on her hand while instant tears poured down her face. Sally ran inside for baking soda and Band-Aids, and Anna gathered Lucy onto her lap, all her concerns about Jesse shoved aside by Lucy's screams.

"It hurts," Lucy whimpered, pressing herself closer. "It hurts." And the summer Lucy was four, somehow even that was a pleasure, for Anna to be holding her crying daughter and comforting her, for her to inhale the smell of Lucy's hot, damp head, to hug Lucy's little body against her suddenly tender breasts and murmur words of love and solace and reassurance, secure in her knowledge that she could make things better, safe in her conviction that everything would be all right.

* * *

JAKE HAD BEEN SO MUCH FUN AT FIRST—AND FUNNY, TOO—ASKING everyone at the bar he took Cerise to that first night if they'd had their bowel movements in exactly the same tone as the nurse at Woodland Manor whose daily chore it was to poke her head into all the rooms, yelling that question for the benefit of the hard of hearing, and then charting their mumbled answers on her clipboard.

"Have you had your bm?" Jake asked the bartender, and the whole bar roared, and Cerise felt proud—and lucky, too—to have been asked out by someone who could make a roomful of people laugh.

The second time Jake spoke to her, she was mopping her way down the long south hall, oblivious to anything but her memory of Melody wrestling drunkenly with her ruined boots the night before. It was only when she paused to rinse her mop that she realized she was being watched. She looked up to see the house painter she'd talked to in the staff room, the tall one with the kid's grin, leaning against the wall. His body seemed to make another wall perpendicular to the one she was mopping alongside, as though he were adding a private room for the two of them in that public place.

"I thought my job was bad," he said when her work brought her to a standstill in front of him. "But maybe yours is worse." His voice was low, as insinuating as though the two of them already shared some kind of secret.

"Why?" she asked stolidly, planting her mop and leaning on the handle while she waited for him to move out of her way.

"It's like painting the Golden Gate Bridge, isn't it?"

"What?"

"They're never finished, either—get to one end and then just start over again." He grinned down at her, and added, "But at least they get breaks."

"I get breaks," Cerise answered staunchly, and he pounced. "When?"

It was nice to spend time with someone who wasn't senile or dying. It was gratifying to have someone who could laugh about what went on in Woodland Manor without scorning what she did there all day. It was a respite to go with Jake to the bar after work instead of going home to

Melody's anger or her absence. And it was astonishing—like finding a diamond ring glittering in the street—to discover that someone liked her height, liked her long feet and thick breasts and the deep curves of her waist.

The first time Cerise brought Jake back to her apartment, she'd felt a guilty relief that Melody wasn't home. Later, after they'd made love, she told him it was her first time. "The kid's not yours?" he asked in puzzlement, and she had to explain, though her whole bare body grew hot and flushed, that what she meant was, it was the first time she'd liked sex, the first time she'd come.

Jake claimed condoms cramped his style, and though Cerise insisted on using an arsenal of creams and gels, before the day came for her appointment at the free clinic, it was too late to need the birth control pills she was going there to get. This time, she suspected right away that she was pregnant, and instead of calling LifeRight, she took the money Jake had given her to pay the cable bill and bought a home pregnancy test instead.

Working in the steamy bathroom after Melody left for school, Cerise read the directions the kit contained and then followed them as exactly as she could, balancing her equipment awkwardly on the rim of the sink. After she dipped the plastic wand into the little vial that contained her pee, she held her breath and dug her fingernails into her wrist, trying to will the tip of the wand to stay white. When, despite all her yearning, the pink line appeared, she whispered, "Shit," and sank down on the closed toilet seat, the wand limp in her hand.

After his initial shock, Jake reacted to the news that he was going to be a father with surprising good humor. He said he hoped the baby would be a boy because he wanted someone to go fishing with, and he seemed pleased by the ability of his sperm to outwit all the traps Cerise had set for them. "Little guys slipped right on through," he marveled proudly.

"It's okay, darlin'," he added, reaching for Cerise. "What's one more baby in this whole mess? While we're at it, let's just see if I can give you twins."

But when Cerise told Melody that she was pregnant, it was as though Melody were the furious mother, and Cerise were once again the wayward girl. "How could you do it?" Melody stormed, and when Cerise answered with a rare attempt at wit, "In the regular way, I guess," Melody snapped, "That's disgusting."

"You're going to have a little sister or brother," Cerise said. "It'll be nice. We'll get a bigger place. You can have your own room. We'll be a family."

"I don't want a family," Melody answered. And then she said the thing that wrenched Cerise's heart, "Whatever happened to just you and I?"

Jake the Fake, Melody called him, Jake the Snake, and Jake the Jerk, and all of Cerise's attempts to gather them into a family were like trying to sweep up the skittery ball of mercury left after someone dropped a thermometer at work. But despite that, and despite the morning sickness that made her have to puke into the toilets as she cleaned them, a part of her was happy to be pregnant. This time she could trace the swell of her stomach and imagine the baby hiding inside. This time, her pregnancy seemed like a second chance, like an opportunity to get it right, to be again the good mother she'd been when Melody was young, instead of the woman who had somehow ended up raising a bitter stranger.

When her water broke, she was cleaning the dining room after lunch. She hadn't expected the baby to arrive for another few days at least, and she stopped to mop the puddle from the floor before she wheeled her cart to the storage room, punched out, and called Jake and the doctor.

This time, she wasn't scared during her labor, wasn't drugged and whimpering as she had been when Melody was born. Abashed by Cerise's intensity and by the doctor's authority, Jake fed Cerise chipped ice and rubbed her back, and this time, when the hurt threatened to rip her apart, she managed to fix her thoughts on the coming baby, to remember what all her work was for. She recognized when it was time to push, and she rode the waves of her final contractions like a surfer.

"Come on, baby," she cried as she bore down with a thousand muscles she had only just discovered. "Come on, come on!" she yelled, as though she and Jake were alone in the apartment with the bedroom door closed. At the moment when she was the widest, she reached down and shoved the doctor's latex-gloved hands away, thrust her own hands between her thighs. To a rising chorus of protests, she bore down one last time, her whole self taut and straining as she pushed the crowning head into her hands, pushed again and felt the hard slither of shoulders, and then pushed one final time and caught her baby herself, guiding its slippery body out of hers, laughing as she lifted it up and laid it, hot and wet and whimpering, against her chest.

She crinked her neck to peer down into its puffy, stunned face, and all her pain vanished. Lying in the hospital bed with her legs still splayed, she had the odd sensation that everything was ascending—the room, the building, Jake and the baby—everything rising up to soar among the stars, even as the doctor stitched, the nurses scolded, and Jake slipped out to have a smoke.

But before Travis was six months old, the job Jake was on finished up. "Don't worry, darlin'," he said, when he gave Cerise the news that he'd been laid off. "There's always something that needs a coat of paint."

But either the building boom had begun to sag or Jake's luck had soured, because he couldn't seem to get hired anywhere. He took to spending his days at the bar with his laid-off buddies, all of them celebrating their enforced vacations by drinking their unemployment checks and commiserating about the fucked-up state of everything—especially bosses, the government, and women.

Jake and Cerise's schedules didn't mesh too well once Jake lost his job. After the bar closed, it was too late for him to stop by the apartment very often, what with Melody and Travis hopefully asleep and Cerise tired out by getting up with Travis in the night. Sometimes Jake would come over in the afternoon, after he was up and before much else was going on, and sometimes when he did, Melody would be at school and Travis would be napping and Cerise and Jake would make love. Afterward he could be so tender it brought tears to both their eyes, when he told Cerise she deserved a better man than he was, and claimed he wasn't worthy of her love.

But other times he was too hungover for sweet talk, or so pissed at how the world worked that he was ready to slam walls, and when Cerise tried to shush and humor him and beg him not to wake the baby, he called her a bitch and raised his fist, held it trembling in the air between them before he turned and slammed out the door.

With Jake out of a job, when her maternity disability payments ran out, Cerise had to decide between going back on welfare or giving almost half of her paycheck to someone else to watch Travis while she worked. As much as she hated welfare, she couldn't bear the thought of being away from Travis all day long, so she applied again for AFDC.

"What the fuck?" Jake demanded when he found out that Cerise had named him as Travis's father on the Statement of Facts form. "What the fuck did you do that for?"

It was not the afternoon she would have chosen to tell him if she could have helped it. His face looked pale and greasy, and he smelled as though he were sweating alcohol.

She explained, "They won't give us any aid unless I say who his father is."

"And what business of the state's is that? Seems like they might leave it up to you, where you get your jism from."

"It's a new rule," said Cerise, glad that Melody wasn't there to hear how he was talking. "To try to make sure the dads help out with child support."

"Haven't I been helping, every bit I can?"

"Sure you have," Cerise answered swiftly. "But with you—you know—I mean, it's just not quite enough. Besides," she added wistfully, "I thought you were proud to be his dad."

"So now I'm going to have to send child support to the fucking god-damn state of California. Well, that just gravels my ass no end, you god-damn bitch."

She tried to stay understanding as long as she could, but finally it got to where whenever he came over, they spent their time together sniping at each other like angry siblings, each of them blaming the other for all their troubles. Even so, she cried when he left Rossi in hopes of getting in on all the new construction going on down south. Before he left, he claimed he would come back and marry her as soon as he got a job. But later, when he called, he said that work was so spotty he couldn't even afford a place to stay, that he had to crash at friends' houses or sleep at the work site in his car. He was never able to send either her or the state much of the child support he owed, but occasion-ally he called her late at night, when the bars were closed and the phone rates were the best, and talking to him on the phone, she sometimes thought that missing him was nicer than being with him had been.

When Travis was twenty months old, Cerise received a letter with her AFDC check saying that the whole welfare program was being revised and informing her of the date and time of her appointment with the eligibility worker who would explain her situation to her and outline her options. During her appointment, Cerise sat on the chair in front of the eligibility worker's desk and struggled to contain Travis on her lap while the eligibil-ity worker explained that the state understood that Cerise would rather be a productive member of society than waste her life on welfare, and as a consequence, she only had twenty-four months of benefits left.

"But in twenty-four months he still won't be old enough for kindy-garden," said Cerise, grabbing Travis's hands before he snatched her file off the eligibility worker's desk.

"You'll need to find a job," the eligibility worker said, speaking as distinctly as though she thought Cerise were deaf.

"I had a job, before I had him. But I can't pay for his day care with what I could make at work," Cerise answered.

"There are programs," the worker explained, "to train you for a higher-paying job. The state can help with your expenses. But you have to hurry and apply, before the grant runs out."

"Oh."

"What do you want to study?"

"I never finished high school," Cerise said, trying to interest Travis in one of the weary toys she'd brought from home.

"Something in computers or food service? How about child care or office management?"

"Maybe child care?" Cerise said, prying a letter opener out of Travis's fingers. "That way I could keep him with me when I went to work."

"Maybe," the worker said dryly. "But right now the important thing is to get you working at all."

The only welfare-approved program for training child-care workers that would still accept Cerise for summer quarter was at a community college just south of San Francisco. At first the thought of moving seemed impossible, but the counselor at the community college was so reassuring and her eligibility worker was so unyielding that Cerise filled out the forms and made the phone calls and found the documents to get herself in. She called collect to Rita in Florida and asked to borrow money, though she knew she could not ask again in some greater emergency.

"If you would only get married," Rita said before she agreed to make the loan, "none of this would be necessary."

"Travis's dad got laid off."

"So find someone else."

"I'll try," Cerise lied. "But right now I need that child-care certificate, or we'll end up on the streets."

She called Jake and asked him to come back and help them move, though she dreaded the sting she would feel when she saw him again.

But even so the hardest part of moving was Melody.

"There's no way I'll leave my friends," Melody announced when

Cerise told her what she was planning. Melody was in the bathroom, where every day she spent a longer time with the brushes and creams and cosmetics she kept stashed among Travis's plastic ducks and bags of diapers, and Cerise was in the front room, hunched on the toy-strewn sofa with the community college course catalog in her lap, marking and remarking the classes she'd have to take, as though by memorizing their section numbers and the times they met, she might have a better chance of passing them. "You'll make new friends," she called to Melody. "I've got to get this certificate."

"Why can't you just go back to Woodland Manor?" Melody asked.

"I can't afford to pay for this apartment and child care, too, on what I made at Woodland Manor."

"Then stay on welfare till Trav starts school, like you did with me."

"I can't. The rules changed. You think I want to leave Travis with someone else all day?"

"I'll watch Travie while you work," Melody said, emerging from the bathroom in a leather miniskirt and a velvet halter top. She'd grown her hair out blond again, and with her perfect makeup and her lean legs, she looked as remote and gorgeous as the model Cerise had once dreamed she'd be. Only now Melody's beauty reminded Cerise of a loaded gun— as much a danger to the person who possessed it as to anyone else.

When Melody bent and swung Travis up out of the pile of toys where he'd been enshrined, Cerise caught a glimpse of black silk panties beneath the supple hem of her skirt. More and more of the clothes that Melody wore were ones Cerise hadn't bought for her. Suede jackets, designer jeans, and sequined shirts, they were clothes that Melody said she'd borrowed, said were gifts or hand-me-downs from friends Cerise had never heard of.

Melody said, "We'd have fun, wouldn't we, Travie?" and Travis burst into a chortle of joy as she swooped him toward the ceiling.

Cerise asked, "Where did you get that skirt?"

"Oh, this," Melody said, glancing down at it and then setting Travis back on the floor and shrugging. "Justine gave it to me. She said she was tired of it."

"You sure?" Cerise asked.

"What do you mean, am I sure?" Melody snapped. "Like I wouldn't know if my own friend gave me a skirt?"

"I just want you to be sure," said Cerise doggedly.

Coolly Melody changed the subject. "So I'll watch Travie for you, and you can go back to work."

"You have to go to school," Cerise answered. "The new rules say if there's a minor who's not in school, the assistance unit will lose that portion of their aid."

"What the fuck's an assistance unit?"

"Don't use that type language around the baby. An assistance unit's a family—like us."

"I hate school."

"You have to finish high school," Cerise repeated. "You don't need to do things the hard way, like me. With your brains and looks, you—"

"Brains and looks—" Melody tossed her hair down her back and straightened up to face her mother. "Get real. What kind of stupid TV la-la land do you live in, anyway? I'm not going to get one goddamned chance—"

"You've got to take it," Cerise pleaded. "You've got to make it for yourself."

"Look," Melody said, spitting out the word as though it were rotten, "I could be a good girl. I could go to school and study until I'm fucking blue in the face. I could get good grades. And maybe if I'm real good and I'm real lucky, I can go to the community college, too. Oh, goody.

"And then," Melody went on nastily, "I can bust my butt and work two jobs and study a bunch of meaningless shit and get a little piece of paper so I can work my ass off at some stupidfucking job for the rest of my life. Thank you very much, and no fucking way. I hate school. School's a hoax."

"Your report card came in the mail yesterday," Cerise said. "You're failing every subject."

Melody spun around, "No way. What about art? I got an A in art."

"Art's not a subject."

"What?"

"English is a subject," Cerise said. "Math is a subject. History is a subject. Science is a subject. Art is like—PE. Or band. It's not anything real. Not real work."

"I work hard at art."

"What—taking apart toasters? Drawing pictures of Dumpsters? If I were your art teacher, you'd fail that, too."

"I can't believe this." Melody rolled her eyes toward the ceiling as though up there she would find an impartial judge.

"Art," Cerise said, "is not going to get you anywhere."

"Oh, right. Like you're an expert on how to get somefuckingwhere."

"That's what I'm trying to do, right now. Get somewhere. And," Cerise said loudly, to drown out the waver of terror in her voice, "I'm going to take you with me."

SIX WEEKS AFTER ELIOT WAS DENIED TENURE, ANNA STOOD IN FRONT OF the bathroom sink, a pink-tipped plastic wand dangling in her hand. She leaned toward the mirror, and the face that met hers there was strained and stunned. Dark half-moons hung beneath her eyes, harsh lines framed her mouth, and the flesh of her cheeks looked soft and pulpy. Catching her lower lip between her teeth, she pressed it until she felt the hurt, wished she had the courage to bite for blood. Her eyes sought their reflection as if she still hoped she might find some kind of answer there. But her eyes were only holes that led directly to her brain, and her brain was only a meaty tangle of despair.

A little plastic vial half filled with urine sat on the counter in front of her. She picked it up, emptied its contents into the toilet, and closed the lid. She fitted the vial and the wand back into the box they had come in and tucked the box beneath the other trash at the bottom of the wastebasket, where no one else would see it. Then she sat down on the toilet, buried her face in her hands, and tried to think.

She was at least eight weeks along—maybe as much as ten, or even twelve. When she first realized that her period was late, she'd assumed she'd been so worried about what was happening with Eliot that she'd made a mistake about the dates, and later, when her period still hadn't started, she'd thought it was stress that was keeping it away, had thought that stress was making her feel weary and nauseous and uneasy.

But now the pink line claimed otherwise.

"I don't know who's the bigger fool," Eliot said back in February when he'd told Anna the news about his job. "Me, for thinking I could get away with working on a project that might take half a century to show results, or the college, for pretending they can stick to quick fixes, even now."

They were in the kitchen, where Anna was fixing supper and Lucy was making a cottage for Noranella beneath the breakfast table. Still in his jacket, Eliot stood in the middle of the room and said, "One-third of the world's arable land has been lost to erosion in the last forty years, and Spaulding University denies me tenure because they claim my research doesn't show adequate relevance."

"They're wrong," Anna answered, wiping her hands on a dish towel and reaching for him. "We both know that. Besides, your teaching evaluations are the best in the department."

"Teaching doesn't matter to a tenuring committee," Eliot answered. He gave her a perfunctory hug and moved away. "We know that, too. Nothing matters really, except funding. And," he went on bitterly, "there's lots more money available for splicing mouse genes into tomatoes than there is for developing perennial wheat."

"Yes, but—"

Eliot interrupted her. "The bottom line is that I've lost my job." His voice was harsh, but his expression was so desolate it frightened her. "I have no idea what we'll do," he said, staring past her to the window above the sink.

"We'll think of something," Anna said. "We still have my job. We'll find something else for you."

"Not around here," Eliot answered grimly. "Not unless they're hiring genetics professors to flip burgers at McDonald's."

"We'll find something," Anna promised through all her fears. "We'll work it out. It will be okay."

"What's wrong?" inquired Lucy's voice from beneath the table. "What happened?" Poking her head out from between the blankets she'd draped over the tabletop, she asked, "What will be okay?"

"Everything will be okay," Anna answered, picking up her knife and trying to resume her work on the salad. "It's just that things have changed a little."

"What changed?" Lucy asked, her face scrunched with concern.

"I said this might happen," Eliot said, ignoring his daughter and speaking to his wife. "But I guess I never thought it really would."

"It shouldn't have," Anna said staunchly.

Eliot said, "We'd have to move, for me to get another job. Or at least I would," he'd added tentatively. Startled, Anna looked up from her work. "Only you?" she asked.

"Have you thought about all you'd be leaving, if you moved, too?" he answered.

It was a question that left her dizzy. Of course she'd thought about what might happen if Eliot didn't get tenure, but only dimly, only from a distance. Eliot was too good a scientist, too well respected by his colleagues and his students for her to believe he could really lose his job. In a way it had even seemed wrong for her to think too much about it, as if imagining the worst would somehow cause it to happen. But suddenly a hot anxiety bubbled up inside her. This is real, she thought.

Her eyes swept the room and settled on the window above the

kitchen sink. Outside, sunset was burnishing the frozen hills. For as long as she could remember she had loved that view, loved the way the seasons moved across it and the way it looked in every light. She thought of the show she was preparing for—in the most prestigious gallery she'd shown in yet—and once again it struck her how entirely her art depended on what lay outside her kitchen window. She thought of all the photographs she still wanted to make of that land—hundreds of photographs—each one leading to the next like an endless magic, like the inexhaustible pasta pot in the story that was Lucy's current favorite. She thought of her own job at the university, of her colleagues and her students and her friends. She thought of Sally and Mike in Salish and her parents so close by, in Spokane.

She thought, I'd lose everything if I left.

Lucy said, "Are we moving away from here?" Her voice sounded appalled.

Anna tore her gaze from the window, looked blindly around the room until she met Eliot's eyes. For a moment she didn't know him, he seemed so tired and sad, so stricken and alone. She looked down at Lucy, standing waist-high in front of her, the worry on her face deepening as she waited for an answer.

"We might have to move," Anna answered, squandering every other future and looking directly at Eliot as she spoke. To Lucy she added gently, "We don't yet know."

Lucy asked, "Who will live our lives, if we move?"

"They'll always be our lives," said Anna, infusing her voice with more certainty than she felt. She wiped her hands on a dishcloth and reached her arms around Lucy. "We'll take our lives with us, when we go."

In that moment she felt a kind of triumph, a surge of hope. She promised, "As long as we're all together, everything will be all right." But then Lucy squirmed out from under Anna's hug to stand alone in the center of the room. "Noranella won't go," she said.

"Why won't she?" Eliot asked, reaching for Anna's empty hand.

"Noranella won't leave her home," Lucy answered.

"Oh, Lucy," Anna begged foolishly. "You could make her come."

"I can't," Lucy had answered with great dignity. "I would not never do such a increnulating thing to Noranella."

"Lucy," said Eliot wearily, "people can feel two ways about a thing."

"Not Noranella," Lucy answered, folding her arms like a grown woman and turning away.

Now, alone in the bathroom, Anna raised her head from the cradle of her hands and looked around the room. She saw the collection of Eliot's starts and cuttings that lined the windowsill, saw the piles of bath toys and the towels hanging crookedly on the rack, but no meanings for those things registered in her brain. The plastic wand had appeared so innocuous when she'd taken it from the package, like a child's toy or a game piece, like a baby's rattle. Thinking of it now, she felt an odd little tug of temptation, like a strain of far-off music. She resisted the urge to dig through the trash, find the box she'd buried there, and look at the wand again.

It was all impossible.

It would be impossible for her to have a baby if she couldn't take time off work to care for it. But it would be impossible for her to ask for a leave of absence from the university now that her job would soon be their sole support. It was impossible for her to finish the photographs for her Los Angeles show if she couldn't work in the darkroom, but it was impossible for her to work in the darkroom without exposing a developing embryo to poisonous chemicals and heavy metals. It was unthinkable to cancel such an important show, but it would be impossible to finish it if she were pregnant.

If Eliot were miraculously offered another position somewhere, she could not ask him to turn it down just because she didn't want to move, especially since Eliot was already battling such brutal failure. But she could not imagine moving with a newborn, could not imagine having another baby without the support of her family and friends.

It was all impossible. It would be insane and irresponsible and wrong for her to bring a baby into the world right now. So she had to stop it. For the good of their family—for Eliot's sake, for Lucy's, and for her own—she had to send that little possibility back to where it had come from, like a misdelivered letter, like a message that had been meant for someone else.

It would take courage and some contriving, but she thought she could manage it so that no one else would ever have the burden of knowing what she'd had to do. She could make the necessary appointments for times when Eliot was at work. She could schedule the procedure for an afternoon when she had no classes to teach, could arrange for Lucy to go home from kindergarten with a friend that day. That evening she could claim she'd come down with the flu and go to bed. With the work and stress of all that was facing them, it wouldn't be too difficult to keep from making love until she'd healed. Later, she promised herself, when things were more settled, they could have another baby—just not right now.

But before she could stop herself, she was thinking about babies, was remembering how delicious newborns were, at once so goofy-looking and so wise. She remembered Lucy as an infant and as a round-cheeked toddler, remembered her imp's grin and her wide-open eyes. She thought of Lucy now, how utterly herself she was, how inevitable she seemed, and how crucial, and she felt the lust for a baby rise up in her, that craving that defied all logic. Suddenly and beyond all reason, she wanted a baby's flesh, a baby's scent, wanted the promise and comfort of a baby.

We could make it work, she pleaded with herself. Pressing her palm against her abdomen, she let herself imagine the bean-sprout-size embryo hidden there, let herself wonder what kind of person was rising toward the world. She remembered the drifting bit of tissue she'd allowed the doctor to excise, remembered how lovely it had been, and how lorn, and she felt a surge of mother-worry to think of the long hours she'd been spending in the darkroom, of the dektol and selenium that little sprout had already been exposed to. Stop it, she thought sternly—remember how impossible it is. But already, in some far-off, treacherous corner of her being, she was aware of an inordinate delight. She felt a welcome widening inside her, and also a splinter of reckless thrill, to see the future veer so far from her control.

CERISE FOUND A TWO-BEDROOM TRAILER AS CLOSE TO THE COMMUNITY college as she could afford, in a little pocket of a trailer court crammed with weeds and dust and broken cars. She packed their things in grocery sacks and liquor boxes, and Jake came up in a borrowed pickup to help her move. He brought a dozen red roses for Cerise, a bottle of light-sensitive fingernail polish for Melody, a half-rack of Bud for himself, and a battery-operated laser power blaster for Travis, who spent the afternoon in amped-out ecstasy, pulling the trigger and shrieking gleefully each time lights flashed inside the plastic barrel and an electronic voice announced *Attention. Drop your guns. Fire. Target.*

Cerise felt a twinge of sadness to leave the apartment that had been their home, though as she rode through Rossi for the final time, crammed into the pickup cab with Jake and Travis and Melody, she looked out the window at the new malls and dirty palms, and it seemed strange to think she had ever lived there at all.

The trailer was half the size of their apartment. The appliances in the kitchen would have fit inside a playhouse—the refrigerator with a freezer that couldn't hold a quart of ice cream, the stove with its two burners and its doll-size oven. Cerise let Melody have the bedroom at the back, and she and Travis shared the one in front, although it was so small that her mattress and his crib were only a few steps apart.

At the drugstore where she went to buy diapers and toilet paper and shampoo she found flower seeds on sale, ten cents a package. She bought a dollar's worth and planted them below their bedroom window, studying the directions on the envelopes and then breaking up the hard dirt with a hand trowel, patting the seeds carefully beneath the soil, and watering them with pans of water she carried from the kitchen sink. She caught Travis trying to dig them up again the next day, but by midsummer a few of the sweet peas had begun to bloom, and one of the zinnias had developed buds that looked like thick green thumbs.

The first time she went on campus, she kept waiting for someone to realize she shouldn't be there and tell her she had to leave. Weathering Melody's scorn, she dressed for her first class even more carefully than she'd dressed for her dates with Jake. But even so her hands felt as slick as if they'd been in rubber gloves all day, and she kept her elbows pressed to her sides to try to hide the perspiration that steeped dark circles into the armpits of her blouse. Unsure of where she was going, she hurried along the crowded sidewalks, her new textbooks pushed against her breasts as though she were twelve again.

But she managed to stumble into the right classroom. And she managed to come back the next day. Slowly her terror began to ease, and she even started to think that maybe her program counselor was right— maybe anything was possible, if you only tried hard enough, if only you wanted it with all your might.

What she liked best about school were the hours she spent with the preschoolers in the on-campus day care. Once the children got to know her, they ran to greet her whenever she arrived, lifting their arms and faces to her like clamoring sunflowers. They filled her lap at circle time, showed her their invisible owies, told her rambling stories about the dreams they'd had and the videos they'd seen. And halfway through the summer her mentor teacher said Cerise must be some sort of magician, the way she could get them to settle down at naptime.

Despite how angry Melody had been about the move, she also seemed to be doing a little better that summer. She watched Travis while Cerise was in school and found an evening job at a fast-food restaurant not too far from where they lived. She made new friends—not, this time, with leather-clad kids who owned loud cars, but with a pack of dreamy teenagers in ragged clothes. These new friends went barefoot, wrote poetry, and wore their pale hair matted into dreadlocks, though some of the girls shaved their heads and some of the boys wore skirts.

Melody said their goal was to save the earth. She said they wanted to live the way people were meant to live, at one with nature, in tribes. They called themselves the Lost Children, which made Cerise think of the movie *Peter Pan,* though when she mentioned it, Melody reminded her scornfully that in the movie it had been only boys.

By the Fourth of July, Melody said she was in love with one of them, a willowy boy with raven-colored ringlets that Melody called Tree. He owned an old school bus that Melody helped him paint, covering it with sinuous flowers and dark-eyed animals and geometric patterns she said had sacred meanings. Tree also had a tattoo gun, and he sold tattoos at concerts and street fairs. Melody told Cerise that sometimes Tree used her designs for his tattoos, and she claimed she was going to start her own business soon, airbrushing those designs on T-shirts and silk scarves and canvas bags.

One night in mid-July, long after she'd gotten Travis to sleep, Cerise was scrunched on the sofa, so engrossed in studying that she barely looked up from her textbook when the front door opened and Melody came in.

"Hi," Cerise said, pausing to highlight a section about maternal-infant bonding before she added, "How was work?"

"Work sucked," Melody answered. "But—check this out." She tossed something on the sofa next to her mother.

"What is it?" Cerise asked, glancing up from her book to see what Melody had thrown. Her first thought was that it was an ornament for some weird Christmas tree, but when she picked it up she saw it was a grapefruit, although its coarse pink skin had been decorated with a sinuous, many-pointed star.

"It's Celtic," Melody said, pointing at the star. "It's very magical.

Tree says I'm learning fast," she added proudly. "He says I'm almost ready to try a real tattoo. I just have to get my depth a little more consistent first."

"Try a real tattoo?" Cerise asked warily.

"There's lots of money in tattooing. If I get good at giving tattoos, I can make way more money than I'll ever make selling burgers at McVomit's. Even teachers and bankers want tattoos these days. Tree says my designs are deeply cool."

"Just as long as you never get one yourself," Cerise said, studying the star embedded in the grapefruit's sallow rind and thinking of Melody's perfect skin. She remembered the tattoos on the flaccid biceps and wrinkled forearms of the men at Woodland Manor, the blurry purple anchors and flags that had always reminded her of the mimeographed worksheets her teachers used to give her back in grade school. She said, "If you get a tattoo, you can never get rid of it. You're stuck with it, your whole life."

"That's the point," Melody answered primly. "It's important to have things that will be in your life forever. But don't worry—if I ever get one, it'll be small and easy to hide. Tree says tattoos are sexier if you have to hunt for them. Some people practice on chickens," she went on, "but I've quit eating meat."

"Quit eating meat? What? When?"

"When I met Tree."

"Why?"

"Do you have any idea the kind of poisons they pump into meat? Hormones and drugs and crap like that? Besides," Melody said, retrieving her grapefruit and examining it proudly, "Tree says its bad karma to eat someone else's flesh without getting their permission first."

It made no sense for Melody to quit eating meat, especially because for every shift she worked, she got a free Quarter Pounder and a large drink and a fries. And it made Cerise sick to think how even a little butterfly tattooed on Melody's ankle or her shoulder blade would deface her lovely daughter. But at least Melody had a job. At least she wasn't coming home drunk, though sometimes Cerise thought she recognized the scent of marijuana in her hair. At least the clothes Melody wore were her own, or were so flimsy or tattered it didn't frighten Cerise to wonder where she got them. At least Tree didn't carry a knife or suck bruises into Melody's neck.

And once or twice after that, on nights when Travis went to bed on time and Melody happened to be home from work, nights when Cerise was too tired to even try to study, they found some old movie on TV, made popcorn, sprinkled it with the cheese powder packet from a box of macaroni and cheese, and sprawled together on the collapsing sofa, watching the movie in companionable quiet, the popcorn bowl between them, and only their jaws moving as they gazed at the screen, their fingers occasionally brushing when they both reached for popcorn at the same time.

But before August was half over Melody got fired for helping the Lost Children picket the restaurant where she worked with signs that said "Unfair to Animals" and "Eat Your Own Meat."

"Lost your job?" Cerise said, when Melody told her. "You mean you were fired."

"I couldn't take it anymore, working at a place that sells murdered animals. Do you know those cows never even see the light of day? They spend their whole lives standing in their own shit. They can't even walk."

"You were doing so good," Cerise mourned. Travis, who had been watching cartoons while Cerise tried to study, slid off the sofa and trundled across the room to where his laser power blaster lay.

"Oh right," Melody scoffed. "Like a job at McNazi's is doing good."

"It was a start. It'll be harder to get another job, now you got fired."

"Ask me if I care."

"Mama. Meedee," said Travis, pointing the laser blaster in their direction. He pulled the trigger, the lights flashed, and the electronic catechism began once again, though the lights seemed weaker, the voice deeper and more slurred than usual.

Cerise said, "Don't point that thing at people, Trav." To Melody she added, "School's starting soon. How're you going to buy school clothes without a job?"

Travis fired again, and the lights strobed wearily. "Tar-get," the voice drawled, dropping an octave lower.

Melody said, "There's a boutique at the mall, and the lady's said she'll sell my T-shirts."

"You lost a good, steady job," Cerise said, wavering between fear and anger. "You got fired."

"Just back off, okay? You should be proud that people want to buy my art. I don't give a flying fuck if I got fired. Besides, it's my life."

"Well, it's my life, too," Cerise said, snapping her textbook shut, sending the yellow highlighter spinning across the room. "And I—" she began, but suddenly Travis let out a shrill wail.

"What's wrong, Travie?" Melody asked, turning toward him with eager solicitude as Cerise leapt up from the sofa.

"What's the matter, baby?" Cerise said, snatching Travis up before Melody could reach him. Imagining black widows or scorpions or hornets, she asked urgently, "What's wrong?"

"Anh, anh," Travis howled, his face red and hard with frustration as he pulled the trigger of his silent power blaster.

"Let me see, Travie," said Melody, tugging the power blaster away from him and trying the trigger herself. "It's not working," she announced above his cries. "You have any more batteries?"

"Are you kidding?" Cerise called back. "I don't even have money for diapers."

"Baddies," said Travis, snatching the word. Shaking the toy in his dimpled fist, he clung to Cerise and cried, "Baddies, baddies."

"Let me see, Travie," Melody said, reaching for the power blaster and sliding the battery cover off the bottom. "It takes one of those square kinds with the little snaps. What else uses those?" she asked, her eyes roving the room.

"Nothing we got," Cerise shrugged. "It's okay, Trav," she added, patting his back. "It's just a toy."

"I'll fix it," Melody said, spying the smoke detector that hung from the ceiling at the entrance to the narrow hall.

"You leave that alone," Cerise snapped as Melody reached up to take the cover off.

"Oh, come on," Melody answered, her hand pausing in midair. "Just for tonight. I'll get a new battery for the smoke detector tomorrow. It probably needs one anyway by now."

Coldly Cerise asked, "And just what do you plan to use for money, now you don't have a job?"

"I'll have money soon—lots of money now that I'm working for myself. I'll be able to buy all the batteries you'll ever need as soon as my shirts start selling."

"Baddies," Travis cried, stretching out his arms to Melody.

Cerise twisted her torso to keep Melody from reaching him, and Melody shrugged and dropped her arms, headed past them toward the tiny kitchen.

"You leave that smoke detector alone," Cerise said over her shoulder to Melody. "I mean it," she added grimly, as she hauled the screaming toddler off to bed.

"Don't worry, Travie," Melody called after them as she opened the refrigerator and bent to peer inside. "Meedee'll get you a new battery. I promise."

BEYOND THE
END OF
EVERYTHING

THE WHOLE TIME THEY WERE PACKING, ANNA WAS CERTAIN that at some point Lucy's imaginary friend would relent and decide to move to California with them. But even after the house had emptied to an echoing shell and they'd said good-bye to Sally and Mike and Anna's parents and all their friends, Noranella remained resolute.

On the final morning, as their loaded car pulled out from under the shelter of her great-grandfather's spruce and down the driveway to the road, Lucy craned her head to watch the only home she'd ever known receding down the valley. "Bye, Noranella," she said from the backseat in a voice so small and sad that for an unhinged second it seemed to Anna they should find a way to stay for Noranella's sake alone.

"Oh, Lucy," Anna begged as they crested the hill and the house disappeared from view. "Please make Noranella come."

"I tried," Lucy answered wistfully. "But she refuses to adubricate."

It was August, and Anna was nearly nine months pregnant, so full of baby that she could barely breathe. Eliot had suggested that she and Lucy should fly to California and he could drive the car down by himself, but Anna had wanted them all to stay together. She'd hoped, too, that it would make the move feel more real if they traveled the whole way by car, though now, as she tried to adjust her seat belt around her swollen belly, she gazed out the window and wondered if she'd made the right decision.

They drove on into the shining morning, but even before they reached Salish, Anna felt like a stranger, passing through a land that was no longer hers. Harvest was in full swing. Pickups were parked at casual angles on the freshly stubbled hills while combines lumbered over the fields like packs of dinosaurs. Anna remembered the harvests she and Sally had spent as kids, riding the loaded trucks to the grain elevator. She remembered her grandpa joking that he was a multimillionaire because there were a million kernels in every bushel of wheat. She remembered the summer suppers her grandmother used to fix, the ice cream she used to churn by hand. She remembered later, making love with Eliot on the slope of the butte, remembered helping Lucy spread her sleeping bag beneath the stars, and it was less like being uprooted than having the roots ripped out of her to be leaving all of that to live in California.

"California," she'd echoed blankly when Eliot first told her about the job he'd found, as the director of the USDA Plant Germplasm Center at UC Santa Dorothea.

"Plant Germplasm Center?" she'd asked. "What's that?"

"It's a seed bank, the government's attempt to try to promote research and maybe preserve some genetic diversity. It won't pay well, but it's a pretty good job for someone who just lost his head on the tenuring guillotine."

"In California," she'd repeated, trying to find a way to make her enthusiasm match his own.

"Northern California," Eliot had qualified. "North of San Francisco."

After months of strain and worry, it was marvelous to think that Eliot might have a job, but northern or southern, all Anna could imagine of California were palm trees and freeways and Ansel Adams's photographs of Yosemite. She'd had never been to California. She'd planned on going to the opening of her Los Angeles show, but because of her pregnancy she'd had to call and cancel it instead. Later, when Eliot went down to Santa Dorothea to find a house for them, she'd had to stay behind to finish teaching and clean out her office for the new photographer.

The baby gave a lurch inside her. Reaching down, she pressed her hand against the spot where the movement was most distinct. When she first told Eliot that she was pregnant, he'd turned pale and opened his arms to her, holding her not in celebration but as though some great disaster had just struck. "A baby?" he'd echoed dumbly. "Are you sure?" But at the sight of the fear and yearning that trembled in her face, his whole bearing had grown firmer and more solid. "We'll manage somehow," he'd promised, and his voice had held more certainty than she'd heard since he'd lost his job.

"How are you doing?" he asked now, reaching across the front seat to lay his hand on Anna's knee.

"Okay," she answered in a voice she'd intended to be hearty but which sounded wan. "I'm all right." Later that afternoon, the house that had sheltered four generations of her family would be unlocked by strangers. Strangers' hands would open the cabinets and drawers her great-grandfather had built, strangers' feet would climb the stairs and claim the rooms, and some time that evening, strangers would catch the scent of her grandmother's roses wafting across the yard.

"How about you, Monkey Buckets? How's it going back there?" Eliot asked, tilting his head and speaking to the backseat.

"Okay," came Lucy's forlorn reply.

"Do you want to listen to a tape?"

"No."

"Are you hungry? Should we get your mom to rustle up some grub?"

"No."

"Are you thirsty?"

"Uh-uh."

Eliot shot a glance at Anna, who roused herself enough to ask, "Are you sure you don't want anything?"

"Yeah."

Lucy sounded so sad. Anna wished she could gather herself and try to comfort her, but she felt inert, too stunned and stupid. All morning she watched listlessly as the hills flattened and the harvest light grew thin and the land became drier and rockier and less lush. They drove for a hundred miles along the dammed Columbia River, and Anna stared dully at its torpid power. At Biggs Junction they left the river, and by midafternoon they were driving across a high plateau filled with rock and sagebrush.

"It's empty country, isn't it?" Eliot asked. "Maybe it's a good thing we let Jesse sell us that cell phone, after all."

At the mention of Jesse, Anna felt a familiar twinge of remorse. After a few more scrapes with the law, he had joined a church, married a girl he met in Bible class, and bought a cellular phone franchise. Last summer he hired his mother to decorate his showroom, and now the family's consensus was that he'd turned out all right. But Anna still remembered the ardor in his voice that night he'd talked about his art. She wondered if he ever craved the thrill and satisfaction of painting in the dark. And then she wondered which was sadder—for him to miss it or for him to never think of it at all.

Lucy broke the silence to announce, "Guess what?"

"What?" Eliot asked.

"Guess who's coming with us?"

Anna heard the tingle of discovery in Lucy's voice and forced herself from her torpor to ask, "Noranella?"

"Nope."

"Then who?"

"Noranella's ghost!" Lucy announced triumphantly.

"Her ghost?" Eliot asked.

"Yep," Lucy answered. "And Noranella's ghost is starfing for M&M's."

Maybe it will be all right, Anna thought, staring at the desert unspooling in front of them and listening as Lucy divided her candy between herself and the ghost of her imaginary friend. The baby thumped against her bladder, and she reached across the seat to lay her hand on top of Eliot's.

"Okay?" he asked, glancing over at her. But before Anna could answer, Lucy spoke. "Where are we?" she said in a small, bleak voice. "Noranella's ghost wants to know."

"We're in central Oregon," Eliot said. "Just north of Shaniko."

"Where are we going?"

"We're going to our new home," Anna answered patiently. "Remember? We're moving to California."

"Is that beyond the end of everything?" Lucy's voice held a streak of panic, and when Anna heaved around in her seat to look at her, she saw that her daughter was gazing out across the barren landscape, her exquisite little face pinched with despair.

AFTER MELODY LOST HER JOB, SHE SPENT LESS AND LESS TIME AT THE trailer, and when she was at home, she seemed sadder than Cerise had ever known her to be.

"What's wrong?" Cerise asked one evening when she looked up from her algebra workbook to see that Melody was staring at the TV news with tears glittering in her eyes.

"The world," Melody answered bleakly. "Everything." But when Cerise tried to ask her what she meant, she shook her head impatiently and left the room, and Cerise, who had a test the next day, could only look after her with an aching heart.

The summer term ended, and when her grades came in the mail, Cerise opened the envelope with the same sense of doom she'd always had when she was a kid and her report card arrived. But this time she could hardly believe what she saw—two B's and three A's. She felt an enormous upwelling of pride, and then, a second later, a little prick of disappointment when she realized that no one else would value those letters as much as she.

Fall semester was approaching, but when Cerise offered to go with Melody to the local high school and help her get enrolled, Melody told her about the alternative school where Tree had gone. It was deeply cool, she said. At the alternative school she could study what she really wanted to learn. She could avoid all the crap—the pep assemblies and study halls and cliques—and still graduate ahead of the other kids her age.

"What about college?" Cerise asked, and Melody answered breezily that Tree had been accepted at MIT.

"So he'll be leaving soon," Cerise said hopefully.

"He's not going yet," Melody said offhandedly, tossing her head so that her hair rippled down her back like a river of blond light. "He's got more important things to do."

"What—"

"Besides," Melody said, changing the subject with another flick of her hair, "do you have any idea how dangerous high schools are these days? Kids get killed all the time, going to high school." She reminded Cerise of the Columbine massacre and the shootout at Jefferson High and claimed that last year two boys had been stabbed in the lunchroom of the school Cerise wanted to send her to. She said that the biology teacher had found a bomb in his car, and that all the girls she knew who went to that school developed bladder infections rather than use the lavatories where the gang girls hung out. She said, "I can't believe you'd want to risk my life by sending me to a place like that."

"I don't want you to get hurt," Cerise answered. "But I just—"

"Anyway," Melody said, "The spaces were going fast at the alternative school, so I went ahead and enrolled."

"You enrolled? Without telling me?"

"You were busy studying, so I just faked your signature. It's all taken care of," she added blithely.

"Well," Cerise answered, teetering between her pleasure at Melody's initiative, her terror of Melody getting hurt, her concern about Melody's future, and her guilt about not staying more involved, "just make sure you keep your grades up. You have to stay in school, or we'll run into trouble with our aid."

"Don't worry—you'll get your money," Melody promised, the sarcasm of her words almost neutralized by the affection in her voice.

Then fall semester began, and Cerise was engulfed once again, so immersed in her studies and other responsibilities that she had no choice but to assume that everything was okay with Melody, and to be grateful that Melody's schedule allowed her to spend so much time watching Travis that Cerise did not have to find a day care for him.

But late one Friday night in September, when Travis climbed over the permanently lowered railing of his crib to crawl into bed with Cerise, she woke up enough to notice a rim of light outlining the edges of her closed bedroom door. She lay awake beside her sleeping toddler until her irritation with Melody's carelessness and her worry about the electric bill prodded her to her feet. Crossing the room on tiptoe to avoid waking Travis, she eased the door open so that it wouldn't creak and then stopped in the little hall, stunned by what the light revealed.

Melody was standing in front of the stove, her back toward Cerise. At first Cerise assumed she was cooking something, but before she could find her voice to ask what, Melody cocked her wrist and plunged her forearm against the red spiral of the element. A long half-second later she yanked her arm from the burner. Holding out her wrist, she studied the stripe she had branded in her skin as dispassionately as if she were examining a new manicure.

"Melody!" Cerise gasped, as though she were warning Melody of a danger she had not yet seen for herself.

Startled, Melody flung herself from the stove. She swung around to face her mother, and Cerise watched the expressions flick across her face, shifting with breathtaking swiftness from satisfaction to shame and then to a kind of animal furtiveness before finally hardening into defiance.

"What?" Melody asked belligerently. "You scared me."

"What are you doing?" Cerise asked.

"Heating water. Where's the cocoa mix?"

"Did you burn yourself?"

"N—yes. It was an accident. Where're the Band-Aids?"

Cerise cried, "Oh, Melody, why?"

"Why what?"

"Why did you—hurt yourself?"

"What do you mean?" Melody asked indignantly. "I said it was an accident."

"But I saw—"

"What did you see?"

But in that second all of Cerise's faults and lacks as a mother, all the flaws of her love, came bristling round her. Suddenly it seemed she remembered every scolding she had ever given Melody, every shriek of blame. She remembered every time she'd said no, every time she'd made a mistake by saying yes. She remembered every instance of her ignorance, her impatience, her exhaustion, all the million ways she'd failed her daughter. And she felt the shame of what now seemed the largest fault of all, that somehow, without intending it, she had passed on to Melody the need—and even the method—with which to hurt herself. She felt the dare in Melody's gaze and looked away, unable to meet the hard need in her daughter's eyes.

Back on her mattress, she lay awake beside the inert warm heap of Travis. The rim of light that framed the bedroom door had vanished, and for a while she could hear Melody rummaging in the bathroom. Then a thick silence reigned as Cerise stared up at the darkness, trying to imagine what she could do to help her daughter. But just before dawn her plans were lost in a series of sharp-edged dreams, and when Cerise's alarm rang at five, Melody was already gone.

All that day, as Cerise studied and shopped for groceries and played with Travis and tried to clean the apartment for the week to come, she wondered what it meant, for Melody to burn herself. Part of her said it was not all that important, that Melody would be fine. After all, Cerise had done the same thing once, and she was no drug addict or outlaw. But another part of her ached with pain both current and remembered—not the sting of blisters on tender skin as much as the hole in her soul those burns were meant to cauterize. She knew she needed to do something for Melody, but she was afraid that anything she did might only make things worse.

That night, after Travis had gone to bed, Cerise was sitting on the sofa, trying to memorize Piaget's stages of cognitive development, when she heard Melody's key in the door. At first she felt the slump of relief she always felt when Melody got home safely, though in the next instant she tensed herself for whatever might go wrong next.

Even so, she was not prepared when she glanced up from her textbook and caught sight of Melody's swollen face. "My God," she gasped. "What happened? Did Tree hit you?"

"Of course not," Melody answered staunchly. "Tree wouldn't hurt a fly. I did it all myself." Cocking her discolored cheek toward Cerise, she added, "It'll be perfect, once the swelling goes down. After it heals, the contrast will be way better. I used good inks," she went on, reciting the colors as though she were ten years old again, naming crayons. "Emperor green, sea blue, Texas blue, and pelican black."

Tattooed below Melody's left eye was a raw blue teardrop outlined in black.

Inside the tear a miniature earth was suspended, the darker blue waters of the oceans rising out of the pale blueness of the teardrop, the green continents of North and South America minute but recognizable against the seas.

"I had to do the whole thing backwards," Melody went on, as Cerise stared in growing horror at the ruin of her daughter's face. "In the mirror. I thought my arm would fall off." She laughed. "It hurt so much I couldn't stop crying, and the tears made my cheek all slippery."

The trailer began to spin. Cerise's whole life was suddenly reduced to that single awful moment in that stifling room. Nothing could ever again be right now that her shining girl—her perfect baby—had trashed her own face.

"Why?" Cerise said finally. "Why on earth?"

"Hey!" Melody laughed, "Exactly. Why on earth? Good one, Mom."

Ignoring her, Cerise said, "Why did you do it?"

"Don't you get it? I'm crying for the earth."

"But your face—you'll never be able to get it off."

"That's the point."

"You've wrecked your face."

"It's not wrecked. The earth is wrecked." Melody grinned, and added, "Tree says it's sexy."

"How dare you!" Cerise exploded.

"Mom, it's something even you should face," Melody said primly, "what's happening to the earth."

Savage with the need to hurt the thing that had ruined her daughter, Cerise slapped Melody, hitting her so hard across her tattooed cheek that her head snapped back. Melody gasped and threw both hands against her face as though it were something precious she had to catch before it fell and shattered.

"What have you done?" Melody asked, clutching her face and rocking with the pain. "What have you done to me?"

But before Cerise could gather an answer, Melody turned and ran into the night, slamming the door so that the whole trailer shook and Travis woke wailing from his sleep. Dashing into their room, Cerise snatched him up and jammed him on her hip. Shouting Melody's name, she ran with Travis into the dark road. But although she saw curious faces pressed against the lighted windows of the nearby trailers, she could find no sign of Melody.

Finally, she had no choice but to retreat into the trailer, nurse Travis back to sleep, and hope that Melody would be home by morning, and then, when Melody did not return, to try to live inside the anguish that was Melody's absence. She made what calls she could, but none of the Lost Children were listed with directory assistance, the secretary at the alternative school said she had no record of a Melody Johnson's enrollment, and the lady at the mall boutique said she didn't know a thing about buying airbrushed T-shirts from a girl named Melody.

Cerise was afraid to call the police and say her daughter had run away for fear it would get Melody in some worse trouble, and she was afraid, too, that if the welfare office learned that Melody was no longer part of her assistance unit, their aid would be reduced. She couldn't quit her program, couldn't possibly find a cheaper place to live, couldn't jeopardize the future for Travis and herself because Melody had run off. So she found a day care that could take Travis on such short notice, and then, worrying and working, she waited for Melody to come back home.

PUSH, THEY KEPT SAYING—ELIOT AND THE DOCTOR AND THE CHORUS of nurses—push, push, keep pushing. And hour after hour Anna pushed, bearing down with every muscle and sinew, pushing until she shook with the effort. She pushed her way beyond exhaustion, beyond expectation, pushed into the very heart of pain, pushed until it seemed her life would never again be anything but that cruel squeeze and peak and plunge, that awful push.

"I've already done this once," she'd gasped, back when she could still speak. "Why is it so hard this time?"

"Maybe this baby's a little bigger than your last one was," a nurse answered, slipping a blood-pressure cuff on her arm. "Or it could be positioned differently. Every labor's unique," she added, calmly turning her attention to her stethoscope.

"What—" Anna began, but before she could shape the rest of her question, she was under the waves again, clinging to Eliot's hand because only Eliot could keep her from slipping forever out of reach.

Push, they all urged—push.

Easy for you to say, she thought with a final bitter particle of something resembling humor. But she roused herself and pushed—not because she believed that pushing would change anything, but only because she could think of nothing else to do, only because pushing was inescapable, pushing was life's one certain thing. Century after century she pushed, pushed with every cell and fiber of herself, pushed as though she were pushing the mountain to Muhammad, as though she were Sisyphus pushing the stone uphill.

And all the while they yelled, Push, push now, push harder, make this one count. With some last wisp of everyday consciousness, she was aware that a new tension had entered the room, that the doctor's orders were more clipped than before, that the nurses had given up talking among themselves and were guarding their monitors intently, and she felt nearly gratified that finally they all seemed to realize how dire her situation really was.

Eons after she'd pushed everything else out of her—shit and spit and pee and hope—she bore down one last time with every muscle she'd ever owned. Shaking so hard that Eliot had to hold her to keep her from falling off the bed, she pushed, and suddenly she felt something give, felt an exquisite near-relief that made her desperate to continue pushing.

"There's the head," someone announced.

"Stop," the doctor commanded, harsh as a sergeant. "Stop pushing now."

"Pant," a nurse added quickly. "Pant to keep from pushing."

"Stop pushing," echoed Eliot in Anna's ear while another nurse darted in next to the doctor at the end of the delivery table. "You've got to stop, Anna. They need to clean the baby's lungs."

It made no sense, but even so she tried her best to comply, panting and trembling and moaning while her body ached to continue pushing. The nurse at the end of the table ducked her head between Anna's legs, and Anna thought she caught a glimpse of her sucking on a length of plastic tubing.

But before she could try to understand, another contraction swept over her. "I can't," Anna gasped. "I can't not push."

"Just—" the doctor answered. But already Anna was bearing down against the thing that filled her past bursting. She pushed, and suddenly it broke free of her burning labia, slithered out of her in a warm delicious gush. The doctor caught it—"a girl!" a nurse announced—while Anna sank back among the pillows on the upraised bed, utterly spent.

It's over, she thought. I did it. She closed her eyes and floated in a relief sweet as ecstasy while Eliot bent next to her, rocking her in his arms. "She's here," he murmured. "She's with us. Our baby's here," and Anna, far out in her private sea, remembered the reason for all her work.

"Our baby," she croaked, opening her eyes and glancing between her sprawled knees to where the doctor held their child.

But the thing that dangled from the doctor's gloved hands looked more like a discarded rag doll than a newborn human being. Its wrinkled torso was the dark bruised color of steak, its purple face as expressionless as an idol. It looked inert, as dead as mud. It looked as though it was never meant to live. What's that? she thought wildly. There's been a mistake. Where's my baby?

She and Eliot had planed to cut the cord together this time, their hands clasped on top of each other's as they had been when they'd cut their wedding cake. But before Anna could rouse herself to stop him, the doctor had already snipped it as unceremoniously as though it were a chicken neck.

"We'll need to suction," he muttered to the nurse who stood beside

him as he rushed the baby to the steel table in the corner of the room. A
sudden crowd of people were flinging words around the room, a terse jumble of words that Anna was too spent to follow—*deLee, heart rate, now.*

"Can I see her?" she asked thickly.

"In a minute," the doctor answered, leaning over the limp creature
with his stethoscope.

"What's wrong?" Anna begged Eliot, clinging to his hand as though
she were having the worst contraction yet.

"What's going on?" Eliot asked the room. "Is everything okay?"

"It should be fine," a nurse said, tossing the answer over her shoulder as she twisted a suction bulb into the baby's mouth and gave a deft
squeeze. "She aspirated some meconium, and now she just needs a little
resuscitation to get her going."

Meconium? Anna thought, her brain stunned dumb. Resuscitation?
She tried to get her mind to remember those words, felt, in the midst of
her growing horror, another stab of failure for not having managed to
take a childbirth refresher course before the baby came. But there was no
time, a corner of her mind pleaded helplessly. We only got here two
weeks ago. I barely managed to find a babysitter for Lucy. Meanwhile, a
nurse began to scrub the baby with a towel, rubbing it as though she
were shaping dough, seemingly oblivious to the way its tiny limbs
flopped against the steel table.

"Bag her," the doctor barked.

Anna heard more words, a flurry of words—*oxygen, falling, come on.*
She watched in helpless agony as they covered the dark face with a tiny
mask, watched as a nurse encircled the small torso with her hands and
then pressed a quick, insistent rhythm on the blue chest with her paired
thumbs.

"Oh, please," Anna moaned. The air was suddenly thick and viscous,
as though all the oxygen had been sucked from the room. Sharp scraps of
thoughts rattled through her mind. It's my fault, she thought. I spent
those days in the darkroom before I knew. I didn't always want this baby

enough. I was too worried about the move. I lifted too many boxes. I didn't push hard enough. I couldn't stop pushing for long enough. She thought, This can't be happening. She thought, I would give anything.

"I have to help her," she said, struggling with the twisted sheet, trying to will her body to let her rise.

"Lie down," a nurse commanded, pressing her hand against Anna's shoulder and speaking to her as though she were simple-minded. "You still need to deliver your placenta."

Another nurse leaned over Anna. "She's in good hands," she said.

But I'm her mother, Anna thought. A contraction hit her broadside. "Please," she whimpered as the placenta spilled out of her like a large warm liver. "Please."

More people pushed into the room. They spoke to each other in terse tones, and then whisked the baby away before Anna had a chance to touch her, before she could see whose eyes she had or how much hair.

"Where are they taking her?" Anna begged one of the nurses who remained.

"NICU," the nurse replied.

"What?" Anna asked, vainly trying to turn the letters into words.

"Neonatal intensive care," the nurse said, her voice so full of patience and warmth that Anna instantly hated her. "This happens sometimes. The neonatologist will be back as soon as he can to explain things to you."

"What are they doing to her?"

"They're just trying to get her lungs cleared, to help her breathe." The nurse bent over Anna's abdomen and began to knead her uterus.

Anna craned her neck to watch the nurse's hands bear down on her empty, doughy belly. Her uterus cramped as though the nurse were pressing against an open wound, and she grimaced and winced automatically, but at the same time the pain felt remote, a thing apart from her. It felt as though her life were happening to someone else.

They moved her into another room, helped her to change into a clean gown, helped her to arrange a fresh pad between her legs, asked if she'd like to take a shower. "You'll feel better after you've had a chance to clean up," the nurse said.

"I won't feel better until I have my baby," Anna answered. Even to her ears, her words sounded desperate and pathetic, her voice so tight she could hardly recognize it as her own.

"You'll have your baby as soon as possible," the nurse answered, and Anna felt the grating of impatience and condescension in her tone. "Right now, the most important thing is to get your daughter stabilized."

My daughter, Anna's mind echoed. The most important thing. Unable to speak, she clutched Eliot's hand until it seemed the bones of their fingers would be permanently twisted by the tightness of her grip.

After what felt like many lifetimes, a new doctor came into the room. He introduced himself to Anna with a grave formality and reached out heartily to shake Eliot's hand. Anna tried to follow what he told them, but the few words she managed to catch made little sense, a barrage of phrases that only sounded frightening—*staining below the vocal cords, supplemental oxygen, IV glucose, pneumonia, dehydration, pulmonary infection*. She clung to Eliot's hand and tried to look intelligent and pleasant and grateful for all that the doctor was doing, tried to keep from screaming, Give her back to me, tried to keep from keening, Please make her live.

"I'm sorry," she said to Eliot after the doctor left.

"You heard what he said," Eliot gestured toward the door. "It was nothing anyone did. These things happen."

"But—"

"It'll be okay." Eliot's face was sharp and shrunken.

"How do you know?" she snapped in instant fury. "How can you possibly say it will be okay?"

His eyes met hers. They were bleak and dark, like holes that led nowhere. "Hope?" he said, his voice teetering between plea and irony. They stared at each other for a second, and then he shrugged helplessly, his expression melting into utter pain. With a sudden slash of insight she realized how vulnerable they were—he and she—how easily their marriage could be shredded, how thoroughly their whole world toppled by the loss of one tiny child.

"I need to see her," she said, struggling to her feet. Standing up, she felt as though what little was still left inside her might flop out, organs spilling down her legs onto the shining linoleum. She wove like a drunkard, and clutched at Eliot's arm.

"You sure you're okay?" Eliot asked.

She thought, Nothing will ever be okay again. "I'm fine," she said, leading him down the hall. "I just need to see my baby."

Wire mesh was embedded in the windows of the neonatal intensive care unit, and the door was locked. Like a prison, Anna thought as they waited in the hall for a nurse to let them in. Inside the dim room it was unexpectedly loud with a varied cacophony of monitors and ventilators. The nurse had them wash their hands, and then she led them past an oak rocking chair, and through a labyrinth of equipment. Babies lay in some of the incubators and radiant warmers they passed along the way. Some of the babies were so impossibly small they seemed more alien or simian than human, while others looked nearly normal except for how still they lay, except for the maze of tubes and wires and probes and sensors that kept them attached to life.

"Here she is," the nurse said, stopping beside a radiant warmer at the back of the room and waiting for Anna and Eliot to catch up. "It's okay to touch her gently, but don't pick her up."

"When can—" Anna began, but suddenly an alarm sounded in another corner of the room. Eliot flinched, and Anna gasped, but the nurse only said, "Excuse me," and moved off, leaving them staring down at their daughter.

She was no longer the dead blue color of a bruise, but lying prone beneath the radiant lights she looked weary and utterly worn, like a shipwrecked traveler washed ashore in a storm. She was naked except for the huge white plastic diaper that dwarfed her bent legs. A blood pressure cuff encircled one little thigh. A needle was taped into her frail arm, a battery of probes and sensors were taped to her sides and chest, and a tube snaked into her mouth, held in place by more tape on her cheek. Her eyes were closed, and she was panting as rapidly as a dog on a hot day, panting as though simply lying there—simply living—was an exertion almost too great to be endured.

I did this to her, Anna thought. I made her be alive. She remembered having a similar thought after Lucy was born, though then her emotions had been pride and awe, not trepidation. Tentatively, she stretched out a forefinger to touch the little shoulder, felt for the first time her daughter's skin beneath her fingertip. It was impossibly soft, like butterfly wings, like rose petals, like tears. She ran her finger wistfully across the brief back, felt her own tears burning in her sinuses. Beneath the infant's frail skin Anna felt her tiny ribs, and she thought of all the hardness and sadness that still waited for them, of all the sorrow they would have to endure even if the baby managed to live, to thrive, to grow into an ordinary girl. This is only the beginning, she thought, and for a dizzying moment she wished the baby were already dead, wished the worst had already engulfed them, so that the worry could be over and all she would have left to face was grief. A sob burst from her, inadvertent as a sneeze.

"You heard the doctor," Eliot said. "This isn't all that uncommon. She has a good chance of being just fine. It's just this next few weeks that'll be touch and go." He strengthened his grip on Anna's hand.

"But what if—" Anna faltered, unable to bring herself to find words for what could happen next. She remembered her grandmother's daughter, the Lucy who died before she could be named. It happens, Anna thought, tearing her gaze from her baby to cast a glance at all the other struggling babies in the nursery. It happens all the time. Why did I ever think we would be spared?

Standing above the Plexiglas box that contained her daughter, she saw what she couldn't believe she had never seen before, how perilous life was, how unpredictable and uncertain. Always before her problems had been with the complexities of living, not with simply staying alive. It was as if she had somehow assumed that dying could be avoided—or at least postponed for so long that the fear of it had never really reached her. Dying was what people did if they were old, like her grandmother, or if they were careless enough to let bad things happen.

But now she saw how ignorant she had been to think that way. She had been naive and stupid and insensitive, and she realized with a jolt so mean and sudden it was like a car wreck that death was always lurking behind all of them, that they were each only a breath away from darkness all the time. Standing over her panting daughter, she marveled that anything else could have ever mattered, that she could ever have cared about photography or where she lived or the color she chose to paint her living room.

After Eliot left to pick up Lucy from the babysitter, the nurse sent Anna to her room to get some rest. She went with a reluctant obedience, in the superstitious hope that if she did what she was told, her daughter would be okay. A bouquet of homegrown roses was waiting on the tray beside her bed, and for a strange, chaotic moment, Anna thought her grandmother must have sent it. But when she read the card, she saw that it had been delivered to the wrong room, that the roses were meant for someone else.

The room was as impersonal as a room in a cheap hotel. She missed her friends back home in Salish, missed her mother and her sister, both of whom had planned on coming later, after the baby was born. She felt like a husk, a vacant shell. She couldn't bear to lie down, alone in her empty body. Instead she went to the window, opened the heavy plastic drapes, looked out beyond her dark reflection into the night. The city of Santa Dorothea stretched away below her, its streets aglow with yellow house lights, white and red car lights, the cold orange-violet glare of streetlights. Above her, the sky was stained with the blending of all those lights, its sickly glow saturating the blackness, concealing the stars. She thought, I live here now.

The lights of an ambulance pulsing in the distance snagged her attention. She watched as it pushed single-mindedly up the boulevard toward the hospital, racing through the bright night with its desperate load. She could not hear its siren behind the window, but as she watched it draw nearer, she felt an answering pulse of fear. Anything is possible, she thought as the ambulance turned into the hospital drive and vanished from her view.

Her eye was caught by a group of teenagers ambling along on the sidewalk below her. The streetlight illuminated them as though they were passing through a spotlight on a stage, and Anna could see the glint of bottles in their hands, could see the red pulse and glow of their cigarettes. Watching them, who had so recently been babies and who had now taken their lives into their own hands so stridently, she felt a panic in all her bones. What's next? she wondered.

And suddenly a million threats suggested themselves to her. It was as though she were still dilated, still open and unfiltered, as though she were a lens that admitted all possible light, and every shadow. She thought of SIDS and AIDS and hidden heart defects, of strange viruses and untended swimming pools, of childhood cancers and E. coli–laden hamburgers. She remembered all the appalling numbers that filled the newspapers, the thousands of extinctions and billions of pounds of toxic chemicals that threatened the world. She thought of global warming, nuclear winter, and silent spring. Clutching the windowsill and staring down on the city stewing in all its ugly light, she wondered how she could ever feel safe again.

WHEN THE ALARM RANG, THE ROOM WAS BLACK AND COLD AND CERISE was still so tired—was always so tired—was aching with exhaustion even as she woke. It was cruelly early, but even so her first thought was that she should have been up at least an hour ago. She should have used that extra time to shower and dress and study, to assemble Travis's diaper bag and make his breakfast and pack his lunch. She should have washed the heap of bowls and spoons and bottles that spilled out of the trailer sink and choked the tiny counter, should have tried to address the disaster in the little living room, to unpack the stacks of boxes that had sat untouched since she and Jake and Melody had heaved them there, four months before.

She should have spent a quiet moment trying to decide what to do next about Melody. Three weeks, she thought as she clutched Travis's sleeping body—tonight it would be three weeks since Melody had run out into the darkness, that awful teardrop bleeding on her cheek.

Beneath the snarl of blankets, Travis began to stir. She pulled him closer, folding him into the pocket her body made when she drew her knees toward her chin. Burying her face beneath the blankets, she inhaled the scent of him, the clean, tealike fragrance of his breath, the aroma of his head like the smell inside a bakery.

"Mama?" he asked.

Without opening her eyes she lifted her T-shirt, thrust her chest toward him, let him nuzzle until he trapped her nipple in his mouth. With Melody, even if Cerise had not been too shy to nurse, she had never really believed that her breasts were capable of making milk. But Travis had latched on just minutes after she pushed him into her hands, when it seemed like just another miracle of birth that her body could feed his. For months he had lived on her milk alone, and she had felt a secret pride to be his only food. The blond curls that sprouted on his head, his round tummy, even the orange smears of wax inside his ears—all of him, she'd liked to think, had come from her. Now he was eating lots of other foods, and she felt a guilty compunction that she hadn't weaned him yet. When Jake came up to help them move, he'd said, "That boy should be chewing on a steak. It's time he left the titty to his dad."

She cupped the back of Travis's head in her palm, felt the milk rising in her breast and tried to concentrate all her love for him into her wish that he would have a good day. The day care she had been able to find for him after Melody left was not a place she liked to leave him. It was loud and crowded, and more than once his diaper had been so heavy when she picked him up that she was sure it hadn't been changed all day. Every morning, when they finally reached the Happy Factory after their long bus ride, Travis clung to her like a desperate monkey, and only her fear of being late for class would allow her to peel him from her neck and hip and race away, his final cries magnifying in her memory so that it was their sound, and the image of his tear-smeared face, that haunted her all day at school.

Suddenly Travis pulled away from her breast, letting her nipple pop out of his mouth like a cork from a bottle. He cocked his head and laughed at the sound he'd made, at the way her nipple bobbled on her breast.

"Meedee?" he said, pushing away from Cerise to stand teetering beside the mattress in the new gray light that entered the trailer through the high window above the crib. "Meedee?"

"Meedee's gone," Cerise said, "you should know that by now." But grinning like a drunken cowboy, Travis lurched out of their bedroom and down the miniature hall to the room at the back of the trailer that still held all of Melody's things. Cerise sighed and heaved back the blankets. Pushing herself off the mattress, she pulled a sweatshirt over her T-shirt and set off after him.

Melody's room was a clutter of posters and scarves, its cold air dense with the lingering scent of incense. Travis was sitting in the half-dark on Melody's mattress, intent as a mystic as he draped himself in beads and chains and bracelets.

"Those are your sister's," Cerise said, stripping off his finery, dropping the bangles back in a heap on the mattress, and scooping him up. "You better leave her things alone."

She carried him, protesting, back into their room. Plopping him on their cooling nest of blankets, she unzipped his sleeper, unpeeled the tabs on his soggy diaper, and tried to fit a dry one onto the wriggle he became each time she changed him. Then, his diaper finally fastened and his sleeper rezipped, Cerise lifted him from the mattress and carried him out to the sofa.

"Mama needs a shower," she said, flicking the remote until two dueling space aliens appeared on the TV screen. "Be a good boy, and watch this till I'm done."

In the shower the heat of the pounding water made her skin red, although the parts of her the water didn't reach were puckered with cold. She'd used the last of the shampoo two days before, and now she filled the empty bottle with shower water, shook it, and poured the limp soup over her head. Wadding her heavy hair at the back of her neck, she tried to make it lather, calculating, as she scrubbed her scalp, when she'd next be able to afford shampoo.

She stepped out of the shower stall and, shivering, grabbed a towel. "Trav?" she called, "Are you okay?"

It was not yet six, and she was already late. She could feel the tension gathering in her shoulders. She had a quiz in basic English today, a child-development test tomorrow, and a report about her observations of three-year-olds due at the end of the week. She had to put in four hours at the school day care, and then had to retrieve Travis from the Happy Factory before it closed at six, had to feed and bathe him, to play the games with him that she hadn't been able to play with him all day, had to rinse out clothes for both of them in the salad-bowl-size sink because there was no money for the Laundromat, had to nurse Travis to sleep and then study until the words on the pages of her textbooks blurred into her dreams, had to do all that today so she could do it all again tomorrow.

As she yanked on her clothes in the bedroom, Cerise could hear above the TV the electronic voice of Travis's laser power blaster commanding, *Attention. Drop your guns. Fire,* and then, a second later, proclaiming, *Target.* It sounded a little slow, the voice wearier than it had been the day before. Even though Travis would probably have another tantrum, Cerise hoped that meant the battery Melody had got for it was finally wearing out. She hated that toy. She still resented the fact that Jake had given it to Travis instead of buying him diapers or food or clothes, and it worried her that Travis loved it so much. She wondered what it meant to him when he pointed the barrel at her and pulled the trigger. In her child-development textbook it said that toddlers had no concept of the permanence of death, that they couldn't tell fantasy from reality. But she couldn't figure out whether that meant that every death was pretend, or that everything that Travis imagined was real.

From the front room there was a crash, a long moment of silence, and then the inevitable exhalation of Travis's wail. Dropping her sweater, she ran from the bedroom to find Travis flailing beneath a collapsed stack of boxes.

"Goddammit," she screamed, snatching him up from the floor by his shoulders so that he dangled from her hands. At the sound of her anger, he cried louder.

"Look what you've done," she shrieked. She wanted to shake him, to hurt or frighten him. She wanted to make him cry. For a poisonous second she wanted to drop him and walk out the door, to run off as Melody had, into a fresher, easier, more promising life. But suddenly her own tears needled their way into her eyes, and she pulled him against her chest instead, held him close while her face twisted with the effort of not crying.

Startled by her silence, Travis quit bawling to squirm around in her arms. Peering up at her in concern, he said in a worried voice, "Mama? Owie?"

"It's okay, baby," Cerise answered, pressing her face into his little shoulder.

"Mama? Bannay?" Travis asked. For a moment she held him close enough to feel the calm, firm bones beneath his flesh, and then, releasing her grip, she answered, "No, Trav. Mama doesn't need a Band-Aid. It's okay. I'm all right. Come on, buddy—we've got to hurry. We can't be late."

Back in the bedroom she traded Travis's sleeper for a clean T-shirt, a pair of sweat pants, and his Batman jacket. She counted three more diapers into his diaper bag, and tried not to wonder where the next package of diapers would come from. She replenished the supply of wipes, searched for two clean socks and for his shoes while Travis practiced the words his laser power blaster was teaching him, "Tentin. Fie-o. Tawgit."

Cerise turned on the burners of the stove and laid a slice of bread on top of each of them. When the slices were branded with the elements' spirals, she snatched them off and wiped them with peanut butter. Travis's she cut in strips and set on a plate for him to eat while she studied for her quiz. Hers she swallowed without tasting while she tried to memorize the rules for apostrophes.

When the phone rang, Cerise was writing "the men's cars" in the final blank of the study sheet, and Travis was watching space aliens destroy the universe. Someone was selling something, she thought, as she rose to answer.

"Hello?" she said.

"Mom?"

Cerise made a noise into the receiver, a gasp involuntary as a belch.

"Mom?" the voice said again. "Is that you?"

"Melody?" she answered. "Where are you? Are you okay?" She clutched the receiver in both hands, careful not to drop it or make any sudden moves, as though Melody's voice were a feral kitten she might accidentally scare off.

"I'm fine," Melody said. "I got a lot of poison oak. But I'm fine. I'm having fun." The phone-voice laughed, and it was both amazing and appalling that Melody could laugh, could even think of having fun.

Cerise croaked, "Poison oak?"

"I was gathering firewood," Melody explained, "after dark."

"Where are you?" Cerise repeated. "Where are you calling from?"

They were staying in the state park north of the city, Melody said, the whole tribe of them, in a campground on the mountain.

"It's so beautiful," Melody said. "Real woods, with trees and everything. You and Travie should come up sometime, and visit."

They slept in tents and on Tree's school bus. They ate their meals all together. The guys were talking about starting a band, and Melody had seen a deer. She'd found a puppy, a little black one she'd named Circle.

When Cerise asked how she was paying for food, Melody laughed again. Tree was giving lots of tattoos, she said, and as soon as they got settled somewhere, she was going to start painting murals. She'd realized her artwork deserved a lot of space.

"Everybody shares their food. We take care of each other," Melody said, and added with a mixture of awe and pride, "we're a family."

"You left a family," Cerise answered, coldly enough to hide her hurt.

There was a silence so long and dense it seemed that Melody had vanished once more. Then she asked, "How's Travie? Does he miss his Meedee?"

Of course he misses you, Cerise wanted to say. But I miss you more. She wanted to say she was sorry, wanted to ask Melody to please come home. But she was afraid of how the meanings of her words would be altered once she spoke them, like the nail polish Jake had given Melody that changed color when it was exposed to light. And she was afraid of how Melody might answer, afraid of the hurt she'd have if Melody told her no.

She said, "Trav's okay. But we're late. I've got to go. We'll miss our bus."

DURING THE TWO WEEKS THAT ANNA AND ELIOT SPENT ENCAMPED IN the neonatal intensive care unit, it came to seem more like a home than the unfamiliar house they stumbled back to every night. They discovered where the quietest restrooms were, and which foods from the cafeteria were most nearly edible. They learned which babies were the sickest, which families seemed the sanest, which nurses were the friendliest. They learned what all the machines were for, learned which numbers they should hope for when the monitors gave their readings, what words to dread when test results came back. Anna even learned to find a kind of comfort in the corny posters above the nurses' station and in the row of stuffed animals that adorned their desk.

Sally left a decorating job half finished to fly down and stay with Lucy, who was too young to be allowed in to see her baby sister. But Anna was so absorbed in her newborn's struggle, she hardly noticed when Sally arrived. The first three days of Ellen's life, the alarm on her respirator rang so many times that Anna got almost used to the sickening flush of terror that swept over her each time it sounded. It came to seem almost routine for her and Eliot to be shuffled into the hall until the crisis had passed, almost routine when, after a wait as excruciating as drowning, a nurse came out to tell them it was okay to go back in. Anna grew used to the sight of tears on strangers' faces, and she became so accustomed to seeing babies attached to lines and tubes that once or twice she nearly panicked when, on her way through the hospital, she passed an open doorway and caught a glimpse of a newborn lying unencumbered in a bassinet and breathing on its own.

Adrenaline kept her body jangling with unspent tension, but instead of fighting or fleeing, instead of building a palace in a single day or slaying a dragon or separating kernels of wheat from grains of rice, she could only fit the shields of the hospital's milk pump over her stiff breasts and let it suck her empty. She could only stroke Ellen and whisper that she loved her. She could only wait and hope. But surrounded by sick babies and their frightened parents, she began to wonder if hope were any more than desperation's twin. After days of incessant hoping, hope seemed like the hardest labor yet, more harrowing and demanding than giving birth had ever been.

Then suddenly the neonatologist was signing the papers to send Ellen home. "She's basically a healthy little girl," he explained to Eliot and Anna as he passed Ellen's chart to her beaming primary nurse. "But her lungs will still be susceptible to infection for a year or so. You'll need to try to limit her exposure to viruses. Keep an eye on her, and she should be just fine."

"We've been very lucky," Anna answered, gratefully bending to claim Ellen from the bassinet she had graduated to once she proved she could breathe on her own. Anna and Eliot thanked the nurses with hugs and candy, said good-bye to the other parents, and then left, walking out of the hospital into the blaze of midmorning sunshine, the first living light that Ellen had ever seen.

But surviving a catastrophe meant that life went on. Sally flew home the next day, and Eliot, who had stolen time he could not spare from his new job to keep the vigil beside Ellen's isolette, vanished into his work.

"Now you can go back to your normal life," Ellen's primary nurse had exclaimed as she hugged Anna good-bye. But alone in a strange city with a weak-lunged newborn and a lonely first-grader, Anna realized she had no normal life to return to. Stranded in a house that did not feel like hers, in a place that was a thousand miles from her home, it was hard for her to keep in mind how lucky they had been.

On the websites Eliot found about meconium aspiration syndrome, other parents had written that having a sick baby had shown them how truly precious life really was, how they should never take a single second for granted. But instead it felt to Anna as if life were now too precious to relax into, too precious to be enjoyed. Home from the hospital, everything still felt dire and off-kilter, as though another greater crisis were looming.

"Look at me!" Lucy announced on Monday morning as Anna was leaning against the counter, buttering a toasted bagel for Lucy's breakfast. She looked up to see Lucy entering the kitchen, wearing the dress Eliot's mother made for her sixth birthday party instead of the school clothes Anna had set out for her.

Ellen had been awake since two, and Anna had been awake with her, rocking her and nursing her and trying not to panic when Ellen cried so hard that she began to cough. Now, at seven-thirty, Ellen had at last fallen into a fretful sleep, and Anna had just managed to ease her out of her arms and into the baby seat on the counter. "Shhh," she said to Lucy, casting a fearful glance in Ellen's direction. "That's a lovely dress," she added softly. "But you can't wear it to school."

"Why not?" Lucy asked, spreading the pink skirt like wings between her outstretched hands and bending her head to study it. A panel of smocking lay across her flat chest, and a wide pink ribbon encircled her sweet belly. Standing in the middle of the kitchen, she was so beautiful, so purely and unabashedly herself, that for a moment Anna was almost able to lose herself in admiring her daughter. But then she remembered that school started in less than an hour, that traffic could be bad on Monday mornings, that Lucy hadn't yet had breakfast. She remembered what happened the last time Lucy wore a special dress to school, and she said, "You'll ruin that dress if you wear it to school."

"No, I won't," Lucy answered passionately. "I love this dress. I wouldn't never ruin it."

"Keep your voice down," Anna said. She felt thin and gritty and bubble-headed. "You wouldn't mean to ruin it. But it would just happen. Remember when you wore your Christmas dress to kindergarten?"

"I was a baby then," Lucy said indignantly. "And besides, it was a accident."

"It would be an accident now, too," Anna answered. "Do you want to wear the purple pants I set out for you, or would you rather wear your daisy dress today?"

"I want to wear this," Lucy answered, standing in front of her mother like a stubborn pink stump.

"Lucy," Anna said firmly. "You still need breakfast, and we need to get you to school on time. You have to go get ready, right now."

"I'm already ready right now."

"No, you're not. You need to go upstairs and change your clothes."

And suddenly they were embroiled in an argument of such intensity and complexity it made Anna dizzy. Dozens of questions tangled in her sleep-starved mind. Was wearing a party dress to school Lucy's attempt to make herself feel special in the wake of her sister's arrival, or was it just another of Lucy's many whims? Was it a play for power inside the family, or a desperate effort to make herself feel lovely and loved at the school where she still spent every recess by herself? Would it be good for Lucy to see that Anna cared enough to protect her favorite dress, or would it be better for her to feel as though at least some small part of her life were in her control? And if Anna let Lucy have her way today, what would she want tomorrow? What would she demand when she was a teenager? How would she behave as an adult?

"I want to wear my birthday dress," Lucy yelled, her chest heaving beneath the pink smocking. In her infant seat, Ellen gave a jolt as though she had just been dropped. Her eyes flew open, and she began to cry.

"Now look at what you've done," Anna groaned. Between clenched teeth, she said, "You need to go upstairs and change into something else, and you need to do it right now."

Lucy's face crumpled. She fled from the room, and suddenly the whole day was in shambles although it was not yet eight o'clock. Mechanically Anna lifted Ellen from her seat and carried her, wailing, out of the kitchen. Standing in the center of the living room, she swayed with the screaming baby. Croaking a lullaby, she stared dully out the window at the oleander bushes that some previous owner had planted beside the house. They were dusty and lusterless in the late autumn heat, and despite the earliness of the hour, the light that fell on them seemed strained and thin.

It had been months since she'd seen light that moved her. Back in the never-never land before they'd left Salish, Anna had promised Eliot—and herself—that once the baby was born and Lucy was settled into school, she would split her time between setting up the house and exploring the California countryside for subjects for her new photographs. Back then she had even hoped that this baby's birth would invigorate her work as Lucy's birth had done. But now, as Ellen's crying veered toward another coughing fit, it was impossible to remember why her photographs had ever mattered.

Life was too dire to include anything as superfluous as art. Jobs could be lost, babies could die, the species in Eliot's seed bank could all become extinct, and still supper needed fixing, still the laundry needed folding and the dishes needed washing, still the boxes in the bedrooms had to be unpacked. Still behind every image Anna could imagine there lurked her memory of Ellen's fixed, blue face.

"I'm ready," she heard Lucy say over the swell of Ellen's cries. Lucy's voice was small and hollow, and when Anna turned to look at her, she looked so little, standing in the doorway in her purple pants. She looked defenseless, so negligible and crushable that Anna had to fight the impulse to beg her to go upstairs and put her party dress back on.

Instead, she answered as cheerfully as she could, "Thank you, Lucy. I really appreciate it." Still swaying with the baby, she glanced at her wristwatch and added, "There's a bagel in the kitchen for you. Give me a minute to calm Ellen down, and then we'll really have to run."

But instead of subsiding, Ellen's wails intensified, escalating until they echoed off the empty walls, and all of Anna's love, all her patience and intelligence, all her devotion and desperation, couldn't do a thing to stop them. Looking into the rigid, red face of her screaming daughter, Anna felt like a stranger, stranded in a life that wasn't hers.

WHEN THE SMOKE FIRST FILTERED INTO CERISE'S SLEEP, HER DREAMS recognized it. It was a nasty smoke, the smell of cheap things burning, and for a while her dreams engulfed it, offering weird dream-reasons to explain its presence. It was an explosion that finally woke her, a blast that left her unmoored in the darkness, adrenaline prickling her flesh, dread clinging to her bones. A bad dream, she told herself as she struggled to find a way out of its grip.

Beyond the blackness she heard roaring, a smooth sound like a hurricane wind, punctuated by explosions like bottles hurled against a wall. In a daze she fought with the blankets, struggling to remember where she was—in Rita's house, or her apartment, or back at Jake's?

Swaying and trailing blankets, she rose. Her arms flailed, groping the hot dark. She tottered forward and almost fell. Her hand bumped a door frame, scrabbled lower, and found a knob. She twisted and pushed. The door gave, and she tumbled into a narrow hall, looked down it to a place of searing heat and wild orange light.

For a long moment she stood paralyzed. The thing she faced was so fierce, so urgent, so huge and loud and frightful and strangely beautiful that it seared even the word *fire* from her mind. It was like a huge beast bearing down on her. Standing before it, Cerise was small and feeble and awestruck and alone.

Stop, the shred of a thought finally came. I have to stop it. Now.

She stepped forward, stretching out her arms as though she could force her way through the fire to its source. But before she could enter it, the awful heat seared her palms, although she felt no pain, but instead a quick sense of pressure, of pulling in. A moment later some instinct—some last scrap of what others might call luck—pushed her out of the fire's path. She stumbled backward to the door that appeared behind her like a gift. Without pausing to question where it led, she turned and tore it open. Bursting through it, she tripped down the trailer's back step, landed on the dark grass at the bottom.

The door slammed shut behind her, and in that instant she remembered—

"Travis!" she screamed, and leapt to reclaim the door. Grabbing the knob, she turned it and jerked. But it would not give. She tugged and twisted, pulling, pushing, yanking savagely, kicking, but still the door held fast, locked by her own hand before she went to bed to protect them from intruders. Banging her fists against the door, clawing her fingers under the metal flashing, she fought with it as though it were a living thing. "Travis, Travis, Travis," she shrieked.

Suddenly the night was peopled. Like the shifting sequence of another dream, lights pulsed, voices behind her yelled and called. Over her shoulder she cried, "My baby's in there," and all the while she beat the door.

A clumsy creature in thick gear caught her in an embrace, pulled her from the door, held her while he yelled, "Which room?"

"Inside. There's fire."

"Where is he?"

She understood, cried, "The window!" and tore away, ran barefoot and sobbing through the cold grass to the other side of the trailer, trampling the last of her feeble garden as she jumped to beat at the bedroom window with her fists. It shattered with a tiny, immediate sound, and the firefighter was beside her again, pulling her back from the hole.

The night pulsed with light, a radio crackled. A ladder appeared and slammed against the trailer. Cerise reached to climb it, but other hands grabbed her, held her back. The firefighter climbed instead. He swept the last shards of glass from the gaping frame with his thick-gloved hand while she watched, struggling to yank her arms from the man who restrained her, and sobbing, "Travie, Travie, Travis. My boy is in there."

The man who held her asked, "Anyone else?"

"What?"

"Is anyone else inside?"

"Anyone else," she gasped, trying to think, unable to focus on anything but Travis.

"Do you have other children?"

"Yes."

But the pulse of his shock got through to her, and she added, panting, "No. I mean, my daughter. But she's gone. You've got to let me get my boy."

"You can't go in there."

"I have to. I'm his mother."

He wouldn't let her, though she begged and wept, though she thought she heard above the shriek of the flames the shriek of her son.

From somewhere came the sound of water, the push of steam, the widening stench of burn. People yelled. Lights swept the night. The firefighter disappeared in the empty window frame, and another one climbed up behind him, stood on the ladder, training a flashlight inside the window. Cerise whimpered, "Get him, get him, please get him."

The light changed. There was the sound of an ax smashing, more yelling. A bundle was being passed to the firefighter on the ladder.

She moaned and surged forward. "Oh, Travis," she wept.

"Stay back," they warned. "Careful. Don't touch him."

"Burn kit!" a voice called. "Sterile blanket."

The firefighter gasped, "He was hiding. Under the crib. At first I couldn't. Find him."

A crowd had gathered, a semicircle of strangers. They stood just at the edge of darkness and watched Cerise rave. Her hair wild about her head, her face contorted, her burned hands imploring, she pleaded to be allowed to touch him, to see him, to comfort him.

But she was only his mother. These strangers knew how to save him. When the EMTs arrived and strode across the grass to kneel around him, the thought flickered through her mind that Travis would love these men, with their sirens and big trucks. But Travis was collapsed under the sterile blanket, unconscious, but still alive—or rather, still capable of being made to live when they caused his heart to beat and his scorched lungs to accept their oxygen.

THERE HAD BEEN A KIDNAPPING. TWO WEEKS BEFORE HALLOWEEN IN A nice neighborhood on the north side of Santa Dorothea, a twelve-year-old girl had been taken from her bed while her family slept. A week later her photograph was everywhere—on trees and telephone poles, on the sides of buildings and supermarket bulletin boards, alongside the goblins and pumpkins in the windows of all the stores. Reproduced a thousand times, it was an enlargement of what must have been the girl's school picture. Her gap-toothed face smiled from every handbill as if she were still having fun, though below her in bold letters were the words *Missing,* and *Reward.*

"What's that say?" Lucy demanded the first time she noticed it, posted in the side window of the Volvo stopped next to them at a traffic light. As always they were in a hurry, late for Lucy's school and Ellen's doctor's appointment. Now Anna was driving impatiently, her foot pivoting from accelerator to brake as she glanced at the dashboard clock, tried to remember what was on the grocery list she'd forgotten at home, tried to decide whether she had time to stop at the store before Ellen's appointment or whether she should wait until afterward, when Ellen would be tired and fussy and ready for a nap.

Lucy spoke again, "Mommy, what does that say?"

Anna glanced to where Lucy pointed and answered absently, "It says, 'missing,' 'reward.' "

"That girl is missing her reward?" Lucy's voice was puzzled.

"I guess so." Anna silently cursed her heedlessness and imagined all the things she might have told Lucy instead to forestall the coming conversation.

"That's not fair," Lucy said indignantly. "She should get her reward. Is that picture to make her get it?"

Anna felt a wisp of relief. "I suppose so," she said, trying to keep her voice light and noncommittal. "I don't really know."

The light changed. As they pulled away from the beaming paper girl and entered the bright haze of exhaust left by the car in front of them, Lucy asked one final question, "What is her reward?"

The girl's name was Andrea. The newspapers said her father was a lawyer, said her mother stayed home with her younger brother and her baby sister. Andrea was on the soccer team. She sang in the church youth choir. She had friends, grandparents, aunts and uncles and cousins, who loved her. All her teachers liked her, too. She had lived at the center of a charmed ring meant to keep her safe, but the earth had swallowed her. Since her abduction the news each night was choked with editorials, police reports, pleas from her distraught parents, but no clues.

Those poor parents, Anna thought, remembering the days after Ellen's birth, how excruciating hoping had been, how the waiting had flayed her. She was driving through the center of the city, and she looked with repugnance at the sound walls and overpasses that surrounded them, at the trash that flapped up from the roadbed like maimed birds in the traffic's manufactured wind. Billboards flashed past her, and bumper stickers—a montage of anger and desire that made her glad Lucy hadn't yet learned to read. The brake lights on the car in front of her came on. Her foot found the brake pedal, her car slowed, and she watched helplessly as her rearview mirror filled with the grille of yet another big rig.

She sat in the unmoving traffic, watching a dark cloud of exhaust billow from the pickup in the next lane. Even with the windows of the car rolled up, she could taste rubber and carbon monoxide. She wondered what it was doing to Ellen's tender lungs, to have to breathe that air. She wondered what Andrea was feeling at that moment, what kind of loneliness or terror or despair. She wondered where on earth Andrea was, while the whole city searched for her and her parents wept on the nightly news. She wondered how they could possibly survive, if they never saw their daughter alive again.

The cars began to creep forward, though by the time Anna reached her exit, she was gripping the steering wheel so tightly her arms were aching. She turned down the street that held Lucy's school, and the instant she pulled up in front of the flagpole, a buzzer began to sound.

"Oh, no," Lucy cried, tearing at her seat belt, "I'll be late."

"Tell Ms. Ashton it was my fault."

Lucy cast her mother a withering glance. "She knows it's your fault. It doesn't matter. Late is late," she said, ramming her shoulder against the door to open it.

"It's okay, sweetie. Slow down."

"We get red circles on our good citizen stars if we're late."

Leaving the engine running, Anna got out of the car to help Lucy gather her backpack and lunch box.

"Watch out for Noranella's ghost," Lucy commanded as Anna leaned into the backseat. "You're squashing her!"

"I'm sorry," Anna said, trying to adjust her arms to avoid Lucy's wraith. "Is she going to school with you?"

"No," Lucy said, hopping and twisting with impatience as she watched the playground of children converge at the doors of the school. "Noranella's ghost feels too sadful at school, but she waits on the swings and plays with me at recess."

"Does anyone else play with you at recess?" Anna asked, and held her breath.

"No," said Lucy flatly. "Everyone else already has a friend. Bye," she added, gearing to dash away.

"Wait!" Anna cried. She bent to hug her, but Lucy squirmed out from under her embrace. "I'll be late!" she cried, and sped off after the flock of vanishing children, leaving Anna to stand empty-armed beside the throbbing car.

"Bye," Anna called after Lucy's running heels and streaming hair. "Have a good day. I love you," she added, though only the air was there to hear.

Another bell rang, and Anna watched as Lucy vanished among the final throng of kids, the doors closing behind them with the finality of possession. Anna stood on the asphalt, smelling her car's exhaust blending with the freshness of the morning. She had an impulse to snatch Lucy back from behind those closed doors and spirit her away so they could spend the day together—just the pair of them—giggling and snacking and napping in each other's arms. But it wasn't easy to reschedule appointments with Ellen's doctor, and besides, even if Anna could somehow convince Ms. Ashton and the principal that she needed Lucy back, she wasn't sure that it would be good for Lucy to take her out of school.

Out on the playground, the empty merry-go-round continued to circle, and the vacant swings arced back and forth with the momentum of their final occupants. Anna thought of Noranella's ghost, waiting there until Lucy came out for recess, and for a second she considered returning with her camera to shoot those empty, yawing swings. But when she examined that image most closely in her mind, she saw how easily it could become mundane, and when she thought of all the work that getting out her camera would require, she dismissed the whole idea. Behind her in the car Ellen was beginning to fuss, and by now Ellen's appointment was so soon that Anna didn't dare to even stop to nurse her. In the end there was nothing she could do but climb into the car and race back down the freeway.

SOMETIME THE NEXT AFTERNOON, IN THE BURN CENTER IN SAN Francisco where Travis was transferred as soon as he was stabilized, the attending physician described what they were doing for him.

"Burn wounds evolve over the first few days," he told Cerise, "especially in children."

"He'll be okay?" Cerise pleaded.

"As I said, it's hard to predict. We'll do our best."

He went on to talk about respiratory insufficiency, about analgesics and debridement and sepsis, about eventual grafts and possible donor areas, but Cerise could not listen to his words. Instead her gaze clung to his eyes. She stared at his eyes as though he were her lover, as though she were waiting for him to promise her the world.

His eyes were dry and veined, and the skin surrounding them was etched with a network of frail lines. He described the respirator and the monitor and the heat shield, told her what those machines were doing to save her son. But as he spoke, an image bullied its way into her mind, and she couldn't help but see the doctor's face in flames. With a jolt of horror she realized it was not the machines that were keeping Travis alive, but people—men and women—and that people were really nothing more than weary-eyed animals. Animals were trying to save her son's life, animals whose minds grew tired or anxious or confused, animals whose bodies were only containers for their own future pain.

The attending physician left, and a nurse came to bandage Cerise's hands. She held them out obediently, and while he cleaned her palms, she tried to soak up all the pain he caused, as if any hurt that she could feel would be that much less for Travis to endure. As the nurse was taping gauze pads across each palm, he nodded at Cerise's chest and asked, "What happened there?"

She looked at him in astonishment, assuming, for the tiniest of instants, that he was interested in her body. In bewilderment she followed his gaze, bending her neck to look down at herself, and saw the dark spread of fluid across her shirt, a wild bull's-eye centered above each breast.

She said, "I'm leaking."

"Leaking?"

"Milk," she whispered, futilely trying to cover the wet spots with her arms.

"You have a baby somewhere?" the nurse asked in alarm.

"Only him," she whispered, looking at the bandaged boy pumped alive by the whooshing respirator. "He's my baby."

Jake came. He'd brought a remote-control race car for Travis—a toy for a boy four times Travis's age whose price could have bought Travis's diapers for a month. It was the first time she had seen Jake since she'd moved. He seemed subdued in the way she remembered hangovers sub-

duing him, his brashness momentarily leached away by pain. She tried
to remember the pain he had caused her, how hard it had been for her to
give up on him when she had been so hungry for what she thought
could be a family. But despite his height he seemed so insubstantial now,
so colorless and flat. She looked at his blunt hands, at the bunchy muscles of his biceps and the rim of pale skin she could glimpse above the
sleeves of his T-shirt as he stood, stiff-faced and wary, at the foot of
Travis's bed. It was odd to think she had ever laughed with him, had ever
drank and danced with him, had ever let him inside her. It was odd to
think that Travis was his boy, too.

"Where's Melody?" he asked, holding the toy car in front of him like
a shield.

"With friends," Cerise answered, staring at the bundle that was her
son, sedated so he would not fight the respirator tube, dwarfed to almost
nothing by the gleaming machines and long white bed.

Later that evening after Jake had left to get some sleep, two nurses
arrived to change Travis's dressings, sending Cerise out to wait in the hall.

Standing like a sentinel outside his door, she heard him moan, and
her vagina contracted at the sound. She remembered his birth, the feel
of him moving through her, remembered the triumphant moment when
she'd pushed him into her hands, and suddenly her whole being needed
a baby, needed to hold or smell one, or even just to look.

Leaving her post outside Travis's door, she roamed the bright corridors and impersonal stairs until she reached a hall cut off by a set of
locked doors. A sign said "Nursery—Buzz for Admittance." But when
Cerise pushed the button and asked to be let in, the voice beyond the
door asked her who she wished to see.

"A baby," she answered, speaking into the grating of the intercom. "I
wish to see a baby."

"Name?"

"Cerise," she said.

"Last name?"

"Johnson."

"I'm sorry, ma'am," the voice came back. "There is no infant with that name here. Are you sure you're at the right hospital?"

"No. I mean yes. I'm in the right hospital. That's my name. Cerise Johnson is my name."

"What is the name of the infant you wish to view?"

"I don't know."

"Mother's name?"

"My mother's name?"

"The name of the mother of the infant you wish to view."

"I don't know. I mean, I don't know any of the babies there. Please, I just want to see one. Any one. I need— There's been an accident, my boy—"

"I'm sorry. Hospital procedure will not allow unauthorized strangers to view the babies."

"Oh, but please—"

"It's a policy of security. I'm sorry."

And as Melody had so often pointed out, *I'm sorry* was just a bullshit way of saying no.

AT BEDTIME LUCY SAID, "THAT GIRL WAS STOLEN."

She was lying beneath soft blankets and white sheets, and her nightgown was on inside out. Anna had just read a book to her and one to Noranella's ghost, and now she was sitting beside Lucy on the bed, lingering one final moment before she said good night, switched off the light, and turned her attention to Ellen and the dozen other details that had to be addressed before she, too, could go to bed.

"Did you hear me, Mommy?" Lucy said, reaching over to tap her mother's leg. "I said, that girl was stolen."

"What girl?" Anna said, trying to keep the caution from her voice. "What do you mean?"

There had been another lead. The evening paper said that two boys playing in the woods along the highway had found a roll of electrician's tape, a corkscrew, and the pillowcase from Andrea's bed. Reading that, Anna had been struck by all the sickening uses her own bland mind could suggest for electrician's tape, a corkscrew, and a pillowcase.

"The girl in the pictures," Lucy said. "She wasn't missing her reward. She was stolen, from her bed."

Stolen, Anna's mind gulped, like a jewel or a purse.

"Who told you that?" she asked.

"Everyone. Ms. Ashton says we all have to be extra careful."

"Well, you know you'd never get in a car with a stranger."

Lucy shook her head so violently her hair splayed across the pillow, and for a second Anna allowed herself to wonder if the parents—perfect as they sounded in the newspapers—weren't hiding something.

Lucy was saying, "Ms. Ashton says if a stranger stops to talk to us, we have to scream and run."

It's like a war, Anna thought, as she laced her fingers through Lucy's glossy hair, only now the enemy was everywhere and nowhere, like one of those movies where aliens infiltrated the bodies of honest citizens, and suddenly the mail carrier, the old lady at the end of the block, even members of your own family, might be a threat.

It was because they were in California, Anna thought bitterly. There were too many people in California, too many cars, too much dirt and noise. No one knew anyone, and because of that, no one mattered. Everything was crowded and hurried, everything greedy and ugly and out of control. Even the weather was unnerving—still as hot as midsummer, though October was nearly over.

To be fair, she had to remember that the weather wasn't typical, even for California. The newspapers said that the whole country was in the grip of the hottest fall in history—another proof that global warming was a reality. But tonight that only increased her panic, to think she was stranded in a place that was not her home while even the weather went awry.

"Brianna says that girl is dead," said Lucy, watching Anna carefully.

"Oh, no," Anna answered, pumping conviction into her voice. "Lots and lots of people are looking for her. They'll find her, and everything will be okay."

In the tiniest possible voice Lucy said, "I don't want them to find her."

"Oh, Lucy," Anna said. "Why not?"

" 'Cause then I'll be next."

"Of course not. Why would you say that?"

"That man that took her will need someone else."

"The man that took her will be in jail," Anna answered.

Lucy said, "He's not in jail now."

"No. But he will be, very soon."

But it seemed as though he were in the room with them already, as though Anna were fighting him for Lucy as she spoke.

Lucy said, "You couldn't stop him."

"Why not?" Anna asked, feeling her blood rise, imagining the satisfaction of tearing into him with her teeth and nails, the pleasure of destroying him for what he could do—was doing already—to Lucy.

"You're not big enough."

Anna offered, "There's Daddy."

"Maybe he's not big enough, either."

"Lucy, there are policemen, and dogs, and lots of other men—good men," she added hastily, "like Daddy and Uncle Mike. There are lots and lots and lots of people to make sure that bad man doesn't hurt anyone, ever again."

"Mommy?"

"What?" Anna could hear Ellen beginning to cry downstairs with Eliot, could feel the tension gathering along her temples.

"I'm afraid to go to sleep."

Anna took a deep breath, for balance, for forbearance, for inspiration. She said, "There's nothing to be afraid of."

"If I go to sleep, he'll get me. What will he do to me, Mommy, after he gets me?"

"He won't do a thing. I mean—he won't get you. You're safe. And now," Anna said, infusing patience into every word, "it's time to go to sleep."

"I can't sleep. If I go to sleep, he'll get me."

"No, he won't. Of course not. You're safe at home."

"Andrea was safe at home."

"Yes, but that was random."

"What's 'random'?"

"It means it was an accident—just bad, bad luck. It could never happen here."

"Why not, if it was just bad luck? We could have bad luck, too."

"We won't," Anna promised, though it felt feeble as a lie.

"Why not?" Lucy persisted.

"Because I love you," Anna blurted before she could think.

"Love won't keep you safe," Lucy said.

The image of Ellen's livid face and limp blue body crowded into Anna's mind, and it was all she could do to keep from telling Lucy that she was right, that the world was dangerous and life too risky to ever relax into.

"He could come in right there," said Lucy, pointing at the window.

Crossing the room, Anna rechecked the window and pulled the curtains tighter. "He can't come in. The window's locked. Besides, we're on the second floor. We'd hear him if he tried to climb up."

"You wouldn't hear him. You'd be asleep."

Downstairs Ellen's cries were escalating, and it was as though Anna's brain were a machine that had suddenly seized up. She could feel her sympathy start to drain away, could hear the impatience begin to rasp in her voice when she said, "Lucy, it's bedtime."

"I can't sleep," Lucy whimpered, curling into a ball and looking up at her mother with an expression so pathetic it almost seemed calculated.

"Look—you're in your own room. In your own house. The windows and doors are locked. I'm here, and Daddy's here. Your night-light's on, and I'll leave the light on in the hall, too. Tomorrow is a school day, and now it's time to go to bed."

Lucy's shoulders began to shake, and although it seemed theatrical, it still squeezed Anna's heart. Part of her wanted to stay and gain a kind of courage from comforting Lucy. But Ellen's cries were growing urgent, and Anna could feel her evening unraveling if she could not get Lucy to go to sleep. Besides, she was afraid that if she gave in now, tomorrow night Lucy would expect the same treatment, and the next night she'd want more, in exactly the way the books and magazine articles all warned. She stood to go. "Okay, Lucy. I'll give you a kiss, and then I'm going to leave. I love you, and you'll be fine."

But when she bent to kiss her, Lucy rolled to face the wall, her back stubborn as living rock.

Anna asked, "Don't I get a kiss?"

The shiny head shook no into the pillow.

"Okay. Good night." Anna crossed the room, pausing at the door to turn off the light. "I love you," she said. But there was no answer from the white bed.

IN THE FINAL FLURRY OF TRAVIS'S DEATH, PEOPLE CAME HURRYING FROM all over the hospital—doctors, nurses, even the housekeeper. At first they pushed Cerise out into the hallway, but later, when all their efforts to keep the life trapped in his little body had come to nothing, they let her back in the room, left her alone with what was left of him.

Tears already racing down her face, she gazed at him. He was so impossibly small beneath the white sheet. The monitor and respirator were still, and a raw new silence clung to everything. She grabbed the railing of his bed in both bandaged hands, squeezed until her arms shook and the blisters tore beneath the gauze. But the bed held, the building did not fall, his tiny chest did not rise. She threw her head back on her neck and howled.

She had never thought that he could actually die. In all those awful hours she had never thought he would really leave her, had never for an instant believed he would not live. From the moment Travis had first entered the world, it had been inconceivable that the world could exist without him. Now it was inconceivable that she could remain after he was gone.

Someone was speaking from the doorway. It was the young nurse, the one who'd called Travis "Cowboy." Timidly she said, "We've called Travis's father, Ms. Johnson. And sent for the social worker and the chaplain. They'll be here any minute, to talk with you. Is there anything—should I stay with you until they come?"

Savagely Cerise shook her head. She didn't want the nurse to stay with her, didn't want to have to see Jake or the chaplain or a social worker, didn't want to have to do any of the things words were used to do— explain, defend, excuse, or soothe. She wanted to be as alone in the room as she was in her anguish, wanted only to scream and howl and moan.

But the nurse's question had diminished her to silence. Tentatively, mutely, she reached to touch Travis with an unswathed finger. Part of her was still aghast at how the fire had hurt him, though another part was afraid, even now, of making it hurt worse. She bent to kiss him, but the thought came that she was kissing him good-bye, and her body convulsed, propelling her back from that abyss.

She turned and stumbled from the room, Travis for once unprotesting at her departure. She walked down the halls like a purposeful zombie, the tears already so familiar it never occurred to her to wipe them from her face.

She passed hurrying nurses, passed clusters of families standing awkwardly in the hallways with their cones of flowers and their Mylar balloons. She entered the lobby, passed the registration desk where, at some point in the last two days, she'd had to remember the numbers and recite the facts that summed up her right to claim care for Travis. When she reached the entryway, the hospital's main doors slid apart, and she stumbled outside.

It was not until she stood on the street that she realized she had nowhere to go. "Totaled," the fire chief had said, as if their trailer were a car, as if she'd been traveling instead of sleeping when it happened. When he'd said it—with Travis still breathing—it had been only an annoyance, a fact as inconsequential as the flies that slipped through the torn window screens in the afternoon or the mosquitoes that hummed in their bedroom at night. But now, standing dazedly on the sidewalk in the feeble sunshine, Cerise had no idea what she should do next.

At Woodland Manor the routine of death had been simple and immutable, her part in it clear. But now it was as though death were a test she hadn't yet had time to study for. There were things she should do—she was sure of that—things that were expected of her. But when she tried to think what they were, her thoughts skittered off like spit on a hot iron.

She began to walk, her footsteps thick with shock. A mean wind stung her cheeks with grit. She was shivering, her shoulders and knees shaking, her teeth chattering unstoppably. A carload of teenagers careened past. She felt the throb of their music, heard their reckless laughter. Other cars passed. In some of them were children, living children.

Her feet slapped the concrete. She was walking past a row of restaurants. Their warmth and smells assaulted her. People brushed by her, laughing and talking, as oblivious of her suffering as if she were a ghost or another druggie or a drunk. They did not realize it was they who were ghosts, the food they ate already turning to shit even as its flavors lingered in their mouths, their laughter fading like smoke as it left their rotting lungs. She looked at them, and images swarmed unbidden into her mind. She imagined them burning, saw how their clothing would flare and how their skins would char. She could not help but hear how they would scream.

The hospital Travis had been taken to was in a part of the city Cerise did not know. For many blocks it had not occurred to her to wonder where she was going, but gradually, as she pushed down the unfamiliar streets, she realized she was heading north, toward the bridge. In a campground, Melody had said, on the mountain. It was impossible to think, impossible to plan. She made her feet keep walking. Small details snagged her awareness—a pink rose bush blooming in a pot beside a doorway, a whole banana rotting in the gutter, a poodle yapping behind a gate. They seemed significant, but when she tried to understand what they meant, her mind slid sideways.

She was moving up a street lined with pastel-colored row houses whose windows and doors were decorated with curls of iron grating. She could smell food cooking, could smell the scented steam from someone's shower. She tripped over a toddler's riding toy abandoned on the sidewalk, and felt a surge of rage against all that domesticity, against all the smug happiness she imagined those iron gratings were intended to protect.

The thought came to her that she had been wrong to leave the hospital. She'd made another awful mistake, like in those dreams she'd begun to have after Melody left, where in her hurry to board the bus on time, she forgot Travis on the sidewalk, and then, no matter how loudly she screamed, no matter how hard she pleaded and pounded the closed doors, the driver of the bus either failed to hear her or refused to stop, and she had to watch in frantic helplessness as Travis grew smaller and smaller until at last he vanished out of sight.

Surely Travis was still alive. Surely he was sitting up in bed by now, yanking at his IV lines and respirator tube and calling for his mama, crying because she was not there to comfort him. She stood paralyzed while her mind raced back along the sidewalks, across the streets, and through the hospital corridors, back to the room where she had left him. But then she imagined the faces of the nurses looking up at her in surprise.

She saw the solid bodies of the orderlies, felt the judgment of the doctors, slammed back again into the fact that Travis was gone.

For a second she wanted him so savagely she was ready to return anyway. But when she tried to imagine freeing his body from its tangle of lines and tubes, she realized how impossible it would be to claim even that husk of her boy. Standing on the sidewalk, she remembered Jake's sorry helplessness in the face of Travis's suffering, and odd words came to her from somewhere, perhaps a movie she'd seen but could no longer remember—a horror movie, maybe, or one of those old dramas she and Melody used to watch together late at night—*let the dead bury the dead.*

It was almost evening by the time she neared the northern edge of the city. In a broad plaza overlooking the bay, clusters of people were laughing and pointing, gnawing on ice cream bars or pizza wedges. Standing alone or intertwined in groups, they posed for photographs, and unwittingly Cerise pushed her way into their pictures. Ahead the bridge loomed. She raised her eyes to the towers that soared above the crowded roadway, saw the cables swooping between them, and suddenly everything shifted into focus. She began to walk with greater purpose, following the sidewalk that led out of the plaza and across the eastern side of the bridge. Traffic passed less than a yard from where she walked, and yet already the world was growing distant. People pushed by her— joggers, clots of tourists, loud groups of teenagers—but she moved among them inside a charged stillness, conscious only of the promise of the bridge and the hammering of her heart.

She ran her bandaged hand along the rib-high railing as she walked, and when she was halfway across, she paused to look down. At the level of the roadbed a steel ledge jutted an arm's length from the bridge. But beyond the ledge there was only a waste of open air, and beyond that, the distant water. Her cheeks were stiff with the residue of tears. The wind tore her hair from her face, molded her clothes against her body, chilled her leaking breasts. A bird flew beneath her. She thought of Travis crawling over the lowered railing of his crib to try to hide from the heat and flame. She imagined crawling over the railing of the bridge, imagined swooping down to meet the water, imagined filling her arms and lungs with ocean and finding Travis in that embrace. With her teeth she tore the gauze and tape from her hands, flung the bandages over the railing, watched them flutter toward the water. Lifting her arms high as she could reach, she grabbed a steel cable, and, gritting her teeth against the pain of her seared palms, she tried to scrabble up the railing.

When hands clasped her waist, she thought at first that they were the hands of angels, come to help her over. But instead of boosting her up, they held firm, not yanking her back but simply steadying her, as though they were only there to help her keep her balance until her feet touched the sidewalk once again.

She released the cable and wheeled around to face whatever it was that had interrupted her. A man stood chest-high in front of her, his hands already quietly by his sides. He was an Asian man in tidy clothes. He spoke to her in his language, a phrase that sounded like a question. When she did not respond, he shook his head gently as though he were reminding a child of some small mistake. He said something more, and his eyes were friendly and curious and calm. Cerise stared into them, and for a moment it seemed so simple for him to save her.

But a thick shame rose in her. In that instant she was aware of the press of bodies as separate people, of the traffic-roar as the roar of many cars. She realized that hundreds of people had watched her scrabbling at the railing, and suddenly she was certain they all knew why she wanted to die. She knew they could see the guilty, howling woman inside her, who, when she turned and began to run, seemed to spill an ugly trail of blood behind her. She ran until she reached the north end of the span. Panting and sobbing, she made her way away from the crowds and beneath the deck of the bridge. When she found herself in a weedy parking lot on the ocean side, she stopped, gasping, and looked around, trying to make sense of where she was.

She had assumed that crossing the bridge would bring her to

Melody. But instead of the forested mountain and the campground Melody had described on the phone, Cerise saw only looming hills, empty of everything but windblown grass. Behind her, the freeway still roared its condemnation, but at the far end of the parking lot a road led up into the empty hills. She began to trudge along it, her head bent to face the gravel and weeds. A pair of bicyclists flying down the grade in the thickening dusk shot her looks of curiosity as they swept by, though the cars, their headlights newly lit, passed within inches of where she walked without slowing.

By the time she neared the top of the hill, it was almost dark. Next to the road was a gravel pullout with an information kiosk. Posters advertising campfire lectures and flyers warning about rattlesnakes and poison oak shook in the wind beside a wooden map routed with a web of trails and roads. In the failing light she tried to decipher it, though her mind was as stiff as her tear-roughened face.

A car slowed to a stop beside the pullout. Its driver leaned across the passenger's seat. Rolling down the window, he asked, "Where ya going?"

She ignored him, and he asked again.

"The campground," she answered over her shoulder.

"Going camping?"

Her eyes on the map, she shook her head as though his voice were a mosquito whine she might chase from her ears.

"Come on," he said. "I'll take you there."

She started toward the car, but when she saw the driver's leer and the jumble of blankets and beer cans in the backseat, a final scrap of caution made her veer away instead.

"Get in," he commanded, reaching across the front seat to open the passenger's door. At the sound of his voice, she turned from the road and began to run up the hillside. Cursing, he slammed the door and the car tore away, gravel spitting like shot from beneath his tires.

Lungs burning, she ran uphill in the waning light. She was accustomed to pavement, and her feet slid and twisted on the chert and sage.

When she finally sagged to a stop, she was beyond the crest of the hill, overlooking a valley more barren and uninhabited than any place she had ever seen. The first stars pricked the sky overhead. A moon slender as a shard of glass hung low above the opposite hill, while all around her the wind continued, stealing her breath and savaging her hair.

She staggered down into the empty valley, calling for Travis, screaming his name to the broken moon. Sobbing until her guts heaved, she lurched and stumbled through the darkness, collapsing finally beneath a lone tree to sleep outdoors for the first time in her life, to sleep on the dirty ground below a sky filled with an appalling multitude of stars.

SOMEONE WAS SCREAMING.

At first the screams came from such a great distance that it was possible for Anna to sink deeper into her sleep and pretend they could not reach her. But rapidly they grew louder and nearer and more urgent until each cry was a knife hacking her awake, leaving her aching and prickling and thick with confusion—the same sensation of unbearable interruption she felt when one of the girls woke while she and Eliot were making love. The black room spun, and Anna struggled to reconstruct herself inside its spinning. Even so, she was out of bed and running before she could find the reason why.

She was running toward the screams, running to meet the trouble because she recognized the screams were Lucy's, and when at last she reached the open door of Lucy's room and saw that Lucy was still there—unbroken and unbleeding—sitting up in bed and sobbing beside her bunny night-light, a little of Anna's terror left, though she rushed to grab Lucy as if she might still be stolen.

"What is it?" Anna rasped. "What's wrong? What happened?" In her arms Lucy's body seemed so small, her bones so sharp and frail. Trembling like a sparrow, Lucy cried, "He killed her!"

Ellen, Anna thought like a shot, and her heart surged toward the baby's room, but before she could leap from Lucy's bed, her voice croaked, "Who?"

"Andrea," Lucy sobbed. "He killed Andrea."

"It was a dream," Anna said, relief gushing through her. Pressing Lucy against her, she added, "You had a bad dream."

But Lucy pulled away to stare in horror at the shadowed wall. "It's true," she cried. "It's true. He cut off her head."

"Whose head, sugar?"

"Andrea—Andrea's head."

Anna felt a prickle of premonition. "Of course not," she said firmly. Gathering Lucy deeper in her arms, she insisted, "It was just a dream."

"It's not," Lucy sobbed. "It's true, it's real. The grown-ups said."

"What did they say?" Anna asked. She tried to make her body big and calm, tried to make her flesh a protective barrier between Lucy and the world. She felt the press of Lucy's elbows, the bones of her shoulders, her sweet, sharp chin. She wanted to murder Ms. Ashton, with her safety rules and her stranger awareness program. She said, "Tell me what the grown-ups said."

"They said he had Andrea. They said—" Lucy paused, looking puzzled.

"See?" Anna murmured, making her voice smooth as cream. "See? It was only a dream."

"Things are wrong," Lucy persisted, bewildered.

"Nothing's wrong," Anna murmured, stroking Lucy's head. "Everything is fine. Go back to sleep."

But instead of relaxing into her mother's words, Lucy sat up straight and stared at her with horror. "I can't do that," she gasped.

"Why not?"

"He's waiting for me there, inside my dreams."

"Of course not," Anna said. She thought, I love this child too much to be her mother. Casting wildly for inspiration, she offered, "Noranella's ghost will keep you safe."

For a moment Lucy looked confused, and then her whole being seemed to deflate. "Mommy," she said, a mask of desperation stiffening her face, "this is real."

WHEN CERISE WOKE, IT WAS AS THOUGH SHE HAD BEEN SUBMERGED IN dark water, and were now rising toward a small circle of light. At first she only knew that she was cold, and she reached instinctively for Travis, for the solace of his breath and flesh. But instead of his body, she felt the prickle of wild grass, the grit of poor soil. Groping again, she felt the pain burned deep in her palms, and tried desperately to descend back into sleep.

But there was no more sleep.

Sickened that she had ever slept at all, she opened her aching eyes, looked out at the foggy world. Through the blur of new tears, she saw that she was lying against the snag of an old tree. Its lichen-spotted trunk had been split almost in two, and one half was angled along the ground, its branches making a crude curtain that had sheltered her from the worst of the night wind. Using her forearms, she pushed herself to sitting and choked as memory descended like another toxic smoke.

She buried her face in her blistered hands and cried, the rough sobs tearing her chest, the new tears stinging her palms. It was like a sickness, like a fever rising. For whole seconds the horror seemed almost bearable, but in the next moment some new thought or realization would spike, and it seemed she could stand it no longer.

When she finally raised her head from the darkness of her hands, she caught a whiff of past-ripe fruit. Hunger cramped her stomach, although it was followed a moment later by a sweep of revulsion. Spread across the ground was a coarse crop of fallen apples. Most were discolored and swollen almost to bursting. But a few, though bruised and bee-stung, still looked firm. She watched dully as a line of ants swarmed one of them. Finally, filled with self-loathing, she took an apple in her unblistered fingertips, blew the ants away, and ate it in ravenous bites, oblivious to bruises, worms, and fibrous core. She ate another, and then one more.

The fog was growing brighter when she stood. She steadied herself for a moment against the tree, and then set off. It was a relief, almost, to walk, a relief to submit to the mindless conviction that action would accomplish something, though when she tried to think what she was walking away from and what she was approaching, her footsteps slowed in dread.

The fog lifted in shreds and rags. When she gained the crest of the hill, she caught a glimpse of sea, wide and blue and rimmed with a silent white line of surf. In the bottom of the next valley, she saw a green band of willows and weeds. When she reached it, she smelled moist air and heard the murmur of water. Pushing her way through the cattails and sedges, she found a sluggish stream. She knelt in the muck and lapped the algae-thickened water from her cupped hands, its coolness first shocking and then soothing her stinging palms.

Then, oblivious to the hot smell of sage that rose beneath her feet, oblivious to the liquid call of red-winged blackbirds and the tender breeze, she pressed on down the valley. Her body was stiff, and her hands throbbed. Her clothes were scratchy with the seed casings of the million grasses she'd passed through, and her swollen face itched with unwashed tears. Her T-shirt clung to her chest, and her breasts were hard as fists, the nipples chafed raw from the rub of wet fabric. But all those pains were nothing, such tiny hurts compared to what she'd lost.

There had to be a way to get back home, to return to the trailer and her life before the fire. There had to be a way to fix things so the fire never started, or so they both got out in time. If you want it badly enough, you can make it happen, her program counselor had promised, her eyes melting with conviction as she showed Cerise how to apply for yet another loan. You can do anything you put your mind to, her welfare eligibility worker had snapped when Cerise mentioned how hard it was to try to study with a toddler. Now it seemed impossible that need alone would not make Travis come alive—if she only knew how, if she only tried harder. It seemed it was her fault, yet again, that she could not bend time and save her son.

One step. And then another. A snake slithered beneath her feet, a quick, cool rustle across the dirt. Lizards, their heads as erect and grinning as Travis's plastic dinosaurs, watched her approach and then scurried out of her way. Once she heard a hum, smelled the sweet, thick scent of rot, and looked down to see a fawn's carcass swirling with flies. She screamed and vomited a hot broth of creek water and apple. Three vultures passed above her, their shadows braiding a pattern on the ground.

It was late afternoon by the time she neared the woods. She had been walking for miles along the top of a high ridge. On her left the hills sloped down to the far-off sea, and on her right they rose up toward the forested mountain. Ahead of her was a dark line of trees that for hours had seemed to come no nearer. She had long since abandoned her fight with the wind and sun, and now she was simply moving in an endless dream of breeze blown grass and thirst.

Once, much earlier in the day, she had been walking along the gravel shoulder of a road when a car slowed to a crawl beside her. Remembering the man at the information kiosk, she'd kept her head down, continued to trudge while the car crept next to her. Suddenly an arm had reached out the rolled-down window, thrusting at her a can of soda so cold it stung her blistered hands like fire. The car sped off, leaving Cerise to pry at the pull tab with swollen fingers. She'd drunk in a daze, grateful not to the people in the car so much as to the soda itself for allowing her its infusion of liquid and sugar. But that had been hours ago, and now her tongue filled her mouth so thickly she could hardly swallow.

She had become so used to the constant wind that when she finally reached the forest, its stillness was like entering a closed room. After the openness of the hills, the air smelled heavy and cloyingly sweet, and already the woods were filling with shadows. She heard the creak of branches rubbing together like old doors being opened.

Being in the woods reminded her of the campground, and of Melody. As she walked along the road that curved between the trees, she tried to plan how she would tell Melody about Travis and the fire. At the hospital, when the fire chief talked with her in the hall outside Travis's room, his first question was if she had ever inspected the battery in the trailer's smoke detector. For a moment it had been hard to even understand what he was talking about, and then, startled, she'd had to admit she'd thought the landlord would have taken care of that before she moved in.

"It was empty," the fire chief said, his voice carefully flat. "There was no battery."

"Melody!" Cerise gasped, clapping her bandaged hands to her mouth.

"What's that?" the fire chief asked, his pen poised above his clipboard. But Cerise could only clutch her mouth and shake her head, and when he'd asked her the number of people residing in the trailer, she'd answered, "Just two."

But all day her need to see Melody had been increasing beneath her shock and grief until it was a sensation even greater than her thirst, a longing as physical as lust for her daughter's breath and flesh and living bones. A baby, she'd said, I wish to see a baby, and now she knew the baby she longed for was her own. She wanted to gather Melody in her arms for safekeeping, wanted to press Melody to her aching breasts and never let her go. She wanted to lose herself again in loving her little girl.

But along with that need Cerise also felt a growing desire to make Melody suffer. She could not bear to be so alone inside her anguish. She wanted someone to share her torment, wanted to bludgeon Melody with the truth of what had happened. The parenting magazines always said that children must be held accountable for their actions. Melody needed to know—and to acknowledge—the monstrous consequences of what she'd done. Now, as Cerise stumbled on through the hushed and fragrant forest, the only respite she could imagine for herself was the little relief that would come when she confronted Melody with what the fire chief had said.

It was nearly dusk by the time she reached the campground. She had never been in a campground before, and it seemed she had arrived in a foreign land, as she walked the road that circled the campsites and saw people clustered around picnic tables, saw tents glowing like paper lanterns. Someone was playing a guitar. She heard soft talk, the laughter of families, the happy shrieks of children. But she found no tribe of kids, no painted school bus, no black puppy.

At the far end of the campground a narrow path led off into the trees. Cerise took it only because if she didn't, she would have to retrace her steps, and she couldn't fathom leaving the campground without finding Melody. She followed the path for a hundred yards or so until it intersected a weedy road that led through the woods like a green tunnel to a final campsite hidden in a thick circle of shrubbery.

There was no tent at this site, and no campfire. But a dusty Nissan was parked beside the picnic table, its trunk open. On its bumper, stickers announced "The Old Ways Are Not Forgotten," and "Magick Is Afoot." Moving closer, Cerise saw that a woman sat cross-legged on the bench in front of the picnic table, her dark hair loose around her shoulders, her back to Cerise. A blue cloth was spread on the table, and arranged across it was a puzzling array of objects—crystals and wildflowers, a silver cup, a votive candle, a figurine of a bare-breasted woman holding two snakes out at arms' length. A little cone of incense sent a fragile trail of smoke into the forest air.

Cerise reached the car and then paused, uncertain how to proceed. Swaying with the odd sensation of not-walking, she waited until she heard the low growl of a dog coming from the shadows beneath the table. The woman shook herself as though she'd been napping and cast a startled glance over her shoulder. Then she bent and murmured something to the dog before she turned around a little defiantly to face Cerise.

She had bright blue eyes and a skin that had seen too much sun, though it was impossible to say if she was old or young. She was upright and trim, dressed in a gauzy purple dress and leather sandals. Encompassing her head was a slender circlet of silver from which a pendant hung, its green stone tapping against her forehead when she moved.

"How can I help you?" the woman asked, rising to stand in front of the table as if she might somehow shield its contents from Cerise's view. Her words made Cerise think of a salesperson in a store, though something about her demeanor reminded her of Sylvia at the LifeRight center all those years ago.

Bewildered, Cerise peered past the woman to the picnic table. The quiet flicker of the candle at the foot of the little statue caught her eye, and the sight of even that tiny fire caused the tears to resume their path down her stiff face.

"Do you share my reverence for the Great Mother?" the woman asked, her tone suddenly warming as she noticed Cerise's tears and the focus of her gaze.

"I'm looking for my girl," Cerise answered. It had been so long since she had spoken that she could taste the bitter taint of her breath on her words, and her tongue felt thick and sticky in her mouth. "Is that water?" she croaked, pointing to the cup next to the candle while the tears rolled unheeded down her face.

"It's moon water," the woman answered. She sounded affronted, but when she saw how intently Cerise gazed at the cup, something in her expression shifted, and a second later she lifted the cup from the table. Holding it toward Cerise with both hands, she gave her a formal little bow. "May you never thirst," she said. Clumsily, Cerise accepted the cup, drained it in huge, rough swallows. The water tasted stale, as if it had been stored in a plastic jug for a long time.

"Who did you say you were looking for?" the woman asked when Cerise handed her the empty cup.

"My girl," Cerise answered. "My daughter."

The woman frowned. "Is your daughter little?"

"Yes. No. Not really. She's—I guess she's turned seventeen. She was supposed to be—she said—at this camp."

"There was a group of young people, camped down at the other end." The woman gestured back the way Cerise had come. "I spoke with them last night."

"Was there a girl with them?" Cerise asked hungrily. "Long hair? As tall as me?"

"Blond? With a tattoo on her cheek?"

"That's her!"

The woman said, "Her puppy tried to eat my candles. She's your daughter?"

"They've gone?" Cerise asked incredulously.

"They left this morning."

"You're sure? Where did they go?"

"Your daughter told me they were headed north. To Arcadia, she said."

"Where's that?"

The woman gave a quiet laugh. "Near Elysium, I think."

"Where?" Cerise choked.

"I think she meant Arcata," the woman answered. "Young people like to go there. There's a university they can make a point of not attending, and lots of other similarly souled people to meet. Your daughter said they were going to build tree houses, and live in the woods."

"How far is it from here?" Cerise managed to ask, though the words came out a broken whisper.

The woman studied Cerise for a long moment. "It's a ways," she answered finally. "Three or four hundred miles. Are you okay? I've never seen an aura darker than yours is right now. It's really quite astonishing."

Helplessly, Cerise shrugged and shook her head.

The woman asked, "Where's your baby?"

Cerise started as though she'd been slapped. "What—"

"I can tell these things," the woman answered almost smugly, though she added, "Besides, that's milk, isn't it? On your shirt."

Beyond the curtain of bushes someone was building a campfire. Cerise smelled the first tentative wisp of smoke, and her gut clenched. She said, "My baby—" But the next word was too huge to be spoken.

The woman leaned forward. "You've lost your baby somehow?" she suggested. Her voice was tender but insistent.

Cerise nodded, still grappling with the word that was too large to fit inside her, too big to be gotten out.

"Did it die? He? Or she?"

"He." Cerise stared at the scatter of twigs and redwood fronds littering the forest floor.

The woman asked, "How does that make you feel?" It was the question Cerise recognized from the news shows, the question that harvested others' emotions, but it was irresistible. She said, "I want to be with him."

The woman nodded. "It's not as hard as we sometimes think. This society," she scoffed, "with its dependence on technology—guns and pills and plastic bags. The woods have better gifts."

"What?" Cerise croaked, struggling to understand what the woman was talking about.

"Hemlock's probably best. Though there's oleander and nightshade, too. And of course the amanitas." She paused and peered more closely at Cerise. "Do you mind me talking like this?" she asked. "The ascendant culture is so squeamish and suicide is the last taboo. Too few people understand that it's okay to be the mistress of your own destruction, as long as you're clear on what you're doing, and why."

The woman waited until Cerise gave an uncertain shrug, and then she asked, "Why do you want to die?"

"I just—I want to be with him."

"You already are, you know," the woman said kindly.

"I'm dead?"

"No, though it might feel that way right now. I mean, he's still with us."

"Where is he?" Cerise asked urgently.

The woman gave a smile that was both sad and serene. "His energy hasn't left the universe. His life force is still with us, as are all the atoms he borrowed to incarnate. He's closer to us than ever, really, entering every breath, each drink of water. And of course you have your memories."

"Where is my boy?" Cerise persisted.

"Look at these trees, look at the stars." The woman swept her arm in a wide arc. "He's all around you, even now. He wants you to be happy."

Cerise glanced where the woman pointed. But there was nothing of Travis in the looming trees, nothing of him in the sharp and distant stars.

"Hemlock's feathery," the woman said. "It looks like carrot tops or parsley, a little like fennel. But it smells like mice, not licorice. Look for the purple splotches along the stem. It'll kill you, but it won't be pretty.

"But then you already have the knowledge of Our Lady," she went on, the pendant on her forehead swaying as she spoke. "The Mother-Destroyer—Kali with her necklace of skulls. Demeter's rotting swine's flesh and sprouting wheat. Birth and death, that's the whole story. Now you just have to find a way to hold it. But we women are containers. It's our work.

"Let me see your hand," she commanded.

Dazed by her own exhaustion and by all the woman's talk, Cerise could hardly recognize the hand she held out, palm down, in front of her. Taking Cerise's hand between her own, the woman turned it over, gently easing the fingers flat, tilting it toward the light that lingered in the sky above them.

When she saw the oozing blisters and shreds of dirty skin, she gave a little gasp. "Is the other one like that, too?"

Cerise nodded.

"Just a minute," the woman said, crossing the campsite to her car. "All things were meant to be," she called back as she rummaged in her trunk. "My coven meets tonight, and I packed before I came up here." A minute later she returned with a basket and a bowl of water.

"Lavender and aloe," she announced, pulling a towel, a tiny bottle, and a jar from her basket. "I wish I had my Saint-John's-wort with me, too," she added, swirling a few drops from the bottle into the bowl, and then submerging Cerise's hands in the pungent liquid. "You'll want to pick up some Saint-John's-wort as soon as you can." She lifted Cerise's dripping hands, daubed them on the towel, and then opened the jar and smeared them with a colorless gel. "There," she said once she had finished. "Now, before I cover them, let's see what they have to tell me."

Cerise watched as the woman studied her burned palms. She felt the stir of the woman's breath and the movement of evening air stinging in the chill gel on her hands. She heard the sound of an ax, more laughter, a barking dog. She had walked so far to reach this place, and now Melody was gone. Her tears returned, warm and almost soothing to her eyes.

"It's hard to tell much until they heal," the woman said. Her voice sounded round and full, as though there were more people in the clearing than just Cerise. "But what I see is promising. Your palms say you are an important person. They tell me you have a long journey ahead, and that you're smarter than Socrates."

The woman paused, waiting patiently until Cerise croaked, "Who?"

"A stubborn, ugly old man who had inklings about the soul," the woman answered. "It's his blood you'll find on the hemlock stem." Despite her tangle of words, her hands were cool and gentle.

Then she fell quiet, bent above Cerise's hands for so long that Cerise found herself staring at the little figurine, watching the flicker of the candle, listening to a wind she could not feel as it ran like a distant river through the treetops. Abruptly the woman said, "I think you should go north."

"I don't really believe this stuff," Cerise said, finally reclaiming her hand.

The woman smiled and nodded, as though Cerise were a student who had just given the right answer on a quiz. "Excellent," she said. "You're making boundaries. You can't keep them, of course, but you've got to have them to start from. And *don't* might be better than *do* or even *want* for you right now. *Don't* is probably what you need to keep going," she said while Cerise stared past her to the darkening forest.

"You and your daughter parted unhappily," the woman continued. "You're still angry with her for her life choices. You think she's made those choices to hurt you. You don't yet see how much she learned from you, how much she needs you, even now. And you need her, too—though not in the way you imagine."

Some of her words snagged Cerise's awareness, and a protest rose up in her throat, though when she tried to speak, it sounded like another sob.

"Justice is the business of the Goddess," the woman said, her voice ringing in the clearing. "Healing is the human task. Your job is to heal. You need to find a new way to align yourself with the intention of the universe."

"I—" Cerise tried.

"Later, if you find you truly can't, you know what hemlock looks like. It doesn't take much," the woman went on. "And it's easy to harvest. The whole plant is toxic, though probably the roots are most effective.

"First find your daughter, that's my advice. Find her, and then decide if you're still hungry for hemlock. It's always in season."

She gave Cerise a sad, steady smile. Then, frowning, she twisted her wrist to check her watch. "I've got just time enough to bandage your hands, and then I really have to fly. Can I give you a ride back to the city?"

Cerise shook her head. For a long moment the woman watched her, studying her as though she were trying to balance something in her mind. Finally she said, "I'll worry if I leave you here."

Cerise shrugged, and when the woman continued to wait, she whispered, "I'll be okay."

The woman nodded. Spreading her arms wide, she tilted her face back to the patch of pale sky still left above the dark weave of soaring branches. "Earth, wind, fire, and sea. As she says, so mote it be."

Taking gauze and a pair of tiny scissors from her basket, she wrapped Cerise's hands until they were as shapeless as clubs and only her thumbs remained uncovered. Then the woman returned to her car, rummaged through the trunk, and returned with a pile of clothes. "Here's a clean shirt," she said. "And a jacket. It'll be cold tonight. There's a blanket, too, though I'm afraid it smells a little doggy.

"This is my card," she added, slipping a stiff rectangle on top of the heap of clothing. "I know some rituals that could help you, and I also read tarot and do a little channeling. I work on a sliding scale."

Her voice shifted again, grew clear and resonant as she reached out to lay a hand on Cerise's head. "May Isis and Osiris guard you in all the empty places through which you must walk," she said, and then she removed her hand and turned her attention to packing the things from the table. Cerise watched numbly as the woman snuffed the candle with a silver snuffer, wrapped up the cup, replaced everything in the basket, and folded up the cloth. Finally the woman picked up the figurine of the goddess and, cradling it in her arm like a doll, nodded at the dog, who crawled from under the table to follow her to her car. "Merry meet and merry part and merry meet again," she called out the window as she drove away, leaving Cerise alone in the darkness while the scent of exhaust and incense lingered in the cooling air.

Cerise slept that night beneath the picnic table, wrapped in the blanket and jacket that smelled of dog hair and fabric softener. When the birdsong began, she rose before the campers could build their morning fires, and though her bandaged hands were as awkward as paws, she managed to change into the woman's shirt. Then, bundling the blanket in her arms, she headed north, dropping the woman's card and her own milk-sodden clothes into a garbage can as she left the campground.

All that morning she walked through the state's forests, impervious to the splashing streams, heedless of the redwoods' soaring height and the flit and twitter of birds, unmoved by the meadows of wild oats that whispered in the breeze and caught the sunlight in their empty bracts. Hawks sailed in the wide air, a doe halted like a momentary statue to watch Cerise approach, but she ignored them all and kept on walking.

It was a relief, finally, when the woods gave way to homes, when the winding roads yielded to the freeway and she could stumble along the edge of the cyclone fence, assailed by the endless traffic roar, breathing carbon monoxide and dust, tripping over scraps of tire tread, burger wrappers, and the shimmering loops of gutted cassette tapes, stumbling past empty cans, shards of glass, and the desiccated bodies of little animals, past the fluttering pages of old magazines and the tatters of a million plastic bags.

Mile after mile she walked, passing car lots, prisons, and strip malls, passing factory outlet malls, golf courses, and sleek office buildings, passing beneath billboards and by a thousand gas stations and fast-food restaurants, passing new developments with their miles of raw studwork and scraped earth, and sad old neighborhoods whose backyards were crammed against the freeway.

Twice cars swooped to a stop ahead of her and waited until she trudged up alongside them. Past caring about her fate, she climbed obediently in and then sat in silence, waiting patiently until, after twenty or thirty minutes, they pulled over again, and she gathered her blanket and her jacket in her bandaged hands, got back out on the shoulder of the freeway, and continued walking as though the rides had been only an interruption in her work.

One of the drivers offered her a bag of chips. Another gave her a bottle of warm water and a dry sandwich, which she drank and ate mechanically as she trudged. Hour after hour she walked, walked until she couldn't remember how to not walk. When night came she kept on walking, stumbling alongside the current of traffic, oblivious to the blast of exhaust, the urgent sweep of headlights, the cold night air. She out-walked exhaustion, outwalked thought, walked until it seemed impossible to be in the world without taking the next step, without pushing on, step by step by step, alone beside the whining, growling, roaring traffic.

IT WAS STRANGE TO BE ALONE. WITHOUT THE GIRLS BUCKLED IN THE backseat, the car seemed preternaturally quiet. Anna felt empty and adrift, as if she'd left some essential thing behind—her purse, perhaps, or her keys, or even an organ or a limb—though at the same time she could sense some cramped part of her unfolding to fill the space where her daughters had been.

She was flying down the freeway, her foot firm on the accelerator, her hands easy on the steering wheel. The window was down, and a warm wind bashed in at her, slapping her hair against her face. Her field camera rode beside her, the squat, unwieldy box of it filling the passenger's seat like a vaguely remembered alter ego. But despite its presence, and despite the luxury of being the only person in the car, she saw nothing that sharpened her desire, nothing that made her want to stop the car.

It seemed pointless to be doing what she was doing, cruising a countryside she did not love, looking for images to harvest. But Eliot had insisted. "You need a break," he'd said. "You'll feel better once you get back to work." She'd wanted to tell him it was not that simple, but when she tried to express her doubts in words, they'd sounded either too tenuous, too spoiled, or too shrill.

She reached for the radio, and the Rolling Stones surged into the car, Mick Jagger drawling a dirge to lost love. She had passed beyond the southern edge of the city and was driving now through a wide valley ringed by pale ungainly hills. Dark trees were spread across the hills like scabs—oaks, she guessed. She missed the glisten of pines and their clean, uncomplicated lines. She missed the elegance of the land around Salish, missed the rhythm of the hills, their generous curves and sensuous textures.

The traffic had thinned, although the cars were moving even faster. She passed a golf course. She saw a travel trailer in an open field, bare-chested men milling around a smoky fire. An exit sign appeared. She tried to look ahead, to get an idea of where that road might take her. She wanted a road that wandered among the hills. She wanted to get lost, wanted to find something that stirred her enough to stop the car. She hoped that Eliot was managing to get the kitchen cleaned, hoped that Ellen wouldn't cry the whole time she was gone, hoped that Lucy was doing her home-work so that they wouldn't have to struggle about that at bedtime, too. There'd been no news about Andrea for several weeks, but still Lucy was afraid to go to sleep, still she woke up screaming in the night.

Anna was nearly abreast with the exit. She glanced at the watch on the dashboard and then swerved onto the off-ramp, spilling out along with several other cars onto a two-lane blacktop road that led east toward the oak-studded hills. It was good to escape the push of the free-way, but the road felt wrong somehow—too sleek and congested to drive slowly, too narrow to drive fast. She missed being the sole car on the road, missed the grip and slide of gravel beneath her tires, missed being in a land she knew how to look at, and how to love.

The Stones song ended and was instantly replaced by a blast of advertising. She turned the radio off, tried to focus on the landscape she was passing through. The road led past new vineyards staked and wired in strict rows, and then past a field covered with pale tarps that shim-mered like sinister water beneath the lifeless sky. As she neared the hills, she passed brand-new houses looming above raw expanses of dirt. A good eye can find a good image anywhere—semester after semester she'd stood in front of her classes and made that proclamation. But now, when she considered stopping to shoot those staked vineyards or tented fields or soulless houses, it only made her weary.

Even after she entered the hills, a film of resistance like a sheet of plastic kept her separated from all she saw. She passed oaks the size of houses, their branches twisting in the air like tortured filigree. She passed an upright wooden church, its windows boarded over, its gravel parking lot paved with weeds. But she'd seen those images already, in other people's work.

Her car crested the top of the hill, and she found herself in another valley. It was filled with weeds and ragged trees. These trees were smaller than the oaks had been, crowded together and nondescript in their brokenness. The sky above her was flat as a floor, the light inert. For a moment she wished her daughters were with her, missed them for the distraction they would have provided, for the way they could have shielded her from herself. She reached for the radio again. The final bars of a commercial filled the car, and then the announcer came on. Even before she realized what he was saying, she was aware that his smooth voice sounded shaken. "We're just getting news that hikers in the eastern Sierras have found an abandoned car that appears to be connected to the Andrea Brown case. Neither Andrea nor any suspects have been located, although according to police, a nightgown that her parents have identified as belonging to Andrea was recovered in the trunk, and there is evidence of violence both inside the car and in the surrounding—"

A ragged gasp escaped her, and Anna snatched blindly at the radio. But even before she turned it off, she knew she was too late. More clearly than she'd seen anything all day, she saw that scene inside her head—saw the wadded nightgown, saw the damp dirt of the little-used road, and the solemn rock and tangled forest, saw the wide seats of the sedan, the car's ripped headliner and cracking dash, saw the burger wrappers and soda cans scattered on the floor, saw the blood. In an instant her eyes were so hot and thick with tears that the road in front of her was nearly washed away. She twisted the steering wheel desperately to the right, and the car lunged off the road, coming to rest almost by luck alone on a dirt track that headed off through the weeds and trees.

She was already sobbing by the time she stopped the engine, crying in great raw gasps that tore her insides out and ripped her throat. She leaned her head against the steering wheel and cried—cried for Andrea and for Andrea's parents, cried for their fear and their despair, cried for the ugliness of the car and the emptiness of the forest where it had been found. She cried as though Andrea were her own daughter. She felt the lonely sting of milk rising in her breasts, and pressing her palms against them to staunch that flow, she cried for her daughters, too.

She cried for how tired she was, how homesick, how worried and sad, cried because she had lost her ability to fall in love with light. She cried until her eyes grew dry and her face felt tight and itchy and the light was beginning to leach from the flat sky, cried until she began to feel foolish, sitting alone in her car in the middle of nowhere, weeping for a child she would never know, weeping for her own privileged life. There are people really suffering, she thought sternly.

She rubbed her face with her hands, blew her nose on a paper napkin she found tucked between the seats, and raised her eyes to look out the windshield at the place where her car had come to rest. She had managed to pull off onto a faint road that seemed to lead through the scraggly trees. The trees were little more than snags, but as she studied them in the gathering dark, she saw that they had once been arranged in rows. She was in an orchard, she realized—or what must have been an orchard, long ago, though now all the trees she looked out on were dead, their trunks splintered like weathered bones, their broken branches draped with lichen instead of leaves. It's a graveyard, she thought, a cemetery of trees.

She thought about setting up her camera and trying a shot or two. But it was a stunted, busy landscape, with nothing strong to hold the eye, and the light was already long past its feeble prime. Instead she turned the key in the ignition. The car leapt to life, and she backed onto the road, left the dead orchard to the thickening darkness. Driving home through the hills without having exposed a single sheet of film, she felt a sour triumph. The headlights of approaching cars stabbed holes in the evening's shadows. As she came down into the valley, she could see Santa Dorothea spread out below her, its lights vulgar as a carnival, so much light it extinguished all the stars.

It hurt her, all that ugly light. Looking down on the festering glow of the city, she thought of the photographs she'd seen of the earth at night from outer space, every continent outlined with light, all the cities glowing, the whole world lit up like an all-night supermarket. Alone inside the dark capsule of her car, she felt an inordinate sorrow to think that in spite of all that unrelenting light, Lucy was afraid to go to sleep, and Andrea was still lost somewhere in the darkness.

THE PLACES CERISE PASSED THE NEXT DAY ALL CAME TO LOOK THE same, the drive-ins and gas stations repeating themselves like late-night reruns on TV. The crowded houses, the overpasses and cloverleafs, all seemed so similar they might have been paper scenery scrolling past. Only the green signs above the freeway changed, proclaiming places Cerise had never been, a jumble of cities whose names she'd heard but whose distance or proximity to each other had no order in her mind.

Finally, when it seemed impossible that she had not walked far enough, she began to think she had missed Arcata entirely, to worry that maybe she'd taken a wrong road and was headed to Nevada or Mexico instead. Just south of Santa Dorothea she stopped at a freeway exit gas station to ask how much farther to Arcata.

"Maybe two hundred miles," the attendant shrugged. "Two-fifty, one-fifty, something like that. Why?" He chewed at the edge of his mustache and watched with minor interest when, in response to his offhand words, Cerise's face began to twist and lurch.

"Car break down?" he asked. When she didn't answer, he added, "You wanna call a tow?"

She shook her head and stumbled off, carrying her tears with her like a final possession.

The exit was one that seemed to exist only to feed travelers and refuel vehicles. After she fled the gas station, she found herself on a wide, little-used frontage road. It was separated from the freeway by a concrete sound wall lined with oleander bushes still studded with dirty white blooms.

She followed the road away from the freeway services, walking until she spied an opening in the hedge. She had to go down on her knees to enter it. A weave of branches scratched her arms, and spiderwebs broke against her face and against the blanket and jacket and water bottle that she carried. Inside the oleanders it smelled musty and private, though the roar of the freeway still filled the air. She pushed on until she found a little open place tucked up against the sound wall, a hidey-hole strewn with dried leaves and trash.

Heaving herself into that space, she leaned against the oleander trunks and let the last tears come, tears of anger and frustration now, hotter and sharper than before, with sobs that tore at her throat and ripped her guts. They were ugly, useless tears, and when they were spent, she wiped her eyes with the back of her hand, stared at the mesh of leaves, and tried to gather herself for the final push to Melody.

Straining until the leaves melted into a mass of green and her stomach cramped with effort, Cerise focused her whole being on Melody, concentrating until the vision that filled her mind was so real her burned hand twitched to touch it. She saw Melody bent over a coloring book, her smooth braid tied with a velvet bow, and when Melody raised her head to look in Cerise's direction, her face broke into a smile so brilliant that for a whole moment Cerise smiled back. But then she yanked that image from her mind and slumped to the ground as though she'd been punched. She lay curled like a pill bug in the oleander duff while her feet swelled from not-walking and the truth she'd tramped down with every step ballooned inside her: the Melody she longed to see was gone.

The baby Cerise had loved so fiercely, the little girl who had loved Cerise so ardently in return, that shining child with her crayons and her happy smile, had vanished long ago. That Melody—the true Melody—lingered only in Cerise's memory, and if the other Melody still existed, the one who had dismantled the smoke detector, ruined her face, and run away from home, then maybe she was better off left lost. That Melody was a stranger, an impostor, and even if Cerise were able to find her, even if she walked another two hundred miles and somehow managed to locate her, all that could possibly exist between them was recrimination and resentment. Maybe, to protect her love of the real Melody, she should leave the other Melody alone.

Besides, Cerise thought as she stared at a crushed paper cup half buried by oleander litter, it would be easier for Melody if she never had to cope with losing a brother, if she never again had to deal with having a mother. Maybe the last loving thing she could do for Melody was to let her be.

Her mind went loose. For hours she lay in a stupor, unmoving and barely breathing, because it was as close as she could come to disappearing from the world without the effort of making herself go. When darkness came, she roused herself enough to pull her blanket around her. Huddled beneath its folds, she could smell the sour tang of her armpits, the freeway stench of her clothes, and, tangled so deeply into her hair it seemed no amount of wind and time could ever erase it, she was certain she still smelled smoke.

Below the freeway din she heard the rustle and skitter of the little lives that filled the oleanders, the insects and rodents and small reptiles. But instead of disgusting or frightening her, they seemed almost like a comfort, the way they went on about their business despite her presence. Swaddled in her blanket, it was as though she were six years old again, huddled beneath the covers of her canopy bed, her knees drawn to her chin, her whole self still and secret while her father shouted and her mother screamed, the house shook with curses and sobs, and Cerise knew only that she had to wait for those sounds to stop before it was safe for her to crawl back out into the light.

Dawn arrived, and she woke from another drowse. A few birds rustled and chirped among the bushes while beyond the wall the traffic continued, ceaseless as a sea. A ladybug came into view. Cerise watched it scramble over the duff, its enameled wings parted slightly to help it balance. She took a twig in her bandaged hand, reached out, and poked the ladybug so that it flipped over on its back. "Your house is on fire," she croaked inside her head as she watched it flail. "Your children will burn." But even after the bug finally managed to right itself, she could not bring herself to crush it.

She was weak and sick. Her gut cramped and her abdomen ached, so many hurts she could not keep them straight, could not think, My stomach hurts because I'm hungry, or My legs are sore from walking. Sometime that morning, when a backfiring truck roused her from another doze, and she found her bladder throbbing with an insistence she could no longer ignore, she crawled farther into the oleanders, worked her sweat pants down below her hips, and crouched to pee. As the urine flowed from her, she was startled to catch sight of a smear of red inside her thigh. Her first thought was it was another injury from the fire, and for a moment she felt almost gratified to see more proof of what she'd suffered.

But when she caught sight of still more blood, its true cause occurred to her, like the punch line to a tasteless joke. Scooting back to the spot that had become her home, she remembered the day in junior high school when, perched on the cold toilet in the girls' restroom, she had first discovered blood in the crotch of her panties. She'd panicked then, not because she thought she was hurt or dying but because she was afraid that, despite all her efforts, the blood would run down her legs or stain her skirt.

She felt blood leaking from her vulva, soft and warm as tears. She told herself it no longer mattered if it caked her thighs and soaked its telltale stain into her pants, and there was a luxury in that fact that was seductive, a giving up almost as cozy as dying. But then the thought of

Travis brushed her mind. She winced to think that someone might see her, blood-smeared and stinking, and conclude that she deserved to lose her son.

She began to look for something she could use to hide her blood. But the oleander leaves were not absorbent, and she recoiled at the bits of filthy paper. Finally, though it was clumsy, painful work with her bandaged hands, she untied her shoe, eased the stiff sock from her travel-blistered foot, and stuffed it inside her panties like a napkin. Then, tucking her empty water bottle into her jacket, she crawled from her nest on her elbows and knees.

Forcing herself to stand and blinking in the unfiltered sunlight, she brushed herself off as best she could and limped back down the frontage road. She went first to the gas station she'd stopped at before, but the bathroom at the back of the building was locked. The bathroom at the second station was also locked. At the third she entered the convenience grocery and tentatively asked for the key. The woman behind the counter flicked her eyes across Cerise's clothes and hair, and her face shut tight.

"Customers only," she said.

"Please," Cerise pleaded, startled by her own courage and by the awkward grating of the word in her throat. Then, lowering her voice to a shamed whisper, she added, "I've got my period."

The woman made a quick sound of impatience, reached beneath the counter, and then held out a grimy board with a key dangling from one end. "After this, you go somewhere else to do your drugs."

"I don't," Cerise whispered, clutching the key in her clumsy paw. "I don't do drugs."

"Oh, right. And I'm the queen of England." The woman turned to the man who had come to stand behind Cerise, saying as Cerise pushed past him toward the door and the woman took the twenty from his outstretched hand, "Tell me how you manage to look like that, if you don't do drugs."

"Booze'll do it," he answered, and as Cerise left the store, the sound of their shared laughter was sharp as a slap.

The bathroom was a small, cold cubicle at the back of the building, with a stained toilet and a sink with a single faucet. The concrete floor was damp and grimy. The enamel paint on the cinder-block walls was stained brown with cigarette smoke. A tampon dispenser, a condom dispenser, and a perfume dispenser hung next to the sink. Cerise shook the tampon dispenser, but it was both padlocked and empty.

Her sock was soaked in blood. Working gingerly with her damaged hands, she wrapped it in paper towels and buried it at the bottom of the overflowing trash basket. First she tried wiping her legs with the squares of rough tissue she pulled one at a time from the metal dispenser beside the toilet. Then, holding a stiff paper towel in her fingertips, she wet it in the icy tap water, sprinkled it with powdered soap from the dispenser by the sink, and washed between her legs. The water seeped through the gauze and stung her hands, and the soap scratched like sand in her crotch and on her thighs, but once they were clean she wet another towel, dusted it with more soap powder, and scrubbed her face and neck and armpits.

She was refilling her water bottle when someone rattled the door. She jumped as though she'd been kicked. Hurriedly she capped the bottle, crammed her pockets with wads of paper towels, and then left, averting her gaze and pushing quickly past the woman who waited outside the door.

AFTER THE RUSH OF GETTING THEMSELVES SHOWERED AND CLOTHED— Anna in a rayon dress and Eliot in a sports jacket and tie—after nursing Ellen until she finally fell asleep and then easing her down by breathless increments into her crib, after settling Lucy in with a nice snack and a special video, after showing the new babysitter around the house, tiptoeing back to check on Ellen one last time, and then dashing through the unfamiliar countryside as they tried to connect the minimalist map that came with the Laughlins' invitation with the poorly marked roads that twisted past vineyards and wineries and finally meandered up almost a mile of private drive, Anna and Eliot were the first guests to arrive.

"This had better be the right place," Eliot said, as they crested the final hill to confront a house that rose like a ship—all jutting angles and wide decks—from a sea of shining lawn. "If not, we'll probably get shot for trespassing."

"This guy had your job?" Anna asked, gazing skeptically at the looming house.

"Yeah, but his wife had a trust fund, and I think she may have done something in real estate, too." Eliot parked the car at the edge of the drive and turned off the ignition. "Apparently she's also something of an art patron, at least that's what Phil said."

"That's nice," Anna said mechanically.

"Thank you for coming to this," Eliot said, reaching over to squeeze her hand before he got out of the car. "I know it's not your first choice of how you'd spend your Saturday afternoon."

Carole Laughlin was fastening a bracelet as she came across the lawn to meet them, her clothes fluttering around her as though she were an important bird.

"I'm afraid we're early," Anna apologized.

"Why, no," Carole said. "You're just on time." She smiled at them indulgently, as if being on time was something that clever children did.

"It's nice of you to—" Anna began, but suddenly the musicians arrived behind them with their music stands and instrument cases.

"Excuse me," Carole said, reaching out to touch Anna's arm. "I won't be a minute." She endowed them with another smile, and then turned and led the little procession of black-clad musicians toward the house.

The lawn where they were standing spanned a ridge top. Behind them the view ended in a forested hillside, while in front of them a panorama of golden grasses and thick-trunked oaks sloped down to a wide valley striped with rows of wine grapes. In the center of the valley Anna caught a glimmer of river.

"Pretty," Eliot said when he saw where Anna was looking.

"Yes," Anna murmured, "it's pretty." For the last three weekends she had managed to leave the girls with Eliot for a few hours while she drove out looking for something to photograph. But each time she'd come home without exposing any film. Now, when she looked down into the quiet, sun-soaked valley and tried to imagine how she might frame that image on the ground glass of her camera, she could not hear the click of a shutter that had once meant, Try this. It was a landscape that had nothing to do with her, like a stranger's pretty child.

"I hope the girls are okay," Anna said to shift her thoughts. It was the first time she'd left Ellen with anyone but Eliot, and thinking about it now, she felt a little swell of panic.

"The babysitter seemed fine," Eliot answered.

"She said she's joining the Peace Corps in January," Anna answered with a sigh.

"That's nice."

"For her," Anna said wryly. "And for some developing country. But for us it means having to start the sitter search all over."

There were tables set up under the oaks next to the front deck, and half a dozen caterers were busily filling them with food and flowers. Watching them, Anna almost envied their clear sense of purpose, their busyness. She thought of Jesse's cell phone nestled in her purse and resisted the impulse to call home.

More guests began arriving. The first few came up the lawn as awkwardly and bravely as Anna and Eliot had, and then suddenly the whole hilltop was filled with gusts of laughter and the sound of conversation, sharp and light as the perfumes and aftershaves that wafted around them in the oddly balmy air.

Anna said, "It's bizarre to be at a garden party this time of year. What would they have done if it rained?"

Eliot shrugged, "Move it inside. But according to the locals, we still have at least a few weeks before the rains usually arrive."

"We're too dressed up," Anna observed, looking across the lawn at the groups of laughing strangers in their linens and cotton sweaters. "We look like tourists."

"We are tourists," Eliot answered.

"Nope," she said. "Not anymore. We live here—remember?"

"Invasive exotics, like eucalyptus and French broom."

"Invasive, maybe," Anna agreed. "Though I doubt they'd consider us very exotic. Look at this place."

A strong light emblazoned everything. The autumn flowers glowed in their beds as though they had been polished. Even the temperature was perfect, warm as bathwater, with a breeze that posed no threat to the tablecloths and cocktail napkins. Carole sought them out again.

"Phillip will be along soon," she said to Eliot. "He's dying for news about the center. But don't tell him too much, or I'm afraid he'll decide to come out of retirement and reclaim his job—and that would be disastrous for both you and me." She waited while they laughed politely. Then, turning to Anna, she said brightly, "Let's see—you've just escaped from somewhere. Nevada? Kansas?"

"We moved from eastern Washington," Anna answered, trying to keep her voice smooth. "Near Spokane."

"Oh. My. Well, welcome to California. I'm sure you'll love it here."

"I hope so," Anna answered curtly. Down in the valley she caught sight of a tiny figure in the vineyard, and when she looked more closely, she realized there were many of them—a battalion of ant-size people moving purposefully among the vines.

Carole looked at her sharply. "You're an artist?"

"A photographer," Anna said. "And I taught at Spaulding University until we moved."

Carole raised her head just slightly, as though she were acknowledging Anna for the first time. "I'm a bit of a collector myself," she said. "I don't know if Phillip told you. Californian photographers are one of my interests." She gestured toward the house. "I've got a few things up inside. You're welcome to take a look, if you'd like. I'd love to know what you think of them."

Then, turning back to Eliot, she thrust her face toward him and asked, "And how are things going at work?"

At the sound of Eliot's voice going deep with satisfaction, Anna felt a wash of unexpected sadness. She wasn't resentful of Eliot's luck, but still it hollowed her somehow, to hear him talk so happily about his work when she was so adrift. He deserves this, she reminded herself. After all he's been through, he deserves to have found another job he loves.

After Carole left for other guests, Eliot said ruefully to Anna, "I think you'll like Phil better."

"She's okay," Anna answered, reaching out to give Eliot's hand a loyal squeeze. "At least she buys photographs."

"Maybe there's more to her, once you get to know her better."

"Maybe," Anna answered, looking out across the party. The autumn sunlight shone in the women's hair, glinted off the men's watches and rings, glowed in the bowls of the guests' wineglasses. Down in the valley the little figures moved slowly among the rows of vines.

Anna said, "I do think I'd like to look at her 'things.' Do you mind?"

"Want me to come, too?"

"I'd rather go alone. Not that I don't love your company," she added. "But you should probably wait and talk to Phil."

The grass was so thick her feet couldn't feel the earth beneath it as she crossed the yard. Even the linen-covered tables seemed to be floating above the ground. She wove her way through packs and clumps of strangers, passing through pockets of conversation like different temperatures in a lake.

"Great access—"

"—at the top of his class."

"All the lawyers say we should, but we aren't that—"

"—last time we were on Santorini."

"A tad too oaky—"

The food, when Anna passed it, still looked unapproachable, the platters garnished with flowers and curls of vegetables, the napkins still arranged in symmetrical fans. She accepted a glass of wine, a merlot so dense and silky that the first sip of it seemed reason enough to have left her daughters with a babysitter she'd only just met to race off to a party filled with people she did not know. Glass in hand, she drifted toward the house. She passed a hedge of white flowers, and a fragrance like living perfume wafted after her. She took another sip of wine, let it loll in her mouth, and then, when it was warm as saliva, she swallowed it, felt it glow inside her.

On the wide deck a flautist and a cellist and a guitarist played, their music drifting above the chatter and laughter. Anna smiled in the direction of the musicians and slipped inside the house. It was quiet, cool as a mausoleum. The air smelled vaguely sweet. A sculpture sat in the tiled entryway, a rough-hewn boulder from which the faces of many animals peered as though they were watching all who entered or were waiting for some safer moment to emerge themselves. An armful of lilies filled a vase on a table of polished mahogany. On the tiled floor a stuffed heron lifted one yellow leg, its delicate foot permanently curled for its next step.

A dozen photographs hung on the walls of the room, each framed immaculately and illuminated by a little light. Adams. Stieglitz. Weston. White. John Sexton. Some of the prints she'd seen before, and some were new. Her eyes darted greedily to the signatures even as she soaked in the images—the open doors, the dunes, and stones, and hands. Slowly she circled the room, standing before them one by one.

Each photograph was perfect, so lucid with the authority of its own vision that she moved from one to the next as though she were in a chapel or in a dream. It wasn't until she returned to the door that she remembered the nearly finished darkroom waiting in the basement of their new house, remembered the camera she hadn't used since Ellen was conceived, remembered her fruitless drives through the countryside. She circled the room again, but this time as she passed from one print to the next, she felt not encouragement but a mounting defeat. Those photographs had already surpassed everything to which she had aspired. The conversation had been completed long ago.

And who was listening anyway, she wondered, as out on the lawn, perfectly dressed strangers drank amazing wine, and down in the valley, anonymous workers toiled beneath the sun. What did it matter that someone had once cared enough about a corner of the world to make a photograph? What did they mean, those patterns of shadow and light trapped in silver halide?

When she reached the entryway again, she forced herself to turn back and face the room one last time. She saw each photograph hanging in its pool of light, silent as a tree falling in an unpeopled forest. She heard the sounds of the guests outside, their gusts of laughter like a fickle breeze, and for a moment, standing in the doorway, she felt like sobbing.

CERISE SOON LEARNED WHICH OF THE BATHROOMS OFFERED THE BEST amenities, which of the Dumpsters were most apt to yield food, what times of day she was least likely to be seen. Furtive as a timid ghost, she spread her needs among the half-mile of gas stations and restaurants that clustered round the exit and tried to evade the service workers and freeway travelers who swarmed there, too.

She was as continually exhausted as she'd been when her babies were newborn, so woozy from broken sleep it was as though she were neither asleep nor awake but had instead entered some new state that shared qualities of each, a waking dream in which things loomed and shifted and made no sense. She tried not to let her mind touch on her children, and yet there was never a moment when she was not encompassed by the loss of them. But even so, she learned to make detours inside her mind to avoid thinking of them directly, and sometimes she could evade a little of the pain that way.

The bandages on her hands grew raveled and black, and one day she roused from a doze and rubbed her eyes and was startled to discover that her palms did not hurt. It was an emptiness as surprising as if the freeway roar had suddenly ceased. She tore at the dirty gauze with her teeth, and when she had bitten the bandages off, she saw that tender skin was beginning to form around the edges of the scabs on her palms. It was another defeat, that she should heal. Staring at that fickle pink skin, she hated her own hands for their dumb insistence on living.

Perhaps time passed, though in her efforts to avoid both the past and the future, the present seemed endless, and it was hard to tell. The roar beyond the sound wall never stopped, but one night she woke to find water on her cheeks. At first she thought she had been crying in her sleep. But a second later she remembered rain, heard the winter's first rain filtering through the leaves, felt the splash and roll of raindrops on her face.

Rain changed everything. The oleander droppings became a wet mat beneath her sodden blanket. Inside her damp clothes, she shivered and shrank into the smallest corner of herself, and all the food she found that day was soggy. She tried to rig a roof of salvaged plastic sheeting over her head, but the plastic ripped and leaked, and all night the oleander leaves tipped little loads of water down on top of her.

At dawn, when the rain finally eased enough that Cerise could leave her nest in search of food, she found a woman waiting for her next to the Dumpster behind Denny's. The woman wore a short brown polyester dress covered with an orange apron, and her bare arms looked almost purple in the early morning light. "Here, look," she said, her words appearing as puffs of pale mist. "You need to leave before something happens. Some of the others're starting to say you're not good for business. Don't you know there's places for homeless people—soup kitchens and shelters and stuff—downtown?" She shoved a flyer toward Cerise. "It tells right here where you can go."

It startled Cerise that someone would choose to speak to her, and it was hard to follow what the woman was saying. It baffled her, to have her plight reduced to the lack of a house. She remembered the homeless people she'd seen back in Rossi and in the city, with their shopping carts and old coats and missing teeth, and it seemed strange that there was a name that simple for what she was. She took the flyer the woman offered and tried to read its numbers and letters, but they wouldn't clump together into meanings. She tried to speak, but her throat felt seared shut.

The woman shifted impatiently and shot a glance toward the back door of the restaurant. "My shift's over in a few minutes," she offered. "I'll drive you downtown."

It felt wrong to leave her hole in the oleanders, but Cerise's bones had grown hollow with shivering, her hands were rigid with cold, and the threat and compunction of the woman's concern made it impossible for her to stay. So she waited, huddled beneath the overhang in back of the building, until the woman returned, a jacket slung over her restaurant costume.

"I got some food for you," the woman said, holding out a bag cautiously, as though she were offering something to a feral dog, "and some clothes, too."

She drove an old sedan, its seats and floor littered with fast-food bags and broken action figures. As she drove, she talked, a quick barrage of complaints about her old man and her job and her kids that clattered around Cerise like a bucketful of Ping-Pong balls while Cerise huddled in the warm car and tried to remember how she was supposed to answer all those empty, bouncing words.

The center of Santa Dorothea was such a wet confusing wilderness of streets and strangers it made Cerise long for the privacy of her oleanders. She missed the bugs and birds and lizards and the constant anonymous sound of traffic. In the city, the people weren't all hidden in their cars. Instead they pushed past her so closely that even in the rain she could smell their sweat or their perfume. At first she felt exposed and raw among them. She expected that she would be noticed, that her grief and guilt would be as conspicuous as her filthy clothes, and she cringed and looked for places where she could hide. But she soon realized that if it weren't for the fact that no one ever bumped into her, she might have been invisible, for her presence registered on no one's face.

There were seconds as she wandered the unfamiliar streets that she panicked when she realized Travis wasn't with her. Each time, her first thought was that she'd been negligent or forgetful and that somehow she'd let him wander away. A moment later, when she remembered the reason for his absence, her relief that he was not lost and scared and crying twisted back into such agony that she tried not to remember him at all.

In the windows of the stores and malls, pilgrims and turkeys competed with Santa Clauses and reindeer, but the approach of the holidays barely registered in her mind. Instead, on every wall and pole, she was haunted by the same picture of a girl, the words *Missing* and *Reward* blaring below her rain-worn, smiling face. Each time Cerise saw that girl, a fleet thought of Melody crossed her mind—the young, dear Melody who could never be found, that smiling child whom no one would ever see again.

In a chilly restroom in a wet little park she changed into the blue sweat suit the woman from Denny's had given her. The knees of the pants were threadbare and the sleeves of the shirt were too short, but it was warmer than what she'd been wearing, and it was clean and dry. As she shed the shirt the woman in the campground had given her and pulled the new sweatshirt over her puckered skin, she had the dizzying sense that she was fading into a stranger. After she'd completed her change, she stood for a long while in the little cubicle, staring at the obscenities scratched into the wall and trying to understand what was left of her.

At noon she entered the soup kitchen reluctantly, her head down so that she could see only the grimy floor and her own torn shoes. She was so terrified that the whole roomful of strangers would recognize her as the mother who had no children that only the fierceness of her hunger managed to force her through the door. It was strange to be inside a building. The air was warm and damp and thick with the steam of heavy food, a smell that made her stomach clench with the nausea of hunger.

A line of people straggled along one wall, and Cerise claimed a timid place at the end of it, took a fork and a paper napkin when the person in front of her did, got a tray from the stack and then slid it down the aluminum tubing of the counter, watching as the strangers on the other side assembled plates of food. When it was her turn, she took a plate in her tender hands and gave a ragged nod of thanks.

Long rows of tables filled the room. She found a place at one with empty chairs on either side of her, and as soon as she sat down, she bent her head over her tray. It was a gift she kept waiting to be snatched from her—food that hadn't come from the trash—a scoop of macaroni salad, a pile of brussels sprouts, a bun covered with a circle of pink bologna and a square of orange cheese. The food reminded her so much of Woodland Manor that when, halfway through her meal, she raised her eyes timidly from her plate, she felt a moment's confusion because the faces that surrounded her were not all old.

A few were elderly, and some looked as grim and weary as she, but others appeared no different from people who might be eating at the food court in the mall. There were women in well-kept outfits, men in clean T-shirts and jeans. Children threaded among the chairs, and several families clustered together, eating intently. Across the table from Cerise a man sat with closed eyes and a half smile, as though, amidst the clamor, he was praying. Beside him, in front of a well-cleaned plate, was a large dark woman in bright clothes. Her hands were busy beneath the table while she studied the room with unmasked curiosity. When Cerise sensed their eyes were about to meet, she glanced away as though she'd just ducked a blow.

She spent the afternoon wandering the damp streets. Toward

evening, as the light above the buildings began to seep away, she found two Dumpsters at the end of an alley and tucked herself between them, sat with her legs folded against her chest and her arms wrapped about her knees while the night city throbbed around her.

Because her life was a scrap she would gladly do without, the shouts and sirens did not frighten her. But after a while, beneath or beyond those sounds, she thought she could hear the sound of a telephone ringing—maybe in an apartment where no one was home to pick it up, or maybe in an unlit room where someone sat ignoring its plea. On and on it rang, echoing relentlessly through the darkness, begging someone to answer.

Huddled between the Dumpsters, Cerise could not help but think of the stranger named Melody and the phone call she would surely make, calling home again to brag about her new life. She wondered when Melody would place that call, and she wondered what would happen when she did—would Melody hear the ringing of a phone that no longer existed, or a message announcing that the number she'd called was no longer a working one?

Sitting on the cold asphalt, Cerise tried to ignore the endless ringing that seemed to fill her head, tried not to imagine Melody's call groping toward the heap of ashes that had once been their home, tried not to see the person who was no longer her daughter shrugging and turning away from the phone. Shivering in the darkness, Cerise tried only to endure till dawn.

THEY WERE STOPPED AT A LIGHT ON SANTA DOROTHEA AVENUE ON their way to Lucy's dance class when Lucy caught sight of the woman standing on the traffic island next to them. It was raining, and the woman's hair was clumped with water, her face so slick and chilled and expressionless that it reminded Anna of Ellen's birth face. The woman was wearing a torn raincoat, and she held a tattered square of cardboard with a crayoned message scrawled across it.

"What's that say?" Lucy asked from the backseat, and Anna winced in anticipation of what was coming as Lucy slowly sounded out the words on the woman's sign, " 'Home-less. Bad Heart. Will work for food.' "

"That's good reading," Anna said lightly. "You're really learning fast."

"What's a bad heart?" Lucy asked, staring out the window at the immobile woman.

Cautiously Anna answered, "I guess it means her heart's sick."

"Heartsick means sad, like homesick," Lucy said.

"Sometimes. But she's probably saying that her heart doesn't work as well as it should."

"She's not sad?" Lucy asked, studying the woman whose stony gaze was lifted above the roofs of the cars toward the flat gray sky.

"She might be sad," Anna answered. "I don't know for sure."

"What does homeless mean?"

As gently as possible Anna said, "It means that she doesn't have a home."

"How could she not?"

"Some people don't. They lose their homes, somehow."

"They lose their homes?" Lucy sounded astonished.

"Not like misplacing them," Anna explained. "But maybe they don't have enough money to pay for them, so they have to move out." She felt a sudden complicity, as if her very explanation was turning people out into the streets.

"Where do they sleep?" asked Lucy.

The light finally changed to green. Anna stepped on the accelerator and pulled into the intersection, leaving the woman standing motionless as a weary statue. "Under bridges, maybe, or in deserted buildings. I don't really know."

"Like camping?" Lucy asked, twisting her head to get a last glimpse of the woman.

"Kind of, I suppose. Though they probably don't have tents."

"In the rain?" Lucy persisted.

"If it's raining, yes," Anna answered reluctantly.

"Oh," Lucy said in the smallest possible voice. A minute later she asked, "Why does she want to work for food?"

"I suppose she doesn't have any money to buy food. And she's hungry."

Anna glanced in the rearview mirror at Lucy's expression, saw the horror of a new understanding creep across it.

"She's hungry?"

"She could be hungry, if she wants money for food."

"Why doesn't she have any money?"

"Well, I doubt she has a job."

"Why doesn't she have a job?"

"I really don't know. Lots of reasons, maybe. Sometimes people have problems that keep them from being able to work."

"We could give her a job," Lucy said brightly. "She could work for us."

"We don't have anything for her to do."

"She could clean my room."

"You need to clean your room."

"She could take care of me and Ellen so you could work in your new darkroom."

Anna felt a jolt of alarm. Carefully she said, "I'm not sure that lady would make a very good babysitter."

"Because of her bad heart." Lucy nodded knowingly. She looked worried for a moment, and then she brightened. "I could give her some of my food, Mommy, couldn't I, if she's hungry? Couldn't I give her some of mine?"

For a moment Anna considered turning back. She imagined handing the woman a few dollars or giving her the package of rice cakes and the apple she'd managed to grab from the kitchen for Lucy to eat after her class. But they were on a one-way thoroughfare. To turn back would cost at least ten minutes. They'd be late for Lucy's class if they turned back, and then it all got complicated so quickly—because what if the woman were drunk or belligerent, what if she started crying, or begging for more than Anna felt safe to give? How was Anna to know if her sign was the truth, that her heart was truly bad? How could she be sure the woman would really spend Anna's money on food? How could she encourage Lucy's generosity and appease her worries without lying to her, or adding to her fears?

But as they pulled into the parking lot outside the dance studio, it was Lucy who asked the hardest question of all. With a kind of astonished horror in her voice, she said, "Is the world bad?"

"Oh, no," Anna replied. She turned off the ignition and fumbled an answer about love and beauty and the goodness of people while the rain dashed the roof of the car and the windows fogged with the steam. She talked about the importance of hope and tried to explain how there were reasons for bad things to happen that human beings couldn't always understand. But even as they unbuckled their seat belts and raced across the parking lot to Lucy's class, she knew that nothing she could say would erase the woman standing in the rain.

THE NEXT TIME CERISE WENT TO THE SOUP KITCHEN, IT WAS SO CROWDED that there was no place for her to sit where she could put a chair between herself and the person next to her. For a moment, as she clutched her tray and faced that mob of diners, she considered leaving without eating. But she couldn't think how to abandon her untouched meal in a way that no one would notice, so she pushed herself blindly into the first empty chair. Snippets of conversation battered her as she ate.

"The whole city blames me. But I came here with a bank account. I came here with good in my heart, with democracy, and caring for others—"

"—give you a bag on Mondays, but it's always moldy."

"That's where I place my faith, in God the—"

"—condemned to life—"

"—the prettiest wedding. I'd grown all the roses, too."

"If I could just talk to a lawyer—"

"Packed, ain't it?"

It took a moment before Cerise realized the words were meant for her, and when she did, she jumped and bent her head further over her food. A second later she ventured a quick glance at the person beside her, and recognized the woman she'd noticed across the table the day before. Her wide lap was piled with an afghan whose colors were as loud and variegated as the lights on a carnival fairway. In one hand she wielded a crochet hook that flashed like a fishing lure, while a length of acid yellow yarn danced between her dark fingers and the accreting rim of the blanket.

She said, "Know why, doncha?"

Cerise kept her eyes on the silver hook and yellow yarn and made her head shake no.

"End of the month. Plus rain. That's what drives 'em to this restaurant. Your check must've run out, too. I've only seen you here once before."

"I don't get a check," Cerise whispered, though the words rasped in her throat like sandpaper, and she suddenly feared she'd be told to leave because she didn't have a check.

"Me, neither," the woman said complacently, as her hook darted in and out. "Goddamn state made it so hard to play their game, I told the lady she could play with herself instead. Ha!" she added in a harsh burst of humor. "That's cutting off my nose to spite my face, I know. State don't give two farts in a shithouse if old Barbara freezes to death on the streets. But fuck 'em.

"Butt fuck 'em, I mean," Barbara went on, pleased with her pun, "Someday the truth will out, someday they'll know the plain, pure, unadorned truth about our lives, and then they'll get down on their knees and beg us for forgiveness.

"Homeless," she scoffed while her fingers kept up their twist and dance. "The homeless. What kind of dumbfuck word is that, anyway?

"What's the opposite of homeless?" she asked.

"Homeful? Homed?" she went on when Cerise looked bewildered. "Homemore?" She cackled, "Used to wish my old man'd be homemore."

"They have a 'no home' box on the food stamp application," she said. "When I saw that, I told the lady we've been institutionalized. They count on us, see, the feds do. They need us to make this great country what it is."

She shifted her thighs on the seat of her chair and paused in her crocheting to dig a fist into the small of her back. "But what the holy fuck do I know? My mama said it, a million times, 'If you're so goddamn smart, why ain't you rich?' "

A towheaded toddler in blue overalls lurched past them, pausing for a moment to steady himself by clasping Cerise's knee as casually as if she were a piece of furniture. She caught her breath and tried to empty her mind of everything, tried to hold herself still as stone even as his touch scorched every cell. The wad of yarn in Barbara's left hand had diminished to a final tail. She smiled benevolently at the baby, and then with a grunt she leaned down to reach into the shopping bag that sat on the floor beside her.

The toddler turned as if he'd heard a voice he knew in all that noise, and his face bloomed into a grin. Cerise glanced in the direction he was looking, saw a young woman kneeling down, her tattooed arms stretched out toward him. He grinned and pitched joyously toward the woman, and Cerise felt so dizzy she wondered if she would faint.

Barbara was tying one end of a cantaloupe-size ball of brick red yarn to the yellow tail. "Little fucks," she said, her voice round with good humor.

Cerise croaked, "What?"

"Well, they are. No matter how much some might want to deny it, we're all sex acts of some kind or another. Came from sex, got sex wired in us. You got kids?"

The question tore Cerise's entrails and seared her lungs. The question took her answer away.

Barbara went on, "Me, I don't have kids. Couldn't. Though I sure tried," she cackled. "Had a grand time trying. Hell, I still try a little every now and then, give me half the chance.

"I should of had me a kid," she said in a different tone, her eyes looking inward and her face going soft, "and that kid could of grown up and saved me from all this crap. No kid of mine would stand it for a minute, for his own flesh mama to have to live like this."

She made a little movement with her hand as though she'd just caught herself doing something foolish, and when she went on, her voice was loud again, public, as though she were speaking to more people than just Cerise. "But see, I tried so hard for babies all those years, I guess I come to thinking they're all my children. I could just kill people who hurt 'em. Hurt the whole world when you hurt a kid. All the kids here, all the kids you see, all the kids you've ever seen, all those little fucks are mine, and people better damn well treat 'em right, or they'll have me to say so.

"What's your name, honey?" Barbara asked, looking at Cerise.

Cerise sucked breath, but her name wouldn't come. Barbara was looking at her, waiting for her to answer the world's simplest question.

What's your name, honey? echoed in her head, and all she could do was repeat the echo, to offer it up and let chance name her.

"Honey," Cerise said, fast and flat.

"What?" Barbara asked sharply.

"Honey."

"That your name?"

When Cerise nodded, Barbara gave her a shrewd split-second glance. "You mean I knew it before you said it?"

"Honey Johnson," Cerise said stubbornly, though inside it felt as though she was abandoning the person she had been even as she was shielding that person from whatever happened next, like protecting an organ by lopping off an arm.

Barbara said, "I always knowed I was a goddamned prophet. Honey Johnson—what the fuck." She shook her head, her shoulders heaving with laughter. Holding up her blanket, she gave it a brisk shake. The colors clattered and crackled against each other.

She asked, "This make you laugh?"

Cerise heard the sounds of forks scraping plates, the gleeful shouts of children running around the tables, more scraps of talk. She looked at the blanket and shrugged uneasily.

"I try to make my blankets funny," Barbara went on, "like big jokes. To cheer up people. It's fucking cold out there, in the goddamn rain."

Barbara chortled and then made her voice high, her words mincing, " 'Why don't your colors match?' the lady said." Then she let her own voice boom out again, "Colors match, heck—I mean fuck—colors match? Match what, I'd like to know. Match your Goodwill jacket and your Salvation Army slacks? Match the goddamn ground you're sleeping on? Way I figure is, if it exists—if it's a color in this world—it matches. If it's a color, we need it, just like in the right world we'd need every person, too.

"Look," she said, raising the blanket to her lips to bite off the red yarn in her teeth and speaking to Cerise out of the corner of her mouth, "you take this blanket and tell me tomorrow if it makes you laugh."

"Oh, no," Cerise said, startled. "I—"

"You sleep warm last night?"

"No, but—"

"But's for assholes. You think it don't mean something that I was finishing this up just when I met you? Or what—you want me to give it to one of those losers over there?"

"I'm a loser," Cerise whispered.

"Well, shitfire, Honey. Course you are. You don't eat here if you're on a winning streak. But there's losers and losers. You know that."

Cerise shook her head. "You don't know," she said.

"Course I don't," Barbara said, grabbing the handles of her shopping bag of yarn and rising with regal difficulty to her feet. "No one ever does."

When Cerise left the soup kitchen, she carried Barbara's blanket folded in her arms as carefully as an American flag. That night, in order to keep her new blanket clean and dry, she found a square of cardboard to sit on and rigged a roof of plastic between the Dumpsters. Toward dawn she even managed to sleep a little, and when she woke she felt the weight of Barbara's blanket anchoring her to the world.

AFTER MONTHS OF DUST AND BRITTLE LIGHT, AT FIRST THE RAIN SEEMED like a miracle. The night it began, Anna woke from another dream of home to the sound of water murmuring on the roof and the scent of wet earth sweeping in their open window like a blessing. Lying beside Eliot while their daughters—for once—slept peacefully in their beds, she thought that maybe things would be easier, now that a new season had finally begun.

But after four weeks of unremitting rain, it was clear her late-night hopes had been in vain. Lucy was still plagued by nightmares more nights than not, and she hadn't mentioned making any friends at school. Anna's darkroom was finally plumbed and wired, and the counters and shelves had been installed, but the winter light was so thin and wan that she'd given up even trying to find anything in California to photograph.

And then, the Sunday after Thanksgiving, as she was on her way downstairs to fix breakfast, she stepped in a patch of soggy carpet on the landing at the top of the stairway. Cold water oozed between her toes. Looking up, she saw an ominous stain spreading across the ceiling, dirty water dripping from the center of it. Abandoning her plans for pancakes, she went back to wake Eliot.

While she set out buckets and tried to sponge the water from the carpet, Eliot climbed onto the roof in the rain to make an emergency patch with plastic sheeting and mastic. He came inside an hour later, dripping and looking glum. "I think that'll keep the worst water out for a while, but we'll have to get a new roof before next winter comes."

"A new roof?" Anna asked, handing him a towel. "Where can we possibly find that kind of money?"

Eliot shook his head. "Rob a bank, maybe, or sell one of the kids." But all afternoon, as Anna raced through the rainy city running errands, she worried about where the money could come from. She and Eliot had used their savings to make the down payment on their leaking house, and still their mortgage payments were twice what they had been in Washington. Moving to California and installing her new darkroom had edged their credit card to its limit, and they were spending every penny Eliot made just to reach the end of the month. Christmas was coming, the transmission on the Subaru was getting loose, the washing machine wasn't emptying properly, and Lucy's dance class—which these days was the only thing she seemed to love—cost a hundred dollars a month. Driving from the hardware store to the grocery store to the drugstore to the bank, Anna sorted and resorted that same set of facts as if she could find the extra money hidden somewhere behind them.

It made her hot and nauseous to think of taking out a second mortgage or asking her parents for a loan. It made her weary to think of having to take the kind of job an unemployed professor of fine arts could find, and it broke her heart to think of having to be away from Ellen all day just for the sake of money.

It wasn't until she was driving home through the dark, wet city, the car loaded with groceries, nails, plastic sheeting, and an electric space heater to dry the clammy carpet, that she realized where the money could come from. At first it was a shock as sickening as cold water on her bare soles, an idea nearly as appalling as selling a child. But it made sense, too, she thought grimly. It made sense, and maybe it was the only way.

Her field camera was worth nearly half a year's salary. If she sold it, they could reroof the house and fix the car and pay off their credit card.

Maybe then, if they were very frugal, she could manage to wait until Ellen was talking before she found a job. She might as well sell her camera, she told herself as she turned down their street, since she wasn't using it, since owning it only filled her with regret.

She parked the car, loaded her arms with groceries, and dashed through the rain toward the back door, opened it to find Lucy sprawled on the kitchen floor, drawing. Her chin was propped on one hand, crayons were strewn in a wide fan across the floor, and she glanced up listlessly when Anna heaved her damp bags onto the counter.

"Hello, Sweetness," Anna said, forcing cheer into her voice as she shrugged out of her jacket. "How was your afternoon?"

"It was okay," Lucy answered, her hand hovering above the sprawl of crayons.

"What did you do?" Anna asked.

"Oh, just a bunch of things," said Lucy, choosing green.

On the stove the stainless steel pasta pot was steaming. Three crimson tomatoes, a head of romaine lettuce, and a sheaf of leeks sat on the cutting board, and a loaf of crusty bread waited on the countertop beside them. Eliot had got that far, at least, with supper.

"Where's your daddy?" Anna asked, opening the refrigerator to put away the milk.

"On the computer," Lucy answered absently.

"How about Ellen?"

"She's still having her nap."

"She is?" Anna glanced at the clock above the sink and winced to think of the price she'd pay tonight because Eliot had let Ellen sleep so long. To Lucy she said, "What are you working on?"

"Homework," Lucy answered, putting down the green crayon and taking up a red.

"Good for you." On the stove the water had begun to boil. Anna salted the bubbling water, rummaged through the bags of groceries until she found a package of fettuccini. When the water had recovered from the salt and risen back up to boiling, Anna emptied the pasta into the kettle and gave it a quick stir with a slotted spoon.

She was crossing the room to put the canned goods in the pantry when she noticed Lucy scrubbing wild spirals of red across her drawing. She said, "You don't need to press so hard, Lu. The crayon just flakes off the paper if it gets too thick."

"But there's a lot of blood."

"Blood?" Anna asked, stopping in the middle of the kitchen, the bag of cans lumpy in her arms. "Why blood?"

"Because," Lucy said firmly.

"Because why?" Anna asked cautiously, looking down at Lucy.

"Because the girl got hurt."

"That's too bad," said Anna, peering at the drawing. Scribbles of red were curling across the page like crimson smoke, nearly obliterating the stiff-looking figure lying prone on the green ground. "Who is that girl?"

Lucy shrugged, "Just the girl in my picture."

"How did she get hurt?"

"The man that napped her hurt her."

"The man that napped her?" Anna echoed.

"You know—like Andrea."

"You're doing this for your homework?" Anna asked incredulously, setting the bag back down on the counter.

"I did my math already. This is extra credit."

"Extra credit for what?"

"For stranger-awareness class."

"Ms. Ashton asked you to draw a picture of Andrea?"

"Ms. Ashton asked us to draw pictures that would teach kids how to be careful about strangers. The best picture in the city will be made into a poster, and then there'll be a pizza party for that whole school. If I win, then everybody will be my friend." Lucy scrubbed the red crayon resolutely.

"I'm not sure," Anna said carefully, "that I like Ms. Ashton making you draw pictures like that."

"She didn't make us," Lucy answered. "This is extra credit. Besides, they're pictures to help keep other kids safe. She said," Lucy quoted solemnly, "that some children didn't understand about strangers, and that if we drew our best pictures, we could teach them."

"Ms. Ashton told you that?" Anna asked.

"It's true," Lucy answered indignantly.

"But it's—kind of sad," Anna said. "For kids to have to think about."

"Kids have to think about it," Lucy said staunchly. "Or else they might get gotten." She choose a yellow crayon from her heap and began to fill a corner of the sky with a circle of sun.

Anna said, "Maybe kids should think about it a little, but not a lot. Not so much they worry."

"Kids shouldn't worry about it?" Lucy asked.

"Well, not too much. They should be prepared, maybe."

"That's what we're doing," Lucy announced triumphantly. "Being prepared. She said it's good for everyone to work together and help. She said if everyone helped, there wouldn't be a problem anymore."

"Well," Anna said vaguely, "I suppose that's true." She looked down at Lucy's bleeding girl and cringed to think what bedtime held in store.

Diligently Lucy began to draw rays from her yellow sun, sending them across the page in all directions so that they seemed to battle with the billowing blood. Suddenly she looked up at her mother, and for the first time that evening, her voice sounded animated. "I know, Mommy," she said. "You could help, too."

"Me?" Anna asked.

"You could make a photograph to help save children."

Anna could hear the pride rising in Lucy's voice, could see a new light growing in her face, and she felt a little stab of yearning. But then a thought hit her gut, although her brain clamped shut before she spoke it: Photographs can't save children.

"Will you make a photograph?" Lucy asked eagerly, and out of a swirl of awful questions and inadequate answers, Anna chose the most meager and least cruel. "That's a nice idea," she said. "I'll think about it. But right now it's almost time for dinner. Go tell your daddy."

BY THE TIME A PLACE OPENED UP FOR HER AT THE REDWOOD WOMEN'S Shelter where Barbara was staying, the final scraps of scab had sloughed off Cerise's palms. The skin beneath was shiny and pink and pulled like fabric that had been stretched too tight, and her palms felt both numb and tender, as though they had been borrowed from someone else.

"It's about time we got you in here," Barbara said to her after supper that first night. "Life's gonna be easy street from here on out, you'll see. Breakfast and supper and a bed for three months while they help you find a job. A job," she cackled. "Sweet Jesus and hot goddamn."

It was mid-December by then, and that night when Cerise lay down on her cot in the warm sleeping hall, it seemed so strange to surrender herself to sleep without worrying how she might be wakened that she kept thinking she was forgetting something or doing something wrong.

She sank into the richest sleep she'd had for weeks, but she woke past midnight, wracked with nightmare. She lay awake for a long time then, listening to the snores and moans of the women around her, listening to the whimpers of the children who slept on wobbly cots beside their mothers and clutched hand-me-down toys that smelled of strangers' houses.

In the morning, after a breakfast of coffee and day-old doughnuts, the residents all had to leave the shelter until dinnertime, because, as the director had explained, being out helped them to keep active, encouraged them to continue looking for work and permanent housing.

"Being on the streets all day helps to get you off the streets," Barbara cackled under her breath to Cerise as they all filed out of the shelter into the rain. "That's the kind of brilliant dumbfuck thinking that made this country what it is today.

"Well, good luck," she mumbled, as they reached the first corner and she turned abruptly to go the opposite way. "Hope you find gold."

"Good-bye," said Cerise, looking longingly after Barbara's shambling figure for a moment before she turned to devote herself to the day-long work of staying dry.

Out in the Christmas-colored city, as she moved from one small refuge to the next, she thought she saw Travis everywhere she went. In the mall, whenever a child said, "Mama," her mind gasped, Travis. Time and again she caught a glimpse of him, sometimes holding a stranger's hand and toddling across a parking lot, sometimes gazing out at the rain from the window of a passing car. Each time she saw him, she was herself again, cupped for an instant by a kind of grace, though every time he vanished into a stranger's child, she had to descend all over again into the vortex of her grief.

Sometimes she followed those phantom Travises even after the blissful second had passed when they were hers. She longed to touch or smell them, longed to talk to them. She wished she could give them something—a sticker or a sucker or the quarter she'd found in the gutter. But she was afraid of their revulsion, afraid of the wrath of the adults who held their hands, afraid, most of all, that even if she were to touch or speak to them, they would not notice her. It was as though she had become the ghost, in a world where Travis was still living.

Once she saw a slender girl climbing into a car with a crowd of other kids. The girl's jeans were so tight they made her thighs look concave, and her blond hair lapped her waist, and for a white-hot second Cerise thought she was seeing Melody. She froze in the middle of the sidewalk, longing and terror detonating inside her. But suddenly the girl turned around. Looking straight at Cerise, she tossed her hair and laughed, and a second later Cerise realized that she was staring at a stranger. But for the whole rest of the day she felt as though she'd somehow seen Melody, after all.

At dusk the women all returned to the shelter, gathering together like an awkward family after their day in the wet parks and crowded malls. Their quarrels and kindnesses flared in the dining room, spilled into the TV room, followed them to the bathrooms and the sleeping hall, and it was almost a relief to Cerise to have the flurry of other lives to muffle the anguish of her own.

One night while she was sitting beneath the poster of Andrea in the TV room, some of the other residents came over to ask if she wanted to join their prayer circle.

"It helps," Maria said. "To keep the faith." While the rest nodded fervently, she went on, "We know Jesus has a plan for every one of us. He wouldn't ask us to endure any more than we can bear."

Cerise cast a desperate glance at Barbara, who was crocheting implacably beside her, and finally scraped together the courage to say, "No, thanks."

"What is your story, Honey?" Maria asked tenderly. "You could come to our circle and share it with us and Jesus."

"No," Cerise said, so savagely that Maria did not try again.

"So you got a bit of grit, after all," Barbara observed approvingly after the prayer-circle women moved on. A new blanket, colored like a bipolar rainbow, spilled over her lap and tumbled onto the floor.

"Anyways, I'm like you," she told Cerise, while her hands moved steadily as a heartbeat and her little hook gobbled yarn. "Troubles ain't worth a single damn except to maybe teach us who we are, and if it turns out there's a god puts up with all this shit and thinks it's cute to make us learn the hard way, I'd say he can go fuck himself like he's already fucked us."

Her hook grabbed a loop of orange yarn, yanked it through the turquoise of the proceeding row. She waited for Cerise to speak, and when she didn't, Barbara reached into the shopping bag that stood open beside her and pulled out another ball of yarn. "Plum," she proclaimed, as though she were announcing the winner of a raffle.

"Chenille," she added, savoring the feel of the yarn between her fingers before she tied one end of it to the orange. "Someone spent good money on yarn like that. Most likely her pattern was too complicated," she went on. "That's what usually makes 'em give up, what they tell me, anyways, when they give me their throwaways."

She glanced up from her work to speak directly to Cerise. "Keep your patterns simple," she said, before splicing her way back into her own conversation.

She sighed and dug her fist into the small of her back. "Their hearts are in the right place," she said as she took up her hook again and began looping plum chenille to orange wool, "no matter how deep up their asses their heads might be. Besides," she chuckled, "I always like it when they pray for me."

It frightened Cerise at first for there to be so many children at the shelter. She almost hated them sometimes, for the way their presence taunted her. In the beginning, she tried to ignore them, tried to sit as far away from them as possible, tried not to look at them or listen to what they said. But when little Carmen Diez tripped in the dining room and gashed her lip on the corner of a table while her mother was working in the kitchen, Cerise was flying across the room before she could think to stop herself. She was there before anyone else had even noticed, before Carmen even began to wail. Scooping the astonished girl off the floor, Cerise pressed Carmen's face against her blouse to staunch the blood, shushed her when she started screaming, promised her what Cerise knew to be a lie, murmured, "It's all right, it's okay, everything'll be all right." After that Carmen followed Cerise like a sad-eyed puppy, and soon the other children were also finding reasons to linger near her.

As Christmas approached, Cerise tried to avoid it. At the shelter she shunned the caroling, skipped the trimming of the tree, and when the cardboard snowmen and satin angels went up alongside Andrea's poster, she did her best to ignore them. But one evening a few days before Christmas, a pious Santa in a red polyester suit and a fake white beard swept into the TV room and Cerise was trapped as he ho-hoed and praised Jesus and handed out packages whose labels read, "Boy Aged 6," or "Infant Girl" or "Pregnant Lady."

Only Barbara noticed how Cerise swayed and pressed her hands against her chest as though she had to keep her insides from spilling out. "Hey," she called across the crowded room, waving her crochet hook, "come over here," and when Cerise drew near enough to hear, Barbara began a counter-patter of her own. "True meaning of Christmas up your asshole," she mumbled in Santa's direction, murmuring it soothingly as a mama crooning a lullaby, while her crochet hook flashed in her hand like a knife blade.

"Up your asshole with a bowlful of jelly," she went on so softly only Cerise could hear. "There's plenty of women and babies here tonight who'd be thrilled with a nice dry manger and some swaddling clothes. Plenty of women who'd be Mary in your fucking Christmas play. Up your asshole with a sprig of holly, Santa. Up your asshole with a ho, ho, ho."

But for once she kept her voice low so she would not offend those who, if they heard, would invoke the shelter's rules about profanity and remind her how few chances she had left before she would be asked to leave.

A GLIMPSE OF THE
WORLD'S ROUGH
GRACE

COLUMN OF CLEAR WATER SPILLED INTO THE TUB. CLUTCHING
Ellen to her chest with one arm, Anna knelt on the rug and
leaned over to check the temperature of the bath. Wet light
filtered through the plants that clustered on the sill of the rain-stained
window, and the air was damp and sweet as a child's breath. Outside it
was storming, and the bluster of wind and rain made the room seem so
warm and safe and simple that for a moment everything else seemed
warm and simple, too.

Christmas had come and gone, and the rain had never stopped. It
was the worst rain in ninety years, the meteorologists were saying—
record-breaking, devastating rain. Anna and Eliot had planned to spend
Christmas up in Washington, in the snow. But a week after the roof
began to leak, Eliot discovered an inch of water in the basement and a
damp spot growing on the wall of the laundry room, so they'd had to
use the money they'd set aside for plane tickets to waterproof instead.

Anna had tried to make a Christmas for them in California. She'd bought a tree pruned like a pet poodle from the forest that sprang up overnight in the Kmart parking lot, and she took Lucy to see *The Nutcracker* and to visit Santa at the mall. On Christmas afternoon, while a dull rain fell, Ellen napped, Lucy played halfheartedly with her new toys, Eliot sat hunched over his computer trying to meet a January deadline for another grant, and Anna fixed an elaborate dinner of Californian ingredients—organic duck, sun-dried tomatoes, goat's cheese, and fresh strawberries. But when the four of them gathered around the table, the food had tasted too rich, and their ordinary talk—*Pass the salad; Lucy, don't kick the table leg; Do you think the FedEx office is open tomorrow? Mommy, can I have more strawberries?*—lacked the substance it seemed the dinner and the day deserved. Cleaning up afterward, Anna had felt an empty relief, as though Christmas were another chore she could cross off her list.

And now it was January, and still the rain kept falling. Eliot had met his grant deadline, they'd managed to drain the basement before the water reached the darkroom, and Ellen had miraculously missed the flu that Lucy brought home from school. But despite all those accomplishments, everything seemed as dreary as the rain. Last night after the girls were finally in bed, Anna and Eliot had gone over their finances again.

"I need to get a job," she'd said flatly, staring at the numbers they could not get to fit into their budget.

"Ellen's too little for you to be away all day," Eliot had answered immediately. "Besides, I hate to say it, but I'm not sure what kind of work you could find around there that would even cover the extra expenses of working—day care and transportation and paper diapers and all that stuff."

"Maybe we need to sell the house," she'd offered.

"I thought of that, too," said Eliot, shaking his head. "But housing prices have gone up even since we bought this place. Anything we could afford now would be a total dump, and rent would cost just as much as our mortgage. Plus, we just got your darkroom installed." He shrugged grimly. "I'm going to start calling around tomorrow and see if I can find us a second mortgage."

"How would we make those payments," Anna asked, "if we can barely make our payments now?"

"We'll have to, somehow," he'd answered grimly.

Last night, her only answer had been a sigh. But since then, the idea she'd been harboring since the roof started leaking began to bully its way forward in her mind, growing until it was hard to think of anything else.

Anna lay Ellen down on the bathmat and began to undress her. "Beedo, beedo," Ellen said, smiling up at Anna and twisting her tongue around the sounds, letting the new syllables loll like candies in her mouth. "Beedo, beedo," Anna answered automatically. She removed Ellen's diaper, shook a tidy turd into the toilet, and gave Ellen's bottom a deft cleaning. Relieved of the bulk between her legs, Ellen pulled her foot toward her mouth and began solemnly to suck her toes while Anna leaned forward to check the temperature of the bath.

There was nothing in California she cared to photograph, and Salish was a world away. Besides, she had no time to be a photographer, no reason, in a world so crammed with details and dire needs, to pursue anything as self-serving and uncertain as art. She could keep her 35mm camera for a little longer, and she wouldn't sell her enlarger just yet, but it made no sense to own a camera that cost more than a new car, especially if she never used it anymore. In a way, she thought as she trailed her hand in the warm water and watched the steam rise into the damp air, it might even be a relief to be that definite about things. If she no longer had her camera, it would be harder to feel like a failure for not using it.

Lucy shrugged her shirt off and wriggled out of her pants and underpants. Standing naked in front of the tub, she asked, "Can I get in now?" She was holding herself in a posture that Anna had noticed her using more and more, with her head bent and her shoulders slightly hunched, as though she were trying to close in on herself. With a start Anna saw how skinny she'd suddenly become, her shoulder blades slicing like knives from her naked back, her ribs jutting against her milky skin.

"Okay," Anna answered, turning off the taps and giving the water a final swirl with her hand. "Hop in."

When Anna had asked Lucy if there were anyone from school she wanted to invite over during the holidays, Lucy had only shaken her head. "I don't think that anyone wants to come," she'd said, and Anna had wanted to weep with bewilderment and fury that Lucy could possibly feel that way. She'd wanted to round up Lucy's schoolmates and force them to like her, had wanted to slap them all for making Lucy so forlorn. Now as she watched Lucy climb into the tub, she thought that if she sold her camera, she would be able to volunteer at Lucy's school instead of having to find a job.

"Can Ellie get in, too?" Lucy asked, sitting down in the tub with a plop.

Happy to hear her big sister say her name, Ellen sucked her toes and sang, "Deeble, deebel, deedee."

"You get started," Anna said to Lucy. "I'll put Ellen in in a minute."

Ellen's foot slipped from her grasp, and she looked startled, as though someone had snatched a toy from her. "Guh?" she asked, her voice thick with surprise. Anna lifted Ellen into her arms, and her naked baby-flesh felt smooth as pudding against her skin. Her bottom, resting in the crook of Anna's arm, was cooler than the rest of her, an amazing mix of soft and firm. Burying her face in Ellen's neck, Anna inhaled, drawing Ellen's smell deep into her lungs. An instant bliss surrounded her. She felt a melting in her bones, and thought, Surely all this can be enough.

The phone rang, its sound like a rip in fabric.

"Don't get it," Lucy said conspiratorially as Anna turned automatically toward the door.

"I'd better," Anna said. "It might be your daddy. I'll be right back."

Still carrying Ellen, she crossed the hall to the bedroom, leaving the bathroom door open so that she could listen for Lucy. If it was Eliot calling to tell her what he'd learned about second mortgages, she would have to tell him of her plan to sell her field camera. That would be the hardest part of the whole process, she realized suddenly—not placing the ads or watching potential buyers manipulate the bellows and lenses, but convincing Eliot that they had no other choice.

A nervous dread imploded in her stomach as she scooped the phone from its charger and answered it. Shifting Ellen to the other arm, she tucked the receiver into the crook of her neck and headed back to the bathroom.

"Anna Walters?" a man's voice asked, and her relief that it was not Eliot felt like a gift.

"Yes?" she said with polite expectancy, trying to get the voice on the phone to mesh with any of the faces she'd met in California.

"This is Martin Lee, from the UC Santa Dorothea art department. I met you and your husband once years ago, when I spoke at Spaulding University. I've been a longtime admirer of your work."

For the smallest fraction of time, Anna could not understand what he meant. My work? she wondered, thinking of the swirl of meals and dishes and diapers that made up her days. Then she remembered that other life, her old accomplishments still apparently solid despite Lucy's loneliness and Ellen's precarious health, despite the shambles in her kitchen and her decision to sell her camera. Biting back the irony, she make herself say, "Thank you very much."

Professor Lee was saying, "I'm department chair now. By default, really," he added with professorial modesty. "You know how these things go. The last one to the meeting gets elected. Anyway, I ran into your husband yesterday in the faculty lunchroom, and he said you'd moved here recently."

"Last August," Anna answered, caution and curiosity evenly balanced in her voice. She had a vague idea of who Martin Lee might be, remembered a dapper Asian printmaker with a sprinkling of white in his close-cropped hair. She reentered the bathroom, where Lucy was intently lathering her stomach with soap.

Martin Lee said, "I'm calling because of our photographer—Arnson Hocking. Is he a friend of yours?"

"I've never met him," Anna said. "But I certainly know his work."

"We've been wildly lucky to have Arnie. He's a wonderful colleague, and a fine teacher, too, in spite of all his fame. But he had a stroke the day before yesterday—quite massive, I'm sorry to say. Of course we're all terribly worried about him, but spring semester begins next week, and it's my job to find someone to cover his classes."

"Oh?" Anna asked. She sank down on the closed lid of the toilet, hugged Ellen in her lap, and held her breath.

"I wondered if you would consider it. There's not much glory in it, nor even a great deal of money. But then you already know that about academia, after your years at Spaulding University."

"But I'm not—"

"It's appallingly short notice, I know. But we really need a photographer of your caliber to cover Arnie's classes, and I don't know where else to turn."

A photographer of your caliber, her thoughts echoed. She stared at the wadded clothing on the bathroom floor and wondered how much she should tell Martin Lee about her life.

He said, "I realize you weren't planning on teaching this spring, but I'd like to think there might be some value in it for you, too."

Students, she thought. And colleagues. A salary. She felt something start up inside her, but she caught herself abruptly. "What would I be teaching?" she asked.

"I can find someone around here to take Arnie's intro class. But there's an upper-division seminar we'd need covered, as well as several graduate students who need an adviser."

"Mommy," Lucy said, standing up abruptly as water poured off her in a minor tidal wave. "I'm hungry."

Anna waved a hand at her daughter and touched her fingers to her lips to signal *shh*. Into the phone she asked, "Don't you need to do a search?" Graduate students, she thought hungrily. A seminar. For a moment she could almost smell the Dektol, could almost feel the bite of stop bath in her sinuses, could almost hear the little click of the shutter opening to admit new light, but she snatched herself back sternly. It's not that easy, she told herself.

Martin Lee said, "Normally our hiring process is quite extensive, but under the circumstances—"

"I'm starfing," Lucy said, scrambling from the tub to stand naked and dripping in front of Anna. "You said we'd have snack next."

Anna shook her head at Lucy, grimaced fiercely.

"You said," Lucy insisted. "Right after our bath." Sucking her gut toward her backbone, she clutched her concave stomach and added, "I'm dying of hungerness."

Anna said, "Excuse me just a minute. I'm sorry. I need to say something to my daughter." Raising her mouth from the receiver and speaking in a tone she hoped sounded sweet to Martin Lee and stern to Lucy, she said, "Mommy's having an important call. You go get dressed, and I'll get you a snack as soon as I'm done."

"But—"

"Now." Anna glared so forcefully that—miraculously—Lucy skittered from the bathroom, trailing water down the hall.

"I'm sorry," she said into the phone. "What were you saying?"

Professor Lee continued, "I know we're asking a lot on such short notice, but I must tell you that if Arnie is unable to continue teaching, we'll be looking for a permanent replacement. As visiting faculty, you'd be in an excellent position to apply."

Your last show was four years ago, Anna told herself. You haven't made a print in thirteen months. You're going to sell your camera. She said, "I don't know if Eliot told you, but we have young children. I'd rather not work full-time."

"We would work around your schedule as much as possible," Martin Lee said. "It would be good if you would attend department meetings, but we wouldn't ask you to serve on any committees. Between your seminar and your other responsibilities, I wouldn't expect you'd be on campus more than fifteen hours a week—maybe twenty at the very most.

"I wish I could give you more time to make a decision," he went on. "But if you think you might be interested, I'm afraid I'd need to know by tomorrow afternoon. Otherwise, I'll have to cast a wider net."

"Tomorrow afternoon," Anna echoed. Beneath her growing elation, she felt an odd sense of doom, as if whatever she decided, all her failures would inevitably be laid bare.

Martin Lee said, "I do hope you'll be able to say yes."

Hugging Ellen like a teddy bear, Anna stared at the tubful of cooling water, at the strewn towels, the cluttered counter, the brimming wastebasket. "I'll do my best," she said.

EACH WEEK THE PROGRAM DIRECTOR MET WITH EVERY WOMAN IN THE shelter to review her job-searching skills and to discuss her plans and strategies for finding work, and each week Cerise had to report that all the nursing homes in Santa Dorothea were overstaffed, that all the bars and restaurants said they needed experienced workers, that there were no vacancies for housekeepers at any of the motels she could reach by bus.

"What else can we find for you to do?" the director asked after a month of fruitless searching. Pushing her broken glasses higher up the bridge of her nose, she studied Cerise and said, "How about child care?"

The alarms in Cerise's head were so loud it startled her to realize the director didn't hear them, too. "I don't think—" she began, but then she stopped, afraid of what she might say next.

"You're such a natural with the children here," the director was saying. "Carmen and Tristan adore you, and I've never seen Mary act out when you're around."

"Mary's a good kid," Cerise answered with such fierce conviction that for a moment she almost forgot the danger that she was in.

"You see?" the director interrupted with her forceful smile. "Children are your genius. Have you ever had any experience working with them?"

"I—I don't know," Cerise answered, blundering in her terror. But though her whole soul screamed no, she could find no way of saying no that didn't involve either lying or saying what could not be said, so finally, because the director was waiting with a puzzled expression on her face, she added, "Not working—not for money. But I did take some classes, once."

"There!" said the director happily. "I knew it."

The following Monday, Cerise was invited to an interview at an elementary after-school care program. It was part-time and for minimum wage, but it was close enough to the shelter that she could walk to work, and as the director pointed out, if she saved all her pay, by the time her stay at the shelter was over, she would have nearly enough money to afford a room somewhere.

As she walked the wet blocks to the interview, she tried to focus her mind on that room. She wanted it so badly—a room of her own that she could fix up as she pleased, with a ceiling to protect her from the weather and walls to shelter her from other people, with a window she could look out of when she felt like it and a door she could close when she wanted to be alone with her memories of Travis.

Lately she'd discovered that she could be with Travis without having to relive the hardest times. She'd learned there was a way, like holding her breath and leaping, or crawling quickly through a tunnel toward the light, that she could skip the awful parts, could return directly to how he'd been before the fire—his sunny curls and milk-sweet breath, his firm little shoulders and his smile as bright as light on water.

It was almost as if she'd discovered the place where he still lived, as if she'd found a way to live there with him, though she had to concentrate very hard to get there, and on the streets and in the shelter it was hard to find the privacy to do that very often. As she turned down the street toward the school, she forced herself to fix her thoughts on that room.

Even so, when she reached the school playground and heard the shouts and laughter of all the children, she nearly turned around. But a woman was waiting outside the front doors, and before Cerise could run away, the woman was holding out her hand and smiling. "You must be Honey," she said as Cerise awkwardly offered her own scarred hand in return.

"I'm Ms. Martinez," she continued, and Cerise could feel the tingle of her touch lingering in her palm as Ms. Martinez led her into the school. "I'm so glad you could come this afternoon. We need someone right away."

Ushering Cerise into a room filled with picture books and blocks and tempera-splattered easels she added, "It's amazing. This program is brand-new, and already we have a waiting list. Parents are so busy. The school day just doesn't accommodate their schedules anymore."

After she'd shown Cerise around, Ms. Martinez gave her an application to fill out, and Cerise sat in a tiny chair beside a knee-high table and answered its questions as carefully as though she were taking were a test. She panicked at the first one—"Name of Applicant"—but then an answer came to her, and she wrote, "Honey Cerise Johnson."

After she answered all the questions, she looked back over the completed form and suddenly felt baffled. She had filled in every blank as accurately as the application allowed. She had written down her date of birth and her social security number, had given the street address of the shelter and the number of the message phone the residents were allowed to use there. She'd noted her nine years of employment at Woodland Manor, and the semester she'd completed at the junior college. But reading over her answers was like gazing into one of those mirrors that stretched and squashed her own reflection into a barely recognizable shape. There were no blanks on the application for that other set of facts—the secret set that said everything about who she really was.

She had a vague sense that it would be like lying or cheating not to mention those other things, and she cast an anxious glance at Ms. Martinez, who was busily pouring juice into a long row of paper cups. She hated to trouble Ms. Martinez or to take up her time, but even so she was fumbling in her mind to try to find a way to begin when a buzzer sounded so loudly, it made her drop her pen.

"School's over," Ms. Martinez announced pleasantly. "The children will be here soon."

Suddenly Cerise was desperate to leave that room before the children arrived. Wordlessly she rose and handed her application to Ms. Martinez, who scanned it, nodding. Looking up, she smiled and said, "I think you'll do just fine. I'd have you start tomorrow if I could, but I'm afraid we'll have to verify this first." She gave Cerise's application a quick tap and then tipped her wrist to check her watch. "And you'll need to get fingerprinted. If you stop by the Office of Education this afternoon, there's probably still time for them to print you today."

"I'm sorry," she added when she saw the wince of consternation on Cerise's face. "Sometimes these new rules seem a little excessive. But these days, with things the way they are—" She shrugged helplessly. "We just don't have a choice."

"I'm not—" Cerise began, but Ms. Martinez was saying, "We should have you okayed by the end of the week. Why don't you give me a call on Friday, and if you're checked out by then, you can start next Monday afternoon."

Ms. Martinez gave Cerise the address of the Office of Education, and Cerise escaped just as the first child was entering the room. She went to get fingerprinted only because it seemed easier for someone else to say she couldn't have the job than for her to have to tell Ms. Martinez that herself. But the man at the Office of Education only gave her another form to fill out and then showed her where to wash her hands and how to roll her fingers one by one across the glass plate of a machine that looked like a photocopier. Cerise gazed at the computer screen, where the swirls and lines that decorated her fingertips were magnified to a monstrous size. She knew those patterns held the irreducible truth about who she was, and yet once again, she could not see herself in them at all.

On Friday afternoon she had to ask at four different stores before she found a clerk who mistook her for a customer and allowed her to use the phone. Standing beside a display of leather purses dangling like heavy fruit from an iron rack, she held the receiver carefully in both hands and listened to Ms. Martinez say, "It was a little confusing at first, as you apparently went by your middle name for a while. But when the director at the nursing home realized who you were, he said you were the most reliable employee they'd ever had, and of course the rest of your check came back fine—not even a driving violation. We'll see you on Monday at two-forty-five."

After Ms. Martinez hung up, Cerise stood with the receiver still pressed against her ear, watching but not seeing a woman sort grimly through the purses. Finally, when the phone began to whine, she hung up and slipped out of the store.

It was strange how much the world wanted her back. It was strange that no one saw the truth of who she was. She knew there were laws she'd broken—welfare laws, at least. She'd quit her training program, had not reported her change of address or the decrease in the number of people in her assistance unit, and she felt sure she was a criminal in other, more awful ways as well. But Ms. Martinez had said her background check was fine. Ms. Martinez had said, We'll see you on Monday at two-forty-five.

At some point she was sure that the other set of facts would catch up with her, and when it did, the little life that was accreting around her would crumble back into the dust it had been all along. But until then, nothing really mattered. There were things she was supposed to do—make her cot in the morning, keep her shelf neat, leave the shelter after breakfast, go to work on Monday at two-forty-five—and she would do those things because they were what was expected of her, because it was easier to do those things than not, like water following the simplest path downhill.

IT TURNED OUT THAT THERE WAS A NEW AFTER-SCHOOL CARE PROGRAM at Lucy's school that Lucy could attend on the afternoons when Anna would be on campus, but it wasn't so easy for her to find a place for Ellen. Over the next few days, instead of planning her seminar or moving into her office or talking with Lucy about how she might make friends, Anna examined day cares.

While Eliot hosted a symposium on the regeneration needs of cryogenically storaged fresh stone fruits, Anna studied newspapers and made phone calls and raced through the wet streets of Santa Dorothea, hunting down addresses. She visited places loud as kennels, crammed with kids like packs of clamoring puppies. She looked at homes so spotless it was hard to believe that children had ever stepped inside them until she read the lists of rules posted by their front doors. She went to houses as rank as caves, their blaring TVs their only spots of light.

Finally she found a place she hoped would be all right, in an in-home day care not far from Lucy's school. Safe in Anna's arms, Ellen had peered down at the other children with interest, and she'd even giggled a little when Mrs. Chauncy danced a Big Bird puppet in front of her. But on Monday morning, when Anna dropped Ellen off for her first half-day there, Ellen did not want to leave Anna's arms.

"She'll get over it," Mrs. Chauncy said, reaching decisively for Ellen. But Ellen twisted away from her and burrowed her face against her mother's shoulder.

"I guess she's not quite ready for me to go," Anna said apologetically. She reached down to give Lucy's hand a quick squeeze of encouragement. "I wish I'd been able to spend a morning here with her before I had to start work."

"She'll never be happy about you going," said Mrs. Chauncy briskly. "It's up to you to go ahead and leave. A clean break is easier on everyone than a long good-bye." Setting her hands firmly under Ellen's armpits, she lifted Ellen out of Anna's arms.

"Uh," Ellen cried, twisting back toward her mother, her eyes wide, her face bewildered. She dove toward Anna with such force that Mrs. Chauncy had to struggle to prevent her from dropping on the floor. "You'd better go," Mrs. Chauncy said, as her face clamped shut with the effort of keeping Ellen in her arms. "Before she gets any worse."

But staring at her struggling daughter, and torn precisely in two by her need to meet her first seminar on time and her need to comfort Ellen, Anna froze.

"It's always hardest on the mothers," Mrs. Chauncy said as she edged Anna and Lucy out of the living room. Opening the front door, she added, "In five minutes she'll have forgotten all about you."

"Maaa," Ellen wailed, reaching piteously for Anna. She looked as though she knew what Anna did not yet understand, that if they parted, they would never see each other alive again.

"Good-bye," said Mrs. Chauncy, raising her voice so that she could be heard above Ellen's wails. "Have a nice day." She closed the door, leaving Anna and Lucy standing on the front porch, facing the brass knocker and listening to Ellen's disembodied screams.

"Ellie's sad," Lucy said, a little furrow of worry on her forehead.

"She'll be okay," Anna answered. "It's only for a few hours," she added to herself. She squared her shoulders and took a bolstering breath of rain-soaked air.

"Mrs. Chauncy's right," she continued as they climbed back into the car. "Ellen won't be sad for very long. In five minutes she will have forgotten all about us."

There was a silence while Lucy buckled her seat belt, and then, with a kink of puzzlement in her voice, she said, "I wouldn't want Ellie to forget about us."

"Oh, no," Anna answered as she turned on the ignition and put the car in gear. "She'll remember us when she sees us again. I meant more—like you," she fumbled, "how you can get so absorbed in what's happening in school, that for a while you forget about what goes on at home."

"I don't get so 'sorbed," Lucy answered forlornly. "I never forget."

"That's too bad," Anna said, trying to keep her voice light, "You might be happier if you could forget a little more."

"But what if I forgot to ever 'member you again?"

"You wouldn't," Anna answered, twisting around in her seat and backing out of Mrs. Chauncy's driveway. "When I came to pick you up, you'd remember me then." She hoped that Mrs. Chauncy was being patient with Ellen, hoped she wouldn't leave Ellen in her crib to cry it out. Anne remembered Ellen's dark newborn body dangling between the doctor's hands, and for an unhinged moment she imagined Mrs. Chauncy shaking Ellen or punching her or smothering her with a pillow.

"But what if something happened," Lucy was saying, "and you never came?"

"Nothing like that will ever happen," Anna answered, holding tight to the steering wheel and resisting the impulse to return to Mrs. Chauncy's and beat down her front door.

"It could," Lucy insisted. "You could die."

"I won't die," said Anna.

"How do you know?"

"I just do. I'll always come back to get you," Anna claimed, though even as she spoke she felt a twinge of superstition, for what if she had a heart attack or died in a freeway pileup that very day? What if she had just made the one promise she couldn't keep?

And then it all became so complex. It was impossible to guess which was worse, pretending to Lucy that their safety could be assured, or admitting that no future was certain, just as it was impossible to know whether being at Mrs. Chauncy's would, as Sally promised, make Ellen more resilient or whether, as Anna sometimes feared, it would crush some deep part of Ellen's emerging heart.

As she pulled onto the street and drove off through the dreary morning, Anna thought of how fervently she loved her daughters, how she would do anything for them, if only she could know what the right thing was. She remembered the heroic deeds other mothers had performed for their children. She thought about the Russian woman who, trapped with her son in the rubble of an earthquake, had kept him alive by having him suck blood from the cuts she gouged into her fingertips. She thought of the women in Vietnam who used their own bodies to shield their children from the soldiers' bullets, and of the Eskimo mother who, in the darkest part of winter, made her starving children promise to eat her frozen body and then slipped out of the igloo to lie down in the snow. Anna had no doubt that she, too, would give her life for her daughters as easily as a drifting snowflake, as simply as a petal falling from a rose. In extremity she would know exactly what to do and she wouldn't hesitate to do the hardest thing. But there were times when dying seemed so simple, so clear and unequivocal compared to what was required of an ordinary mother, day after day.

Engrossed in her own grim thoughts, Anna drove on through the thickening traffic toward Lucy's school, and it wasn't until she was merging with the race of cars on the freeway that Lucy broke the silence. "Are day cares like nightmares?" she asked from the backseat.

"What do you mean?" Anna said, tossing an anxious glance over her shoulder and pressing the accelerator toward the floor.

"Are day cares the cares you worry about all day?"

ON MONDAY AFTERNOON, WHEN SHE ENTERED THE BUILDING AND walked down the echoing corridor toward the after-school care room, Cerise felt as strange as her hands still sometimes felt, both anesthetized and excruciatingly raw. She stood for a long time outside the open door, listening to the clamor and laughter that spilled into the hall, and when she finally forced herself to walk into that roomful of kids, it hurt as though she were being skinned alive.

There were times that first day when she was sure she could not endure being in the proximity of so many kids. Twice she had to run to the girls' bathroom, where she hid in one of the cubicles beside a knee-high toilet, shuddering and clutching her mouth shut with both shiny hands until her spike of anguish finally passed and she could return to work.

It was after six by the time the last child left.

"They wear you out, don't they?" Ms. Martinez said kindly as Cerise began to sponge the art table. "Especially at first. It was a busy day."

"I guess," Cerise said, smearing the paint into a muddy rainbow and then wiping the table clean.

"I must say the kids all seemed to like you. I can't get Lucas and DeLong to pick up that well for me, and I've never seen Kaylesha take to anyone so fast."

"They were nice," Cerise said, bending over her sponge, trying to keep the grief out of her voice.

Despite the flicker of pleasure she'd felt at Ms. Martinez's words, by the time she said good-bye and left the room, she was certain she could never go back again. Outside it was night, and raining. Blades and shards of light cast by streetlights and house lights and passing cars glinted on the wet black pavement, and the rain came down like hard, impartial tears.

There was a little park a few blocks from the school. In the dark and in the rain, it was empty and foreboding, as gloomy as a cemetery with its tangle of trees and its looming, rain-smeared swings. Stumbling past it, Cerise couldn't keep herself from thinking of all the children who would never again play there, couldn't keep from hearing the emptiness of their silenced voices echoing in the rain.

That night she was too tired even to try to summon her memories of

Travis to console her. Instead, she lay on her cot listening to the drumming of the rain and trying to plan a way to escape the life that was closing in around her. All night, as she skimmed the surface of her sleep, she imagined leaving, just walking off, imagined finding a way to vanish altogether into the web of the world, though when she woke enough to try to plan where she might go, her thoughts smeared like tempera colors beneath a sponge.

By the time morning arrived and the moans and yawns of the other women rose around her, she was thinking of the spray of freckles across Lucas's soft nose, was remembering Cara's knock-knock jokes and wondering whether Jose's puppy had come back home. All day those children haunted her. At noon, as she sat in the soup kitchen, eating her steamed hot dog and limp potato salad and listening to Barbara's irreverent patter, she thought of Kaylesha's timid smile, remembered how Lucy had leaned against her shoulder as she watched Cerise draw a horse. She wondered if Brianna's cold was getting any better, and by two-forty-five that afternoon, her craving to be near those kids drew her back just one more time.

THE FIRST TIME ANNA SAW A PHOTOGRAPH THAT MOVED HER, SHE MUST have been eight or ten, and she was sitting in the doctor's office, waiting for her turn to go in and get a shot. She understood that shots were good for her, knew she was expected to be a big girl and be brave. She realized that when it was over, the nurse would let her choose a sucker wrapped in cellophane and impaled on a white loop of string, but still dread filled her stomach like gelatinous oatmeal. Sitting beside her mother in the doctor's waiting room, it was all that she could do to keep from crying.

Her mother was reading *Time* and another child had the *Highlights*, so Anna had picked some other magazine at random from the rack. She was riffling through the pages, staring sightlessly at the words and ads and trying not to think of the needle going in, when suddenly she came to a picture that made her stop and stare. It was of a bridge nearly hidden in mist with a few skeletal trees rising up behind it. It wasn't what she would have thought of as an exciting picture, and yet somehow it pulled her in, made her eyes keep working for longer than she'd thought possible to look at a single picture.

And when she finally turned the page, there was another photograph by the same photographer—a boy in short pants walking down a street—and after that one was another, so many pictures in a row that she was still busy looking when her mother nudged her and told her it was time to see the doctor.

Much later, thinking back, she was almost certain that it was Cartier-Bresson's work she'd found that day, that the magazine she had chosen was *Popular Photography*, or maybe *Look* or *Life*. But at the time those names meant nothing to her. All that mattered was that gazing at those photographs was like falling into a quietness, as if the whole room were suddenly filled with the heightened silence of a new-fallen snow.

It reminded her of the message posted at railroad crossings—*Stop. Look. Listen*—only instead of a command, this was an invitation, and behind that invitation was another, so that she kept looking and looking, and each moment she looked, she discovered something more. In some mysterious way, sitting beside her mother and gazing at the rumpled pages, she'd felt as though she were more in the room than she had been before, back when she'd been merely filled with dread.

The swipe of alcohol still stung. It still hurt when the nurse jabbed the needle into the thin flesh of her bicep, and her arm still ached all afternoon. But those hurts were smaller than she'd feared. Afterward she surprised herself by choosing lime, and the sucker tasted even sweeter than she'd expected. Riding home, chewing on the green-stained sucker strings and gazing out the window at the city she'd seen all her life, she realized she was noticing everything as if it were brand-new—a cat crouched under a pickup, a fence entwined with a ragged strand of ivy, a woman in a belted coat standing at a bus stop—each thing vivid and unique and beautiful in a way she'd never seen before.

For years, her whole life had been richer and more real because of the time she spent gazing at photographs, the time she spent looking through a viewfinder or studying the upside-down image on the ground glass of her field camera. That had always been what mattered most—what mattered infinitely more than shows and sales and awards—the way her work kept her awake, and open to the world.

She had thought that her job at the university would be the first step in reclaiming all of that. "This will not only help pay the bills—it will invigorate your art," Eliot had exclaimed when she'd called him at work to tell him about Martin Lee's offer. But after her first few weeks on campus, she began to wonder if they hadn't both been mistaken.

Her students wearied and annoyed her, with their pink cheeks and pierced eyebrows, with their ardent faith in art. It's only a trick of light, she wanted to tell them, it's just another hoax. A photograph is only a residue, a sloughed-off skin. It doesn't change a thing. But instead she reviewed depth of field and discussed principles of composition, while all her words felt like ashes in her mouth.

Rather than encouraging her, the kindness of her colleagues made her feel like a fraud. She cringed when they congratulated her on her photographs and asked what she was doing now. Art is only froth, she wanted to answer. There's a glut of it already in this world. But instead she choked out an answer about the baby and the move and how busy she'd been, and followed it with a lie about how she couldn't wait to get her camera out again.

On Friday night of the second week, when she finally sat down to dinner with her family, Anna was so exhausted her skin ached. Ellen's nose was running ominously, Lucy's mood was manic and brittle, and the weekend loomed ahead like an obstacle course that somehow had to be run by Monday morning.

Only Eliot seemed unfazed by the demands of their new schedule.

"So," he said, as he set a piece of halibut on Lucy's plate and began to work through it with his fork. "How's it feel, to be back at work?"

"Work, lurk, murk," Lucy said, watching her father's progress with her fish. "Daddy, what's murk?"

"It's when things are dark or hard to see," Eliot answered, casting a glance at Anna, waiting for her response.

Anna sighed, "I guess it's harder than I expected."

"It's all still really new," Eliot sympathized, pulling a bone from Lucy's fish and placing it on the edge of his own plate.

"It's more than that," Anna answered, serving him some salad.

"Is someone giving you trouble?" Eliot asked swiftly.

"No, not at all. Everyone's been really great." Anna put salad on her own plate, stared down at the glistening lettuce, the flecks of grated carrot, the nearly invisible grit of salt.

"Then what?" Eliot persisted, adding another bone to his pile.

Struggling to keep her voice light, Anna answered, "I keep remembering a teacher I had back in graduate school."

"Tool, rule, fool," interrupted Lucy, grabbing her milk and narrowly missing knocking Anna's wineglass on the floor.

"Quiet, Pine Nut," Eliot said, setting Lucy's plate down in front of her. "It's your mommy's turn to talk."

Anna spooned a dab of rice cereal expertly into Ellen's open mouth and said, "He was a good photographer, but he was a rotten teacher."

"Teacher, preacher, creature," Lucy sang, jabbing her fork in the air while Ellen watched in moon-eyed adoration.

"Lucy," Eliot said. "Eat your dinner."

"Anyway," Anna said, tucking another spoonful of cereal into Ellen's open mouth and then deftly scraping the residue from her plush cheeks, "every semester at the first class meeting this guy told all his students that the best thing they could do for the world was to never make another photograph. He said no one should be a photographer if they could possibly help it, and that he would give an automatic A to anyone who would quit the class in the next twenty-four hours. After that, they were going to have to work like dogs just to get a C.

"At the time," Anna sighed, staring at her food, "I thought he was a jerk."

"He was a jerk," Eliot answered.

Anna said, "I know. But I have to admit that part of me's been wondering if he weren't on to something, too."

"Seriously?" asked Eliot.

"Maybe," Anna answered, poking at the white flesh of the fish on her plate. "I don't know."

"Foe," sang Lucy gleefully. "Low, woe."

"I don't know," Anna repeated raggedly. "Sometimes I think I'm right, and sometimes I think there's just something wrong with me, like I've forgotten something important that I used to know by heart."

"Heart," said Lucy under her breath, "art . . . fart." She giggled and cast a surreptitious glance toward her parents. But her father was looking at her mother, and her mother was looking out the window at the darkening sky.

It became a little easier, in time. To the children at afterschool care Cerise was like any other adult, a creature so remote and complete it was unthinkable she might have troubles as keen as theirs. But once they learned that she was a tireless jump-rope turner, that she allowed seconds at snack time, and that she didn't make the mistake of always believing the first one who reported a squabble, they accepted her as nearly one of them.

When Lucas told Amanda that the tooth fairy was just your parents, it was Cerise Amanda sought to set things straight, and when Delano fell in the gym and broke his arm, Cerise was the person he ran to first, thrusting himself blindly past the anxious cluster of kids and teachers and pushing his hot, wet face into her solar plexus, trusting her to keep him safe and stop his tears.

During the hours she spent among those children, she could almost share their sense of her, and she was relieved to be reduced to nothing but Honey, pouring juice or cutting construction paper or mixing paint. Sometimes, as she cared for that roomful of other people's kids, she felt almost accustomed to her own children being gone, though at other times she was haunted by the feeling that Travis was still back at the Happy Factory, still waiting impatiently for her to get off work.

Every evening, when the parents arrived to rush their children home, she wanted to stop them, to tell them how utterly precious their kids were and warn them that every minute that passed was one minute closer to the end. Instead, she sorted jackets and helped with sleeves and buttons, found backpacks and library books and homework pages, helped to hurry the children off with their harried moms and dads.

So a little life had begun to accrete around her, like a shell that both protected and shaped the soft animal that lived inside. No one ever asked about her, where she lived or who she loved or what she did when she was not at work, and as time went on, it began to matter more and more that no one ever did. She came to fear those questions not only because of what they would expose, but also because of how the truth about who she was would destroy the haven she'd almost begun to prize.

"Can I give you a ride home?" Ms. Martinez asked one evening after work as they were walking together down the hall. "It's pretty wet out there."

"Oh, no," Cerise said, though she added hurriedly, "I mean, I like to walk."

"In the rain?" Ms. Martinez asked, and Cerise cringed, afraid her secret would unravel like one of Barbara's blankets the moment someone yanked the first stitch.

Back at the shelter every evening, she ate her supper with the other women, and afterward, while the mothers put their little ones to bed and tried to get their older children to do their homeroom, Cerise sat with the childless women in the TV room and let the TV's flicker and murmur soothe her tired brain.

"Notice how there's never any TVs on TV?" Barbara observed while the rest of the women gazed at the screen and scowled at her interruption. Ignoring their irritation, she went on, "Away back long ago, when the government wanted to kill people, they gave 'em blankets laced with smallpox germs. Now all they have to do is just give us this crap-in-a-box instead. Exterminates us just as fast, but keeps us alive to buy shit, too."

Occasionally, beneath the poster of Andrea that hung on the back wall of the room, some of the women would begin to talk about their lives, sorting and re-sorting them as though their pasts were the bags that held their final possessions, rearranging and repacking their troubles until finally they had reduced them to a few words that they could carry with them wherever they went. *My breakdown,* someone would say. Or, *my surgery. Before the car wreck,* another woman would answer, or *After my relapse. When I got laid off. After my old man left. Since I've been clean.*

Sometimes the women cried, and the tears that slid down their tired cheeks and hung from their quivering chins seemed so tiny compared to the oceans of their suffering. Cerise found a kind of comfort in their stories and tears—not because she liked to see more pain, but because suffering was life's true condition. It made sense that people would suffer, made sense that nothing would stay right for very long. Watching the other women gather round the weeping one to pat her back and wipe her little tears away, Cerise could feel almost kin to the crying woman, almost kin to the women who comforted her.

The TV was turned off at ten, and then the women wandered off to bed. All the cots in the sleeping hall had long since been staked out like pieces of real estate—the ones closest to the bathroom or in the darkest corners valued more than the ones near the door or in the center of the room. Cerise's cot was along the back wall between Barbara's and Maria's, and each night it was an exquisite relief to return to it, to lie beneath a roof while the rain came down outside, to sleep on her own bed among other sleeping humans, beneath a blanket that had begun to smell like her.

Lying on her cot, listening to the bluster of the rain and the murmur of the women settling into their sleep, listening to Barbara's mumbled curses and Maria's whispered prayers, Cerise would turn her thoughts to Travis, would try to get her memories of him to come alive inside her mind. Those nights when she managed to find him in that private netherworld between the living and the dead, he was so vivid, so present, and so near that she could almost feel the warm press of his arms around her neck, could almost smell the yeasty scent of him, and she would lie for long minutes, smiling mindlessly up into the darkness while her pillow grew wet with unheeded tears.

Sometimes she couldn't help but think of Melody, too—the young, true Melody whom she would never see again. Listening to the murmurs of the children as they tossed in their sleep, Cerise would remember Melody, worming her way between the sheets to snuggle. Thinking back to how she'd watched the kids coloring that afternoon, she would remember Melody, chanting the names of the crayons like a charm. But each time she began to relax into those memories, another memory would shoulder its way into her thoughts—the girl she'd seen in Santa Dorothea, looking straight through Cerise, and then laughing as she turned away.

Only in Cerise's dreams did the other, older Melody occasionally appear. Sometimes the teardrop on Melody's cheek had grown to cover her entire face, so that whole continents and oceans stretched and collapsed when she spoke. Other times a huge dream-Melody kept trying to scrabble her way back onto Cerise's lap. And once Cerise dreamed she was watching Melody pile up great stacks of garbage on an empty plain. "God doesn't make trash," Melody explained, looking so deep inside

Cerise's eyes it seemed she was peering into her skull. "That's why we need a fire, to get rid of all the trash that God didn't make."

Occasionally, very late at night when everyone else had finally settled into sleep, Cerise thought she caught the sound of a telephone ringing from a long way off, ringing and ringing, ringing wearily and unrelentingly, insisting that someone somewhere should answer its call. But before she had a chance to consider what that ringing phone might mean, she came home from work one evening to find Barbara in the sleeping hall, stuffing her clothes and yarns into plastic grocery bags.

"What are you doing?" Cerise cried. "It's almost time to eat."

"It's been a fine holiday," her friend muttered. "But it's over now. The lady says I gotta look for work or leave. And what the fuck kinda work they think I'm gonna do, with my heart and my legs and my crazy spells?" Her eyes flicked impatiently around the sleeping hall, adamantly refusing to meet Cerise's gaze.

"You can crochet," Cerise offered, dropping to her hands and knees to ferret out the balls of yarn that had rolled beneath Barbara's cot. "Or teach people how."

"Know anyone wants to pay a living wage for crocheting?" Barbara asked, snatching the tangled yarns from Cerise's hands. "Not in this country, let me tell you, not since Jesus baked the cake."

"You can comfort people," Cerise said, but Barbara only scowled.

"No money in comfort," she said. She jammed the narrow strip of the blanket she'd just begun on top of the jumbled yarns.

"I never had no babies," she said fiercely, looking askance at a spot beyond Cerise's shoulder. "But I once was someone's child."

Her crochet hook clattered to the floor, and Cerise asked in panic, "Where will you go?"

"Don't like to tell people my address. I'll be fine. You too," Barbara added, her eyes suddenly drilling into Cerise's, her voice a command.

But a moment later her gaze wavered and slid off Cerise's face. "I'll see you," she said, her voice drifting.

"When?" Cerise persisted.

"At lunch," she answered, heaving up her bags and shuffling from the room. "Sometime. Maybe."

But she wasn't at the soup kitchen that noon or the next, and on Monday when she finally appeared, her clothes were torn and dirty, and her hair was clumped in knots at the back of her head. At the sight of her, standing uncertainly in the doorway while the daylight spilled in around her, Cerise jumped up from her meal. She ran to help Barbara with her bags and to carry her tray through the crowd while Barbara tagged dully behind. When they reached the table where Cerise had been sitting, Cerise dropped one of the bags so that it tipped and hanks and twists of yarn rolled across the floor. Angrily Barbara began to scoop them up, tried to stuff the whole mess back into her bag.

"It'll tangle," Cerise said timidly, "like that." But when she reached to help, Barbara barked, "You let my yarns alone."

"What?"

"Bad as the rest a them," Barbara muttered. "Only you got no shame. At least the others wait till dark."

"For what?" Cerise asked.

"Sneak up on me at night and try to mess with my bag. Sneak in while I'm trying to sleep. Make it so now I can't even rest no more, I got to stay awake to protect my stuff. Won't let my yarns alone, either—tangle 'em, tie 'em up in mean knots. And now they want to paint my skin."

"Paint your skin?" Cerise asked, perplexed and horrified.

"Got an ink that won't come off. They want to paint pictures, poison pictures, want to sneak up and cover me with beautiful bright killer pictures and then watch and see how long I last, like human life to them is just some fucking experiment."

"Who does?" Cerise persisted.

Barbara's eyes narrowed. "You all can go practice your evil arts somewhere else. Won't let you fuck with me."

The whole world felt slippery and tilted, like a ride in the amusement park when the wildest part was over, but even as the ride was slowing down, it seemed the world itself had begun to reel and lurch, spinning on centerless and beyond control. Cerise reached out for Barbara's arm to steady herself, but Barbara shrugged her hand off viciously.

"Don't you come on to me," she hissed. "You go find someone else to do your slut-work with." Abandoning her untouched food, she pushed herself from the table, gathered her broken bags, and struggled off, leaving Cerise aching with worry and helplessness.

FROM HER PLACE IN THE BACKSEAT, LUCY SAID, "THERE'S A NICE TEACHER at after-school care."

"That's good," Anna answered over her shoulder as she pulled out of the school parking lot onto the wet street. "What's her name?"

"It's a sweet name," Lucy said absently. "I forget."

"Do you like her?"

"She's a good drawer."

"A good drawer?"

"She draws good horses," Lucy said, gazing out the window at the rain.

"That's nice," Anna answered, accelerating to enter the freeway. For a moment, as she navigated the curving overpass, she caught a glimpse of the misty, gray-green hills that ringed the city. Last weekend, during a break between storms, she'd forced herself to return to those hills and make a few exposures of the acres of staked grapes, and a few more of the orchard of dead trees she'd wept in when she heard the news about Andrea's nightgown. In the orchard she'd managed to catch that magic hour between afternoon and evening when the light was bold and smooth and the broken trees seemed to glisten in the rain-scrubbed air. But hunched beneath her dark cloth with her finger poised on the shutter release while she watched for the perfect convergence of light and cloud and shadow, she'd realized none of the satisfaction she would once have taken in that moment, had felt none of the pleasure that had once seemed kin to prayer.

"Did you get some good shots?" Lucy had asked eagerly when she got home.

"I don't know," Anna had answered. "We'll see," she'd added, sighing wearily.

"Aren't you happy?" Lucy had asked, studying her mother with perplexed concern. "Daddy said you would be happy if you 'sposed some film."

"Things aren't always that simple," Anna had answered, though she'd instantly hated herself for the way the shine fell from Lucy's face.

Now, as she swerved onto the downtown exit off the freeway, she wondered when she'd ever get a chance to develop those negatives, though at the same time she cringed to think how disappointing they would probably be when she did.

"Why are we here?" Lucy asked in her clear, sweet voice.

"Here, in California?" Anna asked. "Or here, alive?"

"Here, on this street," Lucy answered. "This isn't the way to home."

"Oh," Anna answered, abandoning the half-gathered phrases she would have used to try to explain the move or their existence. "Ellen's got a doctor's appointment."

The week after Ellen started going to Mrs. Chauncy's, she'd got a cold that glazed her cheeks with mucus and dulled her eyes, and last night she'd developed a cough that kept her awake until almost dawn. Today, along with her exhaustion, Anna was plagued by the thought that she'd made a mistake to put Ellen in day care. But what else could I have done? she wondered, perilously near tears.

Ahead a traffic signal changed, the clean red of it glowing through the rain like a color from another planet. When Anna stepped on her brake pedal, she could hear water hiss from the slowing tires. The lines of traffic came to a stop. In the steamy window of the café they were paused in front of, Anna noticed Andrea's faded photograph. Neither

Andrea nor her abductor had been found, although Andrea's rain-smeared picture still haunted the city, lingering on windows, walls, and poles. By now her absence had come to seem as inescapable and oppressive as the rain. It was another sad fact the whole city had gotten used to, another common sorrow to be accommodated and ignored.

The stoplight was a long one. Anna checked her watch and tried to calculate how much time it would still take to reach the doctor's office, park, and get everyone out of the car. When she realized they would be lucky if they made it to the appointment on time, a cap of tension clenched around her skull.

The streetlight suspended in the gray air above the intersection changed from red to emerald green, and the lines of traffic began to edge forward. As she pulled the car through the wet intersection, Anna commenced the old catechism. "How was school today?"

"Okay," came Lucy's voice from behind her. When Anna glanced in the rearview mirror, she could see dark crescents beneath Lucy's eyes, twin bruises that made her seem like someone else's child. Lucy still wasn't sleeping well. Last night she had woken shrieking from yet another nightmare, and today she seemed distant and forlorn. They had tried everything they could think of to reassure Lucy or to distract her. They'd put extra locks on the windows, had bought her a special doll and another night-light and a tape of bedtime meditations for children. They had been loving and soothing and firm, and still Lucy wept as bedtime approached, still she woke up screaming in the night.

Imbuing her voice with cheer, Anna asked, "What did you do in school?"

"Nothing," Lucy answered wanly. "Things."

"Things like what?" Anna persisted.

"Cheetahs."

"Cheetahs," Anna echoed brightly, maneuvering past a car stalled in the lane in front of her. "Cheetahs are the fastest animals on earth, aren't they?"

"They go faster than a car," Lucy said.

"Wow."

"There aren't lots left," Lucy said flatly. "They'll probly get extinct."

"I hope that doesn't happen," Anna said. "They are such beautiful animals."

"Ms. Ashton asked us to describe them—that means say how they look," Lucy said, rousing for a moment from her lethargy. "And I said they had tear streaks down their cheeks."

"Oh, Lucy. What a lovely description."

"The other kids laughed," Lucy said.

"They laughed?"

"Some of them."

Outrage and anguish battled in Anna's chest. "They shouldn't have," she said fiercely. "It was rude and wrong of them to laugh. Even if someone gave a bad description, nobody should laugh. But your description was beautiful."

But Lucy only gave a little shrug. "It doesn't matter," she said, looking out the window at the rain.

THEN CAME THE WET FRIDAY IN MID-FEBRUARY WHEN CERISE ARRIVED at work to find that only half a dozen kids were signed up for child care that afternoon.

"All girls, too," Ms. Martinez said, studying the schedule. "I don't think we both need to be here. If it's all right with you, I'll go ahead and leave. There're cornmeal muffins and apple slices for snack."

Cerise cringed at the thought of being the person in charge if the principal stopped by or the phone rang. But she said okay because that was what Ms. Martinez was waiting to hear. Alone in the room, she sliced apples and set out tubs of crayons while she waited for the bell to ring and end the school day, disgorging the children from their classrooms and sending six of them to her. She read their names on the sign-up sheet—Shannon, Kaylesha, Teresa, Lucy, Brianna, Dolores.

The bell rang, but no girls arrived. Puzzled, Cerise poured juice and waited, anticipating the swirl of secrets and burst of giggles that would accompany them into the room. But when they finally appeared, they came in a silent little clutch, and their faces were flat and small.

Cerise met them at the door. "Ms. Martinez left early today," she said shyly. "So I guess it's just me this afternoon."

Nobody spoke. For a moment Cerise thought they were unhappy to be left with her, but then she saw Kaylesha's trembling chin, and she asked, "Is something wrong?"

Shannon burst into tears.

"They found Andrea," Brianna said.

Cerise looked at the girls' stricken faces, and she wanted to swerve out of the way of the world.

"They didn't really find her . . . ," said Dolores slowly, as though the words she had to say would not fit through her mouth.

"They found her pieces," Shannon whispered.

In that moment Cerise realized she had known from the beginning that Andrea would not be found alive, but still she felt a spasm of horror and disbelief. A throb of thought like an extra heartbeat said, *Melody.* But she tried to ignore it. Looking down at the cluster of bent heads, she heard their sobs and wished Ms. Martinez would return, wished a teacher would come by and hear the crying and rescue her. She wished she'd never left the oleanders, wished she were there right now, huddled in the rain. It was better to live on the streets, safer to keep to places where the worst news would never reach her, to limit her life to the unavoidable work of staying dry, finding food and going unnoticed.

She headed blindly toward the door. At least she thought that she was moving, thought she was pushing her way through the group of girls, but she must have tripped, for suddenly she was kneeling among them. Her arms went out—for balance?—and then she was drawing the whole group toward her, holding her hands as wide as she could reach and dragging them all into the safety of a circle.

There were probably some words, she thought, that she was supposed to say in a situation like this, some way of explaining the awfulness away. But if there were, she could not remember them. She looked at the girls' bowed heads, the black and brown and blond hair tangled from their day at school, and a memory came to her of the hours she'd spent fixing Melody's hair, how content the two of them had been with that as their sole task, and how, once the first mean tangles were out, Melody would grow placid as a petted cat, dreamy beneath the stroking of the brush.

She asked, "Anyone got a hairbrush?"

Several of the weeping girls looked up in surprise.

"I thought," she offered shyly, "that if we had some brushes, we could brush each other's hair."

No one asked why. No one laughed or scoffed or said Cerise was crazy. Instead, the girls all gave themselves up to the little relief of busyness. When enough hairbrushes had been collected, Cerise arranged the girls in a line on the storytime carpet, with herself at the back, behind the dark-haired first-grader named Lucy.

Lucy's back was stiff and tiny, her shoulders sharp and hard with grief. At first Cerise barely skimmed her brush across Lucy's head and down the brief length of her hair, making her strokes gentle as breaths. Lucy, feeling Cerise's solicitude, copied it, brushing Kaylesha's hair with equal concern, and Kaylesha brushed the hair of the girl in front of her in the same way, until they had passed Cerise's care all the way to Brianna in the front, until their strokes were a matched rhythm and their hair was smooth and loose and beginning to crackle with the energy their brushing made.

For a while their work was punctuated by an occasional sob or hiccup, or by someone stopping to wipe her tears or blow her nose on a tissue from the box Cerise had taken from Ms. Martinez's desk, but gradually a calm came into the room, a sense of peace, and even, somehow, of gratitude.

Then Brianna said she wanted to brush someone's hair, too, and Teresa suggested that she could brush Cerise's. Dolores found another hairbrush in her backpack, and they curved their line into a circle. When Brianna eased the rubber band from Cerise's hair and raised her brush to the crown of her head, Cerise winced, afraid the scent of smoke would be released and poison the room. But then she felt the tender prickle of the brush, felt the many gentle pulls of individual hairs unknotting. She could feel Brianna's breath on the back of her neck, could feel the soft hand Brianna ran down her hair after each brush-stroke, and she realized that in all her years of brushing Melody's hair, Melody had never once brushed hers.

BY LATE AFTERNOON, WHEN ANNA WAS FINALLY ABLE TO LEAVE THE campus, the news of Andrea's death was as ubiquitous as her rain-torn poster, and Anna was certain that Lucy must have learned about it in school.

Anna had planned to pick up Ellen at Mrs. Chauncy's before she collected Lucy from after-school care. Yesterday the doctor had given Ellen yet another antibiotic to try, and all afternoon Anna had felt a lit-tle grit of worry, wondering if it was working, hoping it wasn't causing any side effects, chafing to be reunited with her baby. But as soon as she heard about Andrea, Anna knew she needed to get to Lucy first.

Driving through the wet streets on her way to the school, she tried to plan what she would say to ease the horror for Lucy. But it seemed impossible that there were any words that could make things right. As she pulled into the school parking lot, she was reduced to hoping that at least Lucy had been spared the worst details.

The school, when she entered it, seemed oddly normal, the long halls quiet and empty except for the custodian and a passing teacher. In the after-school-care room Lucy packed up her things and pulled on her rain jacket and boots and said good-bye to the teacher and the other girls so mildly that Anna thought it possible that somehow the news hadn't yet reached her, after all. At first she felt a sneaky relief, but as Lucy trailed out to the car and stood quietly by while she unlocked the doors, Anna had to admit to herself that she could not shelter Lucy forever. Already, even in the rain, candles and wreaths and teddy bears were beginning to collect on makeshift shrines around the city.

Anna started the car and pulled out of the parking lot. Glancing in the rearview mirror, she saw Lucy looking out the window at the wet street, her face still, her eyes big and dark and heartrendingly beautiful, and she felt a pang of remorse that all of their most significant conversations seemed to happen in the car—Anna in a hurry, maneuvering through traffic, and Lucy buckled in the back.

She knew that if they didn't talk then, they would not be alone again until Lucy's bedtime, but even so, she drove almost a dozen blocks before she made herself say, "I heard some bad news today." Her voice sounded both too cheerful and too careful, and she winced and shot another look at the rearview mirror.

In the back seat Lucy nodded solemnly. "About Andrea," she answered.

"You know?" asked Anna, more sharply than she'd intended.

Lucy nodded again, and for a moment their eyes met in the mirror. From that angle and in that light, Lucy's gaze looked old and calm.

"Who told you?" Anna asked, stopping at an intersection and watching for a break in the traffic so she could turn left.

"The big kids on the playground, after school."

Anna said, "It's very sad." It was rush hour, and the traffic was thick and steady. Each car that passed in front of them splashed a curtain of water across the windshield.

Lucy was saying, "I know. We wish it hadn't happened."

"Me, too," Anna said, as the cars streamed by. "Who's 'we'?"

"Me and the other girls at after school. And the new teacher."

"The new teacher?"

"Uh-huh. I said about her already."

"Maybe so. That's right. What's her name?"

"Honey."

There was a break in the traffic just large enough to scoot through, but Anna hesitated for half a second too long. "So the new teacher—Honey—talked with you about Andrea?"

"No."

"What did she say?"

"Nothing."

"She didn't say anything?" Anna turned around in her seat to watch Lucy shake her head.

"She had us brush our hair," Lucy said.

"She had you brush your hair?" Anna asked perplexedly.

"We all brushed someone else's."

"You brushed each other's hair?" Anna heard a honk, and shot a glance at the mirror to see a Lexus waiting impatiently behind her.

"We sat in a circle," Lucy explained.

"That's what you did about Andrea?"

"Yeah."

"Oh," said Anna. "Well, how do you feel?"

Lucy shrugged, "I'm sad for Andrea."

"Me, too," Anna said. "And for her parents." At last she saw an opening in the traffic.

"Mommy?" Lucy said beseechingly.

"What, Lu?" Anna answered, stepping on the accelerator and girding herself to meet the next onslaught of Lucy's fears.

"Can Kaylesha come over to our house to play with me?"

FRIDAY NIGHT THE RAIN QUIT AND THE SKY CLEARED, AND ON SATURDAY morning when the women left the shelter, they drifted out onto the drying sidewalks and across the steaming lawns as though they were on vacation.

It seemed astonishing to inhabit a world so bright and warm, though to Cerise there was something wrong about it, too, for there to be such voluptuous weather now that Andrea was truly gone. Andrea's faded posters still reigned in every window and on every wall, though many of them were now decorated with ribbons or wreaths, and piles of mementos had begun to collect beneath them.

Each time Cerise came across another of those shrines, she stopped to study it. Gazing at the flowers and letters and handwritten poems, she couldn't keep from comparing Andrea's parents' situation to her own, couldn't help but think of how Andrea's parents had had their daughter for twelve whole years before they lost her, of how they still owned photographs of their girl, how they possessed her clothes and toys and art projects even now.

At noon the dim hall of the soup kitchen seemed to echo with Andrea's name, and as Cerise carried her tray to an empty corner table, she almost envied Andrea's parents' luck, because the whole city was in mourning for their child. She had finished her tuna casserole when she thought she caught the sound of Barbara's cackle. With a sudden spurt of hope, she raised her head and scanned the hall, and when her first quick look was unsuccessful, she began to study the diners one by one, her eyes traveling up and down the length of every table. In the end, she had to accept that Barbara was not there, but the sight of all those heads—black and brown and blond—bent above their food made her think of the girls at after-school care the day before.

Outside again on the shining streets, snippets of that afternoon kept returning to her mind. She remembered the shock on the girls' faces when they'd come into the room, how even Kaylesha's complexion had looked pale. She remembered the horror with which Shannon had whispered the awful news, remembered how stiffly Lucy had stood beside her, as if a single word would shatter her.

Resting on a bench at the edge of the park, she felt the warm press of sunshine on her head, and her scalp remembered the gentle prickle of

Brianna's brush, remembered the little solace she'd found in that sensation. She thought of how willingly the girls had done what she suggested and with what tenderness they'd stroked each other's hair, and she knew the tiniest shine of pride. She remembered how smoothly her own hair had lain across her shoulders when Brianna had finished brushing it. She remembered the clean, smokeless scent of it, fresh as a city after rain.

When the light began to thicken and she could no longer feel the warmth of the sun against her skin, she turned her steps back to the shelter. Walking through the fragrant evening, she passed another memorial to Andrea and paused to study the jumble of flowers and stuffed animals that strangers had left there.

One of the teddy bears had toppled over onto its face, and she knelt on the sidewalk to prop it back up and to rearrange the cellophane cones of flowers in a less haphazard way. She wished the city shared her anguish about Travis, wished that even one person had left a teddy bear or a rose for him. She wished she had a single snapshot of her son, or that she could have had just one more hour with him before the fire. But gazing down at the browning petals and wilting stems of the bunch of daisies she held in her hand, it occurred to her that compared to Andrea's parents, maybe she'd been lucky, after all.

Because at least she'd been near Travis when he died.

DESPITE THE WONDERFUL WEATHER, ANNA SPENT THE WEEKEND INDOORS, in hopes that staying inside would help cure Ellen's chest infection. The new antibiotic seemed to be working its magic, though it gave Ellen diarrhea, and the diarrhea caused a wicked diaper rash, and between Ellen's rash and her cough and the tooth she was working on, Anna was kept busy all weekend simply trying to prevent Ellen's whimpers from evolving into screams.

But despite her preoccupation with Ellen, she couldn't help but marvel at how happy Lucy seemed, so easygoing and unworried it was still hard to believe she'd heard the news about Andrea. By Monday morning Ellen's cough was gone, her tooth had finally erupted, and her rash was so much improved that Anna was able to promise Lucy that if the weather held they could stop by the park on their way home from school.

That afternoon Anna could hear the noise pulsing from the after-school program as soon as she entered the building. When she reached the doorway of the room, she paused, trying to identify Lucy before she plunged into the mob of kids. It was Ellen, perched like a chimp on Anna's hip, who spotted Lucy first, sitting at a low table strewn with crayons and colored paper and talking animatedly to the woman squatting next to her. At the sight of her sister Ellen squealed with pleasure, and at the sound of Ellen's voice, both Lucy and the woman looked up.

"Hi, Mommy," Lucy called, and added proudly as Anna drew near, "This is Honey."

The woman met Anna's eyes and nodded, although her face was devoid of the professional smile Anna had come to expect from Lucy's teachers. She held her hands in near-fists by her sides, her blond hair was pinned in a thick old-fashioned circle around her head, and when she stood, her jeans creaking on her thighs, Anna saw how tall she was, broad-shouldered and thick-hipped, her T-shirt hanging on her torso like a blocky rectangle.

"Of course I've seen you here before," Anna said, thrusting out her hand. "But it's nice to have a minute to talk. I've really wanted to thank you."

Honey looked startled, though she took Anna's hand softly in hers and held it for a brief, uncertain instant. "Thank me for what?" she asked.

"Lucy," Anna said, "go get your things." When Lucy scampered off, Anna turned back to Honey. "For helping Lucy with Andrea," she answered quietly.

The woman glanced across the room to where the program coordinator stood talking to another parent. "I'm sorry," she faltered, "I made a mistake. I didn't mean—"

"She dealt with it amazingly well," Anna continued. "I have no idea how you did it, but she hasn't had a single nightmare since she heard the news."

"It's okay, then," Honey said, in a voice so low it was as though she were talking to herself.

"Why?" Anna asked, "What's wrong?"

"I'm supposed to quit. After today. For inappropriate touching."

"Inappropriate—what?"

Honey said, "A family complained."

"About what?"

"I had them—the girls—brush their hair."

"But—"

"I should of known better," Honey said doggedly. "I've taken classes."

"In child care?" Anna asked, shifting Ellen on her hip and burying her face for a brief second in her hair.

Honey winced and glanced away, as though it were a man Anna was fondling in public instead of a baby. She said, "And child development."

"And the classes say you're not supposed to comfort children who've experienced trauma?" Anna asked, raising her voice.

Honey gave another quick look in Ms. Martinez's direction. "They say you're not supposed to encourage touching in a day-care setting."

"But hairbrushing—that's absurd!"

"Well," said Honey flatly, "and sharing brushes. That's how kids get head lice. I should of known that, too."

Lucy returned with her sweater and her backpack and a sheaf of artwork and worksheets. "Okay," she said, "I'm ready."

Anna asked, "What will you do? I'll be glad to help you appeal—"

"No," the woman said quickly, and added, after an awkward pause, "It's okay."

Impulsively Anna said, "We were just going to the park, to celebrate the sunshine. Maybe you would like to meet us there when you get off work?"

IT WOULD HAVE BEEN SO EASY TO SAY NO. CERISE COULD HAVE SAID thank you, but she was busy. She could have said that she was sorry, but she had to get home, had to fix dinner for her husband and her kids. She could have said that she had already made plans to rob a bank or fly to the moon. She could have done anything but nod her head and agree to meet Lucy and Lucy's mother and Lucy's baby sister at the park. After her head made that nod, it seemed like the most dangerous thing she'd done yet in her new little life. The whole time she was helping children clean up and find their jackets and backpacks, she kept telling herself she shouldn't go. As she said good-bye to the kids with the hollow knowledge that she would never see them again, she knew that she should just walk back to the shelter a different way. Her life was quicksand and poison and filthy smoke, and it was absurd to pretend it could ever be whole and simple and solid like other peoples'. Even after the last child was gone and Ms. Martinez had left to make a phone call and Cerise was gathering her things, it felt like her whole body was bristling with warnings, like sirens were shrieking inside her head. Don't go, she told herself. Go anywhere else instead.

She'd signed her time sheet, put on her jacket, and was on the brink of slipping out the door when Ms. Martinez came back in.

"I'm so sorry," Ms. Martinez said, her eyes brimming with warmth and sadness. "I'd give you another chance in a minute if I could, but there're just so many regulations we have to follow, especially since you were still a probationary employee to begin with. We have to take parental complaints very seriously, and it turns out that the parent who complained is on the school board. We'd be serving no one if the state were to shut us down. I hope you understand." She looked so upset that for a minute Cerise was afraid that she was going to cry, and she felt another layer of regret, for making Ms. Martinez feel so bad.

"It's okay," she answered gruffly.

"The children will miss you a lot," Ms. Martinez said, watching Cerise with her kind brown eyes. "And I will, too."

"I'll miss—everybody," Cerise said. Then, in order to prevent either of them from breaking into tears, she turned away abruptly and stumbled from the room.

The hall was long and cool and echoing. She'd failed again, failed without even trying, failed before she'd even completely realized how much it might matter to be Honey to a roomful of other people's children. She came to the end of the hall, passed through the silent foyer, and stepped outside. She'd meant to turn left, away from the park, had meant to take the long way back to the shelter where the doors would be opening for the evening and the supper crew would have begun to chop and stir. But before she could turn left, her legs went right, heading west down the street toward the sunset that was just beginning behind the trees and buildings and power lines.

IN THE PARK THE LIGHT HAD THE CLARITY OF MOUNTAIN WATER, AND the balmy air held just an edge of chill that made the grass and leaves seem greener, more awake. The sun was nearly setting, and above the darkening tangle of city, the sky was ribbed with delicate coral clouds. A little fountain murmured a cold music to itself. Anna threaded Ellen's pudgy legs through the holes in the baby swing and helped her to grip the chains with her soft hands, and when Anna gave the swing a gentle tap, a smile opened on Ellen's face. The doctor had looked grave when Anna explained that Ellen spent twenty hours a week in day care. "You may want to reconsider that," he'd said, and Anna had to bite her tongue to keep from protesting how little choice she had.

Lucy climbed on the black rubber slab of a big kids' swing. "Push me," she demanded.

"In a minute," Anna answered absently, and gave Ellen's swing another tap. She thought of Lucy's teacher, Honey, and wondered where the impulse had come from, to invite her to meet them in the park. She knew nothing about Honey except for what little Lucy had said. She could already tell that she and Honey had nothing in common, that they would never become friends. But whatever had happened at after-school care on Friday, Lucy had slept well since then, and when Kaylesha came over on Sunday, she and Lucy had played together as though they'd been best pals for years.

Lucy caught sight of Honey first, approaching across the grass.

"Honey! I'm pumping," Lucy cried gleefully as she drew near. "Look how high I am!"

"You better watch out," Honey called up to Lucy at the height of her arc, "you don't kick holes in that sunset."

Lucy let her legs and head flop down in mock exhaustion. "I'm tired of pushing," she announced. "Honey, will you push me for a while?"

Anna watched as Honey stood behind Lucy and commenced to push, her whole body rocking easily back and forth with the rhythm of her work. She watched Lucy lift her face to the coral-colored sky, her eyes closed, her expression soft with the bliss of swinging. Anna had had a vague idea that she might help Honey somehow. She'd thought she could offer to help Honey write a letter or ask for a hearing, thought she might write a letter of complaint herself, but Honey's silence reminded her that the two of them were strangers. She gave Ellen another little push and tried to think what to say next.

Finally she asked, "Do you have another job?"

"No," Honey answered with a little grunt as she thrust Lucy up into the air.

"What will you do?"

Before Lucy swooped back to earth, Honey shrugged. "I'll find something, I guess. Probably not child care," she added as she pushed Lucy skyward.

Anna asked, "Do you like child care?"

"I like kids," Honey answered quietly.

"Do you have children of your own?" Anna asked.

There was a pause while Honey tossed Lucy up into the air. Then she said, "No."

The swing ascended again, and Lucy called down to the woman on the ground, "Where do you live?"

There was another silence as Lucy fell back to earth and Honey pushed her once more. Then Honey answered, "I live at the Redwood Women's Shelter."

"What kind of a house is that?" demanded Lucy.

The woman was quiet for so long that Anna thought she hadn't heard Lucy's question, but then she answered, "It's not a house. It's a shelter for homeless women."

"Stop!" Lucy yelled. With each pass of the swing she jammed her feet on the ground until finally she was able to leap off her seat. Turning to face Honey, she demanded, "You're a homeless person?"

"I'm not anymore, am I?" Honey said, kneeling down and answering Lucy so directly that Anna felt like an eavesdropper. "If I live at the shelter."

"But you were," Lucy insisted.

"Well."

"What happened to your home?"

Anna said, "Oh, Lucy, we shouldn't—"

"It's okay," Honey answered, though she was silent for such a long time afterward that Anna felt certain Lucy's question had been a blunder. But when Honey finally spoke, her voice was neutral. Looking straight at Lucy, she said, "My trailer burned. I lost my home."

"And now you've lost your job," Anna said softly.

"Mommy, Mommy, Mommy!" Lucy cried, stretching her arm in the air as though she were begging to be called on in class. "I know! I know! Mommy—Honey could have a job from us!"

STANDING BESIDE THE LITTLE FOUNTAIN, WITH THE SUNSET DEEPENING behind her, Anna studying her, Lucy jumping up and down, and the baby watching big-eyed from her swing, Cerise felt both danger and a terrible compunction. It confused her that she'd told them so easily about the shelter and the fire. It troubled her that she'd lied so directly about not having children, and it frightened her to think what she might unwittingly say next.

Lucy's mother was like no one else Cerise had never known, although she reminded her just a little of the woman who'd been her mentor teacher. She liked how Anna looked pretty without appearing perfect. She liked the way Anna treated her daughters, as though she were both amused and pleased by them, and she liked the way Anna treated her, too, as if the world were a thing they shared. She even liked the clothes that Anna wore, and the simple way she fixed her gleaming hair. She liked Anna way too much to disappoint or contaminate her, too much to risk exposing herself to her.

"Please," Lucy pleaded, as though Cerise were a candy bar or another ride at the fair. "Oh, please, please, please, please."

There was a long pause while Cerise stood with her head bent, waiting for Lucy's mother to say the hard words that would free them both. But instead, after another moment, Anna said, "I'm not sure I have any work for you right now, but maybe you'd like to come and spend a few hours with us on Wednesday afternoon? I know Lucy would be thrilled to have you visit. And Ellen, too," Anna added, as she lifted the baby from the swing.

Cerise didn't want to have to spend more time with Lucy, with her funny way of talking, her million moods, and messy clothes. Even though Lucy's eyes were brown instead of blue, and she wasn't anywhere near as beautiful as Melody had once been, Lucy made Cerise think of Melody, her body the size of Melody's, her hair as soft as Melody's, her voice the ghost of Melody's voice back before everything went wrong.

And Cerise didn't want to have to be with the baby most of all. She was afraid that if she touched Ellen, she would never be able to let her go, afraid that if she held her, her hands would somehow twist to claws. She was afraid that in Ellen's presence, she would start to cry and never remember how to stop.

"Please?" Lucy asked turning to her. Her voice was sweet and urgent, as insinuating as Melody's had once been. "Oh, please?" And standing beside the little fountain in the tender purple twilight, the only word Cerise could find was, "Sure."

ON TUESDAY MORNING, ANNA DROPPED ELLEN OFF AT MRS. CHAUNCY'S half an hour early and drove to the Redwood Women's Shelter. It was a low, dull building in a tired neighborhood close to the city center. She parked in front of it, locked the car, and then surreptitiously double-checked the doors. A knot of women were loitering on the sidewalk with their cigarettes and bundles, and as she passed through them, she smiled sympathetically into the middle distance.

Inside was a reception area with a chair-lined wall, a graying carpet, and an office desk on which sat a telephone and a Rolodex file. It all seemed so startlingly normal that Anna realized she had unwittingly been imagining the etchings she'd seen of Bedlam, with wild-eyed women lolling in the straw.

A voice said, "We're not open now." Anna jumped and looked around to see a woman coming toward her down the hallway. She was short and plain, and her glasses were taped at one corner with black electrician's tape.

"I'm sorry," Anna said, "I just need . . . are you . . . do you work here?"

"I do," the woman said, entering the room. "And I'm afraid we're full right now. We can't even take any more applications until our waiting list shortens a little."

"Oh, I'm not—I mean, I have a place to live. I just wanted," Anna stammered, "some information about someone who's staying here."

The woman had been looking pleasantly at Anna, but suddenly her worn face hardened. "And who are you?"

"I was thinking of inviting one of your—Honey Johnson—to my house. And maybe even having her watch my daughters."

The woman pushed her glasses up on her nose. She said, "I'd be breaking confidentiality if I told you anything about any of our residents."

"I know," Anna said, "It's just, I have a responsibility, to my—"

The woman's eyes suddenly softened. "You don't want to endanger your children by helping Honey."

"No. I mean, yes. That's—"

"In that case I'll tell you a little more than I should, though I don't know much."

"I'd appreciate whatever you can say."

"We have to have a lot of rules here," the woman began. "We can't help everybody, so we have to concentrate our energies on those with whom we might have a real chance. If a woman can't follow our rules, we have to ask her to leave, to make room for someone else. It's hard," the woman shrugged, "but there it is.

"Now Honey's never caused a bit of trouble," the woman continued. "She watches out for people, does extra chores, doesn't complain. She's great with the kids—and some of the children here have good reason to be a handful."

Anna said, "What about her—background?"

"Most of the ladies want to talk, to tell their stories. But Honey's never said a word about herself, at least not that I've ever heard."

"She told me she lost her home when her trailer burned."

"If that's what she said, I don't see why we should doubt it. She must trust you, to reveal that. Honey's quiet," the director went on, "but seems sturdy, like a real survivor. She's certainly kind. Her stay with us is almost over, and we'll miss her when she has to leave."

"Why would she have to leave?" Anna asked.

"Three months is the limit any woman can stay with us—three months, as long as she can follow all our rules."

"What are your rules?"

The director adjusted her glasses once again. "The women have to look for work, and when they find a job, they have to do their best to keep it. They have to do chores and maintain their personal hygiene, they can't fight or use obscenities, and they have to stay drug-free and sober.

"I don't think Honey has any dependency issues," the woman continued. "We do drug testing. One dirty catch, and you're out. I'd trust my own kids with her, if I had any."

She paused for a moment, and then she said, "It's good of you to take an interest in her. It's what all these women need—a bridge back. It's communities that make people homeless, and only communities can help them regain what they've lost."

"The government—" Anna began.

But the woman interrupted her, "—is an abstraction. These women . . ." Her voice trailed off as though she'd reached a dead end, but then her thoughts seemed to take a different turn, and when she spoke again, her tone was resonant and firm, "'Be not forgetful to entertain strangers, for thereby some have entertained angels unawares.'"

Anna asked, "Who said that?"

"The Bible, of course. Saint Paul, in the book of Hebrews. It isn't always easy," the woman added, "to try to help. But then it isn't easy to be homeless either, to be stripped to just a life."

"No, though I'd think—I mean, there must be some way. . . ."

The woman gave Anna an appraising look. "There's another thing I try to keep in mind," she said. "It's a legal phrase, oddly enough."

"What's that?" Anna asked.

" 'The right to folly,' " the woman answered.

"Oh," Anna said, though for a moment she was not sure whose folly the woman meant.

IT HURT NEARLY AS MUCH AS STARTING HER JOB, TO HAVE TO GIVE IT UP. When Cerise woke on Tuesday morning, the whole day loomed uselessly in front of her, as eternal and immovable as a mountain.

"Have a good day at work," the director said to her as she filed out onto the sunny streets with the other women, and though Cerise nodded and mumbled, "Thanks," inside she winced as if she'd been slapped.

By midmorning she missed the kids so much, she thought she might sneak back anyway, thought she could lurk around the playground or maybe hide in the hall in hopes of stealing even a peek of them. But as she neared the schoolyard, she veered away again, afraid that someone might notice her and call the police.

She spent the rest of the day wandering the Santa Dorothea that people with jobs and homes and destinations never see—the alleys and weedy lots and vacant buildings, the dank or dusty hiding places, the thickets and wild pockets, the places that could only be reached by crawling or surreptitious climbing.

They were the only places left where she belonged. She'd wanted a place she could go where people would be glad to see her, had wanted a room of her own where she could retreat to pursue her encounters with Travis. But now she saw that she would never have those things. She'd done her best, and she'd lost her job, and it was proof of how little she'd belonged there to begin with that she would do again the thing that made her lose it.

"They say I gotta look for work or leave," Barbara had muttered as she'd packed. But the bars and restaurants hadn't wanted Cerise, the motels and nursing homes hadn't needed her, and even if she could find another day care foolish enough to hire her, she couldn't bear having to start over one more time. "Get real," she remembered Melody scoffing. "Do you remotely think I'd have a chance?" And now Cerise wondered why she'd ever thought she had.

"Where there's life, there's hope," the shelter director was always saying. But hope was a hoax, just a way of trapping people into staying alive. Hope was a mirage, a trick. Hope meant nothing, and still life ground on, still Cerise combed the streets for nooks and hidey-holes, still she went to the soup kitchen at noon to eat cheap food and scan the crowd for Barbara. Forking mealy potatoes into her mouth, watching the others eat, it seemed their only purpose was to fill forbidden toilets with their homeless turds.

When the shelter opened, she slipped inside and snuck the blankets from her cot, took her bag of toiletries and her extra clothes from her shelf, helped herself to a handful of shriveled doughnuts from the pantry, and then stole out the kitchen door before anyone could notice. As dusk came, she made a bed for herself in a stall in a livestock barn at the fairground, sweeping off the wooden floor planks as best she could with a half-rotten grooming brush, spreading a layer of old newspapers along the back wall, arranging her blankets in a tidy rectangle on top.

A little wind skittered through the empty building, stirring trash and dust and then moving on. Otherwise the only sound she heard was the distant growl of the freeway. After the bustle of the kids at after-school care and her crowded life at the shelter, the wide silence of the fairground seemed oddly welcoming, as though it had been waiting for her, as though there were a place inside that silence that was just her shape.

It was a relief to be unknown and unencumbered once again, to be committed to nothing more than caring for the unfortunate pet of her own body. It was a relief to leave the little worries and the heartrending sorrows of other people behind. While the last light seeped from the room, she took off her shoes and crawled between her blankets. Travis, she thought expectantly. She stiffened her body and held her breath, willing herself past the torture of his death to the place where he still lived. Lying beneath her collection of blankets, she waited for his scent, his voice, his smile, to possess her. But this time, though she missed him with a longing so strong it might have severed atoms, she couldn't seem to find him in her mind. She could remember parts of him—the hollow at the back of his neck, his cushiony cheeks and sturdy legs—but those parts kept shifting, refusing to become a whole boy.

No matter how hard she tried to conjure him, he never came. She could remember a million moments with him—changing his diaper, feeding him his dinner, giving him a bath. But she couldn't seem to find her way back inside those times. It was as though her memories were becoming set and flat, like the photographs in the albums that Rita used to have, the little snapshots whose color was slowly seeping out of them, leaving their images pale and yellow-tinged, like fading bruises.

Out on the fairground a lone frog began to sing, its call tentative and plaintive in the dark. A moment passed, and it was answered by a lush chorus. Lying on her paper bed, Cerise let herself be lulled a little by the frogs, let time pass until finally she felt almost used to the awful ache that was her life.

She woke much later to the sound of footsteps and hushed voices. Stiff with adrenaline, she lay in the darkness, pressing her spine against the back wall of her stall and holding her breath, willing herself to disappear, willing her eyes to see through the dark.

"In here," a male voice said, and she was desperately trying to gather a reply when the intruders passed her stall and entered the one beyond it. She heard a girl's giggle and the man's low answer, and her panic ebbed a little.

Terrified of giving herself away, she lay not six feet from where they embraced, trying not to listen and yet unable to hear anything else. At the sound of their shifting bodies, their cozy moans and murmured answers, she almost envied them the little transports she imagined they had in store.

But a moment later the girl gave a whimper. "No," she said, "Oh, please," her voice tight and small and scared as though she'd suddenly become a child.

"You'll like it," the man answered. "Just wait a minute."

The girl made a little cry, a muffled word that sounded, almost, like *Mommy*, and Cerise felt an awful shadow cross her mind. Sick with anxiety, she lay in the darkness, hating herself and helpless to stop a thing, unable to even to put her hands over her ears for fear of making too much noise. She remembered her own introduction to sex, how the bludgeon of Sam's penis had appeared so unexpectedly between her legs, as startling and insistent as a truck bearing down, how she'd been a mother before she'd really understood what Sam was trying to do.

When the thrusts and whimpers ceased, frog-song poured in to fill the silence. After a pause the girl's voice pleaded, "Do you love me?"

But the only answer Cerise heard was an impatient grunt and the quick growl of a zipper being closed.

Long after the couple had left and the frogs had ceased their calling and the stalls were once more silent save for the intermittent wind, Cerise lay awake, tormented by the thought of all she'd been unable to change or stop or save. Before she finally managed to fold herself back inside a thin sleep, she thought she heard, far beyond the distant freeway hum, the incessant ringing of an unanswered phone. Listening to that sound that was so muted it might only exist inside her mind, she felt an uneasy flicker of longing. It's too late for that, she told herself, and pulled her blankets over her head.

She woke to a barrage of birdsong and the thin light of dawn. The air was cold against her face, and the stall smelled of dew and hay and old manure. She huddled beneath her blankets for a long time, watching the slow advent of morning, listening to the chatter of birds and the increasing roar of traffic on the freeway.

She had no reason to rise. She couldn't return to the shelter now that she'd lost her job and stolen one of the shelter's blankets and broken the rule about staying out all night, and there was nowhere else she could think to go. She lay on her newspaper bed and wondered how she could possibly endure the waste of hours that lay ahead before she could lose herself in sleep once more.

The shelter director had said everyone needed plans. She'd said that plans were the ropes you used to pull yourself into the future. But Cerise had no use for the future. The future was only the present stretched out forever, like rubbish scattered along an endless freeway. And yet she knew she couldn't remain forever in her stall. Sooner or later someone would find her and make her leave. Sooner or later her greedy body would drive her into the world.

The rectangle of light the rising sun opened on the floor had almost reached her before she remembered that it was the day she had promised to visit Lucy and her mother. It doesn't matter, she thought, staring dully at the nails angling through the cobweb-covered boards of the ceiling of the stall. They probably hadn't really expected her to come anyway. Lucy's mother would no doubt feel relieved, the baby would never know, and if Lucy were disappointed, she would get over it soon enough. Sitting up, Cerise put on her shoes and then stood to shake and fold her blankets.

But as she stacked the newspaper in the corner of the stall, she kept remembering Lucy's woeful face on the day they found Andrea. She remembered how still Lucy had sat, her whole attention focused on the stroking of Cerise's brush. She remembered how solicitously Lucy had passed Cerise's brushstrokes on, and she remembered how tender the girls had all been with each other, how caring and careful. She would go to Lucy's house, she decided abruptly. She would go to Lucy's house and say good-bye. She didn't have to go inside. She could just stand at the door and explain to Lucy that she couldn't stay. She could say that she was sorry, but she didn't have time to come in, that she was going away, and wouldn't be able to come back for another visit later. And after that, Lucy's disappointment would not be her problem any longer.

It was a long walk from the fairground to Lucy's house. Cerise passed first through neighborhoods where the houses all had grated windows and sagging doors, and broken toys were scattered across their unkempt yards. Worn-looking people sat on the front steps and nodded or scowled as she passed. She walked through the city center, with its thick traffic and slick buildings and grim-faced shoppers, and then through neighborhoods that seemed like different worlds with their wide streets, white sidewalks, and velvety lawns. The brass eyes of sprinklers dotted the grass, and tidy signs warned that the houses were being guarded, day and night.

When she finally reached the right address, in a neighborhood where a street of older houses edged the top of a steep ravine, Lucy came dancing out to greet her even before Cerise turned up the walk.

"You're here!" Lucy cried, circling Cerise like a gleeful puppy. "You're here. You're at my house!"

"Hi, there," Cerise said gruffly. "Look. I came to say good—"

But before she could finish, Lucy grabbed her by the hand, pressed her small warm fingers into the tender skin of Cerise's palm.

"Come on," she urged, dragging Cerise toward the door. "My mom and me made cookies in your honor."

It still felt vaguely wrong or risky to ask a homeless woman into their house. There was a taint to that word—*homeless*—that troubled Anna, as though it meant something worse than being without a home, or as though Honey's bad luck were a kind of contagion they might catch from being in her presence. On the phone the night before Sally had said, "That's nice that you want to help the homeless, but for the life of me I can't see why you'd risk your own children to do it."

"It's not a risk," Anna had answered, standing beside a pile of clean laundry. Holding the receiver clamped between her shoulder and her ear, she'd picked up one of Eliot's T-shirts, given it a brisk snap to shake the wrinkles out.

"How do you know it's not a risk?" persisted Sally.

"Look at how Lucy dealt with the whole Andrea thing. I'm sure that Honey deserves a lot of the credit for that. How could she be a threat to Lucy?"

"Maybe she didn't really do all that much. Maybe Lucy's just relieved that there's finally some closure."

"Maybe," Anna answered, adding the folded T-shirt to Eliot's stack. "All I know is that we were expecting Lucy to freak out, and she didn't— not at all."

"Besides," Sally went on, "you're not a social worker. This woman probably has all kinds of problems you know nothing about."

"How do you know?" Anna asked.

"People don't get to be homeless if they don't have problems."

"People get to be homeless if they don't have homes," Anna answered crisply. She pulled one of Lucy's nightgowns from the warm heap of laundry. It crackled with static and clung to the sleeves of her sweater as she attempted to fold it. "They say we're all about three paychecks away from being on the streets."

"I'm not," said Sally promptly.

"Why not?"

"Because I'd move in with you."

"Oh, great," Anna moaned.

"I mean it," Sally answered. "Don't you see? You and I wouldn't ever be homeless because we have too many resources. Before we became homeless, we'd have to alienate all our friends and family, lose all our life skills. We've got way too much to lose to ever to become homeless. If I were you, I'd be asking why this woman has so little."

But Honey didn't seem sick or drifting or dangerous in the way that homelessness suggested. At the park she had been quiet and direct, but Anna had liked that. She'd liked the unaffected way that Honey spoke to Lucy and the way that Lucy had blossomed in response.

Now, with Ellen on her hip, Anna followed behind them as Lucy proudly led Honey upstairs to show off her room. As she watched the careful regard that Honey gave to Lucy's chatter and listened to Honey's modest replies, Anna thought how groundless Sally's warnings seemed, how pinched and mean and middle-class. Lucy was so happy, so expansive and at ease, showing Honey her Peter Rabbit night-light and her Cinderella sheets, showing her the drawings she and Kaylesha had been working on, and the shell with the ocean inside it that Aunt Sally had sent her from Tahiti.

After Honey admired Lucy's treasures, there was an awkward little pause where they all stood on the landing and tried to think what should happen next. Honey seemed pained, as though she wanted to speak but didn't know quite what to say, and Anna wondered if she'd made Honey feel too self-conscious with her watchfulness. To smooth the moment, she adjusted Ellen on her hip and said, "Lucy and I were hoping you would join us for a snack."

A nearly imperceptible shadow sped across Honey's broad face, and she seemed to hesitate for half a moment before she said, "Okay."

In the kitchen, as they peeled oranges, steeped tea, and arranged the cookies on a plate, it occurred to Anna that there were questions she should ask, things she should find out now, before their relationship went past them—businesslike questions about Honey's background and her qualifications to care for Lucy and Ellen. But it seemed as though it would be a breach in something to make Honey talk about her past. It also seemed absurd to ask Honey for a résumé or references, especially since Anna wasn't yet sure she even wanted to hire her for anything. She worried that questioning Honey so closely would imply that she was offering her a job.

While she was still struggling with those thoughts, Honey cleared her throat and asked shyly, "What's your work? I mean," she added hastily, "besides taking care of your girls."

"I'm a photographer," Anna answered, setting Ellen in her high chair and scattering a handful of Cheerios on her tray. "Or I was," she added ruefully. "Mainly now I teach."

"What grade?" Honey asked.

"I teach at the university."

"At the university?" Honey's voice was tinged with wary awe.

"Well, just part-time." It was hard to sort out how she felt about who she was, talking with this woman who had recently been homeless, who had just lost her job.

Honey asked, "You teach people how to take pictures? Like of weddings and things?"

"I'm primarily a landscape photographer. Fine arts," Anna said briskly. But when she sensed Honey's dismay, she added more gently, "Not that a wedding might not make an interesting subject."

"You're an artist?" Honey asked, as if she were trying to establish an important fact, and though the question cored her, Anna forced herself to answer, "Yes."

"Are these your pictures, on the walls?" asked Honey, staring around the kitchen in amazement.

"There's a photograph of mine in the living room. But these days it makes me homesick to see my work." Anna winced at the blunder of mentioning homesickness to a woman who had no home, but Honey appeared not to notice. Instead she seemed to be intent on a thought of her own. "I knew a girl once," she said, looking at Anna with something oddly near wonder on her face, "who wanted to be an artist." She ducked her head as though she'd said something shocking or revealing, and began to arrange the orange sections on a plate.

"Oh?" Anna said. "Lucy, do you want milk or apple juice?"

"Juice," Lucy answered. "Hey! Juicy, Lucy—get it?"

Honey said, "But it never made a lot of sense to me, the things that girl did."

"What did she do?" Anna asked, pouring juice into a teacup and setting it down by Lucy's place.

"Once she got a lot of junk from the side of the freeway and spray-painted it gold. And then she made a big heap of all that painted trash and called it *Harvest*."

Anna laughed. "It reminds me of the stuff we used to do in college."

"Mel—this girl—she was in high school." Honey answered. It seemed that a veneer of pride stiffened her tone, though when, after a pause, she went on, her voice was lower, as raw as if she were confessing something. "Back when she did it, I thought it was the dumbest thing. But lately—I've been thinking a lot, about trash and stuff, and now it kind of makes sense, what she was doing."

Anna wanted to ask why Honey had been thinking about trash, but something in Honey's voice made her feel she would be trespassing if she did. Besides, it seemed that Honey had already confided something important, although she wasn't exactly sure what it was. Instead she said, "That's one thing art is good for, making us think."

But her words sounded too smug, and the meekness of Honey's answering nod stung like a recrimination.

"At least, that's what I used to believe," Anna said, bending over to pour the tea and feeling the words grate in her throat. "I used to think that art could make us think, and help us feel. I used to think that art could change people somehow. But now it seems like there are a lot of troubles that art just can't touch." It startled her to find herself saying those things to this hapless stranger. She looked up from the tea just in time to glimpse a flicker of pain cross Honey's face. It was like the shadow of a cloud, or the wince after a slap, and Anna wondered where on earth it came from, wondered how Honey's distress could possibly mirror her own.

CERISE HEARD THE PAIN IN ANNA'S VOICE, AND THOUGH ITS SOURCE wasn't clear, it warmed her a little to think that Anna would trust her with something that mattered so much it hurt. But at the same time, Anna's words stung her. For a moment she'd thought that she could learn from Anna how a heap of junk could be transformed into art, and it was disappointing to hear Anna dismissing what she had hoped to understand. She wished she could think what question to ask next, but while she was still pondering that, Anna announced, "It's looks like we're ready. Lucy, go wash your hands."

It was strange to sit at a table with so few people. The room seemed so quiet, and the plates of food all looked so small. Cerise felt cautious, awkward with her cup and with her talk, afraid that she might give herself away with any unwitting gesture, any word. She kept thinking she needed to tell them that she was leaving, but it seemed wrong to blurt that into the middle of their tea party, especially since no one had asked her to stay. Besides, as she rolled the words that she might use around like marbles inside her head, she realized that Lucy would be certain to ask her where she was going, and why, and she suddenly doubted she could concoct a lie deft enough to appease Lucy's curiosity.

"Where did you grow up, Honey?" Anna asked cordially, passing her the little plate of cookies.

"Rossi," Cerise answered carefully, taking a cookie and passing the plate to Lucy, who studied it with great concentration and helped herself to three.

"What was that like," Anna asked, "growing up in Rossi?"

"It was okay." Recovering the plate gently from Lucy and setting it down beside Anna, Honey added, "Rossi wasn't nearly as big back then."

Anna gave an ironic laugh, "That's what everyone says who grew up in California."

Cerise felt pleased to be like everyone, though she wasn't sure what it would be safe to say next. She watched as Ellen intently pincered a single Cheerio between her soft forefinger and her plump thumb and then tucked it deep inside her cheek.

Anna added more tea to both their cups. "I grew up in Spokane," she said, sitting back in her chair and taking a comfortable sip. "Though what I remember most were the times my sister and I spent on my grandparent's farm. That's where Lucy was born, and it's the place I think of when I think of home." Cerise heard a strain of longing in Anna's voice, but before she had time to consider its cause, Anna asked, "Do you still have family in Rossi?"

Cerise winced and hunched into herself. "No," she answered stiffly. Then, because it seemed she had to say something more, she added, "My mom and her new husband moved to Florida."

"You really are all alone, aren't you?" said Anna, and the expression on her face was so kind that Cerise quailed. She buried her face in her teacup, felt its milky steam rising to her cheeks. She would leave, she decided, as soon as they'd finished their snack. She didn't need to tell them she was never coming back. She could just thank Anna for the cookies and tousle Lucy's hair and say good-bye. She was swallowing the last of her tea and trying to scrape together the right words when suddenly Anna spoke.

"I've got some negatives I really need to develop," she said, setting down her cup decisively. "I've been putting them off for a long time now. I wondered if you'd be willing to stay and play with the girls while I work on them. I'd pay you at least what you made at after-school care."

"Well," Cerise said. "But—"

"It's certainly worth that much to me," Anna said warmly, "to have someone we all feel so good about."

Every nerve and shred of instinct told Cerise that she should go, but even so a greedy longing ballooned inside her. She yearned to stay just a little longer, to bask in the feeling of being wanted, no matter how misguided that feeling really was.

"Please," begged Lucy happily, hopping off her chair to throw her arms around Honey's neck. "Please, please, please, please." And with Lucy's cheek pressed against hers and Anna looking at her so expectantly, there was nothing to do but nod.

"That's wonderful," Anna said warmly. "I'll help you guys get settled in, and then I'll go downstairs to my darkroom and get to work." She seemed to give a little inward sigh, as though she were steeling herself to do something difficult, and then she stood resolutely. Lifting Ellen from her high chair, she smiled at Cerise. "Come on," she said.

When Anna mentioned her darkroom, Cerise thought she caught an odd pinch of fear flick across Lucy's face. But in the next second Lucy was flying upstairs to get her toys, and Cerise was following Anna from the kitchen.

WHEN ANNA TURNED ON THE LIGHT IN HER DARKROOM AND SAW THAT her film holders had been opened and the film sheets she'd dreaded having to develop were scattered across the floor, her first thought was that someone else had already decided they were worthless.

It was only when she realized the absurdity of her reasoning that she noticed the lopsided flowers Magic-Markered on each negative, their colors weird and shadowy against the dark opaque surface of the film. Rage rose inside her like a wave, ramming aside every other feeling or thought or caution. The ruined negatives wobbling in her hand, she slammed out of the darkroom, burst upstairs to find Lucy and Honey and Ellen sitting among a scatter of toys on the living room floor.

Sweeping past Honey and Ellen, she stopped in front of Lucy, held out the ruined sheets of film, and demanded, "What happened?"

Lucy glanced up from the stuffed monkey she was dressing, and a quick succession of emotions crossed her face, her expression shifting from shock to guilt to terror. "I don't know," she said, staring at the sheets of film that trembled in her mother's outstretched hand.

It was the first time she had ever lied so boldly, the first time she'd lied about something that really mattered. "Of course you know," Anna hissed, bending down and snatching Lucy's wrist, yanking her to her feet so quickly that Lucy gasped. "You tell me, now," Anna demanded, still holding Lucy up so that she nearly dangled from her own arm.

Honey made a little move, half abashed and half protective, and Anna, reminded of her presence, turned to face her. "Excuse me," she said stiffly. "I need to talk to Lucy." Dropping Lucy's wrist, she added, "Go to your bedroom, right now."

Upstairs, Anna closed the bedroom door carefully, twisting the doorknob so that it would not slam, and then she wheeled to face her daughter. "What on earth were you doing?" she asked, her clenched teeth biting knives into each word.

A look of shocked vulnerability appeared on Lucy's face. "Ellie did it," she began desperately. "I told her not—"

"Ellen did not do that," Anna said. "Ellen can't even crawl. Don't you dare blame your sister."

Lucy's face crumpled as though the bones themselves were dissolving. "I didn't mean—"

"Goddammit, Lucy," Anna exploded. "You are never to go into my darkroom without my permission. You know that." Her chest was heaving, and her fingertips tingled. For a second it felt almost as good as sex to feel the surge of that much righteousness, to feel anything that clearly, to rise above the muddle of everyday into an emotion so keen and strong. She shook the negatives so that they rattled in Lucy's face and said, "There are dangerous chemicals down there. And all my work. These," she panted, "were the first negatives I've exposed in a year and a half. And now they're ruined. You ruined them," she added cruelly.

Lucy's face was wobbling. Her cheeks were slick with tears, and more tears dripped off her chin to land like dark lopsided polka dots on the front of her pink T-shirt. "They were only black," she said.

"They were negatives," Anna answered. "Don't you understand? They hadn't been developed yet."

"Oh," answered Lucy, looking at the floor.

"What were you thinking?" Anna demanded. "What on earth were you thinking, to draw on them like that?"

In feeble whisper Lucy answered, "I don't know."

"You had to be thinking something. What made you do it?"

A look of bewilderment passed over Lucy's face, as though she suddenly found the answer as puzzling as she knew it would be to Anna. "I thought it would make you happy," she said.

Anna's anger abandoned her, and she was all alone in the reeling world, alone in her flushed and trembling body while shame rushed in to take her anger's place. "Make me happy?" she croaked.

"You were so sad. So I thought to draw some flowers to cheer you up."

It was sad and frightening and a strange relief, to sit beside the baby among the sprawled toys and listen to the pound and stab of Anna's voice, listen to Lucy's sobs and small replies. Cerise felt almost as if she were a child again, bewildered and dismayed by the anger of people larger than herself, though at the same time she recognized the echo of her own mother-rage in the tone of Anna's voice. She felt a sting in her palm that was the recoil of the slap Melody had carried with her when she left the trailer, and she also knew a tiny vindication that someone as nice as Anna could get so angry.

This is because of art, she thought, listening to the sounds upstairs and looking in uneasy wonder at the prints and paintings and photographs on Anna's walls. Leaving Ellen to suck on the arm of Lucy's monkey while she gazed expectantly at the doorway through which her mother had vanished, Cerise rose and began to circle the room. At first she felt audacious and a little embarrassed, as though she were sneaking something she had no right to take. But as she moved from one framed image to the next, her curiosity about what she was seeing became so great that she forgot her qualms.

Two of the paintings were so pretty that she liked them right away—the blue bowl filled with crimson tulips that hung above the sofa, and, beside the window, the few brief strokes of misty color that made a duck lifting off a placid lake. But the other two paintings puzzled her. They had no picture to them at all, but only squiggles and slashes and random squares, and their colors were as jangling as the sound of a telephone. *Match the goddamn ground you're sleeping on?* she remembered Barbara scoffing as her crochet hook flashed, and she wondered what paintings as garish as Barbara's blankets were doing on Anna's walls.

Most of the photographs seemed pointless, too. They were only black and white, and one was nothing more than a bathroom sink, one was someone's neck and shoulder, while another was just shadows stippling a concrete wall. The photograph with Anna's signature made a little more sense, though it, too, was all in shades of gray. It was a picture of a strange wide land spreading away in waves of hills that ended at last in a row of gentle mountains. It was pretty, she supposed, but it made her feel lonely, the way the hills went on and on, the way the sky seemed so wide and open. She couldn't understand how a picture like that could make a person homesick, and she wondered if she'd understood Anna right when she'd said that she taught at the university.

She was still studying Anna's photograph when Ellen began to whimper. Cerise glanced behind her and saw that Ellen had toppled over and was straining to reach the doorway, her arms flailing while her legs batted ineffectually against the floor.

"Your mommy will be back," Cerise said, crossing the floor to stand above her. "It won't be long." She felt as though she were looking down on a bomb, and at the same time, watching Ellen struggling on the floor, she felt a pull as strong as gravity, felt a clench in her womb and a twist in her empty breasts. Forcing herself to squat down next to Ellen, she set Lucy's monkey in front of her and tried to animate it with a little shake. But that meager comfort only made Ellen's frustration ripen into real distress.

"Shhhh," Cerise said, leaning over to give Ellen's back a cautious pat.

But Ellen's cries were escalating, and Cerise was afraid that Anna would hear them and be unhappy with her, too. Reluctantly, she sat down on the floor and lifted Ellen into her arms. She had not held a baby since she'd last held Travis, and as she pressed Ellen against her chest, she held her breath, waiting for the agony to sear her, waiting for Ellen's cries to shift to screams of terror.

But Ellen sighed and settled herself against Cerise's chest as though she were only a baby who wanted holding, and Cerise were only someone who could comfort her. Laying her head against Cerise's shoulder, she shifted and wiggled a little, instinctively seeking the way their bodies best fit together, while Cerise sat guardedly, trying not to feel Ellen or smell her, trying to touch her as little as possible while still keeping her on her lap.

Flat thoughts moved through her mind: She hoped that Lucy and Anna were finding a way to forgive each other. If Anna gave her money, she could buy food, which would be nice, since she'd never found a way to cash her after-school care paychecks. If she started to cry, she would frighten Ellen. She wished that Travis had had a stuffed monkey as cute as Lucy's. If Anna gave her enough money, she could buy soap and deodorant, too. She thought that maybe anger didn't have to be the end of everything.

Ellen felt so luscious and cherishable, resting against her body. Ellen smelled of Cheerios and baby shampoo, of Anna's soap and sweat and of her own sweet baby-flesh. She gave another long shuddering sigh, and her head sagged against Cerise's breast. A moment passed a lifetime long, although Ellen did not seem to notice that gap in time. Finally Cerise tightened her arms around her, finally unclenched her hands to cup Ellen's spine and skull. She closed her eyes and felt the sting and tingle in the proud flesh on her palms, like the sensation she'd once had in her breasts when her milk was letting down. But gradually she became almost accustomed to that new ache, gradually almost used to the feel of a baby who was not Travis breathing against her heart. And slowly the density of Ellen's body changed, until she was warm and loose and heavy, asleep in Cerise's arms.

Cerise held Ellen for a long time then, and though her cells did not part to enfold her, though she did not soak the feel of Ellen inside her like a sponge, it still felt good to hold a living baby. She held Ellen until her arms ached and strange needles of sensation plagued her hands, held her as though she could hold the two of them in that moment forever, without the intrusion of Ellen's future or Cerise's past.

AFTER ANNA HAD APOLOGIZED TO LUCY A DOZEN TIMES, AFTER SHE'D forgiven Lucy for ruining her negatives and asked Lucy to please forgive her, too, after she'd hugged Lucy and kissed her and dried her tears, after she'd helped her wash her face and settled her on her bed with a picture book and a bevy of stuffed animals, Anna went downstairs to check on Ellen and deal with Honey.

She'd decided she would give Honey twenty dollars. She would thank Honey for coming and say they had all enjoyed her visit and wish her luck and tell her good-bye. It wasn't as though she'd ever promised to befriend Honey or to offer her a job, she thought as she slipped out of Lucy's room. Honey seemed like a nice person, and Anna was grateful for the help she'd given Lucy, but they were too many worlds apart for there to be a place for Honey in Anna's busy life. Besides, she was too embarrassed by what she'd just revealed about herself to want to be around anyone who had witnessed her like that.

Descending the carpeted stairs, Anna felt a spurt of resentment toward the woman who had observed her failure as a mother. She's homeless, she thought before she could stop herself—and childless— what does she know? But as she entered the living room, what she saw made her pause before she spoke. Honey was sitting on the floor and swaying gently from side to side, humming a tuneless little song to Ellen, who lay fast asleep across her chest. Honey's eyes were closed, and the look on her face was somewhere between rapture and torture, a yearning so intense it seemed to encompass both. Ellen's head lolled against Honey's shoulder, and her hand was hanging open by her side.

Suddenly humbled by the tenderness of a stranger toward her daughter, Anna hesitated in the doorway, groping for the phrases she'd planned to use until Honey felt her looking and opened her eyes.

"I'm sorry," Anna said, entering the room. The words surprised her, they were so far from what she'd intended to say.

"It's okay," said Honey softly.

Anna gave a self-conscious laugh. "You haven't caught me at my best."

"I've seen worse, I guess," Honey answered gruffly. She sat very still to keep Ellen from waking.

"I can't imagine worse." Anna said, though a second later she added, "I mean, I can. Upstairs just now I could have strangled her. But at the same time—at that very same minute—I swear I'd kill anyone who hurt her. Probably even me," she added wretchedly.

"It's hard," Honey said softly. "To be a mother."

"It is," Anna answered, startled by how grateful she felt for Honey's sympathy. "My sister used to say I couldn't possibly understand what it would be like to be a mother until I had kids of my own, and that's true, I suppose—I couldn't. But I sometimes wonder if even mothers can ever understand each other. Even after I had Lucy, I couldn't understand what my sister was doing with her sons. She seemed to love them so much when they were little, but after they got older, it was like she just gave up on them somehow. But see," she gave a painful laugh. "I haven't got there yet. Lucy's only six. Who knows what it will be like when she turns sixteen."

Honey's silence seemed like an open door. "We're all so alone, in mothering," Anna went on, her voice low and raw. "We can talk about how our kids are doing in school and the cute things they say. We can even complain about how they're driving us nuts. But we can't talk about how much it terrifies us to love them as we do, or talk about how much we scare ourselves, trying to stay sane while we raise them. We can't talk about how much they teach us, how much they cost us, how much we owe to them. Or—" She shrugged. "Maybe it's just me."

"No," said Honey looking down at Ellen and speaking so softly it was as though she were talking to herself. "Most mothers are like that, I think."

"Lucy said she wanted to make me happy." Anna gave another naked little laugh. "I asked her why she ruined my negatives, and she said she was only trying to cheer me up."

"She loves you," Honey said.

"I know," Anna exhaled shakily. "More than I deserve."

A new kind of silence opened in the room. Ellen made a little moan and settled even deeper into her sleep. Anna stood staring down at her in helpless tenderness, and Honey sat gazing at the wall where Anna's photograph hung while so much time passed that the shadows in the room had shifted before either woman spoke.

"I could come back tomorrow," Honey said. "If that would help."

"Oh," said Anna, so startled that at first she couldn't understand what Honey was suggesting.

"Maybe," Honey offered, "you could make those pictures again, the ones that Lucy wrecked."

It's not that easy, Anna answered in her head. The light won't be the same, the season has changed. And besides, she thought with a terrible twinge of rue, they probably weren't worth it, anyway. She was trying to find a kind way to thank Honey and tell her not to bother, when Honey spoke again. "It might be good for Lucy," she said shyly. "She feels so bad right now. And anyway," she added with a kind of puzzled and desperate courage. "I would really like to help you, with your art."

WALKING AWAY THROUGH THE DUSK, CERISE FELT WRECKED AND naked, so weary she feared she might flop down in the street and go to sleep. But at the same time she felt lighter, too, somehow more alive. Lights popped on around her—streetlights and porch lights and lights in the kitchens of the houses that she passed. In house after house she saw the cool blue glow of a television, and it made her long to return to the shelter. She yearned to rejoin the other women in the TV room, to lose herself again in that society, to stay safe and small in the little half-life she'd found there.

She stopped at a corner market and used the money Anna had given her to buy a bag of food and a bar of soap and a stick of cheap deodorant. When she reached the fairground at last, the floodlights were already on, ripping the darkness open with their glare, making the weeds and dirt look bleached and cold. Skirting the lights, she slipped through the chink in the chain-link fence and stole her way between the long buildings to the barn where she'd slept the night before.

It was almost like a homecoming, to find her blankets and her bags undisturbed. She had thought it would be safer to move to a different stall, but once she was back inside those familiar walls, she decided she would rather risk staying where she was. She spread her bed in the corner, and then sat on her blankets in the dark to eat her supper. When she had drained her carton of milk, she closed her bread sack, took off her shoes, and lay back between her blankets.

At first she tried to reconnect with Travis, but when she found that once again she couldn't reach him, she turned her thoughts to Anna and Lucy and Ellen and what had happened at their house. She wanted to think about the things that Anna had said and about the pictures on Anna's walls. She wanted to think about what it had been like to hold Ellen, and what had made her offer to return, but she was so tired that for once sleep engulfed her, holding her captive until long after dawn.

ALONE IN THE CAR WITH HER FIELD CAMERA, ANNA FELT WEAK AND A little shaky, as if she were venturing outside for the first time after a long illness. As she sped north up the freeway, the spring light stung her eyes like soap, so sharp it nearly made her cry.

I'm doing this for Lucy, she reminded herself. She felt another wrench of remorse to remember how Lucy had cowered while she'd raged at her, and how delighted she had been this afternoon when Anna explained that Honey had offered to stay with her while Anna tried to replace her negatives. She thought about how happily Lucy had held Honey's hand and waved good-bye to her, though she remembered, too, the odd expression she'd caught on Honey's face, a yearning so intense and private and stoic it startled her. Driving up the bright freeway, she wondered again at her decision to leave her daughters in Honey's care.

When Eliot had finally got home last night, she'd shown him the ruined negatives and watched him wince as he shuffled through them, and then she'd forced herself to tell him about all that Honey had been witness to, and how Honey had ended her visit by offering to help.

"I didn't know how to tell her no," she'd said. "It seemed so generous, so—I don't know—soul-felt, or something. And I was so embarrassed. I swear I've never felt worse. It really was kind of her to want to do something. But now she's planning on coming to watch the girls, and I don't know what to do."

"I'd let her come," Eliot had said. They were in the kitchen, where Anna had been packing Lucy's lunch. Eliot set the stack of ruined film on the counter and began to peel a carrot.

Anna said, "You haven't even met her. How can you say you'd let her come?"

"From what you've told me, and from what we've seen of how she's worked with Lucy. I think everything will be just fine. Besides, you won't be gone for more than what—a few hours? And I can come home a little early tomorrow. I think it would be really good for Lucy to have Honey here, and also I'm sure it would help her for you to redo those negatives right away."

"I can't redo those negatives, you know," Anna said, and though she'd tried to sound matter-of-fact, her tone had teetered between self-pity and resentment.

"I know," Eliot had answered. He'd looked at her steadily for a long moment, and then added, "Maybe these will be better."

"Maybe," Anna had said, still struggling to keep the bitterness from her voice.

She had decided she would return to the dead orchard first. She would expose enough film to replace the negatives that Lucy had wrecked, and when she got home, she would make sure to appear happy with what she had done. That would appease Lucy, and maybe please Honey, too, and later, if Anna never got around to developing those sheets of film, it wouldn't be much of a lie to claim she hadn't had the time.

She left the freeway on the exit she'd used before, although now she hardly recognized the landscape the road led her through. The winter rains and spring sunshine had carpeted the hills in grass and dotted the grass with wildflowers. A mist of budding leaves hovered in the branches of the oaks, and buttercups shone by the roadside. But despite the exuberance of the season, Anna still felt remote as a ghost, a stranger in a land that wasn't hers.

The sun was moving lower in the sky, dark shadows were beginning to stretch across the road, and the light was taking on the dense clarity of early evening. Anna thought of the dead orchard she was driving toward, imagined how the broken trees would look, standing like upright corpses amid the fresh grass. She thought of how once she might have been able to make something of that image, and she felt a longing widening inside her, a nostalgia for all that was now lost to her.

When she rounded the final curve and caught sight of the orchard, at first she thought she had taken the wrong road, or had somehow ended up in another world entirely. Her foot slipped from the accelerator, and a moment later she groaned—a sound so visceral and pleasure-laden, she recognized it as her voice while making love. There before her were the gnarled trees, their branches still broken and lichen-hung, their trunks still sundered and hollowed, the heartwood all but rotted out of them. Only now those broken trees were all alight, laden with a million blooms that glowed like stars in the slanting sun.

She pulled blindly off the road, parked, and stumbled like a drunkard from the car. Stem-sap and the spit-homes of larvae soaked her jeans as she pushed through the waist-high weeds and the green scent of chlorophyll filled her nose.

She had never considered the possibility of flowers, had never thought those trees might be anything but dead. As she made her way into the heart of the orchard, she saw that a few of the trees were truly dead, bereft of even a single petal, although their limbs were still home to a thrumming universe of insects and birds. But most of the trees, however twisted and decrepit, were so filled with flowers that their branches seemed to be floating. It was as if the haggard trees had suddenly broken into song. For a long time she wandered mindlessly, lured deeper and deeper by so much gratuitous beauty. The air was spiced with the tickle of pollen, a smell that reminded her more of grain than of perfume. Here and there, an occasional drift of falling petals caught the slanting sunlight as they fluttered toward the earth.

In a daze of delight, she returned to her car for her equipment. She set up her tripod, loaded the first holder of film into her camera, and as she waited beneath the dark cloth for the right second to open the shutter, she felt a fierce gratitude for her particular life. A moment came when the light appeared the fullest, the shadows as rich as they could possibly be. Pressing the shutter release, she heard the gentle click of the shutter opening, felt her love of the world as it appeared brimming again inside her, and marveled, Where have I been?

ANNA CAME HOME AT DINNERTIME ALL EXCITED ABOUT AN ORCHARD she'd found—a whole valley, she said, of dead trees blooming. It didn't make any sense to Cerise for dead trees to have flowers or for anyone to care that much even if they did, but she could see that there was a new light in Anna's face, and when Anna asked Cerise if she would like a steady job, babysitting Ellen while she was teaching, she could hear an eagerness in Anna's voice that she hadn't heard before.

Cerise knew that saying yes was the wrong thing to do. But she had no idea what to do instead. She needed money if she were to stay alive, and it also felt so good to be wanted—even if the person Anna wanted was not the person Cerise really was. Besides, the thought of spending part of almost every day in the quiet shelter of Anna's house with Anna's baby was an allurement Cerise could not pass up.

Cerise found she even liked Anna's husband, too. He seemed almost a creature from another species, when he changed Ellen's messy diapers without being asked or pulled Lucy onto his lap to read to her or laid his hand so tenderly on Anna's waist. They were his plants, Cerise learned, that filled the house, his cuttings lining the windowsills. Seeing them, she couldn't help but think of the garden she had planted with Travis, couldn't help but remember Travis's rapture at digging in the dirt— couldn't help but remember what all Travis's happiness had come to, in the end. But even that warning was not enough to keep her from promising that she would come back tomorrow.

And so a strange new routine shaped her days. Each morning at dawn she woke in her stall at the livestock barn, grateful that she had managed to pass one more night undiscovered. Shivering in the raw gray light, she folded the blanket she'd taken from the shelter and the blanket that Barbara had given her and hid them beneath the newspapers that made her mattress. She sponged her face and armpits with night-cold water from the bottle she'd filled the day before at the spigot outside the barn. She changed into a fresh set of clothes, ate a few slices from her bag of bread, and brushed her teeth, swallowing the toothpaste so that she would not leave telltale toothpaste splotches on the ground. Then, tucking her possessions into the darkest corner of the stall, she slipped away before the light grew too strong.

She spent most of the time she was not at Anna's trying to stay clean. Washing her hair was the hardest. She'd learned that people thought it dangerous or obscene, if they entered a public restroom, to find her bent over a sink with her soapy head crooked under the running faucet, so she tried to use bathrooms with locking doors, despite the difficulties of having to ask for a key.

Every few days she went to a laundromat to wash her clothes. While her little load bounced and spun, she breathed the humid, cigarette-and soap-scented air and paged through the worn magazines, learning about the successes of celebrity diets, about the ten hottest ways to turn her lover on, about how to use pastels to brighten her breakfast nook and what she should be sure to see the next time she visited New Orleans.

Anna had offered so often to pick Cerise up at the shelter or to drop her off there that Cerise was sometimes sure Anna could see through her excuses when she claimed she needed the exercise, insisted she really liked to walk. Once Cerise had splurged and taken the bus to Anna's house, though afterward she decided it was more important to save her money than to spend it on something she could use her own two legs to do.

Without identification, it turned out to be impossible to cash the paychecks she'd received from the after-school care program, but she carried them with her anyway, zipped safely into the inside pocket of her jacket, and she'd tried to save most of the money Anna gave her, too. She wanted to hoard as much as she could for the room she still couldn't help but dream she would have someday, the room calm as a shrine where she could go to be alone. Other than staying undiscovered, that room was her only goal.

She liked Anna more and more, although as time went on, it seemed she had more—instead of less—to hide from her. It was as if all her secrets had somehow rotted into lies. Now that she'd discovered someone she might almost imagine entrusting with the truth of who she was, she could think of no way to explain her life that would not ruin the refuge she'd found. Sometimes Anna invited her to stay for supper, and then, sitting at the table with Anna and Eliot and the girls, passing the broiled chicken breasts and new potatoes, helping to feed Ellen her bananas and her vegetable purees, pouring milk for Lucy and listening to her rhymes and endless stories, she yearned to be the woman they all assumed she was.

Cerise loved Anna's children as she wished she had loved her own. She loved them tenderly and patiently, but with a detachment that allowed her to tell Lucy no, that let her listen to Ellen fuss herself to sleep at naptime without her breasts swelling in reply. She loved Anna's children carefully and without abandon, and Anna's children loved her, too. Every day when Cerise arrived, Ellen's face lit up like a Christmas tree, and later, when Lucy came home from school, her pleasure at seeing Cerise made her almost manic.

Sometimes, while Ellen napped, Cerise continued to study the pictures on Anna's walls. Standing in front of each of them in turn, she let her eyes flick or drift where they would while she waited for something to strike her—some feeling or understanding. But no matter how long she stood, she couldn't seem to find her way inside them, or couldn't find a way to fit them inside her. Once or twice she tried to ask Anna about the photographs, but Anna's answers never seemed to fit Cerise's questions. It was as if they were talking about two separate things, when Cerise asked why the photographs weren't in color and Anna answered by talking about nostalgia and expectation, about the clarity of vision and the purity of line.

After the hours she spent at Anna's house, it was always both a respite and a sadness to return to the fairground. Each time she saw that the gap in the chain-link fence had not been fixed, a bit of the anxiety she'd been carrying with her all day relaxed a little, and when she entered her stall and found her bundle of belongings still untouched, she felt another small relief. It was as though her essential self were waiting for her in that empty place, the inescapable Cerise she always came to in the end. She ate her supper, made up her bed, and folded herself inside, hoping once again that she would not be discovered in her sleep.

It had been a long while since she had been able to find her way back to the other world where it seemed her son still lived, and there were moments when, lying on her newspaper bed, she missed Travis so fiercely she marveled that it did not stop her heart. There were times when she still worried about him, too. She had the drifting feeling that death was just a chain-link fence separating the living from the dead, and she worried that Travis was on the other side, scared and lonely and wondering why she had abandoned him. It made her sick that she couldn't console him, couldn't reach through the barrier of death to explain what had happened to him in a way he might understand.

But there were also hours when Travis traveled with her like a kind of friendly ghost, like another self inside her. In a strange way he seemed older than she was now, and somehow wiser, because he was outside of life, because he knew what happened when you died. She did not forget him, even for a minute, but sometimes it seemed her memories were growing rounder, safer, less urgent, more like pearls than knives.

For a long time Cerise managed to keep her thoughts of Melody quarantined so that they could not contaminate her other memories or her meager plans. But one evening as she was spreading out the newspapers that made her mattress, a smudged photograph on a back page caught her eye. It was a picture of a slender woman in overalls standing on a ladder with a paintbrush in her hand. The ladder was leaning against the wall of a building on which the rough outlines of a design were just beginning to appear. The woman's back was to the camera, but something about the shape of her shoulders and the way she held her head made Cerise think of Melody. "Muralist at Work," the caption beneath the photograph announced.

Clutching the newspaper in both hands, Cerise hurried to the doorway of her stall. Angling the paper so the article caught the light, she read that the North Coast Arts Council had recently awarded a grant to Melody Painter for a mural to decorate the west wall of the newly renovated Arcata Cultural Arts Center. *Saturday Morning* was the name of the winning design, which had been chosen out of a pool of over one hundred entries.

Staring at the grainy image, Cerise stumbled out of the barn into the exposed space between the buildings, scrutinizing the photograph by what light still lingered in the sky. But although she was certain it was her daughter who stood on the ladder, it was impossible to learn any more about what she was painting, impossible to discern what *Saturday Morning* might mean to Melody.

Cerise lay awake for a long time that night, relishing the proof that Melody was okay, savoring her pride that Melody's mural had been chosen as the best, and trying to overlook the hurt she felt at Melody's new last name. She clutched the article like a talisman and remembered those long-distant Saturday mornings and how happy she'd been back then. Closing her eyes, she let herself be rocked by the swelling round of frog-song, let herself imagine that surely Melody had been happy back then, too.

But when the frogs abruptly quit their calling, startled into silence by a wandering raccoon or a passing owl, her eyes jolted open with a start. Staring up into the darkness from her scanty bed, she made herself admit that her thought about Melody's happiness was only another hope. And then she forced herself to remember how futile hope had always been.

SUDDENLY THERE WERE ABANDONED FRUIT TREES EVERYWHERE. EVEN IN the city, Anna spotted them, blossoming in vacant lots and alleyways and overgrown backyards. Outside Santa Dorothea she found other neglected orchards, and she discovered lone fruit trees, as well—flowering among the oaks on the hillsides, or along the edges of back roads, or deep in secluded stands of fir and redwood.

"Tell me about those trees," she'd demanded of Eliot the night after she'd first discovered the dead orchard in bloom.

"What about them?" Eliot had asked. They were in the bathroom, getting ready for bed. But despite her tiredness and the late hour, despite how early the alarm was set to ring, Anna felt right inside her body again, more keen and easy and alive than she'd felt in months. She squeezed toothpaste onto her brush and said, "Last winter I was sure that orchard was completely dead."

Lifting his chin toward the mirror, Eliot pulled his razor down through the white foam on his face, leaving behind a swath of clean skin from his cheekbone to his jaw. He said, "Not dead, just abandoned."

"But why would anyone abandon an orchard?"

"It's worthless," he said curtly, pausing to rinse his razor.

"Worthless fruit?" Anna asked, her toothbrush halfway to her mouth. "Isn't that an oxymoron?"

"Trees produce less as they age. It gets to where it's not worth the work of harvesting them. Besides, most of those old orchards grow old varieties. They might taste great, but they probably don't transport well. Until someone decides to develop the land, it's cheaper just to ignore it."

"But those trees were loaded with blossoms. I don't think I've ever seen so many flowers."

"They tend to do that, when they're stressed or dying—set more blooms. And they'll burst early, in a warm spell." He gave a bitter chuckle, "You could say it's just another gift of global warming."

Anna asked, "How old would an orchard like that be, anyway?"

"Hard to tell." Eliot jutted his chin toward the mirror, stretched his lip up over his teeth, and ran his razor down his taut chin to his Adam's apple. Relaxing his grimace, he added, "Untended, they can start looking bad pretty fast. Some plum trees'll live a hundred years or more, though I doubt an orchard big as yours would be that old. Maybe back to the Depression, pre–World War II. That's a long time, even so."

"You know how many trees like that there are around here, once you start to look?" Anna asked.

Eliot rinsed his razor and tapped it against the side of the sink. "Sure," he answered. "Lots." He turned and grinned at her, holding her gaze so long that the irony in his expression had melted into tenderness by the time he added, "There's plenty of fruit on this planet that goes to waste."

It became a kind of quest, to find those trees while they still bloomed. In the bits of time she managed to steal from the rest of her life, Anna roamed the countryside, seeking them. Driving slowly and braking often, she scoured the back roads, searching for the apples and plums and pears and figs that had been planted years ago for the years to come, planted by people who lay in graves long gone while their homes and barns and fields sank back into the earth, until now only those old trees remained, like messages sent by strangers or gifts left by ghosts. Disregarding fences, signs, and dogs, she hiked through the hills and draws as though she owned them, and back in her darkroom, each new print made her hungry for the one that would follow it.

The last Sunday in March, Anna left the girls with Honey and headed south, wandering down roads she chose at random until she found herself at last in a land far beyond where she had ever been, a windswept place of vacant hills so broad and steep and rocky they seemed almost like mountains. She parked by a break in the barbed-wire fence that edged the road. Shouldering her camera and carrying her tripod, she set off, hiking up the hill beneath a sky filled with massy clouds. When she reached the top, she looked west, down into a land so big and empty it seemed almost unearthly, a place of rocky soil, sparse grass, and solitude.

The radio had warned that the weather was changing, and she could feel it as she hiked, that gathering tension that meant a storm was coming. She could see it in the creamy strangeness of the light. The terrain was rough, her equipment was heavy, and after a while she became so thirsty that her mouth ached for water. But despite the lack of trees, something drew her on—the desolation of the landscape, maybe, or maybe just the joy of being so alone, of being a solitary body and a single mind wandering through those open, empty hills.

Late in the afternoon, as the western sky grew smooth and fierce beneath the menacing clouds, she came across one lone tree. Halfway up another hill, it stood exposed to the oncoming storm. Some ancient mishap had split its trunk in two, and one half of it rested like a fallen snag along the ground. The cavity where its heart had been was black and gaping, although the damage was so old, the edges of the hole had healed as smooth as lips.

Despite every outrage, it was in bloom. Overhead the clouds were heaped and dark, but beneath them the low-set sun burnished the broken wood and set each frail petal afire. There was something so savage about it that it almost frightened her, that lonely tree glowing beneath the threatening sky. She reminded herself it was only a trick of light that caused that doomed tree to blossom one last time, only a trick of light that made it appear before her now like a kind of earthly glory. But even those ironies could not diminish her awe.

The wind was rising. Her hair stung her cheeks, and her eyes filled with cold tears. She knew a photograph of that tree would never save or change a thing. But she no longer cared. There wasn't much time. The light continued to deepen, and just as quickly it would be gone. Opening her tripod, she planted it on the rocky soil so that the tree loomed above her, luminous against the roiling sky. She had time for one exposure before the wild light slipped away.

BY THE END OF MARCH THE FAIRGROUND WAS FULL OF SQUATTERS.

The first residents had been as furtive as Cerise herself, hiding even from each other, ducking around corners, squirreling their possessions out of sight. But as the days lengthened and the evening air grew balmy and their numbers increased, those new occupants seemed to be gaining an audacity that worried Cerise.

One Thursday night in early April, after she'd eaten her little dinner and climbed beneath her blankets, she could hear people gathering in the open space behind her barn, and she cringed to hear how clearly their voices carried in the dusk air, shuddered to smell the smoke from their bonfire. She lay beneath her blankets in the last dim light of evening and wished she had the courage to remind them not to call attention to themselves. .

She finally went to sleep to the mutter of many voices, although her sleep was shallow and shifting. Sometime around midnight a crescendo of hard laughter punched her awake, and afterward she lay unsleeping for many hours while the whoops and curses of strangers echoed between the buildings. At first she was only worried that the police would come to rout out the revelers or that the revelers would tire of each other and go looking for people like herself. But as the night dragged on, she finally admitted to herself what she'd been fearing all along—this little haven, too, was coming to an end.

As soon as it was light enough to see, she bundled up her things and slipped away, gliding past the people sprawled around the blackened trash barrel. The sky east of the city was reddening with the coming day as she crawled through the fence and hiked into the dawn.

She devoted the morning to doing laundry and trying to figure out where she could spend the coming night. But when the time came for her to head to Anna's, she still hadn't thought of a safe place to sleep. She hid her belongings in a thicket halfway down the steep ravine that ran behind the houses on Anna's street, and for a moment she even considered sleeping there, but the hillside was too steep and rugged, and she didn't want to bring her real life that close to Anna's.

Anna's face was glowing when Cerise arrived. "I just put Ellen down," she said as she let Cerise into the house. "But she isn't quite asleep."

Cerise nodded and followed Anna down the hall. She wondered if Anna had seen her scrambling out of the ravine. But Anna said, "I've got good news." Her voice was bright with excitement. "I just got a call from a woman I met last fall—the wife of the man who had Eliot's job before he got it. She wants to see my portfolio."

Cerise kept her face still and waited until Anna explained, "She's interested in buying some of my new photographs."

"That's nice," Cerise said shyly.

"It is," Anna answered. "It'd be great to sell something to such a good collection, especially right now, when I'm still half a year away from a new show. I just wish—" A shadow crossed her face, and for a moment she looked as though she were thinking very hard. Then she tossed her thought away with an apologetic shrug and smiled directly at Cerise. "Anyway," she continued, "I wanted to ask if you would mind staying with Lucy and Ellen while Eliot and I went over there for dinner tonight. I can come back after my seminar, and help you feed the girls before I go. Of course we can give you a ride home afterward."

Home, Cerise's mind gulped, thinking of her empty stall at the fairground, of her blankets in the ravine. "Okay," she said, to mask the complications in her head.

Anna was looking at her fondly. "You've helped me so much—you've helped all of us. We owe you a great, great deal."

It flustered Cerise for Anna to be talking that way. It almost frightened her. But in the middle of her confusion, she mustered up her courage and said, "Could I see them, too?"

"See them?" Anna echoed.

"Your pictures," Cerise suggested shyly.

"Oh," Anna answered, looking vaguely bemused. "Of course I'd be glad to show them to you. It's nice of you to ask." Glancing at her wristwatch, she added, "I've still got a few minutes before I have to leave for campus."

Anna led Cerise into the kitchen, where a flat black case lay on the table. It was thick as a book, and so long and wide it would hold an unfolded newspaper. Anna was just beginning to unzip it when the baby monitor on the counter crackled to life, filling the room with fretful mumbles and the little sounds of Ellen shifting in her crib.

"I guess I tried too early," Anna said. "Looks like you'll have to put her back down a little later." She lifted the top flap of the portfolio to reveal a stack of prints in mat-board frames. "Anyway, you're welcome to look at them while I get her up."

Anna hurried out of the kitchen, leaving Cerise alone with the stack of prints. She felt nervous about touching then, afraid she might accidentally stain or bend them, and she was worried she would still not be able to understand why they meant so much. While the baby monitor broadcast Anna's murmurs and Ellen's answering coos into the kitchen, Cerise tentatively lifted the first print from the portfolio. It was about the size of the photograph of Anna's that hung in the living room, but rather than being a sweeping landscape, it was only a picture of a row of trees. They were not pretty trees, not the smooth symmetrical trees Cerise would have chosen to photograph. Instead, these trees were twisted and disfigured, broken and blackened and near-dead, though despite all their deformities, their branches were filled with glowing flowers.

One by one, Cerise studied the rest of Anna's prints, letting her eyes roam and linger until finally her gaze disengaged, turned inward in a kind of aching rapture. The monitor filled the room with the intimate hum of loving voices, but Cerise was unable to tear herself away and turn it off. It seemed as though a limb she'd somehow forgotten was part of her body had fallen asleep and was now tingling, buzzing, stinging with the work of waking. It hurt, the yearning that was upwelling in her, and at the same time it seemed to contain the answer to her longing. Looking at those broken, blooming trees was like listening to the saddest music—it made her almost grateful that she was alive to feel such pain.

But when she reached the print at the bottom of the stack, her jaw dropped and she clapped her scarred hand to her open mouth to catch her moan. Her brain seized shut as though it couldn't believe what her eyes were seeing, and still she could not stop staring. It was a photograph of a lone tree on a barren hillside beneath a stormy sky. Sundered almost in two, one half of its trunk lay draped along the stony ground. Of all the trees on earth, Cerise recognized it—though in Anna's photograph it was ablaze with flowers.

"Sorry that took so long," Anna said, entering the kitchen with

Ellen riding on her hip like a round-eyed jockey. "I had to change her, too." She was bending her head to nuzzle Ellen's cheek when she caught sight of Cerise's face and straightened up instead. "You look like you've just seen a ghost," she said, crossing the kitchen to stand at the table beside her. "Are you feeling all right?"

Tears were welling so thickly in Cerise's eyes that for a moment tears were all she could see. "Are you okay?" she heard Anna ask, her tone teetering between tenderness and worry.

"I'm fine," Cerise answered almost fiercely. She handed the last print to Anna. Gouging the tears from her eyes, she added, "I'm just—I mean, it's nothing. I like your pictures."

"You do?" Anna asked perplexedly. "Well, thank you. That's nice of you to say." She studied Cerise for a moment longer and added, "Are you sure that everything's okay?"

IT PUZZLED ANNA THAT HONEY HAD BEEN CRYING. DRIVING TO CAMPUS, she wondered if something had happened at the shelter that was troubling her. Despite herself, as Anna leaned forward to switch on the radio, she remembered Sally's warning, and a little pall of worry descended in her mind.

She had almost reached the freeway when she heard the news. An au pair from Paris had killed the toddler she'd been hired to come to America to care for, drowning him in the bathtub while his parents were at work. There was a sound bite from a spokesperson who said the whole child-care industry needed increased regulation, and then the newscaster began a segment about the record-breaking heat. But instead of the sunny street that lay beyond the windshield, Anna saw Ellen, watching happily as Honey filled the bath.

A thick fear prickled in her chest. There was no excuse for what she had done—opening her home to a homeless stranger, hiring a woman to care for her children who'd lost her job caring for children. There were reasons people became homeless—Anna knew that. In some reluctant recess of herself, she'd known all along that Sally was right, that it must have taken more than simple bad luck for Honey to have sunk so far. She had known, too, that she hadn't hired Honey in order to help her, hadn't hired Honey in order to make Lucy feel better about the world. She'd hired Honey because she needed help so desperately that she was willing to take stupid risks. She'd hired Honey so that she could use her, and now she was going to pay for her selfishness.

She could hear the rill of water filling the tub. In the darkness inside her head she could see the happy anticipation on Ellen's face as Honey lowered her into the trembling water, could see Honey's placid expression grow rigid with resolve, and then the image of Ellen's blue birthface slammed into her mind. Steering with one hand, she jammed the car toward the curb while she used her other hand to dig in her purse for Jesse's cell phone. A truck swooped past her, honking. Frantically she tore the phone from its case, opened it, and then jabbed the pattern of her own phone number onto the grid of tiny buttons.

Her lungs began to burn, and she realized she was holding her breath. But before she could exhale, the phone rang. Honey answered just as suddenly, her voice calm and normal, so loud inside Anna's head it startled her, "Hello?"

Anna took a silent sip of air and dizzily tried to scrape together a reason for her call.

"Hello?" Honey said again. Her voice had gained a little edge of suspicion and impatience that Anna recognized as her own tone when she answered a crank phone call.

"Hello?" Honey's voice was louder now, and hard, exactly as Anna would want it to be to scare off would-be burglars and kidnappers.

"Deedee?" she heard Ellen chirp, and suddenly she was seized with a shame even larger than her terror had been. More clearly than the street in front of her, she saw Honey holding the phone, the small furrow of a frown on her impassive face. She saw Ellen clinging to her as though

Honey were a tree, saw the way the sunlight lay across the floor. With a sudden slap of insight, she saw that her call was the only threat to the happiness of their day.

The wild thought skittered through her mind that Honey would recognize the sound of her breathing and know it was she on the mute end of the phone. Stealthily she took the phone from her ear. But just before her finger touched the button to turn it off, she heard Honey whisper in a voice broken with pain, "Melody? Is that you?"

CERISE PUT THE RECEIVER BACK AND STOOD WITH ELLEN ON HER HIP, staring sightlessly at the bands of sunlight on the kitchen floor. She'd answered the phone only because she'd thought it might be Anna or Eliot calling home. Even after she'd heard the live silence of an open line, she'd had an eerie feeling that the caller was someone she knew, though the thought of Melody never consciously crossed her mind until she'd heard herself croaking Melody's name. It had been so long since she'd spoken that name aloud that it felt odd and awkward in her throat, and in the instant after she'd said it, she'd been appalled by how much hope and dread she'd dredged up with that one word.

On her hip, Ellen began to squirm and rub her eyes.

"It's time for your nap, isn't it?" Cerise said dully, pulling Ellen closer.

Upstairs, she opened the window to let some freshness into Ellen's stuffy room, and then settled into the rocking chair with Ellen on her lap. For a long time she rocked mechanically, staring at the curtains belling in the breeze, and wondering at how stupid she'd been to think it could possibly be Melody on the mute end of the phone. Ellen made a comfortable little sigh. Glancing down, Cerise saw her eyelids slide shut, watched her hand fall open as though she'd just let a ball roll off her fingertips. She felt so warm and simple in Cerise's lap, her little weight as calming as a drug. Arcata, the woman at the campground had said—in a tree house, in the woods—and always before it had seemed like one more proof that the first baby Cerise had loved was lost forevermore.

Now, as she felt drowsily in her pocket for the scrap of tattered newspaper she still carried there, a new thought began to grow in her, a question she couldn't quite shape. But before it could come to anything, Cerise had followed Ellen into the fold of sleep.

ANNA LEFT CAMPUS AS SOON AS HER SEMINAR WAS OVER AND DROVE straight home. I'm being silly, she thought as she parked the car, but when she opened the back door, she was met by a silence so dense it filled the house like an ocean fog.

"Hello," she called, entering the dim kitchen. "I'm home." But the house absorbed her greeting and offered nothing in return. As she climbed the stairs she could feel her pulse accelerate. Walking down the hall toward the unlit bedrooms, she realized she was moving stealthily, and the thought flickered through her mind that if she stayed quiet, she might be able to catch Honey at something.

When she reached Ellen's room and found them both asleep in the rocking chair, her relief was followed by a wave of fierce chagrin. Penitent, she stood in the doorway and studied the two of them. Ellen was sprawled across Honey's lap, her mouth open and her arms out-flung. Honey's legs were akimbo and her head was thrown back, exposing the length of her strong neck and the triangle of tender skin beneath her jaw. Even in her sleep, she was holding Ellen carefully, her scarred palms clasped around Ellen's torso to prevent her from slipping from her lap. They both looked so vulnerable, so utterly at the mercy of the world, and yet they seemed serene, careless and easy in their sleep. The curtains belled at the opened window, the cool, green scent of spring-time filled the air, and the whole room was filled with a tranquillity so keen it made Anna's heart ache.

She was still watching them when Honey shifted uneasily in her sleep, muttering and tossing her head from side to side as though she were saying no to something in her dreams. She groaned, and it was a sound so intimate and anguished that Anna suddenly felt like a voyeur. She turned and tiptoed hurriedly down the hall.

She still had three hours before she needed to pick up Eliot and drive out to the Laughlins', and almost that long before she expected Lucy home from playing with Kaylesha. In the kitchen she paused to zip her prints back into her portfolio. Flipping through them, all toned and signed and mounted in their window mats, she felt a pleasure robust as bread. But she still had an edgy sense of melancholy, too, to think that the best that could befall them would be to end up in galleries or museums or to win places on the walls of collectors like Carole Laughlin. What more could you possibly want? she asked herself sternly, though she could find no answer to fill that little ache.

She'd made two good prints of the lone tree so far, and downstairs in her darkroom, she settled in to spot-tone the second one, patiently teasing the white dust spots with her tiny brush until they disappeared into the grain of the photograph. When that was finished, she turned her attention to housekeeping—cleaning tongs and scrubbing trays and sweeping. She tipped the contents of the dustpan into the overflowing wastebasket and then headed upstairs to empty it. Halfway up the steps she noticed, among the failed prints and old test strips and crumpled film wrappers, the negatives Lucy had ruined. She paused and pulled them from the trash. Looking at the lopsided flowers on their milky-dark surfaces, she felt a hot remorse.

I should keep those, she thought, as a reminder. But suddenly she had an impulse to burn them instead. In the kitchen she found a book of matches. As she backed out the kitchen door with the wastebasket and a newspaper from the recycling bin, the screen slammed behind her, startlingly loud. It was lighter outside than it had been in the house, though dusk was coming fast. Sherbet-colored clouds were heaped in the western sky, and above her she could already make out several stars. The air was cool and verdant, alive against her skin.

An old burn barrel left by the previous owners sat at the back of the yard just before the land sloped into the ravine. Anna set the wastebasket down and began to crumple sheets of newspaper and toss them into the barrel. She wanted a good blaze, wanted it bright and hot. She liked the thought of burning all her struggles and false starts, of starting clean in a new season. She lit a match, savoring the little whiff of sulfur it released into the fresh evening, though as she touched the flame to the nearest crumple of paper, it occurred to her to wonder if it were even legal to have a trash fire anymore.

But the fire was already beginning to take hold. For a moment the edges of the paper she'd lit were etched with flickering orange lines, and then suddenly the whole mass was writhing with flame. Tentatively—at first almost playfully—and then with startling intent and speed, fire spread through the pile of newspaper. There was an inrushing of sound like a giant inhalation and flames rose up, fierce and surprisingly loud, pushing her back from the barrel.

She stood for a moment, mesmerized, feeling the prickle of heat against her skin. Then she stepped nearer. Holding the wastebasket upside down above the flames, she let her trash cascade into the fire.

WHEN THE SMOKE FIRST FILTERED INTO CERISE'S SLEEP, HER DREAMS recognized it. It was a nasty smoke, the smell of cheap things burning, and for a while her dreams engulfed it, offering weird dream-reasons to explain its presence. When the dreams finally turned to Travis and the trailer, she escaped the horror by waking. A nightmare, she told herself as she fought to find a way out of its grip. But instead of fading as she woke, the smell of smoke grew stronger.

Opening her eyes, she cast a wild glance around the darkness and struggled to remember where she was—in Rita's house, or her apartment, or back at Jake's? She rose, swaying. Clutching the baby to her chest, she stumbled down the stairs, floundered through the dark rooms until she found the door, fought with the knob until it gave, and then burst outside, leaving the door gaping triumphantly as she entered the gloaming with the child she had saved.

LONG BEFORE ELLEN'S CRIES REACHED ANNA'S EARS OR REGISTERED IN her brain, she felt them slashing through her body. Quick as instinct, she turned from the flame-filled barrel to see the dark shape of Honey burst through the kitchen door, carrying Ellen in her arms.

"What's wrong?" Anna cried, throwing down her wastebasket and racing up the yard to meet them. "What happened? Is she okay?"

But Honey stumbled dazedly past her. She seemed to be headed toward the ravine when suddenly she caught sight of the fire. At first she veered away in fresh alarm, but then she halted as if she were too stricken go on. When Anna reached her, she was staring wildly into the dusk and panting as though she had just run a long, hard way. "What's wrong?" Anna repeated, grabbing her arm. "What happened?"

Ellen was sobbing, and Anna held out her hands to take her, but Honey gripped Ellen tighter and pivoted away. "I did it," she said. "I did it, after all." Her voice rang with stupefied triumph, but when she looked at Anna, her eyes were blank and hollow.

"What? Did what? What do you mean?" Anna cried, struggling to reach her daughter. But Honey dodged again, clinging to Ellen as though she were a rag doll that she did not want to share. In the jagged light the flames cast, her face was twisted with anguish and exertion and a ferocious determination.

"Mama," Ellen sobbed, reaching piteously for Anna.

"Give her to me," Anna screamed. Seizing hold of Honey's arm, she twisted her fingers into Honey's flesh. "You give me back my daughter."

For a moment Honey appeared bewildered, and then she stared down at Ellen as if Ellen were a stranger, as if she had no idea who Ellen was or how she had arrived in her arms.

"Oh," she said at last, though it sounded more like a groan than a word.

"What is going on?" Anna yelled, jerking her arm again as she reached for Ellen with her other hand. "What the hell is wrong?"

An agony crossed Honey's face. "Oh," she said again, and this time her voice was a croak of despair. Silently she handed Ellen to Anna, who took her daughter and held her fast, soaking the feel of her back into her bones, checking Ellen for hurts or frights that could not be fixed by her arms alone.

"What happened?" Anna gasped, and when Honey didn't answer, Anna clutched Ellen closer and hissed, "You have to tell me. I trusted you."

But Honey only shuddered and bent her head.

"What's wrong?" Anna insisted. Honey looked so stupid and lumpen that Anna wanted to slap an answer out of her. "What's wrong with you? What happened up there?" She glanced back toward the dark house, and then watched in mean satisfaction as Honey flinched and shrank.

"Okay," she said finally after Honey wouldn't answer. "Tell me this—who the hell is Melody?"

Honey grunted and reeled as though she'd been stabbed. "What?" she gasped. "How do you know?"

"Who is she?" Anna insisted, digging in. "Who is Melody?" She watched as Honey wrestled with something, watched as her mouth stuttered open and then sagged shut. Finally, her head hanging, Honey answered flatly, "I guess I had a bad dream."

"A bad dream," Anna scoffed. "A bad dream doesn't make you crazy."

"This one tried," Honey said softly, her head still bowed.

"I don't believe it. There's more to it than that."

"I'm not crazy," Honey answered, looking up suddenly. "Though," she added quietly, as her gaze faltered away from Anna's eyes, "I sometimes wished."

"Are you drunk? Are you on drugs?"

"No. I'm not. I never was." Honey was staring dully at the fire.

"What was your dream about?" Anna insisted. But Honey only shivered and shook her head. A tear ran down her face and wobbled on her chin, catching the firelight for a moment before it fell.

Looking at her, Anna felt a wave of compassion, but she pressed on sharply, "Nothing happened to Ellen?"

"Oh, no." Honey's voice was swift and shocked. "Except," she added remorsefully, "running out here, I made her cry."

"Okay," Anna said, the coldness draining from her voice so that her words sounded only weary. "I'm sorry. It was wrong of me to react so fast. It's just—you scared me. If you're ever a mother, you'll know. You always worry about your children first."

"I know," said Honey raggedly. She swayed as though she were dizzy and hid her face in her disfigured palms.

The final color was fading from the sky, the smoke had vanished, and in the barrel the fire had diminished to a flickering mass of sparks. Anna hugged Ellen and watched Honey rock back and forth, her face pressed into her palms, her shoulders heaving silently.

Suddenly Ellen reached toward Honey. "Deedee?" she asked. Anna moved a step closer so that Ellen could pat Honey's shoulder with her outstretched hand.

A second later, when Anna reached out to hug Honey, she detected no trace of booze or dope in Honey's smell, and the scent of Honey's cheap shampoo and sturdy body was already familiar from all the times Anna had received Ellen from Honey's arms.

CERISE COULD NOT REMEMBER EVER HAVING BEEN HELD BY A WOMAN, and at first she longed for nothing more than to rest forever in the comfort of Anna's arms. For a time they huddled together, Ellen sandwiched between them, their breaths warming the little pocket the three of them made in the chill, new night. But as her shock wore off, she became aware of how she loomed over Anna's head, and grew so embarrassed about how she feared she must smell that she could not keep from edging out of Anna's embrace.

Slowly Anna led her up the yard toward the house, her free arm still supporting Cerise's back. In the kitchen she handed Ellen to Cerise, turned on lights and boiled water and made tea, brewing it in a pot covered with painted roses and pouring it into cups as light as bubbles, adding cream and sugar until it tasted as warm and sweet as human milk.

"Are you okay?" Anna asked when they were both sitting at the kitchen table, Ellen back in Anna's lap and their cups in front of them on porcelain saucers.

Cerise could feel both Anna's probing and her concern. Looking into her cup, she answered quietly, "I'm okay. I'm sorry to be a trouble."

"You're not a trouble," Anna said. "Don't think like that."

They sat in silence, sipping their tea, feeling the steam bloom on their cheek as they put their lips to their cups' rims to drink.

"I would like to know what happened," Anna finally said, though now her voice was calm and tender. "I might be able to help more, if I knew."

A long time passed, in which Cerise struggled inside herself. At last, in a voice so raw it seemed certain that the words would come out bloody, she said, "Please don't ask me that." She cast a quick glance at Anna, but instead of the anger she'd expected to find on Anna's face, she was startled to see that Anna looked stricken, her expression so inward and remote it was as though she were hearing voices from another time.

"I'd like to tell you," Cerise said pleadingly. "I wish I could. I'm sorry," she added in a whisper.

There was a silence so long, it sent a sizzle of warning down Cerise's back. She knows about me, Cerise thought, poised between yearning and terror at the thought of what Anna might say next. But when Anna finally spoke, it was not about Melody or Travis. "I had an abortion," she said, and then she stopped and took an extra breath and gazed into the memory that seemed to fill the space in front of her. "Years ago. I had an abortion. I never told anyone," she went on, her voice brimming with sadness and fierceness and a kind of wonder. "Never. You're the first person I've ever told."

Cerise bowed her head and let Anna's words flow through her heart.

"It's mattered," Anna said. "All this time. It's traveled with me. It's not a thing I'm glad or proud of, but maybe it's helped me in a way, to stay on course."

This time, when Anna broke the silence, it was as though she were speaking to Cerise again, and not to the ghosts that seemed to have gathered in the room. "I don't know what happened to you," she said, and Cerise could feel Anna's gaze against her downcast head. "I'd imagine that it's harder than anything that's ever happened to me, so I probably don't have a right to talk. But maybe—whatever it is—there's a way that it could help you, in the end."

Sitting with her palms curled inside her fists and her fists clasped between her thighs, Cerise could only look into her lap and shake her head.

"Anyway," Anna said after another minute of waiting, "I promise I won't ask you again. Someone once let me keep silent, and now I'm passing that gift on to you."

Cerise answered awkwardly, "I've never had—a friend like you before." After she'd spoken, she cast a quick glance up at Anna to make sure she hadn't said something wrong. But Anna was regarding her steadily, and when Cerise's eyes met hers, she answered, "And I've never had a friend like you."

Later, after the teapot was empty and just before Lucy burst through the kitchen door Anna asked Cerise one final question. "Should I cancel our plans?"

"Our plans?" Cerise asked, casting about inside her head to try to remember what plans they'd made.

"For tonight? Would you rather I just take you home instead?"

"Oh, no," Cerise said, startled.

"Are you sure?" Anna was studying her hesitantly. "It won't be too hard on you, staying with the girls?"

"I'm sure," Cerise said doggedly. "It'll be okay."

ANNA SAT IN THE CAR AT THE BOTTOM OF THE DRIVEWAY WITH THE headlights off, listening to the drone of the engine and gazing back up at the house. The lights from the instrument panel made the interior of the car seem both anonymous and intimate. But despite the calm inside the car, Anna was still brimming with emotions, so many emotions she was unable to release the brake and drive away.

A warm light poured from the kitchen window, melting a small hole in the night and silhouetting the cuttings Eliot had growing on the windowsill. Anna caught a glimpse of Lucy, practicing for her dance class, her arms outstretched as though she were hugging the air, her ponytail bouncing behind her like a friendly pet. She saw Honey moving in and out of view.

When she'd first met Honey, Anna had dismissed her as a person whose life was small and simple, whose little troubles were nobody's but her own. But Honey had done amazing things for Anna and her family. Safe in the darkness of the purring car, Anna remembered the surge of pleasure she'd felt that morning as she'd talked with Carole Laughlin about her work, how after she'd hung up the phone, she'd looked around her living room and realized that what she saw looked like home. She thought of how healthy Ellen was now, and she remembered Lucy bursting into the kitchen that afternoon, her face so radiant it was hard to believe there'd ever been a time when she'd been afraid to go to sleep, ever a time when she'd had no friends. Somehow Honey was connected to all those changes, and yet why and how and what she'd done was still a mystery.

So many mysteries. Anna remembered Honey's voice on the phone, raggedly asking the emptiness, *Melody, is that you?* She thought of how Honey had stumbled like a zombie from the house, how the firelit tears had trembled on her chin. Anna knew in her bones that her daughters were safe with Honey, but she had no idea who Honey really was. Gazing at the glowing window, she saw what was always the case—the closer you got to someone, the nearer you came to the mystery at their core.

She thought of the mysteries of her daughters—those strangers, those guests, those dear and unexpected friends—who had somehow tumbled through her into their own separate lives. She thought how near they were to her, the pitch of their voices and the touch of their hands so familiar, their flesh and breath more precious than her own. And she thought how distant they were, too—their souls inviolable, their secret selves eternally apart from hers. She thought of how much she needed them, how crucial they were to who she was, how even her art depended on them.

She closed her eyes and saw, through the dark tears that welled beneath her lids, the other mystery that she had borne, that long-vanished bit of tissue that had never claimed a sex or risen to a face but that had lived inside her nonetheless, that had somehow helped to shape her with its absence. She remembered swallowing milky tea and telling Honey what she'd never said before. It had faded the shimmer a little to tell, but she was glad she had.

She needed to get going, she thought as she sat. She needed to pick up Eliot, to drive out to the Laughlins' along the tangle of dark roads. She imagined the fine dinner they would enjoy there, the good wine and exotic food, imagined how, in the room that held photographs by Ansel Adams and Edward Weston and Alfred Stieglitz, she would open her portfolio and spread her work across the mahogany table, imagined how her broken trees would shine on the polished wood. But still she sat in the car, too full to drive away.

She remembered a snip of conversation she'd had with Honey a few weeks before. "What's it like?" she'd asked, "living in the shelter?" She'd been merely curious, and was surprised at the dismay that flashed across Honey's face, although when she answered, she'd sounded as placid as ever. "It's okay," she'd said, adding like an afterthought, "They talk a lot about God."

"What do you think about that?" Anna had asked. It had been a long time since she'd discussed religion with anyone, and she wondered if the faith the shelter had to offer was like the faith her nephew Jesse professed, wondered what a person like Honey would think of Jesse's God.

Honey had shrugged, "It's a help to some of them, I guess."

"How about you?" Anna persisted.

"I don't see as how it could ever be much help to me," Honey had answered, and her voice had sounded hard, more nearly angry than Anna had ever heard it.

Now, sitting inside the dim capsule of her car, an odd idea began to grow inside her head, though as it grew clearer, she realized it was what she had wanted her photographs to be saying all along: maybe life created God—and not, as Jesse's church would claim, the other way around. Maybe what made God was life, all of life—every single birth and every death, and all the struggle and delight sandwiched in between. Maybe life made God like a baby made a mother, so that just as it was the baby's coming that turned a woman into something greater than herself, so it was that everything in the world turned the emptiness that had preceded it into God.

It was all so large and hard and lovely, all so strange.

Here we are—alive—she thought, gazing at the light that spilled from the kitchen window, gazing until the light blossomed and smeared, gazing until she began to grin at the craziness of it.

She hoped that Honey would be all right, hoped they all would. Bless us, she begged the darkness and the light. She sat in the humming car for a moment longer, watching the window where Lucy had resumed her dance. She waited until her eyes regained their focus and her grin subsided and her mind felt clear. Then she put the car in gear and drove away, following the path her headlights opened in the dark.

AFTER ANNA LEFT, CERISE BOILED PASTA AND HEATED TOMATO SAUCE and shredded cheese while Ellen watched from her high chair and Lucy twirled in circles in the middle of the room.

Working in the kitchen that was not hers but that she knew as well as if it were, she cut a rib of celery into sticks. She sliced bread and buttered it, poured milk into two glasses and a sippy cup. She set the kitchen table with two plates, placed another plate of cut-up pasta and sauce on the tray of Ellen's high chair. After they had eaten, she gave Ellen a bath to wash the orange sauce stains off her cheeks and out of her hair and from between each chubby finger. Kneeling beside the tub, she watched while Ellen chortled and splashed, and then she lifted her dripping from the water, dried her and dressed her in a doubled diaper and a flannel sleeper, and rocked her until she fell asleep.

Then she played three games of Old Maid with Lucy, retrieved Lucy's favorite nightgown from beneath her dresser, reminded her to throw her dirty clothes down the laundry chute, and watched as she dabbed her face with water and scrubbed her teeth until the toothpaste foamed down her chin. After Lucy scrambled into bed with half a dozen stuffed animals and twice that many books, Cerise turned off the overhead light, turned on the night-light, and bent to kiss her.

"Good night," Cerise said, trying to keep her voice light and smooth.

"I love you," Lucy declared, rearing off her pillow to throw her arms around Cerise's neck.

"Me, too," Cerise said, giving Lucy's hand a gentle pat before she disengaged herself and hurried from the room.

Downstairs in the kitchen, she put away the leftover food, rinsed the dishes, and set them in the dishwasher. As she wiped the table and the counters and Ellen's high chair and swept the kitchen floor, she tried to hold herself apart from everything but the chore that she was doing, the dishcloth wiping its damp arcs across the counter, the broom straws pushing breadcrumbs toward the dustpan.

Finally, after the dishcloth was spread to dry and the broom was back in its closet, she turned off the light and sat at the table in the dark kitchen, staring at the black window and waiting for what would come next. Thoughts drifted and darted through her mind like fish inside the glass walls of an aquarium: It was nice of Anna to make tea for her. She should start the dishwasher soon. Tonight Anna would insist on giving her a ride to the shelter. She hoped her bundles had stayed hidden in the ravine. She didn't want to lose Barbara's blanket. She wished she'd drawn a special picture for Lucy. She wished she could say to Anna what Anna had given her. Maybe there had never been a battery in the smoke detector. Maybe it didn't matter if there had.

When she heard a hesitant noise on the steps, she waited until it reached the landing before she stirred herself to ask, "Lucy, is that you?"

"I can't go to sleep," Lucy whimpered. "Can I sit with you, for just a little while?" she asked, rushing into the room as though she'd already been given permission.

Cerise sighed, "Come on," and Lucy scrambled into her lap. She was so small and knobby, perched on Cerise's thighs, so sweet-smelling and warm, her scant flesh firm beneath her nightgown. Her hair, when Cerise buried her face against the crown of her head, was soft as petals.

They sat for a long while in the half-light that spilled down the stairs, and then Lucy said, "Why are your hands all shiny?" Into the silence that followed she blurted, "Mommy said it wasn't polite to ask, but I thought you wouldn't care.

"Do you care?" she asked worriedly, twisting around to peer at Cerise's face.

"No, I—" Cerise took a breath that felt larger than her body. "I mean, it's all right. My hands got burned," she said, exhaling all that extra air.

"Playing with matches?" Lucy asked.

"No."

"Then what?" Lucy prompted.

"Trying to save some—thing."

"Did you?" Lucy asked, snuggling against Cerise as though Cerise were going to tell her a bedtime story.

"Did I what?" Cerise asked carefully.

"Did you save the thing you tried to save?"

"No," she said, her voice dead.

"Oh," Lucy answered. "Can you get another?"

"No."

"Is that why you're always sad?"

"I'm not always sad."

"Yes, you are—a little. You're always a little sad. You're sad like rain," she added, snuggling in.

"Rain's not sad," Cerise said, staring out the window at the dark.

"It is when you're in it," Lucy said. "I saw a lady once who was very sad, in the rain."

Cerise remembered the time she had spent huddled beneath the ole-anders while rainwater dripped down her face, the time she'd spent seek-ing and avoiding Travis on the wet streets. She pulled Lucy against her and answered, "Rain's only sad if you're sad already."

Lucy said, "When we're dancing and it's time to stop, my dance teacher says we have to make an ending."

"Make an ending?"

"It's supposed to be sadisfying, so you can be glad to stop."

"Oh."

"Endings don't just happen, my dance teacher says. She says you have to make them."

"Sometimes that's hard."

"I know." Lucy nodded sagely. "That's why we practice. You have to make them so you feel sad and fied, all at the same time."

"What's 'fied'?"

"It's when you let the hole be open."

"Did your teacher tell you that?" Cerise asked softly.

"Nuh-uh," Lucy answered, shaking her head. "I teached it to myself."

Lucy lay her head in the crook made by Cerise's hunched shoulder, and was quiet for such a long time that Cerise thought she had fallen asleep. She was beginning to plan how to carry Lucy up to bed when Lucy spoke again. "What did you lose?" she asked.

The words carved Cerise open, slit her from gut to throat.

"My baby," she said finally, speaking over Lucy's head and into the darkness beyond.

"You had a baby?" Lucy asked in wonder.

"I had two." Cerise stiffened, preparing herself for when Lucy leapt off her lap and ran screaming from the room.

But Lucy, resting tranquilly as ever against her chest, only asked, "Girls or boys?"

"One of each."

"A girl and a boy," said Lucy, snuggling in. "What are their names?"

"Travis," Cerise said, and realized that for all she'd thought of him, she had not once said his name since she'd screamed it in the dark hills beneath the broken tree.

"Travis," said Lucy. "And who else? What's your girl's name?"

"Melody." The word came alive on her tongue, like a flavor she'd been craving for so long she'd forgotten how it really tasted and could only remember how much she'd longed for it.

"Travis and Melody," said Lucy contentedly. "Where are they now?"

"Melody ran—Melody grew up. And left. That's what girls do," Cerise said to make herself believe it. "They grow up and leave their mothers. She lives north of here," she added.

"At the North Pole?" Lucy asked.

"No."

"Why don't you see her?"

Cerise shrugged. "She's mad at me. And I—I guess I'm mad at her."

"Why are you mad?"

"Because of the bad things she did."

"She didn't mean to."

"How do you know?"

"Girls never mean to. Only sometimes it's just that things turn out wrong, like a accident."

"Oh," Cerise whispered.

"She's not mad now," Lucy persisted.

"How do you know?"

"Girls don't stay mad," Lucy explained. "You have a time-out, and then you start missing your mom. Where's your boy?"

In the time that followed, Lucy waited patiently while her little question swelled until it grew so big it filled the kitchen, grew so huge it took up all the room Cerise needed to breathe, grew until it crushed against her and forced an answer out.

"He's dead," she croaked. The word was a cruel stone, scratching and grating and choking in her throat. But once she'd said it, she saw how small it was, too, just another human sound—nothing at all like the awfulness it meant. And yet she could breathe after she'd said it, as though somehow that word made the sorrow a little smaller.

Lucy echoed, "Dead?"

Cerise nodded, and then she cringed, waiting for Lucy's horror to set in.

But instead Lucy asked, "How did he die?"

"In a fire," Cerise said quickly, to avoid being crushed. Tears pricked her eyes and plugged her sinuses and clogged her throat, and Lucy watched Cerise's lurching face in fascination. "Your fire?" Lucy asked.

"What?"

"The fire that burned your trailer?"

"Yeah."

"And your hands?"

Cerise nodded, feeling the itch and ache and tingle in her palms.

"He played with matches," Lucy said knowingly.

Cerise rubbed her tears with her fingers, smearing them across her face. "No," she said. "It was an accident, in the wiring. It was just an accident, that's all. It wasn't anyone's fault." The words sounded so simple, so laughably small—an accident—as though Travis had been a big boy and peed his pants. As though there'd never been anyone else to blame. "I tried," she said. "I tried to save him. But—I couldn't." She remembered the triumph she'd felt earlier that evening, running into the gloaming with Ellen in her arms. With a sudden fierce certainty she added, "I would of saved him, if I could."

Lucy nodded solemnly, as if there had never been any doubt. "When's his birthday?" she asked.

"His birthday?" Cerise remembered the slick feel of his body slithering out of her, remembered the slight, wet weight of him as she lifted him to her chest, the umbilical cord still trailing between them. She closed her eyes, and the smell of birth flooded her, rich as grain or semen or fresh blood.

Lucy was saying, "When it's his birthday, me and you can bake a birthday cake. And then we'll take it outside and light the candles and throw it way, way up into the sky and he'll catch it, and then he'll see that you're okay, and he won't have to worry about you anymore. Does he like chocolate?"

Cerise thought of Travis in the sky, eating chocolate cake, and though she knew that was not the truth of where he was, it suddenly came to her that wherever he was, he was okay. With a jolt of excruciating freedom, she understood that Travis was no longer hurt or sad or frightened. Wherever he was, Travis didn't miss her anymore.

She pulled Lucy closer to her, buried her face in the girl's hair. "Yes, he does," she said. "He did. Travis liked chocolate."

Pleased with her plan, Lucy nodded. But then Cerise felt her stiffen with another thought, and she asked in a voice clotted with a sudden new concern, "But won't he be sad if his sister's not there, too?"

Later, long after the business of getting Lucy back to bed, Cerise rose from her seat in the unlit kitchen and headed down the stairs. She had never been inside Anna's darkroom before, and she opened the door warily. Inside it was utterly black, and the first light switch only added amber shadows to the darkness. She groped again and found a real light, though the room it illuminated was not at all as she had imagined it would be.

It seemed more clinical than magical, almost like a hospital with its trays and tools, its looming equipment, cool counters, and vaguely sour smell. At first, when she saw how tidy everything was, she feared she would not find what she'd come seeking. But a second later she saw the print she'd hoped for, sitting on the counter.

When she realized she would have to fold it in half before she could slip it beneath her jacket, she almost changed her mind. But in the end she took it anyway, halving it as carefully as she could, though she cringed at the white scar the crease left on the emulsion. Unzipping the inside pocket of her jacket, she removed the checks she'd received from the after-school care program. She found a pen and endorsed them with the name of the woman who had earned them, and then, adding Anna's name below her own, she left them on the counter in the place where the print had been.

Upstairs she stood for a long time in the dark beside Lucy's bed, gazing into her placid face and imagining the baby Lucy had been, imagining the woman she would become. She realized that if they ever met again, they might not know each other, two strangers standing together in an elevator or passing in a park. And yet she was certain that they would always love each other, even so.

She was in Ellen's room when she heard the car pull up. She bent over the crib railing to breathe the warm steam of Ellen's baby-dreams one last time before she tiptoed from the room and down the stairs. She was waiting at the front door with her jacket on when Eliot opened it.

"How was your night?" Anna asked.

"It was fine," Cerise answered. "The girls are fine. But—I have to go." She looked straight at Anna as she spoke, and Eliot faded back a step.

"It's late," Anna said apologetically. "I know. But if you let Eliot give you a ride, I'm sure you can still make it to the shelter before curfew."

"No," Cerise shook her head. "I mean, I have to leave here. I won't be coming back."

"Not coming back?" Anna said, and Cerise could see a hundred kinds of worry struggling in her face.

"I realized, you—all," she added, glancing back at Eliot, "helped me see. There's something important I need to do."

"What is it?" Anna asked, and when Cerise didn't answer, she added gently, "If you'd tell me, maybe I could help."

"I've got to do this one the hard way," Cerise answered. "All by myself."

"But I—"

"You've done so much for me," Cerise pleaded. "Please do just this one thing more."

"But what are you going to do?"

Anna sounded so bewildered that Cerise teetered for a moment before she answered, "I need to find out what someone means by Saturday morning."

"But I'll miss you," Anna said, her voice shrill with hurt. "And the girls, you can't just—"

"I know," Cerise said. "I'm really sorry. Tell the girls—tell them good-bye."

"Okay," said Anna slowly. A grit of skepticism appeared in her tone. "I'll tell them that."

"I mean," Cerise amended, pushing the words out in a fierce hard rush, "tell them I love them. Tell them I won't forget them, ever. Please," she added.

Anna met her eyes, and their gaze held. For half a minute they looked at each other, each of them silently pleading and then finally conceding, giving way to the mystery that connected them. Anna nodded, and Cerise pushed toward her, reached out an arm to hug her. For the briefest second they stood together, Anna's photograph pressed unwittingly between them, and then Cerise broke away, forced herself out the open door, stumbled down the steps and toward the pool of light at the corner of the street. Because she knew that Anna and Eliot were watching, she did not dare look back. Instead she pressed on until finally she was able to turn the corner, and their house was hidden by other houses in the dark.

The night air was cool and sweet and fresh. It touched Cerise's face like a balm. Casting a quick glance up and down the silent road, she left the sidewalk, slipped across a stranger's yard, and clambered into the ravine. Clutching Anna's print to her chest with one hand, she scrambled along the steep hillside, slipping on the twigs and leaves and struggling to stay upright until she reached the place where she'd left her bundles. She patted the darkness until she found them, and then she climbed back onto the road.

Stopping beneath the next streetlight, she dug the worn rectangle of newspaper from her jacket pocket, studied the picture, and reread the words she knew by heart. Then, replacing the scrap in her pocket, she began to walk. Carrying her possessions in her scarred hands and pressing Anna's photograph against her chest, she left Anna's neighborhood, walked through neighborhoods filled with houses that loomed as large as castles, houses lit by spotlights and protected by alarms, and when she'd passed out of those neighborhoods, she walked past all-night gas stations and convenience grocery stores, past bars and sex shops and lighted lots where acres of cars were planted in tidy rows like fields of corn, and finally she left the city altogether, following the highway that promised to lead her to the coast.

Sometimes she thought of Ellen and Lucy waking in the morning, perplexed by her absence and by their parents' uncertain explanations, and her heart tugged back. It's when you let the hole be open, she remembered Lucy saying, and though she hated to think of Lucy having to practice that lesson quite so soon, in her heart she knew that Lucy could. Sometimes she thought of Anna and the friendship they had made and she hated that of all the women in the world, Anna was the one she had to hurt. But she hoped that in some final end, Anna would understand.

It was late the next morning when she finally glimpsed the ocean. She saw it first as she crested a high hill—a distant rim of gray glinting with light. For a long time she trudged toward it into the wind, and sometimes the wind pummeled her like a romping puppy, and sometimes it battered her like the waves themselves. Sometimes Cerise thought of Melody and the oceans on the tiny planet she had pricked into her cheek. She thought how big the real world was, how hard it could be to find someone who was lost in it, and she was grateful that Melody wore the earth on her face.

By the time she finally reached the sea, the sun was setting. The road ended on a bluff high above the ocean, abutting the narrow highway that ran along the Pacific, north to Arcata and Canada and south to Mexico. The highway gleamed like pewter in the paling light. Cerise crossed it in half a dozen steps, crossed a field of hissing, flattened grass, and stood at the edge of a precipice, looking down. Two hundred feet below her, the ocean looked dark, though far out its waters were still alight. Facing the full force of the wind, she carved out a home for herself inside it. Gazing at the fire blazing on the ocean's distant edge, she stared until her eyes teared from wind and cold and light, and the sun popped below the rim of the sea.

She looked down at the water far below her, saw the shadowy white breakers stretching along the shore like an endless crocheted chain, and though she felt their pull like another law of physics, she ignored that invitation. Instead, turning so that the ocean was on her left, she began to trudge north up the darkening, shining road.

ACKNOWLEDGMENTS

I would like to thank the following experts, whose information and insight were invaluable as I worked to shape this story:

Abortion procedures: Lisa Peterson, Six Rivers Family Planning
Dry land wheat farming: Emmy Michaelsen
Firefighting: Ed Leon, Healdsburg Fire Station
Labor and delivery: Renee Baker
Medical procedures: Monika Balsalmo and Chris Winters
Mothering: Wendy Blair, Penny Chambers, Elaine Greene, Elisa Livingston, Stacy McRee, Melinda Misuraca, Gwen Rosewater, Caroline Draper Swift, Melanie Thornton, Connie Wolfe, Molly Wood
Photography: Heather Fisher, Jackie Kell, Tom Leavitt, Jim Lugo, Belinda Starkie
USDA seed storage: Dr. Rich Hannan, Western Regional Plant Introduction Station, Pullman, Washington

They are not responsible for any of the errors that this book may contain.

I would also like to thank my Beloved Readers: Susan Gaines, Ray Holley, and Sean Swift, as well as Rosemary Ahern, Brenda Copeland, Kate Elton, Virginia Hegland, Bill Horvitz, Beverly Lewis, Kate Parkin, Patti Trimble, Elizabeth Wales, Susan Wasson, and Georgina Hawtrey Woore.

Finally, this novel and I owe a great deal to the clients, staff, volunteers, and director (Susan Lowry) of The Living Room in Santa Rosa, California.

WINDFALLS

JEAN HEGLAND

A Readers Club Guide

A CONVERSATION WITH
JEAN HEGLAND

Q: While your first novel, *Into the Forest*, is a mythical tale about two sisters struggling to survive alone in the redwoods in a postapocalyptic near future, *Windfalls* is very much a realistic story of our time—a profound exploration of the deepest feelings of mother love that also touches upon such timely issues as abortion and the plight of the homeless in our society. Are these two books as completely different as they appear on the surface, or are there any similarities? Do they share any common themes?

A: One of the reasons I love writing fiction is that it allows me to explore so many different aspects of experience. Given that, it makes sense (to me, at least) that my stories would all be quite different, as there are any number of characters and situations that interest me.

But at the same time I'm sure there are parallels between my books that suggest their common source. Some of the most striking similarities between *Into the Forest* and *Windfalls* are that both books have two female protagonists; both put a specific, human face on abstract political issues; and—perhaps most significant—there are characters in both stories who must confront losing the very things that gave the most meaning to their lives. How we humans manage to find the strength and hope to carry on—both in extremity and every day—is a question I could not possibly exhaust in a single book.

Q: What inspired you to write *Windfalls*?

A: The "seed crystal" for *Windfalls* came from a small newspaper article about a woman who had lost a child in a terrible accident. I couldn't stop thinking about that anonymous mother, and wondering how—or whether—she found a way to remake her life after that loss. The more I thought about her, the more I realized that a story about someone like I imagined that woman to be might serve as a container for many of the questions I was currently pondering in my own life— questions about mothering, and art, and home, and the web of circum- stances, choices, and chances that make up our lives.

Q: Do you think that maternal love is the most powerful bond there is? Do you think fathers experience similar feelings for their children, or is paternal love a different kind of emotion?

A: Certainly for many mothers, the love we feel for our children is one of the most powerful and enduring emotions we'll ever have. I know a great number of mothers who have been blindsided both by the fierce, sensual passion and bottomless tenderness they feel for their children, as well as by the dreadful sense of precariousness that having a child intro- duces into even the most secure and privileged of lives.

One factor that helps to establish the intensity of that bond is the profound physicality of most mothers' relationships with their children; pregnancy, childbirth, and nursing all serve to reinforce that connection, and those are experiences that fathers can only know vicariously. But there are also many mothers who did not give birth to or nurse their babies who, nevertheless, feel a connection to their children every bit as profound as mothers who did, and I know that fathers (and other caregivers) can experience those intense bonds, too. In my observation, those fathers who have been able to spend extended periods of time with their children—not merely as babysitters, but as real, in-the-trenches caregivers—develop particularly deep, tender, and vital relationships with their kids.

Q: Anna, one of your two main characters in *Windfalls,* is a photographer who struggles to find a balance between her commitment to her art and to her two daughters. Do you think it is a difficult balance to achieve? How have you managed to find the time and emotional energy to write and teach while raising and home-schooling your own children?

A: It's a wobbly balance, and one I never feel I achieve for more than a few lucky seconds at a time. Every day I try to be ferocious about finding time to write, and every day I also try to be equally committed to giving up my writing time graciously when the rest of my life intervenes. (I love teaching, too, but it's the one part of the equation I would be willing to let go.)

I doubt I could find the energy to try to fit mothering and writing into the same lifetime if it weren't for the fact that both mean so much to me—and also that they are so mutually enriching. I know that for me and for Anna (and hopefully for an increasing number of other women and men), our work makes us better parents, just as our parenting adds a deeper dimension to our art. Both enterprises—raising children and writing books—require creativity, spontaneity, patience, discipline, instinct, intuition, analysis, a profound faith in the process, a deep engagement in the present, a sense of humor, a love of the sacred, and the ability to be steadfast in the face of big messes.

Q: Although *Windfalls* deals with the explosive issue of abortion, you don't seem to take sides. Do you think there is a right and a wrong side to the issue?

A: I personally think that every abortion is a loss, and in an ideal world, a combination of self-restraint, contraception, and supportive social services would make abortion exceedingly rare. But I also believe that much greater losses and even deeper sorrows can result when abortion is not a legal and available option.

But even more important than my own stance on reproductive freedom is my deep belief that abortion is too complex and important an issue to be reduced to a polarized controversy about right and wrong. Every unexpected pregnancy is a unique story, and rather than arguing about abortion as an abstract institution, I believe we should be examining the circumstances of women's lives, and looking at the social, financial, spiritual, and personal factors that go into women's individual decisions to nurture or forgo the potential a human embryo represents. In the recent past, it has been difficult for women who have considered abortion to tell their stories because of the stigmas—and even the threats—they have had to face. For that reason, perhaps fiction is a very good place to begin a healthy and multidimensional *conversation* about reproductive freedom.

Q: For a long while, *Windfalls* reads like two separate stories. In fact, readers may wonder if Anna and Cerise will ever even meet. What made you decide to give *Windfalls* that structure, and to focus your novel on two such very different women?

A: There's an aspect of both inevitability and serendipity to the way people meet that I find very interesting, and I like how the structure of *Windfalls* mirrors that. But perhaps most important, I like how having two characters—whose backgrounds, temperaments, and choices are seemingly so different—helps to suggest which aspects of Cerise's and Anna's experience are universal, and which are particular to their unique circumstances and personalities.

Q: In trying to get inside the experience of your characters, you applied for assistance at the county welfare office and volunteered at a drop-in support center for homeless women. What did you learn from your hands-on approach to research?

A: For me my characters are like imaginary friends. While I'm writing their stories they travel with me everywhere, and one of the reasons I'm able to work so long and hard on a book is that I feel a commitment to my characters to get their stories right. Research is a great aid to my imagination. If I can find a way to experience what a character might actually be seeing and hearing and touching and smelling and tasting in a given scene, it's much easier for me to know how that character would think and feel, and what she would do and say.

Also, I think it's very important to get the facts right in fiction. The sad truth is that a writer can say all kinds of wise things about life and love and human nature, but if—for example—she puts the Golden Gate Bridge on the wrong side of the bay, all her brilliant insights will instantly lose some degree of credibility with those readers who are more familiar with the Bay Area than she is. In that way, I feel I'm always writing for the people who know more about a given field than I do. It's a challenge, but I appreciate the opportunity it gives me to learn about all sorts of important and fascinating subjects.

Q: After Melody runs off with her friends and Travis dies in a fire, Cerise seeks a way to end her unendurable pain and her life. She meets a woman in the forest who reminds her that "healing is

the human task." Is that the message of hope and redemption that you are sending the reader in *Windfalls*?

A: There were many ways in which *Windfalls* was an emotionally challenging book to work on. It contains scenes I was able to write only because I believed they were so crucial to the story and so necessary to any honest examination of the costs and gifts of motherhood. There were moments when I cried as I wrote *Windfalls*, and I've been honored to hear from readers who say they wept as they read it. But despite the sadness the story contains, *Windfalls* is a deeply hopeful and life-affirming book, and I believe that the ability to heal—or at least the willingness to try—has got to be at the heart of hope.

Q: Often a writer sets out to write a work of fiction only to discover that the completed novel is vastly different from the work originally envisioned. How did *Windfalls* evolve as you worked on it?

A: A wonderful thing about the time and work it takes me to write a novel is that it allows me to exceed my own grasp. My initial conception of *Windfalls* did not have nearly the depth and complexity I hope the final work contains. The longer I lived with Anna and Cerise, the better I got to know them and to understand the issues facing them, and also to appreciate their courage and their willingness to grow as human beings and as mothers.

One of the themes that became increasingly significant during the seven years I wrote and rewrote *Windfalls* is how raising children affects parents' lives. For a long time I've been aware that the circumstances under which a woman has children can have an enormous impact on the practical and material aspects of her life, but until I had children of my own, I never really realized how profoundly our interactions with our children can affect our own development as human beings.

Up until very recently, there have been a great number of stories about what *mothers* do to us, but very few stories about what *mothering* does to us. I think there's been an assumption that mothering is too mundane or sentimental a subject to be worthy of a novelist's effort or a reader's time, and yet writing *Windfalls* reinforced my conviction that there are few experiences as meaningful, significant, and potentially life-changing as having and raising children.

QUESTIONS AND TOPICS FOR DISCUSSION

1. Why do you think Jean Hegland chose to call her novel *Windfalls*? Do you think it is a good title for the book? Why or why not?

2. The novel opens with a lyrical description of one of Anna's photographs—of a lone tree on a barren windswept hillside beneath a stormy sky, its trunk split almost in two. What purpose do the tree and its photograph serve in the novel and in the lives of the two main characters?

3. Both Anna and Cerise find themselves facing unplanned pregnancies, but they make very different decisions about their lives. Were the choices they made the right ones for them at the time? Do they turn out to be wise decisions as their lives unfold?

4. *Windfalls* has been described as a deeply stirring novel about the choices that every woman faces. Discuss the ways that life circumstances either force choices on us or take them away from us.

5. Joelle Fraser, author of *The Territory of Men*, describes *Windfalls* as "an elegy to motherhood in all its painful, beautiful complexity." Talk about the rapturous joys and heartbreaking sorrows and terrors of motherhood depicted in *Windfalls*. What other novels have you read or movies have you seen that deal with the theme of motherhood and its rewards and costs? How do they compare with *Windfalls*?

6. What do you think of the way the author deals with the sensitive subject of abortion and a woman's right to choose? Are her own views about abortion made clear in the novel? Should they be? Is it possible for a work of fiction to simply explore the human dimensions of a highly controversial political, moral, or religious issue without taking a stand? If you knew that an author's views on a social issue you feel passionately about stood in opposition to your own, how do you think it would affect your response to her novel?

7. In *Windfalls*, Jean Hegland also explores such volatile contemporary social issues as welfare and homelessness. In an interview she gave after her acclaimed first novel, *Into the Forest*, Hegland explained that regardless of how important an author considers the themes of her fiction to be, "in a novel, it's the story that comes first. . . . It's a challenge because one can get so fervent, but more is less when it comes to fervency." Do you agree or disagree? Do you think she succeeds or fails in *Windfalls* in expressing the passions of her characters while keeping her own fervency in check?

8. Anna's decision to terminate her pregnancy is influenced by her impression of her sister's life. "Sally had been a painter before Jesse was born. She had studied in Italy, had won awards . . . but the woman she'd been then seemed to have vanished into the abyss of motherhood. . . . Anna wondered how much art was lost to the world each time another

baby was born. With a ferocity that nearly frightened her, she'd thought, I could never be like that." Later on, when Anna marries and has two children of her own, how do her views change? How does she balance the conflicting demands of art and motherhood?

9. Why do you think Anna asked to see what was taken from her body during the abortion? Did the request surprise you? How do you think her graphic image of what she saw affected her? Why do you think she never told anyone about her abortion, and why does she finally open up to Cerise toward the end of the novel?

10. When Cerise was a teenager she often would deliberately burn her wrists with a heated iron, a mysterious craving to hurt herself that she could neither understand nor stop, but which disappeared when Melody was born. She is frantic when she witnesses her fourteen-year-old daughter plunging her forearm against the heated element of the stove. "She ached with pain both current and remembered—not the sting of blisters on tender skin as much as the hole in her soul those burns were meant to cauterize." Talk about the overwhelming mix of love, fear, anger, and self-recrimination Cerise—or any mother—experiences as she watches her child behave in dangerous and self-destructive ways.

11. What do you think of the way the novel is constructed—as a series of alternating sections on the separate lives of its two main characters? Talk about the way the author manages to intertwine their lives. How do these two women, of very different educational backgrounds, economic stations, and temperaments, become friends and what does each learn from the other?

12. What life lessons does Anna learn from her grandmother's story of her stillborn daughter? What is the significance of that one quietly spo-

ken word, "Because"? How does the woman Cerise encounters in the forest help her to go on living when she longs to end her life? How does young Lucy help Cerise to cope with her grief over Travis? What does Cerise mean when she says good-bye to Anna and explains, "I need to find out what someone means by Saturday morning"?